Redemption

Also by Victoria Steele Logue
Backpacking in the '90s
Camping in the '90s
Hiking and Backpacking

With Frank Logue
The Appalachian Trail Backpacker
The Best of the Appalachian Trail: Day Hikes
The Best of the Appalachian Trail: Overnight Hikes
Georgia Outdoors
Touring the Backroads of North and South Georgia
Kids Outdoors

With Frank Logue and Nicole Blouin
Guide to the Blue Ridge Parkway

Redemption

A novel

Victoria Steele Logue

Redemption is a work of fiction.
Though some characters are based on the historical,
this work is based solely on the author's imagination.

Copyright ©2011 Victoria Steele Logue
ISBN 978-0-578-09247-8
All rights reserved under
International and Pan-American Copyright

Published by Low Country Press
Savannah, Georgia
www.lowcountrypress.net

Library of Congress Cataloging-in-Publication Data
is available on request.

Manufactured in the United States of America

First Edition: September 2011
9 8 7 6 5 4 3 2 1

This book is dedicated to my husband, Frank,
for encouraging me to bring these characters to life
and to my mother, Laura Kelly Campbell,
for her editorial skill and words of support.

'Tis now the witching time of night,
When churchyards yawn, and hell breathes out
Contagion to this world. Now I could drink hot blood
And do such bitter business as the day
Would quake to look on.

~William Shakespeare, *Hamlet*

When these things begin to come to pass,
look up, and lift up your heads;
because your redemption draweth nigh.

~Luke 21:28

Wolf

THE FOG IS SO THICK he can barely see three feet ahead, but he can hear her footsteps, smell her fear. He senses her accelerated heart rate, the blood coursing through her veins.

In the distance, Coit Tower snakes up through the fog, swaying like an entranced cobra in the swirling mist.

He shakes his head. The fog, which cloaks the city, seems to have insinuated its way into his brain as well.

"Jesus," he mutters under his breath. That's probably sacrilegious. Or is it blasphemous? In my case, probably both, he finds his mind wandering yet again. He chuckles, and shakes his head once more. He looks like a dog trying to shake the water from his fur. In this case, it is the fog. He can feel it there—the mist—creeping through his mind, chilling him with its touch.

He shivers and his flesh crawls into goosebumps. And though it is not the October chill that causes it, he pulls his trench coat more closely to him.

Straighten up or you'll lose her, he tells himself.

And he cannot afford to lose her. It is already late and he would have to start all over again. Now is perfect. Two warm October days have brought the fog rolling across the bay. He enjoys hunting in the fog. It saves him the energy of having to create the right atmosphere, to maneuver the fog himself. He is already so tired, so weak, and unfortunately, he has no one to blame but himself for that.

They are climbing Telegraph Hill. Its narrow alleys and alpine-like inclines are perfect for his purpose. Both the fog and ascending alley will slow her down. But not him.

He can hear her slightly labored breathing and knows it is time.

She can no longer hear his footsteps. She realized she was being followed when she left the bar in North Beach. And, although she glanced over her shoulder a number of times, the fog had always hidden her pursuer. Perhaps she was mistaken. Maybe she was being paranoid, and those echoing footsteps behind her were a hallucination. Only half a block more and she would be home.

If only I hadn't stopped to watch the sun set, she thinks, remembering how particularly striking it had been this evening—neon tones of yellow, orange and red and even purple. It had been completely dark by the time she reached the bar.

If she hadn't stopped to watch the sun set, she would already be comfortably ensconced in her apartment. As it is, her reflexes were dulled by the two glasses of chardonnay she dawdled over at the bar. Now that she thought about it, the alcohol probably made her less cautious, as well. If I get home alive, she promises herself, I will never drink alone again; well, at least not in public, she amends. And if this damn walk home weren't all up hill, she thinks, heart pounding with the effort of the climb, I would also already be there. She can see her building near the top of the incline—almost there.

A strong hand is clamped over her mouth.

Not that I have enough breath left to scream, she thinks with a strange calm. She feels his breath like a chill breeze on her neck, and as his soft lips press against her fog-cooled skin, she is amazed at the wave of desire that sweeps through her. Even her knees weaken at his touch.

Please don't kill me, she thinks when she feels a slight prick on her throat just below her ear, at the corner of her jawbone, and then nonsensically, I'm going to have one hell of a hickey. The fog dances around her, coloring everything gray, then black.

Fog isn't black, she thinks as she slips into unconsciousness.

He doesn't kill her. He never kills. She will wake up cold and damp some hours later, weak and ill but alive.

How many necks, he wonders as he returns to his apartment. How many delicately curved throats has he placed his indifferent lips against—hundreds? Thousands? He laughs out loud but it is a laugh of effect not of feeling. He is full of energy now, and the ruddiness of his cheeks and lips contrast sharply with the extraordinary pallor of his skin.

In the North Beach bar, sitting unobtrusively in a corner, he had surveyed the crowd for his next victim. He'd spotted her not long after he sat down. She wasn't very pretty—a little more plump than he liked, a heavy, doughy face. Only her eyes, dark Italian eyes fringed by extravagant lashes, saved her from ugliness. But she, too, had been trying to appear inconspicuous, and that had attracted his attention.

Wanting only a quiet nightcap and no trouble, she'd sat, undisturbed, in a booth sipping her wine and perusing a magazine. It was a good bar for that, filled mostly with dotcom programming geeks more interested in talking code than hitting up any single females. When she'd finished her second glass of wine, she had closed the magazine and made her way toward the door.

Unless she went to another bar, he knew she was just what he was looking for. He had to be careful these days, especially in this city. He wasn't sure whether AIDS would affect him, but he wasn't about to take a chance. This one didn't appear to be promiscuous; neither did she look strung out on drugs. And, although she had surely heard him following her, she had not panicked. That had happened in the past and it was hell.

He brushes his fog-moistened hair off his high and pale forehead with a leather-gloved hand. A passerby, blinded by the fog, bumps into him, but never quite finishes her pardons when she catches a glimpse of his face. He laughs as she backs away from him.

Until she reaches the end of the block and turns the corner, she finds herself shaking uncontrollably. She could have sworn his eyes were red.

They are not red, but bluish-green. They're the color of the Mediterranean, Hannele, ever romantic, had told him once. He had laughed and pulled her into his arms. "How would you know?" he had teased her. "You have never seen the Mediterranean, much less been out of Fürstensteinbrück." She had silenced him with her kisses, and he had been more than willing to be silenced. But the liquidness of his eyes and their ever-changing color—from the grey of a stormy sea to the placid green of a dead calm—only enhances their inherent power. A smile lingers on his lips at the woman's reaction. It is a practiced smile and although it does not hide the brilliant white of his teeth, it does veil their peculiar sharpness.

An unfamiliar emotion stops him in mid stride. It soon passes and he is unable to identify it as ennui.

The thought of his empty apartment, despite the fact he has accomplished the night's goal, leaves him feeling hollow. With a continued sense of abstractedness, he roams the streets for another half hour, and then enters a video rental store. He heads automatically to the romance section before remembering that his favorite movie is actually on the action shelf.

Once there, he checks for the movie. It's available although he is not sure whether it will help tonight, not sure why he is even checking it out yet again, not sure what has prevented him from actually purchasing the damn thing, and no longer even sure why it is his favorite.

His Akita Inu, Mephistopheles, greets him as he enters his apartment. He pets the brindled dog while bolting the apartment's massive door.

He throws his trench coat, dampened by the fog, over the back of an ancient over-stuffed armchair. The living room has a minimum of furniture—only an old but comfortable leather sofa, a coffee table stacked with numerous books ranging from the latest bestsellers to academic texts. There is even a Bible. Almost seeming out-of-place, a solid oak entertainment center holds a 46-inch plasma TV and a Blu-ray DVD player and myriad DVDs as well as a multi-disc cd player and hundreds of CDs. Another wall is covered by a massive floor-to-ceiling bookshelf bulging with books—contemporary fiction in most every genre, classics, philosophy, theology, and books in a variety of foreign languages. Everything but cookbooks. A nondescript shag carpet covers the floor. It may have been tan once. The ugly avocado kitchen has no furniture, not even an avocado refrigerator left over from the 60s, the last time the place was decorated.

His pulls his gloves off next, tossing them on the coat. He always wears the gloves when in public, even in the summer. But, as he ventures out only at night, he doesn't get too many strange looks.

He studies the long, fine hair that sparsely covers his palms and grimaces in disgust. It is easier to keep his nails filed down. He'd shave his palms, but he knows that the hair will just grow right back and more quickly than for the average human.

In the bathroom, he turns on the shower. There is probably no blood. He is always careful but he has to make sure. He pulls off his mostly black tie and lets it slide to the tiled floor. He tosses his wing tips backwards into the bedroom as he stares sightlessly into the mirror. He removes his suit jacket and begins unbuttoning his now-rumpled shirt. He undresses mechanically, contemplating the most-recent vampire movie he has seen: "The Lost Boys." He has watched it repeatedly, owns the DVD along with a couple dozen other vampire movies. The only ones that even come anywhere close to describing his pathetic life are "Dracula" and "Nosferatu."

He prefers the "Dracula" with Gary Oldman despite the Count's outlandish hairdo. When he'd had the unfortunate experience of meeting that particular legend, the monster had seemed incredibly vain about the long black hair that curled about his shoulders. No, Wolf had shaken his head the first time he'd seen that movie, he just couldn't see the Count wasting his time with something as foolish as styling his hair.

Wolf had mused on more than one occasion that although each of the vampire movies or television series he'd seen managed to dredge up only a modicum of the truth, all were consistent in the vampire's lust for blood.

At the moment he is pondering the flaming eyes, retracting fangs, transformations, consumption of food and smoking in "Lost Boys".

"Hardly," he says aloud. "Not that some of those aren't bad ideas." He smiles at the thought of retracting fangs, a natural smile. Had he been able to see himself in the mirror, he might have been startled to see the ghoulish grin reflecting back at him. He also would have been dismayed at the solemnity and apathy in his eyes.

"But it's never going to happen," he tells the wall behind him as he removes the wool pants that complete his suit. He always dresses up to do his stalking. He has learned from experience that he is more likely to be regarded as a non-threat if he appears "professional."

"A professional," his lip curls in loathing and he laughs at himself. The unfamiliar noise reverberates off the tiled walls as he wonders if a vampire can actually be considered a professional. As the echoes re-cede, his look turns to puzzlement. He very rarely laughs. As a matter of fact, almost never. When was the last time he had laughed? And tonight, he cannot stop. Not that it's been pleasant laughter. Rather it has been damned disparaging.

I don't like myself anymore, he thinks, and the thought shocks him. He contemplates how happy those punks had been in the movie.

"Oh, yes," he says as he steps into the shower. "You never grow old and you never die. You only have to feed."

Vampire movies too often reveal the tongue-in-cheek attitude the world takes toward my kind, he reflects as the hot water pummels his pallid skin. He almost longs for the days when creatures of the night were actually hunted. These days, he thinks, I'd be considered a psycho and committed to some *institution*, what a nice euphemism, where I would die almost immediately.

Or, and this might be worse, he realizes with horror, they would assume I was one of those vampire culture freaks. How much the world has changed, he sighs, when self-proclaimed vampires are just part of a wider underground subculture for abnormal behavior.

He understands that some humans claim to have a real need to consume blood but lucky them, he laughs again, it doesn't have to be "living" blood pumped straight from a human's heart into the vampire's throat. The water is cooling. How long has he been in the shower? He angrily twists the handle on the shower to off and steps, dripping, onto the bath mat.

Toweling off, he crosses the hall to the bedroom where he will sleep until the sun sets the next evening. The door has been reinforced to keep out any unexpected visitors; Mephistopheles employed as both an early warning system and intruder deterrent. No coffin, just a single bed and a dresser occupy the tiny room, but it is what covers the bed that makes him scowl and once more emit that self-deprecating chuckle. A thin layer of soil coats the bed—all that remains of his ties to Fürstensteinbrück. It seems so arbitrary that he must sleep (no, he corrects himself, it is more of a nightly hibernation) on the soil of the land where he was created, so to speak. It has something to do with the grave, but he has never really died. He guesses he will never fully understand. He pulls a robe around his lean and naked body and returns to the living room to watch his movie, "The Terminator." It's still a few hours until sunrise.

Vlad

VLAD STARED AT HIS FATHER IN SHOCK. "You've done what?" he stuttered in anger. His heart began beating, wildly, and his face was flushed with the fury he felt at the most recent of his father's betrayals. In spite of the pervasive November chill, he could feel the sweat start under his arms, sticky and uncomfortable. It was soon sliding down his sides, itching almost unbearably beneath his wool tunic. He wanted desperately to scratch but wouldn't give his father the satisfaction of knowing he had that much power over him. And that, of course, enraged him even more.

"I refuse to go! I will not spend even an hour with those heathen swine . . ."

His father interrupted his tirade with a slap to the face that sent him reeling backwards. He slammed into the wall behind him so hard that his head ricocheted off the stone and he slumped to the floor.

He opened his eyes to find his younger brother, Radu, bending over him, fear and worry making his big brown eyes look even larger. He put a hand to the swelling on the back of his head and groaned. His father glared down at him.

"You and your brother are going to Adrianople. You have no choice in this matter."

"What about Mircea?" he asked, slowly getting to his feet.

"You have no right to question my authority," his father yelled into

Vlad's face, now pale with pain. "I will tell you what is to happen. Do you understand?"

Vlad's cheeks crimsoned again, the brightness of the red contrasting sharply with his pale skin. "Yes, my Lord." He replied, glowering balefully at his father. He made it sound like a curse.

"Be gone," his father ordered, pushing him roughly from his chamber. Vlad stalked back to his room as Radu scampered behind, trying to catch up. Vlad's 13-year-old legs were much longer albeit gangly. His long black curls bounced about his shoulders as he made his way down the cold passageway.

"I need to be alone," he said to Radu as he made a sharp left turn into his own bedchamber and slammed the door in his younger brother's face. The 7-year-old Radu had long since grown used to Vlad's foul temper and skipped, happily, down to the kitchen. Maybe there would be a treat awaiting him there, or at the very least one of the servants might be able to amuse him. He couldn't understand why Vlad was so upset about being sent to Adrianople. Why, they might even have a chance to see Constantinople! He had heard so many stories . . .

In his chamber, Vlad paced the cold stone floor. What a hypocrite his father was, he fumed, doing whatever was necessary to save his own worthless hide; not to mention further himself politically. From killing his own relation, Alexandru, to gain the Wallachian throne to paying tribute to the Sultan, his treacheries were numerous. And all this despite the fact he was a member of the Order of the Dragon, sworn to killing those infidel Turks!

Most recently, Vlad kicked at his bed, his father had sent his own son, Mircea, to fight the Turks in his place at the Battle of Varna, all because he wanted to appear neutral to the Turks. And their forces had been massacred! Vlad was still in shock. There had been more than 120,000 Turkish Janissaries (a number of whom they had provided, he sneered, damn the Turks) to their paltry 30,000 troops. It was no wonder Hunyadi was so furious at his father. And now, the ultimate betrayal—he and his brother were to be sent to those very Turks as hostages.

"He cares more about himself than his own sons," he seethed, watching a large beetle amble its way, laboriously, across the chamber. He lifted his foot in order to smash it into oblivion, but paused. He wanted to make it hurt; he wanted to release on it all the pent up anger he held against his father. How could he do that best? He rifled through the bits of "treasure" he kept in a richly ornamented wooden box that he had removed from the iron-bound trunk at the end of his bed. He might be the son of the Prince of Wallachia, but he had very little in the way of possessions—a few pieces of clothing, even fewer jewels and the barest minimum of weapons that were needed for training as a knight.

As a matter of fact, it had been his tutor, Petru cel Mare, an elderly boyar, who had instilled in him his deep hatred of the Turks. During his apprenticeship, Petru had regaled him with tales of the Battle of Nicolopolis; had taught him not only the ways of war but ways of killing and torturing captives, as well.

He pulled a long, gold hat pin from the box; the small ruby at the end caught the red of the sunset and glinted evilly in the fading light. Vlad returned his attention to the beetle. It was about to disappear into a crevice in the wall. The boy raced over to the wall and scooped up the bug, which, overturned in Vlad's palm, began waving its legs wildly. Fiercely intent on his project, his brow furrowed in concentration, Vlad slowly inserted the sharp tip of the pin into the bug's abdomen. But not all the way. Pushing the ruby end of the pin into a shallow crack between two paving stones in the floor, he silently observed the bug as its weight and its frenetically pinioning legs slowly pulled it more fully onto the pin. At one point, as the room got darker and darker, he dashed to light a candle so that he could watch the drama play itself out to the bitter end. But, as the pin finally protruded through the opposite side of the beetle's carapace, Vlad finally began to get bored. This would be much more entertaining, he thought, if it were a small mammal or bird, instead of an insect. Damn, he frowned, he couldn't even tell if it was suffering. Not much point in this process, he sighed in frustration.

He threw himself on his bed, imagining the tortured shrieks of a mouse. He smiled. Yes, much more entertaining. He would have to try it sometime.

Wolf

HE HAD HAD A FEELING that it wouldn't work tonight. Usually, he finds that watching "The Terminator" makes him feel . . . he finds it hard to articulate. It isn't so much that it makes him experience emotions such as love, passion or even vengeance, but rather it impresses upon him a certain hopefulness. His usual detachment from the world, his constant preoccupation with survival, is lifted and for a couple of hours he feels if not hopeful for his future, at least not hope-*less*.

Tonight, though, as he had watched Michael Biehn and Linda Hamilton, for the first time he no longer wants to trade places with Kyle Reese. He is no longer hopeful that he will be given the chance that Kyle has received to ensure a future for himself, and for that matter, for all mankind. Before this night, he would pray fervently that like the character, Kyle, he would be given the chance to return to the past; to arrive in that clearing before Vlad, and to carry Hannele safely away to a happier future for them both. And, at the end of the movie, when Sarah Conner wept over the loss of her love but resolutely prepared for the future, he would feel his heart swell with the emotion and he would pray, "Please Lord, this is not what I wanted my life to be. Please give me the chance to redeem myself."

But, as often as not, he would wake up the next evening toward sunset and be fully immersed in survival mode—emotionless and cunning—until the next time he watched the movie.

But tonight, as he sits watching the empty television screen, for the first time in a very long time, upon its blank face play his daydreams. There was a time when he used to fantasize about Hannele constantly, but thoughts of her grew more and more painful and for centuries, he has blocked all but the fact she that she existed and was stolen from him from his memory. He hasn't daydreamed in years. But, tonight, upon the screen he sees himself with a woman. She's pretty but she doesn't have to be. He comes home from work, and she is there to greet him. Or maybe, he smiles, she comes home from work and I am there to kiss her, give her a glass of wine. I tell her what I did that day, she tells me what she did. I ask her if she's ready for dinner. Only if you're the main course, she says. Wolf grimaces. The opposite is too close to the truth. And why is he even wasting time thinking this way? He realizes, finally and irrevocably, he is the way he is. He will be a vampire until the end of time unless something happens in the meantime. He will never be human, never be given that chance he so desperately longs for.

He slams his fist into the couch, and jumps up, paces the room. It's not fair, his mind cries. He glances toward the window. The off-white curtains are turning rosy. He yawns. It is that time again. His heart contracts, tightly and painfully. Don't let me feel this way, he screams, silently. God, I haven't felt like this in years, why now?

"Why did it take me more than four centuries to realize the truth of it all?" he queries his dog. "Why on earth am I suddenly feeling this way now? I am not sure I want to spend eternity in hopelessness."

Mephistopheles regards him, solemnly.

"When I wake up, it will all go away, right? This is only a dream. It has to be."

Mephisto barks a reply.

"You're right," Wolf sighs. And the dog is right. Wolf hasn't dreamt in years.

"Watch out for me, Mephisto," he tells the dog. He looks back over his shoulder to the DVD that he has placed on the floor in front of the front door so that he won't forget to return it. He glances at the shelves filled with DVDs he has purchased. Is there a reason he hasn't bought it, he wonders as he bolts his bedroom door? He speculates on what Jung or Freud might have to say about his not wanting to actually own his so-called favorite movie. What were the psychological ramifications of it all, he grimaces, slipping out of the robe and sliding onto the dirt-covered bed. No use dirtying more clothes than necessary. As if it even matters, he thinks, idly, as he falls into his nightly "coma."

The next evening, he will drop his clothes off at an all-night laundry and return the DVD before heading back to Corazon, where he spends most of his days. He feeds only two or three times a week.

Ginny

Tʜᴇ ᴍɪsᴛ ʟɪᴇs ᴀs ᴛʜɪᴄᴋ ɪɴ Cᴏʀᴀᴢᴏɴ as it does up the coast. Ginny's gingerbread cottage looks like a fairy tale gone sour.

A late meeting had kept her at the paper until 11 p.m. And, just as she was heading home for the evening, Abe had walked in. She had groaned, inwardly, and ignored the way his face had lit up when he had seen her still there.

"How about a nightcap?" he had asked.

A nightcap, her brain had ridiculed. Did people still say that? But, she could think of no reasonable excuse to say no to her boss and she couldn't exactly call his pleasure at seeing her 'sexual harassment.' The truth was, they had become friends during the past few years, but it was clear Abe's intentions had moved past the professional and had slowly crept toward personal.

Later, immersed in the ultra-masculine ambiance of The Boar's Head Tavern, and after a bit of small talk over Irish coffees, Abe had visibly taken a deep breath.

Oh Jesus, she had thought, here it comes now. She had known what was coming, had been dreading this moment for such a very long time. And, she had long since admitted to herself, part of the reason she had come to dread this moment was the very fact that it had taken so damn long to come to fruition. Well, it just made her wonder. Between this apparent cowardice (if that was the right word) and the most glaring grounds of all—the fact that she wasn't in the least bit physically attracted to him and had never pretended to be—she had come to dread each of his baby steps toward making his infatuation a reality.

Tonight, as he had physically steeled himself, she had tried to stare into the depths of her drink, searching for a plausible "no" to the question that was about to come. But the Irish Coffee was too murky, or perhaps it was just not the oracle she had hoped it would be. She had studied the eponymous boar's head over the pub's huge fireplace, but its tremendously huge tusks gleamed malevolently in the firelight. Although that had probably been her imagination, as well—the beady black eyes pronouncing doom and gloom. For a second, she had been sure it was laughing at her.

Go ahead and laugh, she had sighed, inwardly. The story of my freaking life.

"Virginia," he'd said, using her proper name. She'd reluctantly looked into the faded blue of his eyes.

"Yes?" she'd croaked.

"Uh, do you, uh, have any, uh, plans, for um, tomorrow night?"

She had tried, desperately, to think of something—another meeting, a breaking story, a previous engagement. Damn! He was only giving her a day's notice for God's sake. "Mary, Mother of God, have mercy on me," she prayed, desperately. But Mary remained silent, she couldn't lie and, more importantly, she knew that Abe was more familiar with his reporter's work schedules and the paper than she was. Besides, she knew that the "I don't date my co-workers" line wouldn't pass with him, particularly as she had gone out with the former sports editor and she suspected, not with a little guilt, just why he was now 'former.' She was nearly 100 percent sure that the offer for a better position from the *San Francisco Examiner* had been via Abe calling in a favor. How could have Scott refused?

"No," she'd replied, nearly sighing and staring at the table instead of his eyes. She could no longer look at him; her reluctance would be too obviously revealed in her big brown eyes. The mirrors of the soul,' she'd reflected, I can't hide anything with my eyes.

So, Abe had talked her into an evening in San Francisco despite the fact she had probably looked like a deer caught in the headlights of a semi. Smash! Road kill. She had felt that a little part of her had died.

now, past midnight and unlocking the door to her cottage, Ginny is seriously regretting her inability to just say "no." One of her many weaknesses and one that got her in a lot more trouble than solitary walks on the beach or champagne and chocolate. Why does she live in such terror of hurting the feelings of others while letting herself be mowed down continually? She wanted to slap herself across the face; kick her own ass.

You're not interested in him, she chides herself. You had no right to go and build up his hopes by agreeing to go out with him just because you didn't want to hurt his feelings. When will you ever learn?

"When will you ever learn?" she sings aloud, paraphrasing Pete Seeger via Peter, Paul and Mary. "When will you ever learn?"

Abe is a nice guy, he really is, she argues with herself. But, that perhaps, is his death sentence. They have been on friendly terms ever since she had come to work for the newspaper close to three years ago now. And while she has tried to maintain her level of interest as no more than subordinate co-worker and friend (he did own the paper, after all), she is just *not* attracted to him. That is it. Pure and simple. She enjoys talking to him, even thinks they could be best friends. But. But, Abe is interested in her as more than a friend. She could read that look in his eyes the moment she was introduced to him.

She had seen it so very many times before, had only fallen for it once when she was a sophomore in college. That was the year she had had the bad judgment to get involved with Ken. Regardless of the fact that she had not been physically attracted to him, she had given in to that "I worship and adore you" look. And it wasn't long before she had realized that despite the fact that Ken loved her, they were meant to be friends, only, and that it had been weakness on her part to be so flattered by his neediness. Well, she amended, perhaps not even friends. She could have remained friends but Ken had wanted so much more and remained perpetually hopeful and so she had had to end it. Painfully, yes, but with so much relief on her own part. So, she was not going to fall for that look again, at least not with Abe.

An incurable romantic who agreeably admits to sappiness, Ginny is still waiting for someone to sweep her off her feet. At night, especially on cold and rainy evenings, alone in her bed, she sometimes realizes that there is no such thing as a knight in shining armor. It is, in fact, the stuff of fairy tales. And she cries. No, it is more than crying, it is heart-rending (or, heart-rendering, as her mother used to joke) wailing. When this happens, she feels as if her heart has been shredded.

"Why can't there be such a thing as romantic love?" she weeps to her cats. "Surely, somewhere in this world there is a man who will want me as much as I want him; someone who will die for me and kill for me as I would die and kill for him; someone who cannot keep his hands off me, even when we're in public. Someone who loses a part of himself each moment he's away from me . . ."

Most of the time she ignores that need in her, and buries herself in her work, her cats and the horse her stepfather had given her when she had earned her Master's degree in journalism.

"**D**amn," she tells her two Abyssinians, as she closes her front door on the fog that seems to want to slither into the house with her. They meow, but it is more of a 'well, it's about darn time you got home and fed us' than a welcome.

"All right, all right," she agrees, leading them to the kitchen. She dishes them up their daily ration of Hill's Science Diet, and warms herself some milk. She has a feeling she will be unable to sleep. Sometimes the fog does that to her. It makes her think more than she wants to, which makes her restless and leaves her feeling frustrated and hopeless. And the events of this night have done nothing to alleviate that feeling.

Half an hour later in her down-comforted bed, she stares at the ceiling, imagining all the terrible conclusions to the next evening.

She could be a real bitch but he might fire her, she thinks. No, worse, he wouldn't fire her and she would have to live with that every time she saw his face. Nope. No way.

She could be nice all evening, and then a bitch as soon as they turned into her driveway and as he was walking her to her front door. How many times had she played that game? "Thanks for the wonderful evening," smiling ever so kindly as her brain yelled, don't you even try to get in my face!" And she would close the door to the barest of cracks, ready to slam it in the face of the offender, rip off his foot if he were even so bold as to stick it in the door. "Good night and thanks again," and shut the door in his face and if that wasn't the biggest clue . . . But, could she risk that with Abe? Is she sure she wants him to think of her that way—the frigid bitch? It is a lose-lose situation. What the hell is she going to do?

Why don't you just enjoy yourself, but never pretend you're more than just friends, play it by ear, be as nice as possible, she finally decides. But then again, how needy is he? Will he take "nice" as encouragement? Oh it's going to be a long night. She wonders if maybe she should get up early and go to Mass. She can use all the help she can get. She tosses and turns, and when she finally sleeps, it is fitfully.

Abe

HIS MOTHER IS STILL UP when he walks in the door. Probably waiting up for him, he thinks, unkindly, brow furrowing.

"You're walking on air," she notices. He stops, his hand on the carved mahogany banister.

"What's that supposed to mean?" he says, warily.

"I mean only that you appear very happy, or perhaps 'ecstatic' would be a better way of putting it."

"So?"

She stares at him, her Wedgewood blue eyes neutral. Only her white-knuckled hands, clenched tightly around the arms of her chair betray the jealousy evoked by her fear of losing him to another woman, particularly a woman like Virginia Hunter.

"I am happy," he gives in. "I am taking Virginia to San Francisco tomorrow evening."

She raises a delicately painted eyebrow, "All the way to San Francisco? Are you sure that is wise?" And, then, almost as an after thought, "She's the type that breaks men's hearts." That was Clara speech for "a good Jewish boy like you shouldn't be sniffing after some Gentile (worse, Catholic) bitch."

His eyes, so like his father's, stare at her uncompromisingly. It was only when he could look at her like this that she would back off. But Ginny is something he feels very strongly about. Clara Bar El's disapproving porcelain gaze cannot keep him from pursuing this woman.

"Where are you going?" she asks. He had won that particular engagement. He would just have to find out the hard way, she grimaces.

"I thought I would take her to that new Moroccan restaurant," he says, face lighting up again. He couldn't wait to be secured in his bedroom. There he might dream of her and of how he was going to win her over. He is not unaware that she is reluctant to go out with him although he cannot figure out why. He has known her for close to three years, and though she dates occasionally, it is quite obvious to him and others that there is no one serious. No one meets her after work, no roses are ever delivered to her small desk, and no gilt-framed picture is given a place of honor. He had managed to nip her short-lived "affair" with Scott Berg in the bud before it got too serious.

"It's late," he cuts short his thoughts and any further questions from his mother. "I need to sleep."

"Goodnight, son," she sighs. He may have won this particular battle but he hasn't won the war. She stands up and makes her way to the master bedroom to begin her nightly routine, deeply preoccupied with just how she is going to get rid of Virginia Hunter.

Once in his Spartan and spotless room, he readies himself for bed. His routine, unvaried for more than ten years, is to undress himself while carefully putting away his clothes. Then he pulls on his pajamas and robe, brushes his teeth and washes up before he crawls on to the firm mattress of his king size bed. Had Ginny known of his nightly routine, she would have had no trouble refusing the date. She has always gone out of her way to avoid becoming enmeshed in any routine. Drink coffee every day! Ha, she'll have tea or orange juice just to spite herself.

Had Abraham Abimelech Bar El been aware of Ginny's scorn for routine, he would have blushed to the roots of his curly auburn hair. He had always been a neat boy, and had never even considered the fact that someone might smirk at his unimaginative habits. Although too late to change, at this point in his life he would have tried to do so, had it meant winning Ginny's love and devotion.

And it is Ginny he is thinking of as he automatically takes his wallet from the inside of his Gucci suit jacket and places it on his dresser. The jacket, he hangs on the valet stand at the foot of his bed. The change comes next, placed in the coin holder, which is part of the stand that holds his watch and other jewelry. He loosens the pale yellow and black diagonally-striped silk tie, placing it neatly on the stand. The white Ralph Lauren cotton shirt is unbuttoned and placed on the same stand for the maid to launder. And the trouser-half of the suit is also carefully hung on the stand for the maid to put away.

Slipping into silk pajamas and robe, he walks into the bathroom to brush his teeth, fastidiously using his Sonicare and flossing before he turns in. Had Ginny known he wears pajamas, she might have been unable to keep from laughing in his face. Her dream man sleeps in the nude when alone; in the nude and entwined in her arms when with his beloved; at least until they have little ones scampering about the house.

Vlad

SITTING ON THE BANKS OF THE RIVER TUNJA, Vlad stared moodily at the setting sun. Nearly a year had passed since he and his brother had been sent as hostages to Turkey. While he and his brother had more freedom than he had bargained on, it still deeply rankled that he was being held prisoner by his mortal enemy. Vlad's father had been admitted to the Order of the Dragon, a semi-secret order of knights created by the Holy Roman Emperor Sigismund, the year Vlad was born. It had essentially been nailed into his head from birth the model of upholding Christianity and defending the Empire against the Ottoman Turks. Hell, he thought, tossing a small stone into the river, his father's coins even bore the image of the order—the dragon, wings extended, hanging on a cross!

And yet here he sat. In Adrianople. He had thought numerous times of running away, but knew the penalty would be severe if he were caught. Death wouldn't be good enough for him; it would more than likely be preceded by a little of the torture the Turks seemed to excel at.

"Duos qui sequitur lepores," Vlad muttered one of the many pithy Latin sayings he had memorized, "neutrum capit." His father had definitely decided the best tactic was to pursue two hares—trying to mollify both the Turks and his fellow countrymen. But, as the saying went, he was bound to catch neither. But, what made him angriest about his father's all-too-obvious, not to mention embarrassingly pathetic, attempts to play both sides was the elder Vlad Dracul's willingness. No. He stopped mid-thought. More than willingness. Eagerness. His excessive eagerness to entrust the care of his sons to a 12-year-old "sultan." And what trebled the humiliation for Vlad was the fact that Mehmed was a year younger than himself! And, not only was that fine with his father but, and this always made him tremble with rage, his father had never treated Vlad as anything more than a child. Worse! He had been handled more like the whelp of a hound than a human. Although, when he actually stopped to think about it, even his father's dogs had been treated better than he.

He stood and stretched, the brows over his heavy-lidded eyes drawn together as he contemplated his next move. The most important thing was keeping an eye on Mehmed. He didn't like the way he looked at Radu. It made him feel oily and unclean. Fortunately, at the present, Mehmed was in Constantinople. On the other hand, he grimaced, they were being watched by the Sultan's even slimier teacher, Iala. Vlad liked him about as much as he liked Mehmed—he despised him. He didn't trust either of them. They were too much like his father—it was all about what they wanted and very little would slow them down in achieving their goals. What was that saying? The end justifies the means? He snorted.

"Habet et musca splenem, father." Yes, even a fly had its anger, he smiled, wickedly, because thinking of flies reminded him of the small forest of impaled insects he had created in the garden that very morning. And the insects reminded him that he had caught a mouse that day, as well. And what better way to diffuse some of this pent-up anger than to teach the mouse some of his recently acquired knowledge on methods of torture? Things that he couldn't even begin to do with a fly.

1447. It had only been three years but a seeming eternity to a teen-aged boy in captivity. He would be 16 that fall, a man in his own eyes, definitely more of a man than Mehmed. And, he was beginning to wonder just how long the Sultan (now that the sultan was once again

Murad II, Mehmed's father) intended to keep him in Adrianople. He was ready to return to Wallachia and begin to set into motion the plan he had been working on that would allow him to wreak his vengeance on these Turks.

Unfortunately, as far as he was concerned, they had not treated him as shamefully as he might have hoped. It would have been nice to have more fuel for the fire but it was enough to him that they requested his being held hostage to begin with. That, along with the fact that these Muslims were his sworn enemies!

His half brother, on the other hand, had actually seemed to enjoy the past three years. He had even become friendly with Mehmed and had consented to being taught Islam. That would never have happened had they stayed in Tirgoviste.

Speaking of his brother, he mused, he hadn't seen him in a while . . . not since they had broken their fast at dawn. Vlad began to hurry down the nearest palace corridor toward the gardens, one of Radu's favorite haunts.

It was a beautiful day in early autumn. The late afternoon sky was cloudless and a deep azure and the air felt crisp, bracing, but still pleasantly warm. As always, the gardens were in full bloom; the vibrant pinks and purples of the bougainvillea seemed to cause the garden to shimmer with a roseate light. The scents of various plants—rosemary, mints, cedar and cardamom—perfumed the garden along with the many roses that bordered its twisting paths. This sanctuary was well-tended by the Sultan's gardeners. Murad II had a contemplative soul and enjoyed spending his evening prayer time, when he wasn't in one of the many local mosques, in the quiet of his gardens. Subsequently, it was forbidden to enter the gardens after sunset.

Vlad had just stepped through one of the archways that led into the garden when he heard a shout that was clearly his brother's voice. The shout was followed by a sharp exclamation of surprise or pain, a pause and then amused laughter. It sounded like Mehmed. Vlad followed the voices to their source deep into the garden at the base of a mulberry tree, which Radu had obviously scrambled up in some haste.

He looked from his 10-year-old brother to the 14-year-old Mehmed, who appeared to be bleeding from a narrow cut on his face.

"Don't let him kill me," Radu pleaded.

Mehmed chuckled again.

Vlad's heart began to hammer in fear. It was obvious that Radu had scratched Mehmed's face with the small sword that lay at the former sultan's feet. But, it was also obvious that Mehmed was amused. And that scared Vlad even more than Mehmed's anger. For Mehmed, despite his apparent youth, was known for his quick and foul temper. He would as soon strike a man dead as deign to gaze upon him once he had taken insult.

Perhaps then, the stories were true and Mehmed preferred boys to women. He felt the blood drain from his face. And that, of course, would mean that he had chosen Radu to be his catamite. It was the final insult and he was absolutely powerless. Standing up for Radu would mean Vlad's certain death and possibly even Radu's. But, if he did nothing . . .

He glanced up at his brother who was still wedged between the trunk of the tree and a large branch. But his brother only had eyes for Mehmed, who was smiling at him, seductively.

"Oh come on down you lovely little boy," Mehmed persuaded Radu. "I promise you that I will not kill you." But there was an unspoken "because I have other things in mind for you."

"I'll bet you do," Vlad retorted, silently, as his scowl deepened, "you sick bastard." And there it was, just the accelerant he had been looking for. It didn't matter to him if Radu was flattered by Mehmed's attentions or not. For Vlad it was just another betrayal. He watched, unemotionally it seemed, as Radu was coaxed down from the tree. But his stomach churned and he was biting his tongue so hard in his effort to keep silent that he couldn't even savor the hot metallic taste of his own blood. It wasn't an unpleasant flavor. He wondered what the blood of a pig tasted like; not that he ever got a chance to eat pork in this God-forsaken country. He couldn't eat pork, drink ale or wine, and most importantly, he wasn't allowed to touch their women. His body longed for that first experience, at times embarrassingly so, and instead he was treated to the humiliation of witnessing the seduction of his younger brother, by a male, no less. It was almost too much to bear.

Radu slithered from the tree into Mehmed's arms and Vlad felt the bile rising into his throat as the older boy pressed Radu's body to his and ruffled his long, dark hair. Mehmed slid a meaningful glance in Vlad's direction as he presented Radu with the sword he had used to cut his cheek.

"Do you know how to clean a wound?" Mehmed asked as he draped his left arm over Radu's shoulder and directed him back toward the palace.

As they headed back down the path and away from Vlad, the two youths seemed oblivious to his presence.

As soon as they were out of sight, Vlad collapsed. Leaning against the mulberry tree, he marshaled his anger and vowed all manner of vengeance against the perverted former sultan. It took him a half hour or so before he was able to pull himself together sufficiently to return to the palace. He was sorely tempted to snatch up one of the Sultan's tame doves as he passed a fountain in which the birds were bathing and drinking. He glanced around, furtively. Surely, it wouldn't be missed. The tricky part would be keeping it quiet until he was once again secured in his room, which more closely resembled a prison cell. The monk-like chamber had been his only place of refuge these past three years. Breaking the dove's neck now would defeat the purpose of carrying it back to his room to torment it. And, he could most definitely use a little session in torture right now. He felt his body responding. Followed by some sexual gratification, of course. It was just a shame he would have to satisfy himself.

Wolf

THE OCTOBER SUN HAS LOWERED its sleepy head as Wolf leaves the building.

"Yet another psychedelic sunset igniting the landscape; how very apropos for San Francisco," Wolf mutters as the last lingering rays disappear beyond the horizon; or in this case, the high rise on the opposite side of the street.

He dresses himself in jeans, t-shirt and leather jacket tonight because he's heading back to the sleepy town of Corazon, south of San Fran, and takes the ever-patient Mephisto for a walk. He decides to feed again, early, just so he won't have to come back to this city as soon. There is something in the air and he can't decide whether or not it is danger.

"Something's going to happen," he tells Mephisto. He sits down on a still warm park bench, letting the dog run free for a few minutes. The fog is gone. It had been a perfect autumn day—turquoise-blue sky with a few lamb's wool clouds skipping across it, warm sun, pleasant breeze—not that Wolf had seen it.

Stretched lazily across the bench, he considers heading toward Geary Boulevard. He yawns, carelessly, then looks around quickly to make sure no one has seen his overly sharp teeth. Particularly the elongated canines. But there is no one but Wolf and Mephistopheles in the park. He thinks about Geary Boulevard again, dreading the following, the tracking. Because there is no fog tonight, San Francisco sparkles like a thousand jewels. Even the stars are no match for the city this evening.

Sitting soundlessly, and now a bit uncomfortably on the slatted bench, he watches a young couple enter the park. In the darkness and silence and utterly absorbed in themselves, they do not see him.

He slowly lets out his breath. This seems almost too easy, a gift from the gods, so to speak, and he doesn't want to pass it up. He can handle the two as easily as one. Just put the boy in a trance and he can easily have his way with the girl. He grins, he likes that—have his way. Hooray for euphemisms, he cheers, silently. Speaking of which, he stands up, I'd better have my way before the other fellow does. The crooked grin on his face is not agreeable.

As silently as his namesake, he crosses the park. He comes upon the lovers' bench from behind. Within seconds, the male has slithered off the seat, nearly comatose; his head makes a dull, thudding sound as it hits the concrete that secures the iron legs of the park bench. The girl soon joins her lover.

He wipes his mouth on the girl's denim jacket, and whistles for his dog. He leaves the park in high spirits, the presentiment that something might happen tonight completely forgotten.

It is past 10 p.m. before he is on his way out of town, the coastal highway weaving him toward Corazon.

Ginny

GINNY GLANCES AT THE DIGITAL CLOCK that sits next to her bed. Three-thirty, the red numerals glow. He is to pick her up in half an hour.

"I don't want to go out with Abe," she informs her full-length mirror. She should never have let him talk her into it.

"What the hell am I going to wear?" she asks her closet, more mournfully than angrily. Not that it matters, but she doesn't want to give Abe any ideas.

A burlap sack or a tent, she thinks, waiting for the perfect outfit to jump off a hanger and say *Wear me.* Her clothes don't move.

They are going to the new Moroccan restaurant in San Francisco, she rolls her eyes, about a three-hour drive from Corazon.

"Jesus, Abe, San Francisco?" she'd said. "Why can't we eat here?"

"I want our first real date to be special," he'd said. So, they are going to pig out on Moroccan food three hours away, which means six hours in the car with him, trying to make conversation. She groans for effect. Might as well rid herself of the histrionics before he arrives. That is probably part of the plan as well; she decides, uncharitably, a way to make sure he has her continued attention. Lord have mercy.

At least it's Friday, and she doesn't have a game to cover tomorrow. The San Jose Earthquakes are away this week. Of course, if she'd had the game, she might have been able to talk Abe into staying in Corazon.

After staring into her closet for another five minutes, Ginny decides on one of her patented (yet always stunning) throw-together looks—a white petticoat skirt, a red lace camisole and a forest green wool vintage dirndl jacket. She can hear her mother now, "You're going to wear that on a date with Abraham Bar El?" and the unspoken, 'one of the most eligible bachelors in California.'

She smiles wickedly at the full-length mirror. "You're damn right I'm going to wear this." She would have liked to have imagined Abe's expression of disappointment when he sees the outfit, but she knows that she could wear a paper bag and he'd look all moon-eyed at her. He understands that she can't afford the designer clothes he wears himself, and that he is used to seeing on his mother and others in their circle of society. And with a flash of insight, she realizes that he would prefer to see her dress the way she did. Anything to irk Clara Bar El, who would only roll her eyes and smirk at Ginny's eclectic manner of dressing.

She does consciously dress on the odd side. Conforming to the current standards of noncomformity, as she likes to say. She also always manages to pull off her strange combos.

Her clear skin and the structure of her face discourage makeup, which is just as well as she prefers not to wear any. It always makes her feel like she is suffocating. Perhaps a little mascara on special occasions. This afternoon, Ginny decides the least she can do for Abe is apply some mascara.

"How come guys always have long, full lashes?" she asks the bathroom mirror, as she applies the make-up to make her lashes look like they, too, are long and full.

Brushing her long, dark brown hair, she ponders securing it with her favorite pair of chopsticks, a gift from her father. He had crafted them himself, using wood from a bough of the hawthorn tree she had so loved as a child because of all the legends attached to it. He had topped each stick with a softly glowing moonstone. They are one of her greatest treasures and a lovely remembrance of her father who had died shortly after she'd completed her Master's.

"I'd better not risk my hair falling in the hummus," she laughs at her reflection, quickly twisting her hair into a bun. When the light catches it, her sun-reddened hair shimmers like burnished copper. Some-times, she wishes it were redder, though. She lays the brush on the tiled counter beneath the bathroom mirror. "But it's really just brown," she sighs with an exaggerated grimace at her reflection, but her eyes sparkle with good humor.

The doorbell rings, and her eyes dim, as if the life has been drained from them. What have I gotten myself into, she worries.

She grabs her purse from the lace-draped bed and heads for the door, cats Tigris and Euphrates doing their best to make her trip, as they dash ahead of her.

Abe hands her a perfect red rose as she opens the door. She smiles in appreciation while thinking, Oh shit, a *red* rose. She's already look-ing forward to later this evening when she can close the door in his face.

"You ready?" he asks. He is exactly on time. Just as she had opened the door, her clock had cuckooed four times.

"Yeah," she replies. He looks nice for Abe, casually rich. His curly auburn hair is perfectly trimmed and his just-too-big nose isn't quite as noticeable as it usually is.

You're going to have a good time, she tells herself, sternly.

He helps her into his immaculate vintage Mustang. Somehow the car doesn't fit her image of him. He's the sedan type. Perhaps a BMW or Mercedes, she decides, but a Mustang? Nah. But then, with another flash of insight, she realizes that maybe there are facets of Abe she has yet, or perhaps, refused, to acknowledge. Nevertheless, she fastens the seatbelt and dreads the next seven to nine hours.

Abe & Ginny

THE DRIVE UP TO SAN FRANCISCO isn't as bad as she had imagined it might be. But, and she freely admits this to herself, this tends to be one of her worst character flaws—the dreading of coming events. Pretty much without fail, she will dread whatever she has made a commitment to, often to the point of nearly not attending at all; to calling and giving her regrets. But then she will screw her courage to the sticking place, so to speak, and keep the dreaded commitment. And nearly every time, she winds up enjoying herself. 'You would think I'd have learned by now,' she silently chides herself.

They mostly talk about the paper—*The Corazon Daily Sun*. Ginny, along with being a staff writer, fills in occasionally as a sports photographer. Abe also owns a couple of radio stations and his late father's construction and development empire. It is through Abe's involvement with the paper, his pet interest, that he had the good fortune of finding Ginny.

The exotic atmosphere of the restaurant envelops Ginny as soon as she enters. The Moroccan archways, colorful tile work and splashing fountain all appeal to her romantic nature.

They are led into a small dining area, richly carpeted in Berber and Rabat rugs. She sits on a low sofa strewn with silk and velvet pillows and admires the carved brass tables and the intricately hand-painted, gold-leafed ceiling. Abe rests his feet on a goatskin ottoman, and gazes at Ginny while she surveys the room. It is important to him that she enjoy this experience; not just the food and ambience but the time spent with him. His breath catches in his throat at the sight of her reflected in the soft light that filters from the cut brass lamps. He still can't believe that she has consented to go out with him. He feels like the luckiest man in the world. If Ginny could read his mind, she would be wracked with guilt.

The scene is completed by the straw baskets from Fez, which are strewn about the small room.

The multi-course feast is served by waiters in traditional costume. It begins with a tea-server washing their hands and handing them each a towel to use as a napkin.

"The entire meal will be eaten with your hands and hunks of bread," the waiter tells them. No silverware allowed."

The meal is excellent and so is the performance by the belly dancers. Ginny feels herself relaxing, enjoying the evening. Might as well, she decides, but not unkindly. She lets Abe do most of the talking—his plans for the paper, the history of Corazon, his hopes for the future. The latter is discussed in general terms: he is too wise to mention that he hopes she'll be a part of those plans.

He enjoys talking to her. She is a good listener, he concludes at one point. That is important to him. He also enjoys looking at her, the way the lamplight catches the red in her hair, turning it to glowing embers. He hopes that she will go out with him again. He wonders how far he might get with her tonight. He doesn't even consider not trying to kiss her.

It is going on 10 o'clock when they rinse their hands and are sprayed with rosewater. Ginny delights in being sprayed with rosewater. She imagines having someone to brush her hair every morning, someone to spray her with rosewater. That would be luxury. She also feels almost unpleasantly full and not a little tired.

Three hours before I can be in bed, she laments to herself.

Wolf

H<small>E IS ONLY HALF AN HOUR NORTH</small> of Corazon when he sees her. She is standing next to an older car, a Mustang, he thinks. She is leaning against the automobile waiting for a male, it looks like, to finish changing a tire.

Their eyes meet and he feels fire course through his veins. Then he rounds the curve, and she is lost from his sight.

Hannele.

No, it couldn't have been Hannele, he reminds himself. Hannele has been dead for nearly 400 years. But oh how she had looked like her.

H<small>e</small> had wanted her for a long time. The thought of her full breasts, deep green eyes and auburn hair almost drove him mad with lust. For months he had been trying to talk her into meeting him here. And tonight, she was finally coming.

He had arrived at the clearing first and it had been frigidly cold as only a night in that part of Germany in mid-autumn could be. It was the last day in October and heading toward midnight. In a little over an hour he would be 28 years old.

The autumn air was so sharp it made his nostrils tingle and he could feel frost on the breeze. It was one of those nights when the stars are like diamonds on black velvet. You could even see the Milky Way.

He smiled when he imagined heaven's diamonds fading only to be re-placed on earth by glittering crystals of dew. She'll have to be home before that, his brow wrinkled. He wanted to spend every moment of the day with her. He wanted to watch the sun rise and set with her in his arms; make love to her just before falling asleep and again upon waking. He wanted so much and it all involved her.

He built a small fire, and waited impatiently for her to arrive.

Steam wisped from his horse's nostrils, and the bit jingled quietly as it cropped some grass not yet killed by fall's frost.

Wolf stamped his feet. They were cold but he was hot with desire. His eyes searched the darkness at the edge of the clearing. He strained his ears for the thud of Erlkönig's hooves. Surely Hannele would arrive on her favorite mount.

I'll soon be her favorite mount, he thought, and he found his face flushing with the thought. God, he couldn't wait to feel her mouth upon his, the warmth of her thighs . . . He stamped again, impatiently, and stretched his hands toward the fire for warmth. The flames caught the emerald in his family ring, and the gem flared and burnt bright for a moment.

The woods were dark but she traveled the well-worn path like a crea-ture of the night. She was on foot because her father had been restless and she was afraid he might hear her taking the horse. She would have preferred to ride the sure-footed Erlkönig through the Bavarian forest but she would not risk being caught. She had promised Wolf she would come, and she never broke her promises. And this was one promise she had been waiting oh-so-long to be asked to make.

She slowed as she neared the clearing, heart-in-throat but blood slowing to a honeyed smoothness, and burning like mead through her veins.

She watched him silently from the edge of the small glade. The pine-needle carpet, silent beneath her feet, had kept him from hearing her arrival. She watched him as he warmed his hands, shifting impa-tiently from foot to foot. She admired his profile, strong yet soft in the light cast by the dancing flames. He was thinking of her, she could see, thinking of making love to her. His desire was so obvious she felt faint. She, too, had wanted him for a long time. She had also fallen in love with him, but would never dare let the word escape her lips. Not unless he confessed his love, first.

Her full lips parted gently in expectation of his kiss. Inadvertently, she had made some sound. She could have watched him forever. He turned. Their eyes locked, burning into each other. It took her but a few steps to cross the clearing. One more to feel the embrace of his arms.

No words were spoken. He pushed the wool hood back from her fiery hair, and pulled her closer to him. Their lips met. Their hands explored. He pushed her cloak back further to reveal her full breasts, thrust upwards by the leather bustier. Her bosom was covered only by the flimsy linen of her blouse. He tried untying the ribbon, which pre-vented him from gaining access to the satin smoothness of her breasts, then impatiently tore it. Spreading her cloak on the forest's floor, he pulled her down with him . . .

A blaring car horn and warning bark from Mephisto jolt Wolf back to the future. He has drifted into the left lane and pulls hard on the steering wheel to keep from slamming into the oncoming car.

"Jesus Christ!" he swears, loudly. He starts laughing, hysterically. I'm losing my mind, he thinks when the laughter has tapered off, and I can't even look in the mirror to see if there is madness in my eyes.

For a microsecond, he considers continuing turning the wheel to the right, sending the Toyota Prius over the cliff and into the roiling ocean below. He can see the fiery hulk of burning metal as it bounces off the rocks below.

"My luck," he says out loud, startling himself, "I'd be thrown clear. Mephisto would die and I would have to walk back home, completely vulnerable and terrified that I wouldn't make it back to Corazon."

'On the other hand,' he argues with himself, 'how unmitigatedly awful would that be?' Would it really be that bad? Because if he is talking about bad luck then he *would* make it back to Corazon instead of dying some horrible death. What were the chances, really, of someone not only realizing he is a vampire but knowing what to do about it? And, once having identified him as such, actually carrying through with destroying him? How many people not only carry the appropriate stakes but know how to use them? He starts chuckling. If he is to die; well, he is going to have to make it happen himself.

"Of course," he tells Mephisto, "if I had a chance to hitch my way home or even walk it, it would be the first sunrise I've seen in nearly 400 years because I've lacked the courage to see any since shortly after I became a vampire."

It isn't that the sun actually bothers him; but not only is he predictably exhausted by sun up (and that near coma is so renewing) but he is just so damn vulnerable during day light hours. Not unlike any other mortal, he reminds himself, and there was a time when he would have thought himself invincible at any time of day.

He laughs loudly. Self-deprecatingly. It isn't in the least bit pleasant. Oh yeah. When he was in love with Hannele . . . nothing else mattered. Nothing else in the world existed. But now. But now he is a pathetic little vampire living his pathetic little existence. Worrying about the sun like some movie vampire. Yet, there is only one vampire that he knows of, and make that "knows" italic, he thought, parenthetically, who would (could?) risk being active during the day. And that would be Vlad. The vampire who had created him. He knows Vlad is an original; he just doesn't know how many "originals" there are nor how many other vampires Vlad has created. His guess would be very few, but that would only be a guess.

The highway has moved away from the cliffs relieving Wolf of that dreadful decision.

"Besides," he murmurs, "I have to find out who that woman is." Mephistopheles barks his encouragement before curling up in the backseat.

Vlad

HE COULDN'T BELIEVE IT. After enduring four long and tortuous years as a prisoner of the Turks, he was essentially back at square one; and exiled to Moldavia no less. And, while his cousin, the prince of Moldavia, had offered him asylum, he found himself frequently in Bacau.

His mistress' brother, Mihai, resided in the ancient town nestled in the foothills of the Carpathian mountains, and Anca had fled to Bacau when Vlad was exiled. Here, Vlad sought the solace only a woman could provide.

On this particular visit, Vlad stared morosely through the leaded glass of the window. Below him, the waters of the Bistrita continued their unceasing journey southward to the river, Siret.

The flow of life, he mused. But, he wasn't quite sure where his particular trajectory was taking him. He wasn't even completely sure how it had all come to end this way so very quickly.

First, he had received the news that his father had been assassinated in a coup led by one of his own relatives—Janos Hunyadi. If he were to be completely honest with himself, Vlad wasn't particularly surprised by that bit of knowledge. Hunyadi had been furious with his father since the Battle of Varna.

"The White Knight of Hungary," Vlad spat, crossing the chamber to the low couch upon which Anca reclined, and grabbing his current mistress by one of her long brown curls and twisting it, angrily. "He's a political manipulator just like all the other boyars and merchants."

Anca stifled her shriek of pain, biting down on her knuckle until tears sprang to her eyes. When Vlad was having one of his outbursts, she knew it was best to keep silent. He enjoyed inflicting pain, particularly when he was aware he was doing so. She would never have made the mistake of kindling his interest had she known when she was introduced to him the type of man he was. But he had been the ruler of Wallachia at the time . . . how was she to know that within two months of gaining the throne the same man he was railing against would appoint yet someone else to the post, another Vlad?

"I was supposed to be Vlad II," he thundered. "But, what I really don't understand," his grip tightened on her hair, "is why they had to kill Mircea. They blinded him with brands *and* buried him alive!" She'd heard this particular tirade a thousand times already and before he could rip the hank of hair he was grasping so tightly loose from her scalp, she began to stroke his arm and murmur soothingly.

He had been released by the Turks upon the death of his father and with the help of Pasha Mustafa Hassan's Turkish cavalry had defeated the boyars and reclaimed the throne.

"Two months!" he screamed, loosing his hold on Anca's hair and aiming a kick at one of her several cats. The feline disappeared, only to be seen a second later slipping through the partially open chamber door. It, too, was accustomed to Vlad's violent tantrums. "How am I to regain the throne? Do you think the Turks will help me again? At this point I'd rather impale myself than grovel at the feet of Hunyadi."

"Here, my lord, drink this," Anca poured him a goblet of wine. "It will help you think more clearly." And as he snatched it from her hand, she added, slyly, "In order that you can more perfectly plot your revenge, of course." She had learned the hard way what to say to distract him from his ravings.

As he gulped down the wine, she nuzzled his crotch, saying a quick prayer of thanks as his member responded. Much better to have him distracted by sex than to risk the bruises his anger promised. Granted, the sex would be more violent than usual but as he was wont to hit her in the face when he was really angry, she was willing to take the risk.

Later, she tried hard to maintain a neutral face as Vlad regaled her with his plans for revenge. The things he wanted to do to the boyars did not differ much in severity to what he wished to do to the Turks. He seemed to despise them equally. Had Vlad known it would be another eight years before he would be able to exact his vengeance, Anca's ministrations would be no match for his rage.

Ginny

S HE IS SHAKEN. Who was that masked man, she thinks, grinning inanely, but her eyes are troubled. Their eyes had met for only a second, perhaps two. But the way he had looked at her had sent her heart triphammering. The brief scene plays over and over in her mind. Despite the fact she was left only with an impression—pale skin, longish wheat blond hair and amazingly red lips framed by a short beard and mustache and those eyes, piercing her to her very core—she can't stop thinking about him. Her legs feel rubbery and weak and there is an unfamiliar throbbing in her groin.

"Well, that's done," says Abe, wiping off his hands on a virgin white handkerchief. Ginny is staring into space. He touches her and she jumps.

"What?" she gasps, eyes wide and staring.

"You must have been a thousand miles away," he says, taking her by the arm and leading her to the other side of the car. She lets him, but she no longer feels the amiability she had reached only half an hour earlier. She had even been considering letting him kiss her goodnight, but that may have been the wine talking.

She slides onto the recently upholstered seat. The interior looks like new, and she sees that she has gotten some dirt on the floor mat. She stifles an inappropriate giggle and wonders, for the first time, if Abe is obsessively neat.

He would probably hang all our clothes up before making love, she realizes, and has to cram her hand into her mouth to keep from laughing hysterically. She glances at him out of the corner of her eye. He has a smudge of dirt on his face and the knees of his pants are dirty. But, instead of this making him more human to her, it makes her want to laugh harder. She is temporarily sobered by this sudden giddiness. She feels unhinged. She feels the hysteria bubbling up again; and laughing as silently as possible, teeth firmly clamped on her hand, the tears begin streaming down Ginny's face.

"Ginny, are you all right?" Abe asks with growing concern. He thinks she is crying; thinks he has done something to upset her.

His earnest consideration strikes her as even more funny. You dope, she thinks, why wouldn't I be all right. Even through her agitation, she realizes that there is no way he could have seen the man in the Prius while completely absorbed in changing the Mustang's tire. And if he had, would he be feeling the same way? As her hysteria burgeons, she finds herself trying even harder to fight back the laughter, which threatens to erupt from around her hand.

Her belly is beginning to ache, and her face is as red as Abe's Mustang, before she finally gains control of herself. "I'm so sorry, Abe," she apologizes, gasping for breath, "I don't know what's wrong with me; too much wine, I guess." She leaves it at that, although it has been more than three hours since she had her last glass.

Please God, just let me get home and into bed, alone, without a hassle, she prays, and I'll . . . What? What will I do or not do? I don't drink too much. I don't smoke. Can't stop fooling around if I'm not getting any . . . she has to bite her hand again. I'm going mad, she looks wildly out the window, and her heart skips a beat. Once again her eyes meet Wolf's. He pulls in behind the Mustang. She turns around to look. He appears as mad as she feels. What's going on? She can't seem to pull her eyes away from his.

"He does seem to be following too closely, doesn't he?" Abe kvetches. "I hate drivers who refuse to maintain a safe distance. What if I have to slam on the brakes?"

Ginny's response is less an assent than a moan. Abe looks at her, worriedly.

"Are you ok? Do I need to pull over?"

Ginny forces herself to turn around and look at Abe. "No, really, I'm all right. I haven't been sleeping well," she lies, "and I guess it's starting to take its toll. Maybe the wine affected me more because I am tired." She feels guilty about lying to Abe, but how can she explain the stranger's sudden sway over her emotions. She can't even explain it to herself.

About a mile and a half later, Abe makes a right turn onto Ocean Drive. Wolf is still following them, but when Abe turns into her driveway a mile or so further, Wolf drives on.

Abe

HIS MOTHER HAS NOT WAITED UP FOR HIM. Thank God, Abe thinks. As he made the drive home, he had worried that she would still be awake, ostensibly "unable" to sleep and pretending to read, curled up in her favorite armchair. She had done that very thing on a number of occasions even though he was well aware that when she couldn't sleep she preferred to turn on the television in her room and watch something overly melodramatic on Lifetime or the Hallmark channel.

He has a false smile pasted on his face as he enters the house but he lets it fade away, gratefully. It had been painful to place there. Besides, she would have known, anyway. She always does; he has never been able to hide his emotions from her.

Upstairs, he sits heavily on his bed and stares morosely into the mirror over his chest of drawers.

What had happened? Everything had been going just to plan until the tire had gone flat and he'd had to stop and change it. Surely the tire hadn't caused her to freak out the way she had. He knows for a fact that changing a tire comes as naturally to her as wiring a ceiling lamp or fixing a leaky faucet; she is a well-rounded woman. It's one of things he loves about her.

It also wasn't the wine. They had only split the one bottle, and she'd had three hours to get over it. No, damn it, it was something else. But what?

He replays the evening over in his head, but he simply can remember no incident that might have caused her to get upset. He is still convinced that she had been crying. He would have been even more bemused had he realized her tears had been caused by hysterical laughter.

"And damn if she didn't manage to get dirt all over the floor mat," he gripes, wiping away the smudge on his face. This would have sent Ginny into gales of laughter, hand stuffed in mouth or not. Had he known the aforementioned dirt incited her hysteria, he may have finally agreed with his mother's impression of his employee.

Feeling confused and somewhat defeated, he heads back downstairs. He could really use a cognac. He had been sure as they neared Corazon that not only would he and Ginny have shared their first kiss by now, but that he might still be at her small cabin, talking, sharing a drink, wrapped in each other's arms . . .

Not yet ready to give up on her, he heads back upstairs with his brandy. Once in his room, he turns on his television to CNN, nursing his cognac for another half hour before he begins his nightly routine.

Wolf

THE DYING EMBERS OF THE CAMPFIRE radiated little warmth. Hannele shivered and Wolf pulled her closer to his chest. She trailed her fingers through the soft hair there, burying her face in his neck.

"I have to go soon," she whispered, moving her face away from the warmth of his neck to watch his face. He tightened his arms around her almost painfully.

"Don't leave me."

"If I'm not back before father awakes, he will know where I've been. He would never forgive me." Had Wolf been the butcher's son or a farmer's or any other peasant's spawn, her father might not have been displeased at her rendezvous.

But, Wolf was the son of Fürstensteinbrück's Gebieter. Being a member of the landed aristocracy was bad enough, but Wolf's family held ruling privileges over that domain, and it was highly unlikely that Wolf would ever marry the daughter of a gamekeeper.

And, as her father had told her too many times to count, there was no use fooling around with someone who could never give you something in return.

Her father had been furious when she had told him that Wolf had been pursuing her; had told her in no uncertain terms she was to steer clear of him.

"He'll only break your heart," he had told his foolishly romantic daughter. "If not worse." And the meaning was clear there. Not only did he not want to worry with the raising of a bastard, it would have ruined his daughter's hopes for marriage. He was already beginning to worry. Very few suitors had knocked upon the sturdy oak door of their woodside cottage. Perhaps he was being too protective. If only her mother were still alive. She would know what to do. But, she wasn't, and he had to do the best he could with his only child.

Wolf turned Hannele's face until she was looking into his eyes.

"I love you," he told her solemnly. "I want to marry you." Her already rosy skin crimsoned more deeply. What the hell was he talking about? He knew he couldn't marry her. She had already gone too far as it was. It wasn't fair for him to tease her like that. A tear escaped her eye, and Wolf kissed it away.

"I am very serious," he said. "I want to spend the rest of my life with you. I don't even care if my father disinherits me. I don't care if he exiles me. I love you."

Wolf pulled the heavy emerald ring off his little finger, and slid it on to the index finger of Hannele's left hand. She looked at it in wonder, the tears trembling, threatening to break the dam of her lids. She searched his face in wonder, seeing in his eyes his love, his desire and his resolve. She smiled, tentatively, and was caught in an embrace so passionate she thought she would melt into the ground like the sun-warmed snow of spring.

But frost, like the crystallized dreams of autumn, began to coat the clearing with its sugar glaze. It was nearing dawn and Hannele reluctantly pulled away from Wolf. She studied, almost shyly, the huge ring that weighed on her finger. It was more than a promise, it was a vow and because of it, her father might actually accept their love.

She smiled, suddenly, and slid her own ring, a pillow-cut amethyst guarded fiercely by a golden dragon, from the index finger of her right hand. It had been her mother's, given to her by her father when her mother had died. It was the only piece of jewelry she owned. Her own mother was disinherited by her family when she chose love over propriety. Hannele smiled, ruefully. It seemed to be a running theme in their family.

She pushed her ring onto the finger vacated by the ring that had born Wolf's family crest—the design carved into the emerald and inlaid with gold.

The love that shone in his eyes was enough to bring the tears to her.

"Why are you crying?" he asked, gently.

"Because I love you," she sobbed.

"And that gives you reason to weep?" That brought the smile back to her face, the dimples to her cheeks.

"I'm happy," she stated, simply.

Wolf lifted her onto the back of his grey stallion. At the gate leading to her father's cottage, Hannele slipped off the tall horse. A final, impassioned kiss from Wolf extracted the promise of another meeting that night. This time she would not have to hide the tryst from her father.

A tear slides down Wolf's unshaven cheek, lodging in his beard. He has not had a more than passing thought of Hannele in years. Be realistic, he admonishes himself, you haven't let yourself really think of her or even dwelled upon that night in more than 200 years.

He had, indeed, tried to block Hannele firmly from his mind, had tried to forget everything associated with 1615. He wipes the tear impatiently from the line of his jaw, where it reflects the red of the slowly rising sun.

He also has not shed a tear in nearly 400 years. He hauls himself from the soft and comfortable leather of his arm chair. Once again, and as it has for the past 400 years, the sun forces Wolf into darkness and sleep.

How nice it would be to see the earth bathed in the warm light of the morning star instead of being perpetually bound to the glacial rays emitted by night, he muses. Why do I fear death so very much? I've lived a lot longer than any person has a right to. Is the survival mode stronger in vampires than in humans? But, his thoughts jump a track, I have to be careful now. That woman, I have to watch her. Her similarity to Hannele is too strong to push aside. Soon, he will know who she was. Is, he corrected himself, absently.

As he does every dawn, he requests Mephisto's care in looking out for him as he imprisons himself in his fortress-like chamber. From the outside, no one would ever know the humble log cabin has a vampire as its resident.

Ginny

GINNY, TOO, FALLS ASLEEP AT DAWN. She has spent the night in turmoil, mind racing and adrenaline pumping. Toward dawn, she runs a scalding bath for herself, sprinkling the water liberally with lavender scented bath salts.

I'd have been fine if it hadn't of been for that damn guy in the Prius, she thinks, sliding carefully into the steaming water. His eyes had really bothered her and when their eyes had broken contact the second time, she was left with an unaccountable feeling of loss, bereavement. Brief though that connection had been, it had still left her feeling frustrated and hysterical.

She was sure Abe still thought he had done something wrong, and feeling unexplainably obtuse, she had not enlightened him on the reason for her hysteria. As if she could have explained it.

Well, you see Abe, this silver Prius passed us while you were fixing the tire, and I looked at the driver and it drove me mad. And then I got dirt on your floor mats . . . The bath is doing its work; the hysteria is fading and she manages a dry chuckle.

What had sent her mind catapulting on its own magical mystery tour, though, was when she caught his eyes again. What if she hadn't glanced out the window at that moment? Shit, she thinks, the hell with that. What was he doing? Waiting for us? Surely, that was what he had been doing. He had pulled in right behind Abe, had looked at her hard and long before driving on.

Perhaps he had been as shaken by her as she by him. But why? The scent of lavender is making her feel drowsy. The slight nausea that had followed her adrenaline rush has dissipated. Languidly, she flips the handle on the drain and stands, wrapping herself in an extra thick cotton towel.

Ginny yawns, hard and wide, eyes tightly closed. Wiping the steam from the mirror with the flat of her palm, she stares at herself for a moment. "You look tired," she informs her self, smiling empathetically. She definitely understands how the doppelganger in the mirror is feeling. It has been a long and emotionally exhausting day.

"You're haunting me," she tells the reflection. "And now that the sun is waking up, I'll go where you can't get me. To bed." Before turning out her bedside light, Ginny lifts her rosary from the small and intricately carved teakwood box she keeps it in. Twining it carefully around her palm, she slips off to sleep, the words, "Hail Mary," still on her lips.

The phone wakes her up at 10 a.m. Her answer is more a grunt than a hello.

"I woke you," her mother says, apologetically.

"No you didn't. I'm still asleep."

"Should I call you back?"

"No, I need to get up anyway," she replies, although she could use a few more hours of sleep.

"We're about to bring Merlin over."

That causes her to open her eyes. She enjoys riding the coal-black Arabian because it never fails to cheer her up. And, afterwards, grooming him, she softly murmurs to him all her troubles. And Merlin always understands. Often she would place her forehead against his broad brow, and arms stretched around the graceful arch of his neck, she would confide to him her deepest, darkest secrets and her terrible longings. She would look into his widely set eyes and find more comfort there than she had ever found in any human.

"I'm on my way to the shower. I'll tell you all about last night when y'all get here," she answers her mother's unspoken question. Raised on the coast of Georgia, she often slips into a Southern accent when she speaks to family members.

She is pulling a cream fisherman's sweater over her head when she hears her mother's knock on the door.

She opens the front door, face still pink from the quick scrub that had been necessary to wake her up more fully.

"The coffee's ready, want some?"

Her stepfather, David, smiles and nods, motioning that he is going to put Merlin in the stall he had built when he had purchased the cottage close to 20 years earlier. Ginny is now buying the house from him.

Her mother had met David when she had still been married to Ginny's father. They had become friends, and when John Hunter had died Ginny's mother, Jessie, had been quick to accept David's invitation to visit him out west. Ginny often marvels at how happy they seem together. But, she is so close to her mother that she never feels even the slightest pang of jealousy. She still dreams that she, too, will meet the man of her dreams. Her mother was lucky enough to have found two.

Her mother follows her into the country-style kitchen, and smiles appreciatively at the aroma of freshly brewed coffee.

"I ought to brew my own." A mug stuck in the microwave and a teaspoonful of instant usually began Jessie's mornings. She is always up at the crack of dawn, helping David with the numerous chores required on a horse farm.

David Tucker owns more than 500 acres in the Corazon valley, less than half an hour's drive from the seaside town.

Ginny tells her mother about the restaurant and about her irrational bout with hysteria. She doesn't mention the guy in the Prius.

"I'm afraid I upset Abe pretty bad," she sighs.

"Call him and apologize, that's the only advice I can offer."

David enters through the kitchen door. "Interrupting?"

"Not at all," Ginny smiles. She likes her stepfather. He has never tried to be more than that to her and she appreciates it. Of course, she was in her early 20s when he became her stepfather, so that probably made a difference. She points to the mug next to the coffee-maker. He helps himself, and sits down at the tiny kitchen table. Actually, it is also her dining room table since she doesn't have a dining room. The tiny cottage holds only a kitchen, bath, bedroom and den. But it is a good size kitchen, and today the warm October sun pours through the windows.

"How was the big date?" David asks, his rough hewn hands swallowing the mug. Ginny summarizes the night's events, then asks suddenly, face blushing slightly.

"Do you know any one around here who drives a silver Prius?"

Her stepfather ponders for a second while her mother looks at her expecting an explanation.

"When Abe had that flat tire last night, a good-looking guy drove by in a Prius," her blush approximates the shade of an overripe peach.

"Here you've got this rich and prominent young man dying to carry you off into the sunset, and you're looking at tourists in hybrids?" her stepfather laughs.

Ginny blushes again and joins in his laughter. So much for that. Who was that masked man, she thinks again. And had he really been handsome? She wasn't sure, she can remember only his eyes.

After another cup of coffee, and hearing updates from her mother on her brother, who recently passed the bar and has been offered a job in Atlanta; and her sister, who is still in college, she waves to her mother and David as they take their leave, promising to call later.

Ginny puts the mugs in the sink for a later washing, and runs out to greet Merlin. She's been on the edge of her seat the whole time, dying to confide to Merlin her latest woes.

A few minutes later, she is swinging into the English saddle and directing Merlin toward the forest next to her cottage. The woods extend along the coast southward from her dwelling. About a mile or so away, they are broken by a large and rambling log cabin. The one time she has ventured near the sprawling home, a ferocious dog, eyes shooting sparks, rushed at her and Merlin, fangs bared and growling fiercely. That was the only warning she had needed. Now, she turns left along that property circling back toward home.

The woods are quiet. Occasionally, the sound of traffic on the coastal highway about a mile away can be heard through the woods, but today, she can't even hear the infrequent cars passing on Ocean Drive, which borders the eastern edge of the woods about half a mile away. The rumbling of trucks and cars is dulled by the tall Monterey and Bishop pines and the miniature Gowen cypress.

She treasures each ride she takes in the thin band of forest, inhaling the pine like a tranquilizer. Today's ride is quieter than most, even the birds seem to be napping. She can even hear the waves pounding on the shore a quarter-mile to the west.

Ginny emerges out of the woods near her cottage looking and feeling tranquil. As she grooms Merlin, they discuss the previous evening. After a nap, she promises, we'll run like the wind.

Wolf

WOLF'S EYES SPRING OPEN just as the sun disappears beyond the western horizon, setting ablaze the Pacific Ocean in fiery tones of red and orange. He showers quickly, not even bothering to shave the stubble growing around his neatly trimmed beard. Most people did not keep his unusual timetable, and he wants to watch that woman for as long as possible before she goes to sleep.

Her house is just a mile away through the woods, and he easily jogs the distance within ten minutes. He is just looking for a good vantage point, when the screen door on the side of the cottage slams shut, and he sees her heading for what looks like a single-stall stable.

She even walks like Hannele, he muses. She moves with the sure grace of someone used to the outdoors. He admires the way the jeans she is wearing cling to her legs. Amazed at himself, he rubs his eyes. Remembering Hannele, and seeing this woman so much like her, has awakened long-forgotten feelings and memories. Mostly, he regrets that he can do nothing about those feelings. Feeding is the closest he can now get to sexual gratification.

He watches from behind a large rhododendron as she leads a midnight black Arabian out of the stable. As the horse passes beneath the stable's floodlight, his heart skips a beat. The stallion looks like Erlkönig.

Well, a lot like him, he corrects himself. Hannele's father could not have afforded such a fine horse as this one.

She mounts, and turns the horse toward the beach. He follows, discreetly. The clean, white sand reflects the moonlight and the two take off like a sirocco on the Sahara.

The first time he had seen Hannele, she had been riding Erlkönig. It had been June, and she and the horse had been racing across a field full of flowers. Marguerites and buttercups crowned the flaming red of her hair, and garlanded the steed's ebony mane and tail.

She had taken his breath away. He had sat, mouth agape, on his dappled grey mount, and as she passed him, she had turned toward him, laughing at the expression on his face. She had said something, flippant about catching bees for honey, and he had raced after her.

Their horses had been foaming when they finally stopped the chase. She had always remained just ahead, just out of reach.

He had handed her a flower, "Who are you?"

"Hannele, die Tochter des Wildhüters." Her eyes were the color of evergreens. He had heard about the beauty of the gamekeeper's daughter; even knew that she was not betrothed. He wondered if she had a lover, he had not heard that she had. In spite of her reputation in the village as being too assertive, most of the rumors at the castle centered around who she would choose as her lover. Now, he understood why.

"I'm . . ." he started.

"I know who you are," her mouth curled in amusement. Of course she did. He was the only son of the lord of the village. She probably knew as much about him as he did himself. Gossip ran high in a hamlet such as this, and he knew most of it centered on what the ruling family was up to, and if that was too boring, excitement was fabricated into their lives.

His eyes were drawn to her full breasts, still heaving slightly from the recent exertion. He could have reached out and caressed them, and she would not have said a word. But, he just couldn't do that to her. He did not want to take her crudely, did not want his position in the village to be the reason he could have her. He wanted her to want him.

He could see in her eyes, too, that she was interested but was unsure of his intentions. Would he just use her or was he interested in something more? He helped her mount Erlkönig, grasping her cotton-stockinged leg, "I want to see you again."

The corner of her mouth lifted in amusement. He wanted to kiss the dimple there.

"You know who I am," she returned, simply, and clucked to the tired horse, "zu Hause, Erl, zu Hause." He watched them ride off.

Wolf follows Ginny out on to the beach and watches her. He stands beneath the sea-gnarled limbs of a cypress, enjoying the sting of the breeze-flung mist against his face. When he appears on the mile-long stretch of smooth sand, Merlin begins to prance in nervousness. A moment later the horse flies southward, the sand spraying upward from his pounding hooves.

He watches as they return, walking slowly toward the cottage. As they near him, Merlin once again begins skipping, white-eyed and skittish. He sees her try to calm the dancing animal; sees her look around for the problem. She cannot see him, at least not in his human form, but when she spies him in his current manifestation, and nudges her steed closer, curiosity winning over her fear, he takes flight.

Disappointed, she soon leads the horse back to the stable, and Wolf follows them there. Watching as the horse stamps and snorts as she grooms him, he observes the way she continues to look over her shoulder as if she feels someone is watching her. Before leaving him for the night, Ginny throws some oats in Merlin's trough and kisses him tenderly on the velvet-smoothness of his muzzle. She seems to be in a hurry to get inside.

He continues to watch her when she goes inside, smiling in amusement as the lights are switched on one by one in each room. He sees her fall on the four-poster bed, stare at the ceiling for awhile, then get up and walk over to her compact disc player. She pulls a jewel case from the rack next to the player, and inserts a CD into the player. He soon recognizes the strains of Saint-Saëns' Danse macabre.

How appropriate, he broods, and sadness or perhaps regret tugs at his heart. He sees her see him, looking startled. They stare at each other for close to a minute as her expression changes to wonder and curiosity. He disappears. Tomorrow I will speak to her, he promises himself. His stomach drops slightly, and his heart beats a little faster. If, he grimaces, I don't scare her away, first.

Ginny

SHE HAS THE FEELING SHE IS BEING WATCHED the moment she steps out the door. The hairs on the back of her neck even seem to prickle. Merlin, too, seems a bit jumpy as she saddles him, the whites of his eyes showing as he continually looks over his back.

She leads him out of the tiny stable, mounts and rides toward the beach. The view leaves her breathless. A not quite full moon reflects off the beach's white sand as well as off the foam which sprays the air with mist each time a wave strikes the rocky shore.

She doesn't even have to speak; Merlin intuits her desire to run, to fly down the narrow strand of beach. He obeys the feeling, and Ginny mistakes his earlier uneasiness for unrelieved energy.

The beach turns rough and rocky a mile or so south. Ginny likes to call this stretch 'mean.' "Just like that big dog that lunged at us not too far from here," she tells Merlin, pulling back to a trot before slowing to a walk and circling back around toward home.

As they near her cottage, Merlin begins rearing slightly, prancing in agitation. His tiny, in-pointed ears twitch nervously.

"Was gibt's?" she asks the horse in German. The language had been one of her majors when she attended the University of Georgia. She had taken up the subject for no reason other than she enjoyed it. She had also majored in journalism and after spending one semester at the University of Heidelberg, honing her knowledge of the language, had considered returning to Germany to work for a year or two. But, it had seemed more practical to go ahead and get her Master's in Journalism, and then her father had died and somehow her dreams of returning to Germany had slipped away.

Merlin answers her query quite vocally and a shiver runs up her spine. He is right, of course. She can sense it again, too, that feeling of being watched. She looks around to see if there is anyone else on the beach. There very seldom is, blocked as the beach is here by a rocky cliff, and to the south by more jagged rocks, not to mention a ferocious dog.

Her heart stands still for a moment as her eyes pass over the lone, tall cypress that stands guard over the path that leads to the beach.

She starts breathing again. It is only a very large bat. You don't see those here very often, she thinks. At first, she'd seen the bat as a troll crouched in the dense spray of foliage protruding from a lower branch. A troll, yeah right, she smiles, wryly, boy is your imagination on over-drive.

She turns Merlin toward the path, informing him that the intruder appears to be nothing more than a hoary bat. She hopes to get a closer view of the unusually large creature, but when it realizes she is approaching, it flies off toward her cottage.

Merlin continues his dance as she combs the sweat from his silky coat. And the feeling has returned. She feels so strongly that she is being watched that the back of her neck tingles as if someone were breathing on it. She has caught herself looking over her shoulder several times, but never sees anyone there, not even a particularly large bat.

Nevertheless, she hurries Merlin's cleaning, dashes some oats into his trough and kisses him briefly, but guiltily, so that she can secure the safety her cottage offers as quickly as possible.

Once inside, she has to turn on all the lights before she feels safe. She still feels as though she is being watched, but the sensation is not quite as strong as it had been outdoors.

Frustrated now that her earlier tranquility has completely vanished, Ginny falls heavily on to the down-filled comforter that covers her bed. Her fingers caress the soft moss green flannel as she stares at the ceiling, wondering what to do. Finding her still for a moment, Tigris and Euphrates leap onto the bed and curl up next to her.

"I'm not tired enough to sleep," she complains as she begins to stroke their silky fur, "and I'm too freaked to concentrate on reading." Unless she wants to watch a DVD, television is out of the question. As a minor form of rebellion, she refuses to pay the outlandish prices charged by the local satellite company. She can keep up with the news at work, after all.

"How about some music? She disturbs the softly purring cats by jumping up to peruse the spines of her more than 100 CDs. She finally selects one from the rack.

"I haven't listened to this in a long time," she mumbles to the cats, who have resettled themselves on her bed. Danse macabre seems to fit the way she is feeling. Since she was a teen, she has loved to imagine the dead crawling from their graves just as the sun sets, cavorting all night—the music reminds her of another song. "What is it?" She asks no one in particular. Oh, yes, "back to back, belly to belly, well I don't give a damn, 'cause I'm done dead already, back to back, belly to belly at the zombie jamboree."

Ginny smiles as she imagines the skeletons coming to a sudden halt with a rattle of bones, gleaming white skulls atilt as they listen to the cock crow, and then reluctantly returning to their tombs. Her smile is frozen on her face as she turns toward the window. She actually jumps, she is so startled, and her heart feels like it is banging against her ribcage.

A huge wolf-like dog is staring at her through the window, massive paws resting on the window frame, its golden eyes luminous. Jesus. She stares back for almost a minute, as her fear fades to interest. Is it dangerous? The cats have now spotted it, as well, and leap off the bed, scrambling beneath it, growling deeply. She takes a step toward the window and the dog leaps off the porch and is lost in the darkness of the forest.

Darn, she pouts. But the feeling of being watched is gone. She glances at her clock. Only 9 p.m., she sighs, maybe she *should* call Abe and try to apologize. She's managed to put it off all day, but the longer she waits, the harder it will be to lift the receiver and make the call.

She keeps a land line because her mother refuses to call her cell phone.

She sits down on her bed, and reluctantly lifts the receiver. I hate apologizing, she moans to herself.

Mrs. Bar El answers the phone, and as Ginny asks sweetly for Abe, she swears the woman is actually considering whether or not to admit that Abe is there.

"Who is it?" she hears Abe in the background. He sounds more than a little bit hopeful.

Well, shit, Ginny frowns, if he wanted to hear from me that badly, why the hell didn't he call me himself? Tigris and Euphrates, who have been hiding since they spied the wolf-dog at the window, re-emerge from under the bed. They rub around her legs before joining her on the four poster bed. She pulls her legs up so she can lie on her side, snagging a couple of toss pillows to cradle her head. Might as well be comfortable. The cats immediately bed down in the curve that she makes, purring loudly.

"Hello?" Abe sounds so stiff in his greeting that Ginny almost laughs, but she says,

"Hello, Abe, it's Ginny."

"Yes." he replies, crisply, obviously trying to sound in control but what he really sounds like is someone who is trying to hold a marble between his buttocks. That's unfair, and Ginny knows it, but the image makes her want to laugh anyway. She pretends a cough, instead.

"Excuse me," she returns, politely, "dust in my throat. I wanted to call and apologize for my behavior last night, Abe. I have no excuse. I really don't know what came over me. Maybe I allowed myself to get more run down than I'd realized. I truly am sorry."

The relief is so obvious in his exhalation that her heart throbs, painfully, with guilt. Oh Jesus Abe, please don't want me so much, she wishes she could tell him.

"Perhaps we can try again," he suggests, "this time closer to home."

"Sure, Abe." She hopes that sounds more enthusiastic than she feels.

"I thought maybe we could have a picnic tomorrow." Tomorrow, jeez he isn't wasting any time, she groans, inwardly.

"A picnic? Where did you have in mind?"

"I thought we could go down to the Point." The Point, that's safe enough. At least they wouldn't be alone. There would be more than enough people around on a Sunday. "And Mother could come along," he continues, somewhat tentatively, as if his mother's presence might be the deal breaker.

If Abe isn't bad enough, she rolls her eyes at her cats, but his mother, too? Honestly, if she didn't feel like it was in her best interests to get their relationship back on somewhat normal ground, she might refuse. Oh, who is she kidding? She knows she'll agree but Lord have mercy, was her behavior last night *that* bad? Did she really deserve to be punished for it?

No, probably not, but she really does have to make up to him for the previous night; if for no other reason than he is her boss.

"Sounds great," she lies, cheerfully. "What time?"

"I'll pick you up around noon." She wants to cry. Never again, she promises herself, even if I have to find another job.

"See you then, Abe. Goodnight." She carefully sets down the receiver. Just for a moment, she gives into a brief fantasy of being able to turn and seek comfort in the arms of the man that had so shaken her the previous night. Something about him set her very soul aflame with desire. Instead, she bumps heads with her cats, who offer their own purring sympathy.

Downcast, she walks into the bathroom to coerce a little sympathy out of her mirror image while washing her face for the night. "What have you gone and done now?" she asks, plaintively, but her only response is her own mournful eyes returning her gaze.

She is well aware of the fact that Abe's mother not only does not approve of her (she's cataclysmically below Abe's 'station' as far as Clara is concerned) but she is also Catholic, and she is more than happy with her faith; it's unshakeable as far as she is concerned and converting to Judaism is not even an option for her. She suspects Clara Bar El would be a bit more friendly towards her if she were at least Jewish. To be fair to Abe, she does know that is not his expectation. Nevertheless, he has now invited the both of them to lunch: Together!

"Give her a break," she reprimands the mournful reflection. "Maybe she's trying to give you a chance."

Or maybe, she thinks, spitefully, this is the old witch's way of keeping an eye on her baby.

Danse macabre repeats itself yet again in the other room. "Ok, that's enough of that," she says out loud and remembers the bat and wolfish dog. Stranger than odd, she muses, using one of her mother's favorite expressions. Stranger than odd.

She heads to the kitchen to make some chamomile tea before settling into bed wrapped in the comforting warmth of her flannel gown, cats snug against her, tea in one hand, a light romance in the other.

She wakes at dawn, just as Wolf is heading to bed. A light mist dances through the trees outside. She decides not only is it a perfect time for a ride through the woods, but she'd still have time to get to Mass. Hopefully, it will calm my nerves before the, da dum, she plays the organ in her head, Picnic at the Point. Here I am getting all worried and it'll probably be just like that "Monty Python" skit, she chides herself.

"When suddenly, da dum, nothing happened," she laughingly tells Merlin. He is no longer jumpy and is pleased to carry her through the ethereal forest. Ethereal, that's a good word, she muses. The woods did look otherworldly this morning. She can almost hear the tinkling laughter of the fairies, and thinks she can hear the rustle of their wings as they skitter from toadstool to toadstool. She dreads the day this land is developed. She doesn't realize it belongs to the person who owns the log cabin. Wolf would be pleased she finds so much pleasure in it. He owns the land for a mile on either side of his house, had purchased it more than a century ago as a refuge from his travels. And as long as he owns it, it will never be changed; just as it has remained essentially unchanged for thousands of years.

The rising sun strikes the mist, sending it swirling and eddying about Merlin's feet. Dew drips from the pines, splashing Ginny and the horse. The cold beads bathe Ginny with the essence of the trees. She wishes there were a perfume that compared.

She turns up her nose at most of the fragrances on the market, especially the ones she sees splashed in advertisements across slick magazine pages. She prefers the sweetness of honeysuckle, the faraway images conjured by sandlewood and patchouli, the clove-like scent of carnations, and the refreshing scent of evergreens.

They are nearing her cottage again. She considers, briefly, a quick run on the beach, but decides against it.

"Too much to do before noon," she explains to Merlin. "We'll have to run later." Depending on her schedule each week, she either keeps Merlin in Corazon or at Half Moon Farms, David's ranch. This week she hopes to keep Merlin with her.

When she returns from early mass, Ginny throws on old jeans and a sweatshirt and makes short shrift of the weekly housekeeping and a bit of stall cleaning. These tasks keep Ginny busy until 11 o'clock. Throwing herself into completing her chores has kept her from thinking of her date, but now she has an entire hour to worry about it.

"**S**o, what does one wear on a picnic when accompanied by one of the town's richest women, and her son?" she is talking to the mirror again, having wiped a shower-fogged spot clean. She admires the way she is able to raise one eyebrow in mock disdain.

"Who the hell cares?"

She feigns shock. "Really!" she says, looking properly haughty. "Listen to the girl speak." Tired of the game, she returns to her bedroom. "You're right," she tells herself out loud, "wear what you feel like wearing. Abe won't mind if you shock his mother, he probably expects you to do just that, and so does she."

She decides on nice-shocking. She pulls on a vintage, wide-wale corduroy mini skirt in slate gray and a cropped polo sweater in chocolate brown. She threads a two-inch wide dark brown belt through the loops of the skirt, and decides on textured grey tights and chocolate brown ankle-high, lace-up boots. She loves shoes, especially boots. But, she rarely wears jewelry, usually only earrings. She pulls her hair back into a pony tail and adds a silver grey grosgrain ribbon for good measure.

Only a few more minutes. He'll be on time, of course. The sound of Ginny popping the top off a can of cat food in the kitchen brings the cats running.

"Oh, yeah," she bitches at them, "you only love me when I'm opening cans. Well, this time you're lucky, because I happen to be feeding you early just in case I get back late from the point." She plops some Science Diet into their bowls, wondering how it could smell so good yet taste like crap. Of course she'd tried it. Who hasn't? She knows them well enough to know they'll be begging to be fed again no matter what time she gets back.

Her door chimes, and she takes a deep breath. Here goes nothing.

Abe, Ginny & Clara

HOW DOES SHE ALWAYS MANAGE TO LOOK SO GOOD, Abe thinks when the door is opened. She is wearing her long wavy hair pulled back with a silver-grey ribbon, and mother-of-pearl glistens on the earrings dangling from her ears.

Abe, himself, is dressed properly casual in white cotton jeans, a black-and-white-striped t-shirt, a red nylon zip-front jacket and a black silk and cotton blazer by Etro, no less. He is wearing a pair of black Gucci loafers, and with those black-framed glasses, Ginny has to admit that he looks kind of sexy in a nerdy kind of way.

And, she is correct when she guesses that he probably has a Burberry mac in the trunk of the car. The question is, did he bring one for her? Now, that would be nice to own—a Burberry macintosh. Never know when it might rain, she smiles, secretly. Wishful thinking, she knows. It is more likely he has an umbrella or two on hand for those unexpected showers that were so frequent here.

He waits for her to lock the door, before escorting her to the car, arm around her waist. That has to be for his mother's benefit, she thinks.

They are traveling to the Point in his mother's burgundy Volvo today. Clara loves the tank-like car but allows Abe to drive, and has even offered to sit in the back. Heaven forbid that Abe think she's trying to sabotage his relationship with Ginny.

"Good afternoon, Virginia," she says.

"How are you, Mrs. Bar El," Ginny's smile is strained. Clara notes she has pretty, straight and white teeth. But the girl's beauty has nothing to do with her inappropriateness for Abe.

"Clara," she corrects, acidly.

"Clara," Ginny says, fastening her seatbelt and grimacing inwardly. This is going to be a long day.

Ginny and Abe try to make small talk during the half-hour drive to the Point but they are met by stony silence from the back seat, as Clara gazes unseeingly out the window. Obviously, the curt greeting she offered is all that Clara can manage at the moment.

Abe is not far wrong in assuming that Ginny no doubt thinks his mother is making it unnecessarily hard on the both of them.

Actually, Ginny is thinking the woman is a dyed-in-the-wool bitch. So, what the heck, she talks with Abe, instead. They've never really had a problem thinking of things to say to each other. As a matter of fact, Ginny thinks, perversely, I won't stop talking. Clara can see for herself just how much Abe wants me.

"What did you say?" she asks, leaning closer to Abe and touching his thigh, briefly. She can almost feel the hatred radiating from Clara.

At Point Lobos, they drive through the reserve. Ginny spots a few black-tailed deer, which despite her vow to appear disinterested, manages to spark Clara's interest. Abe finds a picnic spot, and starts unloading the lunch.

"Would you ask her to put the cloth on the table," Clara says to Abe.

Ginny turns her head to hide the hurt and hate in her eyes. Why couldn't Clara ask Ginny herself? Instead of standing up for her, Abe hands Ginny the red-and-white checked table cloth. Back stiff, she silently spreads the cloth over the concrete table.

The "hers" and "she's" continue. At one point, when Abe requests that his mother call her by name, Clara replies that she feels Virginia is too big a name for such a tiny person.

"Call me Ginny, then," she says through clenched teeth, thinking that five-feet, four-inches isn't all that tiny.

"Will you ask her to pass me the cheese," Clara looks coldly at her son.

"Mother," he begins to protest, but she cuts him short.

"My mother always said that if you cannot say something nice about someone, don't say anything at all."

Ginny blinks back her tears, gulping down the excellent Chianti. Despite the fact Abe prepares a mean picnic, and she has no doubt Abe is responsible, she resolves then and there never to go out with Abe again. Fuck you, bitch, she swears to herself, enraged by Clara's treatment of her, I hope your son never forgives you.

Çlara

T HE RIDE BACK TO TOWN IS UNCOMFORTABLY QUIET. Ginny stares out the window of the Volvo, sullenly, her discomfort nearly palpable. Abe, hands gripping the steering wheel so tightly that it would hurt to remove his fingers later, concentrates on driving. Only Clara seems relaxed, her pale blue eyes shining with victory. She has pulled them apart. At least, she feels, she has alienated Virginia.

A be drops his mother off first, not even bothering to open the door for her.

He'll get over her, Clara is confident.

She stands at the door, and watches until the Volvo is out of sight.

Then, she goes inside and pours herself a sherry. Her hand shakes slightly and her mouth thins in annoyance. She shouldn't let Virginia upset her that way.

But she is so terribly afraid of losing her son, and it doesn't occur to her that by estranging Ginny, she might also be distancing herself from her son, as well. If she could think rationally about it, she would realize that if she loosened her grip on Abe, she might never lose his love. But the more he strains at the leash, the tighter her grip becomes.

The death of her husband, Zev, had left her emotionally at sea. The heart attack had been unexpected. He'd only been thirty-eight. So young. Too young to die that way.

Abe had hidden himself in his room to mourn, leaving her without a shoulder to lean on. The few times she'd knocked softly on his door, he'd yelled "go away" with such pain and hate in his voice, that she crept away like an unloved pet.

Financially, she'd had nothing to worry about. Zev, like his father before him, had inherited the family business along with the family money. The Bar Els had been in Corazon for more than a century. They had made their money in gold, first, when Yitzak Bar El had arrived in California with the gold rush of 1849. Yitzak had used the money from the gold he'd mined to buy huge tracts of land in the Napa Valley. He later sold that land at a large profit, and invested it in a number of interests, including a new industry in California—lumber. And soon, along with the lumber, Yitzak drifted into construction and development.

He then settled on the coast in a small town called Corazon, named after the Franciscan mission that had preceded it—Sagrado Corazon de Jesus.

In the 1870s, Yitzak's son began a newspaper. Although he established *The Corazon Daily Sun* for his own amusement, the paper remained in the family. But, until Abe came along, the Bar Els took no real interest in the daily machinations of running a paper.

Although Abe keeps an eye on the construction and development business that had made the family its money, his real love is the newspaper. He enjoys the people who work on it with him. He loves making suggestions for layout as well as story ideas, and he keeps up with the latest trends in publishing. He retains a membership with the National Press Photographers Association for the one photographer on his staff—mainly so he can see the layouts presented in their monthly magazine.

Clara humors his interest in the Sun, but she would much rather he spend more time with his father's business. If he had done that, she reasons, he might never have noticed Virginia.

And, she suspects that one of the reasons he spends so much time there is because of her. But, that's not actually true. Abe had spent as much time at the newspaper before Ginny arrived as he does now. Only now, he enjoys the time he spends there even more.

What is she going to do with Abe? She wonders what his father would think. In the idolized vision she has of him now, he would support her by telling Abe he must find a woman not only of their social stature but Jewish as well. Either Rachel, their banker's daughter or Leah, the daughter of Daniel Lewis, president of Lewis Pacific Crest Properties, would be thrilled to become the bride of Abraham Bar El.

Clara smiles at the thought of the latter match. Leah is the only child of Daniel and Sarah Lewis. Wouldn't it be nice for my grandchild to own most of the property worth owning in Monterey County, the smile broadens then disappears as she realizes she's grinning foolishly into the gloomy room.

She sinks slowly into her overstuffed armchair. But the way things are going now, that match isn't likely to happen. She stares, unblinkingly, ahead until she suddenly realizes that the sun has set and she can only dimly see the objects in the room.

Had her husband still been alive, he would have been quite happy with Abe's interest in Ginny. Clara has forgotten that she once was the daughter of one of his grandfather's clerks, and that Zev had been so in love with her that he had soon won over his parents' slight objections to her.

Ginny & Abe

AS HE PULLS AWAY from the huge Second Empire-style home, Abe begins to apologize.

"No need to apologize," Ginny says, quietly, eyes down. "It wasn't your fault." Secretly, she is glad of a reason to be rid of him, but she isn't going to make him feel guilty about his mother's behavior. That wouldn't be fair. He isn't a bad guy.

He talks her into a drink at the Boar's Head, the same place he had asked her for their first date. Does he think that is somehow going to make her more amenable? Hard to believe that was only a few days ago, Ginny realizes, shocked, for some reason it feels like ages although not that much has happened since then.

They talk over a bottle of Sonoma wine. A couple of hours pass. Abe orders an appetizer and another bottle of wine.

He is easy to talk to; she'd never said she didn't want him as a friend. Actually, she is hoping the wine will make it easier for her to tell him she really doesn't want to go out with him again. Unless, of course, it is as friends. Another hour passes. Her head is beginning to buzz. She is stalling.

I can be such a damn wimp at times, she thinks, fuzzily. Abe asks her if she wants to remain there for dinner.

She is hungry again and she needs to sober up. Yes, she nods. She refuses wine with dinner, drinking water instead.

"Have to work tomorrow," she tells him. "Can't go to work with a hangover."

"Sure you can," he laughs. She smiles, and skillfully changes the subject each time he appears about to ask her out.

The sun has set when they leave the Boar's Head. Abe takes her home, but decides against asking her out again today. She appears to have thawed toward him, and he isn't about to destroy the progress he's made. His mother has caused enough damage already. He's just glad Ginny is still speaking to him.

"See you later," he says, after she has unlocked the door.

"Goodnight, Abe," she says, stepping inside. Abe feels he is being watched as he returns to the Volvo. He peers into the gloom for a minute but sees nothing. Shrugging, he gets into the car and drives off.

Ginny & Wolf

As soon as the Volvo's taillights disappear from her driveway, Ginny runs through the house to her bedroom, a scream rising in her throat.

She runs into her room blinking back tears of frustration. She again wonders if she is losing her mind.

"Are you insane!" she yells at the wild woman in the mirror. She puts her hands to her face, then pulls them away, whipping her head around, wildly. She has the feeling she is being watched again.

She pulls off the sweater and skirt, throwing them on the floor. Kicking of her boots, she rips her tights off her lean legs and stalks to her dresser.

"Now he thinks you'll go out with him again," she scolds. "You're no better off than you were before you went on the picnic."

She pulls a pair of faded, holey-kneed Levis from the bottom drawer, a white t-shirt from the top. After donning them, she grabs a denim jacket from the closet, and exchanges her nice boots with another pair, which are discolored and ratty-heeled. Wolf, who is watching her through the bedroom window, thinks she looks incredibly sexy and once again curses his state.

Ginny doesn't even bother to saddle Merlin. They take off down the beach reminiscent of Ichabod Crane fleeing from the headless horseman. Ginny finally lets loose an anguished scream and the smile freezes on Wolf's face.

He heard Hannele scream like that once. A scream of frustration and anger, except Hannele's had been tinged with fear as well.

That time, he was the one late for the tryst. He and his father had had a tremendous argument when he announced his intention of marrying the gamekeeper's daughter. But, because he was not affected by threats of disinheritance and exile, Wolf stood strong. So did his father. And Wolf, noticing the hour was getting late, slammed out of the house in the middle of an especially fierce quarrel.

What a perfect birthday, he thought, saddling his stallion.

His ride through the woods struck him as unnaturally quiet. Fear settled in his brain, the chills that coursed up and down his spine made him sit up straighter. He kicked his horse, urging him to go faster.

He heard Hannele scream just as he neared the clearing, and was off his horse with sword drawn in one fluid motion. He was not prepared for what he saw.

Hannele had lit a small fire, and in the light from its meager flames, Wolf could see a man of average height but extraordinary pallor leaning over her. There was blood on his rather fixed and cruel-looking mouth, and blood flowing from Hannele's neck. She hung limply in the stranger's arms.

The expression of surprise on the stranger's face slowly stiffened into amusement.

"I knew she was waiting for someone," he smiled, cruelly. "I cannot believe I allowed my lust for her blood to cause me to lose sight of that fact." And with a exaggerated sneer, he casually snapped Hannele's neck. The sound of her neck breaking broke Wolf's paralysis, and he lunged at the intruder.

The villain laughed, liquidly dodging Wolf. His sharp white teeth flashed in the firelight. Wolf turned and his heart froze. The man was still laughing at him, but there was something in the stance, something in the look that seemed older than time. The knife-sharp canines champed, spraying foamy blood—Hannele's blood. Wolf lunged again, and this time the stranger did not appear as quite as amused. He almost too easily took the sword from Wolf's hand, and smiling disagreeably while licking Hannele's blood from his remarkably ruddy lips, broke it. The creature, for he could not be human, stared at Wolf with a meaning Wolf couldn't fathom.

Wolf came at him again, snarling, and was thrown across the clearing. He landed in a heap near Hannele, and lay stunned for a moment. When his head cleared, and he saw the motionless body of Hannele, head bent in an impossible angle, his anger returned. He jumped up, whipping around to the direction from which he'd been thrown to discover that the fiend had disappeared. A large, black dog now occupied the clearing, teeth bared menacingly.

Almost without thinking, Wolf pulled the hunting knife from his boot and hurled it smoothly at the dog. Had the beast's reflexes been slower, the knife would have lodged deeply in its heart. Instead, the dagger imbedded itself deeply in the animal's shoulder. It's long howl echoed with pain and frustration as it disappeared into the shadows at the far side of the clearing.

Wolf paced the clearing, staring blindly into the darkness where the dog had disappeared for nearly half an hour. He was growing stiff from the cold and he felt as if every muscle in his body ached. When he finally turned to face the reality of Hannele, his heart felt like lead in his chest.

She was as beautiful in death as she was in life. Her red hair blazed and her moss-green eyes still reflected a recently discovered love. He took her in his arms, holding her tightly, desperately. He kissed her cooling lips only once, and cried. The tears edged slowly out of his eyes as if not sure of the world they were about to enter. The trickle soon became a flood, but Wolf did not sob. He cried silently, and when the tide of tears finally ebbed, he had sworn to himself that he would find Hannele's murderer and kill him. Then he vowed never to love again.

He held Hannele by the slowly dying fire until the first rays of the sun began to seep through the trees. As the forest transformed from grey to green, Wolf pulled Hannele up onto his horse with him. Then he carried the bad news home to her father.

When he carried the gamekeeper's daughter up to the tiny cottage, he told the stricken man who answered the door to bury her in the old way—mouth stuffed with garlic and wild roses.

"If you need me to sever her head," he said, reluctantly, "I will do that for you."

Ginny and Merlin are cantering back up the beach when the white face swims out of the darkness at her. Merlin rears, neighing shrilly.

"Jesus Christ!" she screams in fear, "you scared the shit of out me." She reigns in the wildly prancing Merlin, to eye the man, warily. It's the guy from the Prius. Her stomach does a somersault and she feels a nearly unbearable urge to throw herself into his arms. "You could've been killed," she accuses him.

Wolf starts laughing, and Ginny blushes.

"I've seen you before," she says, staring hard at him, "In the Prius, you passed us that night we had a flat tire, and then again, later you pulled in behind us." She realizes the strangeness of the situation, and looks at Wolf suspiciously.

"You reminded me of someone," he speaks. His voice is pleasantly deep with a slight accent.

"And?"

"And, I wanted to meet you," he states. She looks at him for a moment, trying to decide whether to trust him or not. The way he looks at her reminds her of the feeling she has had the past two nights; the feeling of being watched.

"This isn't the first night you've been out on the beach watching me, is it?" she says with dawning realization.

"No." Despite the peculiarity of the situation, she slides off Merlin. She is surprised at herself yet can't seem to stop herself, either. Somehow, intuitively, she knows he won't hurt her. And, even though he looks strange, a little peaked, she senses somehow that she is safe with him.

"So?"

"I'd like to talk to you, if you don't mind."

"I have to get Merlin set for the night. Come along if you like." She leads the trembling black stallion toward his home. When she reaches the miniature stable, she flips on the light. Neither of them had bothered to speak as they walked the short distance to her house. There is something strange, different, about this man, although she can't decide what.

His paleness is even more evident in the light. He, too, is dressed in faded Levis and a white t-shirt. But he wears a leather jacket. She can't decide if she's attracted to him or not. He's tall and slender, easily more than six feet, and his jeans hang enticingly low on his narrow hips. He's not unattractive, there's just something odd about him.

Wolf watches her as she grooms Merlin. The horse has stopped trembling but still eyes Wolf askance. She only resembles Hannele, he realizes when he sees her in the light. Her hair, although glowing here and there with copper and bronze, is not the blazing deep auburn that Hannele's was. Neither are her eyes the deep green of the Bavarian forest. They are golden brown, like the gem, tigereye. For some reason, that makes him feel better. He would not like to feel tempted to compare her always to Hannele. Always, he thinks, ruefully, she may run in fear when she finds out what you really are.

Ginny leads Merlin into his stall, and pours some oats into the trough. Once again, Wolf watches her kiss the silky muzzle, and wonders if he'll ever kiss again.

She closes the stall door, and looks at Wolf. He is looking at her. She smiles, "Well, I don't want to stand out here. I'm getting chilly. This is probably crazy on my part, but you are welcome to come in and talk to me."

Wolf smiles without parting his lips, "That would be nice, thank you." And he is glad because unless invited, he would not have been able to enter her abode.

She leads him into the cottage. It's very much changed since he was last there. When Franz Krumberg had died, he had sold the place, through an intermediary, to David Tucker.

He likes what she has done with it.

"My name is Ginny, by the way," she says, extending her hand. "Ginny Hunter."

He takes her hand in his own gloved one, "I am Wolf Nachttier."

"Wolf?" she smiles, questioningly.

"It's German," he answers. "Actually, it's Wolfdietrich."

"Oh," she smiles in recognition, "like the German author, Wolfdietrich Shnurre." He nods. "Would you like a glass of wine or something?" Ginny asks, heading toward the kitchen. She opens the refrigerator, hand pausing over a bottle of Chardonnay, before selecting bottled water. She's had more than enough wine for one day.

"No, thank you." He has forgotten what wine tastes like, forgotten everything but the taste of blood. He thinks that if he could ever eat again, he would shun red meat.

There are a thousand questions he wants to ask her. She speaks German, apparently. Has she been to Germany; did she attend school there? If so, what is it like now? He hasn't been to Germany in more than 200 years. He has confined himself to the continents of North and South America.

Over the years, customs, security, bag searches, passports and visas, etc., etc., have grown more and more difficult to pass through. Consequently, it has made travel for the contemporary vampire all the more complicated. When he had hired men to care for him, it was easier, but eventually that grew to be problematic. But, when Franz had died, he couldn't face another human, and he had opted for a dog. A hound of hell, he smiles to himself.

"Shall we go in the den?" Ginny asks, heading that way. Wolf follows.

"So I remind you of someone," Ginny prompts, settling herself into the cushions on an overstuffed couch, which has seen better days. Wolf sits in the armchair so he can face her.

"Someone I knew long ago," he murmurs.

"Long ago," Ginny laughs, "you don't look much past 30." Wolf stares at the gloved hands on his lap. How is he going to tell her? He has to do so in order to explain his lifestyle. Why am I doing this, he thinks. She'll freak out; she'll assume I'm insane.

Ginny looks around for Tigris or Euphrates but they are no where in sight.

"What are you looking for?" he asks.

"My cats. They only love me when it's feeding time."

"Cats are very similar to vampires and werewolves," he says.

"What?" she looks confused.

"They're only happy at feeding time," he laughs, but it is not a happy laugh. Ginny laughs but her smile fades quickly.

"My what sharp teeth you have, Grandma," she says, uncertainly. Wolf, unused to laughing, happily or otherwise, has neglected to hide his teeth. She stares at him, warily, and then starts laughing, biting her lip to keep from cracking up. "I'm sorry, but that seems almost too appropriate. It was a *wolf* in grandma's clothing. Something probably fits here but I'm not sure I know what."

Wolf is looking at her with a mixture of caution and hope. He is not sure how she will take what he is about to say.

"I'm not a werewolf, if that's what you're thinking." She looks at him as if that is exactly what she is thinking.

"Silly, there's no such thing as werewolves and vampires and that kind of thing," she says, unconvincingly.

"On the contrary," he replies, grimly.

"What are you saying?"

"I'm saying that I am a vampire."

Ginny does not know whether to laugh, cry or run in fear. How does one respond to that kind of statement, she thinks, mind whirling. The cuckoo clock ticks loudly, filling the silence as the seconds slide by. The seriousness of his tone has kept her from objecting. Is he telling the truth or has she let a madman into her home? She decides that at this point, either way it would be safer to agree with him.

"How long?" she finally asks. Wolf puts his head in his hands. He wants to cry with relief. He suddenly realizes that it has been years since he has been able to confide in someone. He has not realized how important it has been to him just having someone know what he is.

"Nearly four hundred years," he looks at her, and sees that she is still not sure she believes, but is willing to give him the opportunity to prove that he is, indeed, a vampire. He has so much he wants to tell her because he wants to tell her everything—from his childhood until seeing her by the side of the road. He wants her, well, he wants her to be his friend. No. He wants her to be his lover but that is out of the question.

But, first he must prove that he is what he says he is. Then, he'll start at the beginning. And next, he thinks, I'll find out everything about her.

"First," he tells her, "you need to believe that I *am* a vampire. Unless I am crazy, it's not something I would lie about. But you don't know that I am not insane." She studies him, intently. He seems sincere. Appears to be desperately trying to figure out how to prove it to her. She sees him smile, slowly. He does have awfully sharp teeth, especially the canines. Of course, he could have had his teeth capped and filed, but she doesn't really believe that that is what he has done.

"Do you have a mirror?" he asks. She nods understanding. There is no way he could fake not having a reflection. She takes him in to the bathroom and turns on the light. She can see only herself. She turns around to make sure he is there. He is standing right behind her, almost a foot taller. Suddenly, she is very aware of his presence. His golden hair is long, curling strongly around his cheeks yet falling softly against his shoulders. It looks too natural for a metrosexual. On the other hand, she realizes, it looks perhaps not unlike a man might have worn his hair centuries ago. He also has a neatly trimmed beard and mustache.

"What are you thinking?" he asks.

"It's silly," she replies.

"I don't care."

"I was just wondering if it was a choice to wear your hair that way? Most men your age prefer it short. Are you just stuck in your century?" she is unable to keep from running her fingers through his hair. It is softer than she imagined. He smiles, unable to see the razor-like canines. Ginny unconsciously draws back.

"I'm sorry," he apologizes. "I'm not used to being around people."

She relaxes, before thinking, you stupid fool!

He understands the look of fear on her face.

"No, no, no," he states unequivocally, "You're not on tonight's menu. Besides, I never kill, anyway."

"You can do that?"

"I can." He touches her face, and instead of shrinking back in horror, her knees go weak with desire.

Jesus, she thinks, leaning her weight against the bathroom counter for support. He is staring at her intently, and she feels fear again. He pulls his hand away, and the wave of passion she so carefully disguised fades away. God, her heart skips a beat, if that's how it feels when he just touches me . . . But she thinks she remembers, correctly, that vampires are unable to have sex or is that just late-night-movie legend?

Taking his still-gloved hand, Ginny leads him back into the den. She thinks it would be wise to sit down. She doesn't want to do anything stupid.

"Why the gloves?" she asks as she settles on to the sofa, pulling him down with her. She is becoming addicted to his touch. But, Wolf actually blushes at her question.

"I have hair on my palms," he admits, hesitatingly. Ginny guffaws, then claps her hand over her mouth, trying to hold back the giggles. He looks taken aback.

"I'm sorry," she says, still laughing, "it's just that, well, you know, how mothers are rumored to threaten their young sons not to do a certain thing under the covers at night or in the bathroom or they'll grow hair on their palms." Understanding is dawning in Wolf's eyes.

"Or go blind," he smiles, carefully so as to not make her uneasy.

"So, really, you have hair on your palms?" she leans closer, grabbing a gloved hand. "Can I see?" He can think of no reason not to let her. He pulls the gloves off and displays his palms. They are scantly covered with blondish-brown hair, very fine and soft.

She notes the ring on his little finger, a dragon-wrapped amethyst, but her curiosity about his hairy palms, overrides her interest in the ring.

"Can I touch?" He looks at her to see if she is teasing, but there is not the slightest bit of abhorrence in her face, only a child-like curiosity. He nods.

She gently runs her fingers over his palms, and looks excitedly into his face. He can only stare back, breathless.

"Wow," she says, "that's neat. Do you have to wear gloves or are they just for hiding the hair?"

"Just for hiding the hair," he whispers. She is still bent over his hand, face only a few inches from his. The way she is stroking his palm is strangely exciting. Ginny is wondering what that soft hair would feel like caressing her skin, her breasts. She forces herself to drop his hand.

He is disappointed when she drops his hand and sits back in order to survey him, although he realizes that he is not actually feeling any emotions, just remembering them. How nice it would be, he sighs, to actually feel again, feel anything but the need for blood.

"So," Ginny queries, "what happened?"

Wolf opens his mouth to speak, shakes his head and looks at Ginny's cuckoo. It's about to chirp nine o'clock. "Maybe I had better start at the beginning."

"Then I'm going to have to make some coffee. I assume you can't eat or drink anything?"

"You assume correctly."

"You don't mind . . . "

"Of course not."

Vlad.

EIGHT LONG YEARS. But, at 25 he was finally once again on the throne of Wallachia. Ironically, not long after Vladislav II had gained the throne with the help of Hunyadi, he had unexpectedly instituted a pro-Turkish policy—the very thing Hunyadi had despised in Vlad's father. If it hadn't been so unbearable, it would have been highly humorous.

Hunyadi had then decided that Vlad was indeed the more reliable candidate and forged an allegiance with him to take the throne by force. Unbeknownst to Vlad that was going to take awhile but in the meantime he was given the Transylvanian duchies formerly governed by his father and was allowed to return home, so to speak, under the protection of Hunyadi.

Just three years after Constantinople fell to the Ottomans, under the same Mehmed who had corrupted Vlad's brother Radu, Hunyadi decided to invade Turkish Serbia. It was finally time for Vlad to make his move and while Hunyadi was losing his life in the Battle of Belgrade, Vlad was in Wallachia killing Vladislav II and regaining the throne.

And now that he was back in power, he could finally set into motion his plans for revenge. Tomorrow he would celebrate Easter with a very special feast for the boyars of Tirgoviste, his capitol city.

"Miruna," he called.

"Yes, love?" His wife entered the room. Her beauty was a wonder to behold and Vlad watched in open admiration as she appeared to glide across the rough wooden floor toward him.

"Mmmm," he pulled her into his arms, burying his face in her long black hair. As always the scent of her hair, musk and sandalwood, sent a ripple of desire through him.

"Yes?" she prompted, enjoying the feeling of his rising desire against her belly.

"I just wanted to make sure the preparations have been finalized for the feast tomorrow," he groaned into her ear, pulling her more closely to him, and running his hands down her back; squeezing her gently rounded bottom.

"Yes, my love," she moaned as his mouth mapped its way from her throat downward to her breasts, which bulged slightly from her tightly laced bodice.

He was a cruel man, she couldn't deny it, and what he had planned for the next day defied even the most basic human decency. But, he was always good to her and always managed to set her blood aflame with desire. And he was so inventive when it came to their lovemaking. She never knew what he would try next. But most importantly, she shared his hatred for the Turks and the power-hungry boyars. They were meant for each other.

He lifted her onto the cold stone of the window's sill, which overlooked the city below. They were currently in the watchtower, the Turnul Chindiei, because Vlad enjoyed spending a portion of each day watching the goings on in his newly won kingdom.

"Vlad," she protested, half fearfully.

"Don't worry, my love," his voice was rough with desire. "I want to make love to you while surveying my realm." He was already hiking her skirt higher with one hand as the other slid smoothly up her leg.

"Take me now," she demanded, encircling him with her legs and working to free him from his hose.

The neutral expression on Vlad's face hid both his growing excitement and his complete disgust of the people who stuffed *his* food into their mouths. He had spared no expense—the beer flowed, joints of meat, vegetables, fruits, pastries and cheeses filled each table as the boyars of Tirgoviste and their families enjoyed their Easter feast.

"Wouldn't they be surprised," Vlad murmured to Miruna, "if they knew this was actually their "last supper" rather than a resurrection feast? Miruna nodded in amusement, hiding a smile behind a long and slender hand while the other caressed Vlad. She gazed into his eyes, knowingly. It was clear he was highly anticipating his ambuscade. He gave her a kiss, hot with excitement, and pushed back from the head table.

"Ladies and Gentleman," he began, "I hope you have enjoyed this Easter feast. It is but a small thank you in anticipation of your support . . ." Vlad was interrupted by thunderous clapping and the stamping of feet in approval.

"I have but one question to ask you," he continued as the noise receded, "how many princes have you seen rule during your lifetimes?"

The boyars exchanged some confused glances, but numbers began to be called out. The light in Vlad's eyes grew dimmer as he listened.

"So, there is not one of you here who has not outlived several princes?" The Boyars began to stare at their plates, almost guiltily. "Not one, in fact, that has seen less than seven reigns?" Vlad signaled the guards stationed around the banquet hall. "Arrest them all!" he shouted.

Miruna found herself laughing at the mixed reaction—some sat silently, defeated while others pushed back from the table and attempted to escape. Children and women wailed and screamed as they were herded into groups. Vlad had made her well aware that many of these same nobles who had without compunction consumed Vlad's food were also part of the conspiracy that had led to his father's assassination and the burying alive of his brother, Mircea. Many had also played a role in the overthrow of numerous Wallachian princes, including Vlad himself. She felt no sympathy for these greedy cowards.

As Vlad strode around the hall, he gave his instructions to his guards. These, he told them, pointing to the older boyars and their families, were to be impaled on the spot. They were dragged outside where the long and pointed poles waited for them. Thanks to the Turks and his experiments on animals over the years, Vlad had long since perfected his methods for impalement to make the process as long and painful as possible before death.

Vlad's victims were impaled through either the anus or vagina, and it always gave him great pleasure to watch as the their own weight began dragging them down on the thick stake.

Following the Easter feast, the younger and healthier boyars and their families were condemned to a life of slavery and were marched north to the ruins of Poenari, Vlad's castle in the mountains above the Arges River.

Once there, the enslaved boyars were forced to labor for months rebuilding the castle with materials from a nearby ruin. They worked until the clothes literally fell off their bodies and continued to labor, naked. Very few survived the ordeal.

"So," Vlad mused later, once he and Miruna had satisfied the desire galvanized by the mass execution, "I would say that was a highly successful beginning to my reign. I think my people and my enemies will take me very seriously now."

"Without a doubt," she murmured, nuzzling his neck where her head rested beneath his chin.

Wolf

"I TOLD YOU MY NAME is Wolfdietrich Nachttier," he begins, "but actually I added the "Nachttier" when I arrived on this continent at the turn of the century, the nineteenth century, that is."

Ginny laughs, "Now, I understand the *Nachttier*, night animal, that's pretty funny. It seems you have a sense of humor. At least, I hope that's what it means."

"I would like to think so," he says, "I'd be in sad shape if I couldn't laugh at myself. I try not to take myself too seriously. Not only would that make me incredibly boring, it would make me hard to live with. And when you've lived with yourself for as long as I have . . . or should I say when you've been forced to live with yourself."

Ginny smiles, and sips her coffee, "but I interrupted you. Go on."

Wolf inhales deeply, her cottage smells clean, like lavender. She doesn't smoke, Thank God. He detests the odor of tobacco. It hadn't been widely in use before he became a vampire and he'd never grown accustomed to the smell; couldn't understand what would entice someone to breathe smoke into their lungs.

"Europe holds very few good memories for me. It is where Hannele was killed and where I became a vampire. But I'll get to that later.

"I was born on November 1, 1587. My father, Friedrich was a Gebieter, you know what that is?"

Ginny nods, "A landowner, right?" and settles herself more comfortably on the couch.

"We had owned the land around Fürstensteinbrück for almost four hundred and fifty years, at least the family had. For about half that time we had owned a brewery, still do. You may have heard of it—Fürstenbräu?"

Ginny looks surprised and impressed. The beer was a major import here and also was a favorite in Germany.

"I hadn't thought about it before now, but I assume one does have to be wealthy to be able to live as a vampire. You can't have a normal job, that's for sure," she says.

"That's true. One needs some source of income or a place in which to hide out during the day that's inaccessible; that is, a place no one is likely to enter while one is sleeping, if you know what I mean?"

Ginny nods again.

"Anyway, I was brought up the way most rich young men were at the time. I was tutored until of an age I could attend the university. I studied at Heidelberg just as my father had and his father before him."

"I studied there, too," Ginny adds, excited by the fact they already have something in common.

"Good choice," Wolf nods, approvingly. "I didn't really study any one subject while I was there. My father was interested only in that I receive a well-rounded education. For more than four hundred years our family had ruled the area, fairly, we thought, and honestly, there were few complaints. We believed we should keep up as much as possible with what was going on—in the arts, in the sciences and so on.

"Not long after I was graduated, Ursula came of age and I married her. I know I am rushing through my life but until I met Hannele I had never truly lived.

"Anyway, when I celebrated my tenth birthday, it was also arranged that I marry Ursula von Marloffstein. She was born in February of 1597, and was from a family that wanted to join its lands with my father's. I stayed at the university longer than necessary waiting for her to turn 15. And less than a week after her birthday we were married."

"So young," Ginny interjects. She's 27 and still feels rather young herself.

"She wasn't a very healthy child," Wolf continues, "and a child she still was. She died about two weeks after I turned 25. She died in childbirth and the child, a daughter, died with her. Things were different back then," Wolf hurries to add when he sees the appalled look on Ginny's face.

"I do understand," she assures him, "it's just that I can't imagine myself being with child at that age. I'm glad things have changed. I know it still happens but it's nice to know it's not expected of women anymore."

"And, of course, you are fortunate enough to live in a nation and century in which you don't have to worry about producing the next heir to the family name," Wolf acknowledges.

"True," Ginny agrees, pouring more coffee, "times have really changed."

"After Uschi died," Wolf sighs, "I threw myself into my work. Father was teaching me how to run the brewery and how to manage our lands. I wasn't interested in finding anyone else although my mother continued to introduce me to her hopefuls. They were desperate for an heir, I think, because I was their only surviving child. There had been a brother but he died as an infant, and my mother could have no others. I wasn't in love with Ursula, but I was fond of her. I also had been looking forward to having a child, son or daughter. I think I was afraid to put another woman through the pain Uschi had gone through. I thought I was bad luck. Turned out I was right.

"A little more than two years later, I met Hannele. I can't even begin to tell you how much in love I was with that woman. The first time I saw her, she was riding Erlkönig, a coal black horse like yours," he smiles at Ginny, whose heart is already beginning to hurt for him.

"The first time I saw her, I knew that she was what I had been waiting for. Had she been the local whore, I think I would have still wanted her. It was June when I met her, found out she was the daughter of my father's gamekeeper. I had heard of her, probably had met her when she was a child, but I hadn't seen her since she'd grown up. But once I met her, I tried to run into her every chance I got. Her father tried just as hard to keep me from seeing her. If he knew I was coming he'd send her away on some errand. But she always managed to run into me before I returned to the castle.

"Yes, we had a castle," he says looking into Ginny's shining eyes. "But by that point it needed lots of repairs."

"It's like a fairy tale," she sighs, "unfortunately, although fairy tales often have happy endings, there is usually some unspeakable horror in between—Snow White, Sleeping Beauty, Hansel and Gretel—I could name dozens." She sees the tragic look on Wolf's face and suggests that perhaps his fairy tale is not yet over.

"Perhaps," he says, but there are storms brewing in his eyes. He still feels that he carries bad luck around him like a cloak.

"By October," he starts again, "I wanted Hannele so desperately that I was going to ask her to marry me. But, she agreed to meet me on the last day of the month. Halloween. I should have known better.

"I met her in the woods, she had to sneak away from her father's house. She was a little late, but oh it was worth the wait . . ." Wolf trails off into silence, remembering.

A surge of jealousy sweeps through Ginny's veins. No one had ever had that look on their face when they thought about her, not even Abe. She wishes she could tear her heart out to stop the terrible aching. Why can't someone love me that way, she thinks, her eyes brimming with tears.

"Excuse me," she says, rising from the couch and heading for the bathroom. She doesn't even check to see if Wolf's heard her, she might sob if he still had that faraway look on his face.

"The coffee," she explains when she returns to the room, but Wolf notices the slightly reddened eyes, and wonders whether she was crying for him or herself. Perhaps both of us, he thinks and continues.

"This is a painful subject for me," he tells her. "Until I saw you a few nights ago, I had not really thought of Hannele in more than 200 years." Ginny looks guiltily at her hands.

"I asked her to marry me, anyway," he continues his tale. "I realized at dawn, when she said she must leave me, that I wanted her by my side for the rest of my life. I gave her my family ring, an emerald engraved with our family crest. And she gave me this ring."

He looks at the golden dragon on the little finger of his left hand. For nearly 400 years it has faithfully guarded the amethyst. She notes that on his right hand, he has replaced the emerald.

Ginny's romantically-starved heart throbs, achingly. She looks away in case the tears threaten again and spies Euphrates, head poking inquiringly through the door.

"Come here, you rat," she calls, and Euphrates glides into the room, tail held high, completely ignoring Wolf in the arm chair. He stops midway across the hardwood floor to lick his back, before continuing to the sofa. Euphrates curls up in Ginny's lap, and begins grooming his short, reddish-brown fur tipped with small black markings.

"This is Euphrates," Ginny introduces the cat to Wolf. The cat keeps on licking. "I don't know where Tigris is but he's more independent, doesn't like affection as much as Euphrates."

The interruption has helped Wolf regain control of the feelings rekindled by all the memories. He draws a deep breath.

"She agreed to marry me, even though I'd probably be disinherited," he goes on, "and she also agreed to meet me again that night. I could have waited but I didn't want to. I wanted her too much. I had to have her again that night.

"I told my father I intended to marry his gamekeeper's daughter. Mother fainted and spent the rest of the day in bed. Father and I argued. I don't know why I continued to argue with him because my mind was made up, and I know that eventually my parents would have relented. After all, as I was their only son, it was better to have an heir by a peasant than not have one at all.

"Our quarrel broke off midday because there was business to attend to. But, following a very tense dinner, and as I was getting ready for my rendezvous with Hannele, my father burst into my room and started at me again.

"Because I was so in love with her and because I considered her my equal, his arguments held no logic for me. He talked about marrying out of class, he talked about losing the respect of our people, the aristocracy, and he talked about losing the respect of those we ruled over. He begged me to keep her as a lover and marry someone else. That really angered me. I told him I didn't care what 'our' people thought. Even if it meant going to Italy or Spain, or to the very ends of the Earth, I was going to spend the rest of my life with Hannele.

"Then realizing the time, I told him he was keeping me from my tryst with my beloved. His face turned red, and I worried he might have a stroke. But I left him anyway.

"I ran down to the stables and had my stallion saddled. I don't even remember his name. I guess because I associated him with that night, blamed him for not running faster.

"I realized almost immediately that the woods were too quiet, that something was wrong. I spurred my horse on faster, and was almost to the clearing when I heard Hannele scream. Very much the way you screamed earlier this evening."

Ginny blushes. She had screamed out of frustration and anger, and hadn't realized at the time that anyone was listening.

"Except there was also fear in her scream. I realize now that although she was afraid, she was screaming more from fury and defeat. She was in love and before she could savor it, it was twisted from her body. I saw her love for me in her dead eyes. Or perhaps I am too romantic.

"There was a man standing over her when I entered the clearing. He was sucking on her neck. Actually, I realized as soon as he lifted his head that he had been drinking her blood. His mouth was slick with it and it dripped from his chin. I had startled him, and had I not been so paralyzed with the sight of the blood streaming from Hannele's neck, staining his mouth, I might have been able to kill him then and there.

"I had heard of vampires. In those days, they were not yet considered folklore. They were real but not common. Unfortunately, it did not take long for him to regain his confidence and his filthy sense of humor. Hannele was still alive, and I believe the disgust and loathing he saw in my eyes prompted him to break her neck. It broke so easily, like a chicken bone, and he dropped her as if she were nothing more than a sack of flour to the ground. I cannot describe the pain and hate I felt at that moment. I was sure he would kill me but I attacked him anyway.

"But, he had decided to play with me. He dodged me too easily. I was so insane with rage and grief that I wasn't being careful. I stopped for a second, trying to gather my wits, but damned if he didn't start laughing at me again, those sharp white teeth dripping with Hannele's blood. I attacked again, and this time he took the sword from my hand, and broke it. His strength was amazing, but this time he was no longer laughing. He licked her blood from his lips, taunting me, and I went crazy. I charged at him, weaponless. He caught me in a vise grip and threw me across the clearing. He was strong, as strong as twenty men. I was dazed and when the lights stopped flashing, he was gone. Or, at least, he had changed his human form. There was a big black dog sitting in the middle of the clearing."

Ginny makes a noise, she remembers the wolfish dog the previous night, the owl, the feeling of being watched. She looks at Wolf, eyebrows raised.

"We can change our form," he tries to explain. "Kind of like the Indian's manitou, but the animal forms we can use are limited. Does that make sense? I'm not sure why this is, but I seem to be limited . . ."

"To a bat or a large dog?" Ginny tries to remember what she had been doing when she saw the dog at her window, massive paws on its sill. She didn't want to have to be embarrassed. Well, she hadn't done anything then. Listening to music, maybe? But she had once again felt as if she had been being watched earlier this evening. Was it when she was pulling off the clothes she had worn on the picnic? Her eyes narrow, and Wolf blushes.

"You son of a bitch," she says, cooly.

"I didn't know you were going to undress, I . . ."

"Most things done in one's bedroom are private," she says, enjoying his discomfort. She is tempted to kick him out. She is more than a little jealous of Hannele even if the stupid twit had gotten herself killed," she pouts, inwardly, but with a twinge of guilt. Woods were just as dangerous in the 1600s as they are now, perhaps more so, she rationalizes.

"Did you enjoy the show?" she asks, suddenly, spitefully, and is immediately sorry. He looks very troubled. "I didn't mean that, I'm sorry, I . . . This is all so, I don't know, bizarre."

"I'm the one who should be apologizing," Wolf says. "Truly, had I realized, I would have moved away. But that guy in the Volvo, was he the one you were with the other night?" Did she detect a trace of jealousy in his tone? "He had just left. I expected you to be at home when I arrived. But, of course, you have a life; you're hardly sitting around waiting for me to drop by. I have no excuse. To be honest, I was just so pleased when he left without entering the house and I couldn't wait to see you again . . . and I apologize."

Ginny smiles, placated, "Apology accepted. I overreacted, and I interrupted your story. Now, I am sorry. Let me get a snack before you start again."

He watches her leave the room. She is really nothing like Hannele. Hannele had been more timid around men. He had remarked to Hannele later that it must have taken a lot of mettle to have behaved so impertinently to the Gebieter's son. She had told him that her heart had beaten so painfully, she thought it would jump from her breast. But, she had wanted to meet him, had pretended to be braver than she was. It worked, didn't it, she had asked him, coyly. It certainly had. Ginny, on the other hand, was definitely a woman of the new millennium. Had she not been so independent, so sure of herself, he might not be sitting here talking to her right now.

She comes back into the room carrying a plate of sliced cheese and apple, and settles herself on the sofa again.

"All right," she says, smiling. "I'm ready."

"**W**hen I saw that dog sitting there, I knew it must be him. Without thinking, I pulled the hunting knife from my boot and hurled it at him. I surprised him but he was still quick. Instead of killing him, it lodged in his shoulder. He howled and then was gone. I paced the clearing, staring into the darkness of its perimeter for what felt like forever but the dog didn't return. And then I finally had to face Hannele's death. I didn't want to but I cried. I had done it once again; hurt someone who loved me. I probably cried as much out of self-pity as I did for Hannele. But to tell you the truth, it didn't seem fair then, and it doesn't seem fair now. Of course, no one ever said life is supposed to be fair, right?"

I couldn't agree with you more, Ginny thinks. Here I sit listening to a man who loved a woman the way I've always wanted to be loved. And whom do I have wanting me? Abe. Damn it. Abe. Abe would probably shower me with chocolates and flowers if I even hinted to him that's what I want. But there's no feeling there, at least not on my part. And without that, love's just as real as, what? Silk flowers, she decides, it would be like getting silk or paper flowers instead of real ones.

Wolf tells her that he held Hannele until dawn, before he carried her home to her father.

"I told him to bury her with garlic and wild roses," he says. "And her father understood. I offered, to decapitate her if he were incapable of doing so himself."

"Decapitate?" Ginny asks, grasping her throat.

"Yes, unfortunately. Other than cremating her, it was the only way to ensure she didn't become a vampire herself."

"Even with the broken neck?"

"I couldn't take any chances. The rest of the day, I spent making inquiries. Any one recently moved to the area, someone only seen at night. Finally, as it was nearing dusk, I found someone on the outskirts of the village, a farmer, who said someone had taken over habitation of an abandoned keep at the edge of the von Fürstensteinbrück lands.

"I went home to prepare for battle."

He had heard that to kill a vampire a stake must be driven through the heart, and while that kept them occupied, so to speak, they must be decapitated. The vampire could also be burned to ashes, but that seemed more difficult to accomplish.

Wolf asked his manservant to bring him some stakes, preferably made of hawthorn or mountain ash and sharpened to a point at the end. The man acquiesced but out of the corner of his eye, Wolf saw him making the sign against evil.

The sun had fully set by the time Wolf had prepared to hunt

Hannele's killer. He had his horse, the name he had forgotten was Fegefeuer, meaning purgatory, saddled, and started toward the old keep.

He had no plan in mind, he hoped only to catch the man off guard and kill him. He didn't even consider that the vampire might be expecting him.

Candlelight flickered through the windows and gaps in the old fortress. For the past 100 yards or so, Wolf had been forced to lead Fegefeuer. The ground was littered with stones that had tumbled from the walls of the keep during the past century. Many of the rocks were mossgrown and hard to see in the dark. Clouds obstructed the dying moon. Wolf thought he remembered that his great-grandfather had been the last to use the outpost. But even then it had been used as a hunting lodge, and not as a lookout against invaders. The von Fürstensteinbrücks had had no problems with raiders since the late thirteenth century when they had claimed the land as their own.

He slid his horse's reins over an upturned rock, which rose from the ground in a fairly level spot. He played with them for a minute to make sure they wouldn't pull loose, but he knew he was really just stalling. Heart pounding in chest, he stared at the keep for five minutes before he could convince himself to move closer.

If you're so afraid, just go, he thought. But he couldn't do that and he knew it. He thought of Hannele's father, the way his face had turned white when he had opened the door and seen his poor, sweet child lying limply in Wolf's arms. He would blame himself for years, would tell himself over and over again that if he hadn't discouraged Hannele from seeing Wolf, this might have never happened. Wolf would have used her, her heart would have broken, time would have healed her, and so on. But no, they had to sneak out and see each other. Had to meet again, even though they were to be married. He should have offered them his bed. Instead, smiling and proud, he had watched his daughter run happily to her death.

He had buried her as Wolf had directed. He had heard the rumors, never doubted Wolf's word. And, he had removed Wolf's emerald ring from her finger, and returned it to Wolf's father. He didn't want to risk any repercussions from possessing the Fürstensteinbrück crest.

The widow of the village's baker, who had been eagerly seeking his bed, gave him ample consolation. Surprisingly, to him, she helped fill the gap left by his daughter's death. Although even years later, whenever he saw a flash of flaming red hair, he would still call out "Hannele," before remembering that she was long since gone. But, for the most part, he survived, as most people survive when they lose someone they love dearly.

What infuriated Wolf the most, though, and sent him running the last twenty yards to the keep, was the remembrance of the way the vampire had casually broken Hannele's neck, the way he had licked her blood from his lips.

He stepped through a great gaping hole in the side of the keep, carefully avoiding fallen gravel and leaves. He wanted to be as quiet as possible. When he made it to the center of the room, he stopped watching his feet and surveyed the circular tower he was in.

He felt, rather than saw, the eyes boring into his back, and turned to face the vampire, silently cursing his inability to surprise the bastard.

The man stared at Wolf with curiosity. Vlad was actually more upset with himself. He had never before let himself be caught, but he had been so infuriated when he happened upon the whore preparing for what was obviously a secret, and therefore immoral, rendezvous, and in his lust for her blood, had immediately forgotten that her partner had yet to arrive. And although the evening had been more exciting than usual, it had also left him with a wounded shoulder. Wolf noted that the man's shoulder looked especially lumpy, as if there were a bandage beneath his shirt.

I got you, you bastard, Wolf thought, but then the man spoke.

"I had a feeling you would come look for me," he said in badly accented German. "Allow me to introduce myself, my name is Vlad Drakulya." He extended his hand, which unlike the man was broad with short and squat fingers whose nails tapered to sharp points. Wolf shuddered when he saw the hands. The palms were covered with coarse, black hair. But there was something about the man's deeply set eyes overset by heavy brows that nearly joined in the middle over a high-bridged, thin and aquiline nose. Something hypnotic about those deep brown eyes that drew him toward the vampire. Wolf watched his right foot move forward of its own accord. He tried to look away from the man's eyes but the grip of his gaze was too strong.

The red, red mouth under the heavy mustache began to smile in anticipation. Wolf noted that the man's pale ears were slightly pointed at the tips. His chin was broad and strong, and his cheeks firm though thin. He had a lofty, domed forehead with silver-grey hair growing scantily about the temples but dark and profusely elsewhere, bushy black hair that seemed to curl in its own fulsomeness, and it was difficult for Wolf to determine the man's actual age.

Wolf was growing weak looking into those eyes, knew he must look away but could not. As his left foot moved forward, he was ashamed to note the desire that was rising in his blood. He was revolted by the feeling, but at the same time could not control the wave of carnality that washed over him. He could almost smell the vampire's need, and when Vlad took Wolf's jugular between the right upper and lower canines, his knees gave way and Vlad was forced to hold him in his arms like a swooning maiden.

Vlad drank, but only briefly.

"I had planned on killing you," he said, "but I decided you would suffer more for hurting me if I made you suffer as an immortal." The desire had passed, and Wolf looked at Vlad, with fear and with understanding. The monster intended to make him become a vampire.

"No," Wolf tried to shout but it came out less than a whisper. Vlad pulled Wolf tighter to him, like a man embracing his lover. He laughed cruelly as he tore open his shirt with one hand. Wolf tried to pull away but was too weak. Using the keen-edged nail of his index finger like a scalpel, Vlad sliced into his chest over his heart.

"Drink," he ordered Wolf, who shook his head in denial, but Vlad was too strong. And, weak from the loss of blood and the desire brought on by Vlad's proximity, Wolf's lips were soon smeared with Vlad's blood. And Hannele's he thought, but he could not stop. The thirst for blood was too great. Vlad had won.

Ginny blinks away the tears that are gathering in her eyes. Holy Mary, Mother of God, she thinks. Wolf sits silently, a sick expression on his face. She wants to hold him, say something comforting. But what the hell do you say to a guy who's been a vampire for nearly 400 years against his will. She also has to use the bathroom again but doesn't think this is the right time to excuse herself.

He has been staring at his hair-covered palms, he now raises his eyes to meet Ginny's. She still doesn't know what to say, and returns his stare waiting for him to speak.

"I feel like anything I might say right now would be trite," she says, as she stands up and stretches.

"Too much coffee?" he asks.

"Yes," she replies, heading for the bathroom. That was something he hadn't had to worry about in a while.

She stops on her way back through, enroute to the kitchen, "I keep feeling like I should offer you something to drink. I guess I'll have to stock Tru Blood, or do you prefer O positive from the blood bank?"

She starts laughing, more than a little punchy from the lack of sleep. It is already 2:30 a.m. Wolf doesn't join in her laughter, he doesn't even smile. He seems more than a little perturbed. He has never been the brunt of a vampire joke, and isn't accustomed to someone making fun of his plight.

"That was uncalled for," she blushes, making a quick exit to the kitchen.

Wolf forgives her almost immediately. And although he hadn't thought it funny when she said it, is grinning by the time she walks back into the room. It had been a tension-breaker, he realizes. It had actually worked.

Boy, are you slow on the pick up, she thinks, but holds her tongue. She is exhausted, and it would be too easy to say something to piss him off. Besides, the guy really had been through hell. After all, what was the worst thing that had ever happened to her—her father's death when she was in her 20s? Her inability to find her knight in shining armor? The fact that she has had such an easy life is almost embarrassing. Her face burns in shame.

"What's wrong?"

"I'm feeling guilty," she confesses. "I feel guilty for having been comparatively so lucky."

"Actually, since I became a vampire, I have had nothing but good luck, if that's what you want to call it. No one has ever suspected me. I have always had money, a roof over my head, someone to care for me during the day. I've never even hungered. Doesn't seem right somehow, does it? Why, when I am something evil, does everything go right for me? I've considered killing myself a number of times, but the need to live is too strong. I often wonder if Vlad is still around."

"Of course he is," Ginny says.

"What makes you so sure? He seemed as old as time when I, hmm, met him."

"Well, I only know what I've picked up from vampire lore, but supposedly if you kill the head vampire then all the people he has turned into vampires die too. Of course, I could be wrong."

Wolf stares at her hard for a minute, "You could be right."

"So, what did you do after you drank Vlad's blood?" she changes the subject.

"He laughed, quite nastily, and explained to me some of the changes I was going to have to make in my life."

Wolf was weak and he reeked of blood. When he neared Fegefeuer, the horse panicked, breaking its reins and plunging down the rocky slope. The scream of the animal when its leg caught between two fallen stones and snapped, caused Wolf's blood to run cold. Nothing will ever be the same, he thought. He returned to the keep for one of the stakes he had dropped or had Vlad taken them from him? He used the stake to put Fegefeuer out of his misery.

He had managed to wipe his face clean, but the blood still stained his white shirt. When he reached the castle, it was too late to wake his father and he wasn't sure he would yet be able to speak to him rationally.

His manservant fled the room when he entered, staring in horror at the blood, hands flashing the sign against evil. Wolf was too tired to demand service. Instead, he locked himself into his room and prayed that he would be left alone during the coming day. He briefly wondered if he should leave the door open in the hope that he might be put out of his misery. He was so newly undead, had as yet only fed the once on Vlad's blood; that he could still grimace about how disgusted he was with himself and pray for a quick end to his unholy state.

If he had been thinking more rationally, he thought after tossing a handful of dirt on his mattress before he stretched out on his bed, he would have gone in search of Vlad during the day when he was at his weakest. He covered himself with the wool duvet and pulled the curtains closed. As it was, he just hoped that should someone gain entrance to his room, they would assume he was sleeping to escape the reality of Hannele's death.

It never occurred to him that he should be taking advantage of this rare chance, before it was known what he had become, to see one last sunrise. But he was exhausted and overwhelmed by the events of the night and dawn and sleep were calling more strongly than logic. Tomorrow evening, he told himself, you will have to make better arrangements.

He knew it was sunset without looking. Already he could feel the hunger coursing through his veins and cursed it. He would have to wait. Perhaps, if he had time, he would try to feed later. His mind, still unused to his new state, rebelled from the idea of drinking someone's blood. But the survivor, the vampire in him, knew it must be done.

He unbolted his chamber door and glanced out into the hall, warily. Surely the castle must be wondering what had happened to him? But perhaps they had done exactly as he had hoped and assumed he was still grieving for Hannele. Hannele, his heart twisted painfully. They probably thought he had spent the night drowning his sorrows before passing out in his room. His dazed state when he arrived suggested he had indulged in heavy drinking somewhere before he had returned home. They probably thought he had killed Hannele's murderer and then had gone on to drink away the pain. He knew that even had his manservant spoken about his entrance last night, those rumors would have never reached the ears of his parents.

He needed to change, wash up, and find his father. There was water in the pitcher on his dresser, he poured some into the bowl and then looked into the mirror. He wasn't there. He cast no reflection. The realization that he was a vampire finally sunk home. He threw himself on his bed and cried, great racking sobs. He wanted to scream that it wasn't fair. He wanted to throw things. He wanted to kill.

"No!" he yelled into a pillow, tearing the case where his fingers grasped it so tightly. He noticed that his nails were already beginning to lengthen, and slowly, and with a growing horror turned his palms toward his face.

Hair was springing from the palms. It was lighter in color than Vlad's, and sparser, but it was still hair. His stomach heaved, but there was nothing there to expel. A few more tears oozed from his eyes. He slowly ran his tongue across his teeth. His head dropped to his chest. They were sharp. He touched them. Yes, very sharp. No denying it, nothing he could do about it. The only son of Friedrich von Fürstensteinbrück was a vampire.

How was he supposed to tell him? Father, I've got some good news and some bad news. The good news is that I will never die so we don't need an heir. The bad news is, well, I'm a vampire. He laughed, harshly, before pulling himself off the bed. His feet felt like lead. He washed up without the benefit of a mirror. He decided against shaving. As he cast no reflection, perhaps it would be easier to allow his facial hair to grow. In a clean set of clothes, he went to find his father.

His father knew something was wrong as soon as Wolf entered the room. He had heard from the guards that Wolf had entered the gates dazed and blood-stained just before dawn. He had assumed, like most of the castle, that he had found Hannele's killer and taken care of him, then had gone on a drinking binge. The expression on Wolf's face did not bode well for that assumption. Also, his son looked different.

"I think I had better sit down," his father sat heavily on a leather chair, which was within three feet of a huge stone fireplace. It was almost winter, and the castle tended toward chilliness during the fall and winter months. Wolf pulled a chair close to the fire, staring bleakly into the dancing flames until the silence grew uncomfortable.

"Tell me everything," his father demanded, but with resignation. Four hundred and fifty years of good luck were more than most people could ask for. The death of Wolf's brother, Wilhelm, had wrapped a mantle of doom about the Fürstensteinbrück castle. Perhaps Wolf was the sacrifice that would make things right again. Friedrich was willing to do what ever was necessary to help his son, but still wasn't quite prepared for the news.

There was no disputing that his son was a vampire. In the end, Wolf agreed to leave Bavaria forever, and his father agreed to entrust the brewmaster with Wolf's secret. The brewery, they agreed, would be handed down to the Brauers on the condition that Wolf always received a percentage of the gross. The Brauers would keep Wolf's secret and keep him living in the manner to which he was accustomed. And, although Wolf would be the actual owner of the brewery, the Brauers would retain full control of its operations and all profits, except of course, for Wolf's percentage.

It was the best, and only, plan they could come up with. But before Wolf could leave Bavaria, he would need a caretaker. Friedrich suggested his manservant.

"I haven't seen him since I arrived last night covered with blood," Wolf laughed. "I'll need someone who will not be, uh, deterred by my unusual hours and well, you know."

His father grunted. It was certainly unpleasant business, but as Wolf had pointed out, he was still alive and could, conceivably, live forever. His father said he'd find someone.

"**S**o, you left Bavaria forever? You've never been back?" Ginny asks.

"I wanted to go back," he stands up, needing to stretch. "I long to see it again, but at first, it seemed so soon, and later I hated to put the Brauers in the position of having to deal with me personally. And now, it's just too hard to travel." He paces about the small room.

"I used to own this house," he tells her.

"Really?" she smiles, she kind of likes that. "I'm buying it from my stepfather," she says. "He's arranged the payments so I could afford them. He owns a horse ranch in the Corazon Valley, and he built the stable when he used to use this as a beach house. Did you live here . . . where do you live?"

"No, I never lived here. I had this place built for Franz when he was no longer able to take care of me. When he died, well, I just didn't want another human to take care of me. So, I bought a dog. Mephistopheles is the second dog I've owned. Until I got him, the Brauers kept me supplied with a caretaker. Kind of sad, isn't it, when you can't even take care of yourself."

Ginny thinks of something, and suddenly it all makes sense.

"That big log cabin, about a mile south of here, that's yours, isn't it?"

Wolf nods.

"A while back, more than a year ago, I guess. I was riding Merlin through the woods between our houses, and when I got too near your house, that big dog...an Akita?...attacked me."

"Sorry, an Akita, yes, but that's his job. And by the way, I own those woods you've been riding through."

Ginny colors, "I haven't seen any 'no trespassing' signs. I didn't realize that the land belonged to anyone. I mean, I knew it belonged to someone, but I thought it probably belonged to the state or the town."

"No need to apologize. I like the idea of you riding there." They look at one another marveling at how comfortable they feel with each other, especially since he is a vampire. Ginny stands up, excusing herself again.

"No more coffee for me," she says when she returns, "I might float away."

Tired of the couch, she sits cross-legged on the multi-colored throw rug at his feet.

"I was getting too comfortable on the sofa," she explains, "I was afraid I might fall asleep. We've been talking all night and most of what you've told me occurred within a few days. What have you been doing for the past 400 years?"

"That would take many more nights, uh, zu erklären?" he falters.

"To explain. Surely you haven't spoken German in years?"

"You're right, but this is probably more than I've spoken since I became a vampire. And with all these memories of Bavaria, and its being my native language, I have started thinking in German. The truth is, I have kept up with it. Actually, I speak a number of languages. I used to travel a lot and I had plenty of spare time to learn the language before I traveled to a new destination. Sometimes I even forget how to say things in the language I am speaking, and throw in words from another language. Do you understand what I mean?" he asks.

"Sure. When I was going to school in Germany that summer, I had to think and speak in German most of the time. I remember when I first got back to Georgia, it was like I knew how to speak English but every once in a while I would think of the German word, instead, and have trouble remembering its translation."

"Exactly."

"So what languages do you speak besides German and English?"

"When I studied at Heidelberg, and while I was tutored, I learned Latin, classical Greek and French. Since that time, I have picked up Spanish, Italian, some Portuguese. And, of course, wherever I have traveled, I have picked up smatterings of the languages in those countries."

"So, you spent most of your time traveling when you left Bavaria?"

"I had to keep on the move. Too much time in one place could arouse undue suspicion. Things have been easier since the invention of cars. I can travel by night much more quickly and much less vulnerably. I have lived permanently in Corazon since the 1950s, but I bought the land here more than a century ago. Once the Pacific Coast Highway was built, I could get to and from San Francisco in one night, but I keep an apartment there, just so I don't have to push myself."

"Is that where you were returning from the night you passed us?" Ginny recalls that he had passed them from the same direction they had been traveling. "And you waited up ahead for us."

"I wanted to see where you lived. Imagine my surprise when I discovered you were my neighbor."

Ginny laughs, "Pretty ironic, huh? It's like fate or destiny or something."

"There was a time when I didn't believe in fate, but I can't accept that Hannele's death and my becoming a vampire, and seeing you on the side of the road for that matter, weren't meant to be somehow. This has happened for a reason, I just need to figure out what that reason is."

Ginny feels it, too, their coming together like this was not a coincidence. Probably, neither was the fact that she resembled Hannele, but she wasn't about to go so far as to suggest reincarnation. After all, Wolf had never died.

"Can I ask you a personal question?" she inquires.

"I guess so."

"Do you ever get bored? I mean, it seems to me having to hunt for blood several times a week for nearly 400 years would get boring, you know? You can't really have any friends, or at least, you need to be careful that way. I assume you can't have sex. You'll never have a family. Jeez, doesn't that get you down sometimes? It must be strange to be a . . . how old are you?"

"Twenty-eight when I became a vampire."

"Anyway, a 28-year-old stuck in a what? 393-year-old body or actually, I guess you'd say only your mind has aged in a manner of speaking."

"To tell you the truth, until the other day I hadn't thought about it. The years passed by surviving day to day. But, that night in San Francisco . . . I should have known. I started laughing. It was strange. I stopped laughing not long after I left Bavaria. And then the night that

I saw you, I felt something was going to happen. I forgot that premonition almost as soon as I had it. But, I remember now telling Mephisto that something was going to happen that night. And then I saw you, and remembered Hannele, and everything came back to me. Last week, I would not have understood the definition of boredom. Today, I cannot understand how I have managed to survive 400 years."

Ginny cannot comprehend living that long. He had been a vampire for more than one hundred years when the Declaration of Independence was written. He has watched as wars were started and ended—from the Seven Years War to the ongoing conflict in the Middle East. Jesus. It is just beginning to sink in how long Wolf has been around. He has seen Europe fight over Catholicism and religious tolerance, been through the French Revolution, the age of Napoleon. He knew, first hand, almost all of America's history. Had lived through the Industrial Revolution.

She looks at him in wonder. But he has had the time to adjust to the changes that came. He has watched man evolve from a superstitious being to a skeptical, cynical creature.

Wolf has long ago developed the attitude of, "Oh, so they can do that now." Not that he hadn't felt the same wonder as everyone else when a rocket was launched carrying humans, and had landed on the Moon. But, like most people at the time, he had accepted the marvel.

The years of wisdom, knowledge he must carry around in his head, she marveled. Had he been an average human, he might have lost his mind. But he isn't human, at least, not really. He is a vampire, one of the undead, although he did not strike Ginny as undead. He appears very much alive. And very attractive, she decides. The way his hair, the color of sun-ripened grain, curls around his face, falling softly to his shoulders, begs to be caressed. How she would love to run her fingers through it. His liquid eyes are as changing as the sea. His lips are wide and full and when she is near him that magnetic attraction that is a gift of the vampire, is hard to resist. There is something incredibly alluring about him, despite that, and she wonders what it would be like to make love to him.

But of course that is out of the question. He has indicated that her assumption about vampires being unable to have sex is correct. Darn, she thinks, I finally meet a guy that I could actually fall in love with, am falling in love with, she amends, and sex is out of the question. Listening to him speak all night, she has fallen in love with him. Be truthful, she thinks. You've been interested in him since Friday night when you first saw him. Friday, and now it is Sunday. No Monday morning, she realizes. It's Monday morning.

Wolf watches her in silence. She certainly is beautiful. A different beauty from Hannele's, true. Hannele had a beauty as resplendent as her hair. Her beauty burned like a bonfire. Ginny's is a quieter beauty. She is exotic, reminding him of the masked and bejeweled women he had seen when he had traveled in India. A musky intriguing beauty. A glowing ember as opposed to Hannele's burning fire, he decides.

They gaze at each other in friendly silence. He is growing used to her company. He is not looking forward to wasting half the day sleeping. Well, you couldn't actually call it sleeping. It really more closely resembles a coma. It is a dreamless sleep. He hasn't dreamt since his last night as a mortal in November of 1615.

"So, what brought you to America?"

"The French Revolution," he answers, simply.

"I assume you were in Paris at the time?"

"Yes, I preferred, at the time, to stay in big cities. It was easier to hide. After I left Bavaria, I traveled all over Europe—London, Paris, Rome, Madrid. And Eastern Europe—Bucharest, Budapest and so on. Then I made my way through Istanbul, Athens and made a rough trip to India by ship. It wasn't pleasant. I had the crew terrified, but I was never found; my caretaker made sure of that. I eventually found my way back to Paris, just in time for the revolution. When they stormed the Bastille, I decided it was time to get out of there. I made it to London, where I stayed about five years. I arrived in America in 1794. I stayed in New England many years, and as the country moved westward, so did I. I was in California by the time the Civil War started."

"I would have been scared to death traveling around during those times. If I had been a vampire, I mean. Weren't you afraid of Indians? How did you travel, I mean, what did you travel in?"

"Mostly, I traveled by coffin because it receives respect from most civilized people," he explains. "But I have also traveled in trunks, in crates and even in a wardrobe once or twice. I hated being so vulnerable, but even with someone to watch over me . . . I couldn't take many chances. Oddly, though, or maybe perversely, I was never really afraid. There was a part of me that figured, maybe even hoped, that if I was caught, exposed, so much the better. That would be one less vampire walking around or should I say stalking the earth at night. So, of course, since I couldn't have cared less about losing my non-life, I never did. I never even came close except on the voyages to and from India, and to America. My caretaker at the time told me that only a few crewmen suspected something otherworldly. Most people put the bites down to rats, the fatigue and paleness to anemia. Why should I be so lucky when I never had that luck when I was truly human. I would have gladly traded my life for Hannele's."

"Well, I'd like to agree with you there, but I think I'll be selfish. If you had died instead of her, I would never have met you."

"Thank you."

"You're welcome," she pauses, thinking. "How many vampires do you suppose there are?"

Wolf thinks for a moment, "I would say that there aren't that many. Of course, I'm only guessing here. When I was made a vampire I was given a crash course in vampire history, but still mostly had to go by what I know of legend. But, anyway, there are a couple of reasons I feel there probably aren't many vampires. First of all, the more vampires there are the greater the risk of detection. If I turned all my victims into vampires, then suddenly there would be a rash of unexplained deaths. Kind of like in that book, 'Salem's Lot.' Vampires are extremely vulnerable and it would actually be easy to wipe them out during the day, just like Ben and that kid did, with fire. Not only that, if there were a lot of vampires roaming around, it would become more difficult to feed.

"If the entire world eventually became populated with vampires, we'd all die of starvation. So, I would say my case is unusual, that Vlad was not thinking of his survival when he made me a vampire. Most vampires probably do not kill their victims, or if they do, make sure they are truly dead and not undead. But I have never sought out other vampires. I did not wish to become one, and do not want to associate with them. I do believe, though, that you will find at least one or two vampires, maybe as many as a dozen, in any major city in the world. That is where they are safest and can feed without arousing too much suspicion."

Ginny wonders something, and tries to decide whether Wolf would take offense, consider it too personal.

"What are you thinking?" he asks. Her brow is wrinkled, as if she were pondering a tough decision.

"I want to ask you something, but I am afraid you might think it's too personal. I mean, I'm afraid you might get mad at me or something."

That's too much for Wolf's curiosity. What could she possibly want to ask him that might make him angry? He can think of nothing.

"You'd better ask me, because I'll never rest until I know," he says.

"Well, I was just wondering why you never killed Vlad. Even if you were a vampire, it seems as if you would still want to kill him. Is that a dumb question?"

Wolf stares at her hard. The fierce look in those bluish eyes cause her to shift uncomfortably on the hard floor. But he isn't looking at her, he is looking through her. Why hasn't he killed Vlad?

"It was so long ago," he says, out loud, but not to her. He looks puzzled. "I don't guess that I have ever asked myself that question," his gaze refocuses on hers. "I don't know. I know that's a strange thing to say, but I guess I was too caught up in my own predicament at the time, that I didn't even stop to consider the reason I'd ended up that way to begin with. I was shocked and disgusted that night. And, the next night, I was worried only about finding a way to survive. That is probably the first and foremost feeling a vampire has. And, although I have rarely worried about it, it is still something I do without thinking— survive. It's in our blood, and now, thinking about it, it was probably Vlad's major concern as well that night. I wouldn't be surprised, after his anger had passed, if he hadn't realized what a stupid thing he had done, making me a vampire. He probably realized his mistake immediately, and was off our lands by dawn.

"And then, like I said, I soon forgot everything about that night, about Hannele and Vlad, even my horse's name."

"Forgot it, or chose not to think about it?"

"You're right," he says, "it was there, but I just refused to let myself think about it. And after 400 years, it was essentially forgotten; until I saw you, then all the memories came surging back."

It's nearing dawn, and Wolf pulls himself out of his chair.

"Thank you for staying up all night with me," he tells her.

"I know it wasn't easy on you."

Ginny stands and stretches. "Actually, I'm kind of getting used to it."

"Why is that?"

"On Friday, when I first saw you. Gosh, I'm embarrassed to say this now," she blushes, something she does very easily. How could she appear always so self-assured, but still get red-faced so easily. "When I saw you, it really upset me for some reason. I don't mean badly, like you scared me or something. It, you, sort of excited me. For some reason, I felt frustrated and hysterical. I laughed so hard I cried. Abe still thinks I was crying but I was really laughing. It was weird. Anyway, I was in such turmoil when I finally got home that it took the rest of the night for me to finally calm down enough to get some sleep. Just before dawn I took a long bath that relaxed me enough that I was able to fall asleep right as the sun was coming up. Just as it's about to do now. Are you going to make it home?"

"I can always run," he laughs. "You'd better get some sleep."

"Sleep? I have to go to work in a couple of hours."

"Can't you call in sick," he suggests.

"No way. Abe would be sure something is up."

"Abe?"

"My boss."

"Really? You keep saying it with such familiarity."

"My boss that I've dated a couple of times," she says, reluctantly.

"I don't understand. Your boss is your boyfriend?"

"No. No," she assures him. "But he would really like to be and I am having a hard time walking the fine line between being polite and keeping my job and allowing him to think I care for him more than I do. That sounds bad. I do care for him. As a person, as a friend, but *not* as a potential lover."

"I see. And this is this the man you were with Friday night and that I saw dropping you off today?"

"Yes, that's him. He talked me into going on a picnic with him and his mother today. Yesterday. What a fiasco. That woman hates me for many reasons and has no trouble letting me know it."

"And Abe is fine with this?"

"No, I think he finds the way she treats me terribly humiliating. And, unfortunately, I think it makes him pursue me all the more fiercely. Otherwise, I might be able to use her dislike of me as a way to distance myself from him."

"Well, I can help rid you of that particular problem, if you like," Wolf says with a sly grin.

"Very funny," she punches him lightly on the arm. "Suffice to say, to maintain the status quo might be the safest thing to do right now. Which means I need to get ready for work and have an excuse on hand for being tired. At least I'll be off deadline early enough. I can come home and take a nap as long as I don't have any important assignments. I'll see what I can get done early. Do you get the paper?"

"Yes," he says, but now that I know you write for it, I'll have to pay more attention." They are now at the door, and he wants to hold her or kiss her or something, but doesn't quite know how to go about it. He looks as if he might say something, changes his mind, looks down at his feet then into her eyes.

"Can I see you tonight?"

"Yes," she says although she is exhausted. She ought to say "no" but she wants to see him again.

"You can tell me all about yourself, tonight," he says.

"That should take all of about ten minutes."

Wolf smiles his practiced smile because it seems to disturb her less, "Then it will be the best ten minutes of my day." He touches her face again, and she wants to fly into his arms. She wants to feel what it's like to be held by him. She would even like to know the touch of his lips.

She realizes a lot of it has to do with the vampire's sexual charisma, but she doesn't care.

"I'll walk out with you," she says, breaking the tension. "I need to ride Merlin, anyway.

"You dope," she chastizes herself, slapping her forehead in mock dismay. She laughs. "You don't need to walk or run or even fly home. I'll take you on Merlin, if he'll stand for it."

That sounds good to him. He hasn't been on a horse in years, and the thought of being that close to Ginny even if he feels nothing more than her warmth is better than a cold and lonely walk home.

He mounts the horse behind her and clings tightly to her waist. Tiny waist, he thinks and wonders how much like Hannele's her breasts are. The two women are so much alike in size and shape. It is mainly their color that is different. Where Hannele was fair with sun-reddened skin, Ginny is naturally dark. He holds her tighter, yearning to take her breasts in his hands just to satisfy his curiosity.

Control yourself, he warns, but buries his face in her hair.

"You feel good," he whispers. So do you, she thinks. You rat, it's not fair for you to excite me like this when you can't do anything about it.

The mile is much too short, and the sun too quick to rise. When they reach his cabin, Wolf has little time for goodbyes. He kisses her cheek and strides straight for his house, calling to Mephisto. He can already feel the familiar lethargy that sets in with each dawn. The dog is standing, tensed, for a pounce. It is his master on the horse but he does not know the female. He growls, huge white fangs catching the first rays of the sun.

"See you tonight," he says, before bolting the huge wooden door behind himself and Mephistopheles. Ginny's legs feel like rubber, and she is glad she has Merlin to support her.

"You were a very good boy," she praises him, heading back to the house at a slow canter. "Not many horses would carry a vampire so nicely." She laughs, a triumphant, happy laugh. You little fool, she chastises herself, you're falling in love with a vampire. You ought to have your head checked.

Vlad

NORMAL MAN MIGHT HAVE GROWN TIRED of the torture and the death, but the more Vlad killed, and by this point he had killed thousands, the more exciting it became devising new ways to punish those who disobeyed or threatened him.

He had worked steadily over the past six years to remove all the undesirables from his kingdom. From the rich and greedy boyars to the poor, the sick, the handicapped, the vagrants and beggars, he tirelessly tormented and killed those he felt did not contribute to the common welfare.

He smiled as he remembered the burning of the sick and poor. Oh how deliciously well that had gone. Like giving candy to a baby, he'd told Miruna at the time. Of course, that had made it somewhat disappointing as well. By that point his reputation as a prince who did not put up with dishonesty or weakness of any kind was known throughout Wallachia and beyond. He was determined to enforce his own moral code upon his fellow countrymen.

In this particular case, he had issued an open invitation to a banquet, declaring that, "no one should go hungry in his kingdom." Miruna had wondered aloud if the people would shy away from such an offer considering what had occurred that Easter Sunday. Vlad had assured her there was no way the poor would compare themselves to the wealthy boyars killed and enslaved that day. He was right.

As the poor, the crippled, and the just generally greedy poured into

Tirgoviste, Vlad's men ushered them into the great banquet hall. The guests ate and drank late into the night growing increasingly complacent due to their full bellies and the freely flowing alcohol.

It was then that Vlad made his appearance. "My friends," he began, "Now that you are no longer hungry, what else do you desire? Do you want to be without cares, lacking nothing in this world?"

The crowd responded enthusiastically, sending out a cheer loud enough to rattle the rafters in honor of their lord. Giving the nod to his guards, Vlad disappeared and all entrances to the hall were soon boarded up and the great hall set ablaze. No one escaped the flames.

When questioned about his actions by the remaining boyars, Vlad responded, "I did this in order that they represent no further burden to other men, and that no one will be poor in my realm." The boyars were wise enough not to argue.

Later, on St. Bartholomew's Day, having grown weary of the merchants in his kingdom disobeying his trade laws, Vlad had more than 30,000 arrested and impaled, leaving their bodies to rot outside the city gates as a testament to what happened to those who transgressed.

Vlad was aware that rumors abounded about his penchant for eating the flesh and blood of his victims. There was little truth to that, but he did enjoy holding dinner parties next to the concentric circles and other geometric patterns he formed of those he had impaled. It gave him much enjoyment to look upon his handiwork, and the thrill of catching one of his guests displaying even a modicum of disgust at having to eat while looking upon thousands of putrefying corpses was an extra bonus, for they would soon suffer the same fate. And either Miruna or one of his mistresses would enjoy his presence later that evening, for the more he killed, the greater his sexual appetite. It was as if the two had been tied inextricably together.

But even his mistresses had to be careful. Vlad shook his head, remembering. He had had to kill Sanda for lying to him. True, she loved him to distraction. True, she was trying only to cheer him up on one of the many occasions he was feeling down. For when he was not high on death and torture, he was often plumbing the depths of depression. But, Sanda should never have lied about carrying his child.

His beloved Miruna had only managed to give birth the once; every other child had miscarried. When Sanda had claimed to be pregnant, he was, of course, ecstatic, and immediately had her checked by the bath matrons. When they had informed him that she had lied to him, he immediately drew his knife and cut her open from groin to breast, and left her to die in agony. How dare she lie to him about something so important!

And now, a mere six years since he had finally regained the throne, and despite all he had done to fend off the Turks, they were nearly at his door; and led by his brother, Radu, no less. Vlad worked frantically, pulling together what was needed for himself and his young son, Mihnea cel Rau, to escape through the secret passageway he had built into the castle Poenari.

His mistake had been taking on Mehmed II's army the previous year. He attacked them from the Danube River Valley but being outnumbered, had failed to subdue them. That evening, he staged a raid on the Sultan's settlement but attacked the wrong tent. Mehmed was furious and vowed revenge, ordering his men to invade Wallachia.

Vlad retreated northward toward Tirgoviste, destroying his kingdom village by village, burning them to ground and poisoning the wells. He did not want to leave anything behind for Mehmed.

By the time the Sultan arrived in Wallachia, a virtual forest of impaled Turkish prisoners awaited him, their bodies slowly decomposing in the sun, the stench of them permeating the air.

The effect on Mehmed and his tired army was profound. They abandoned the campaign. For the moment. But now the Sultan's army was back and Vlad was backed into a corner.

"My lord," a servant came hurrying into the room carrying an arrow with a note attached to its shaft. "This was shot through the window in your main quarters."

Vlad, who the servant had found standing in a tower room overlooking a tributary of the Arges, snatched the arrow from his hands. Miruna hurried into the room shortly after the servant. "What does it say?"

"It appears to be written by a former servant. It is a warning that Radu's army is fast approaching."

Miruna paled, "I would rather have my body rot and be eaten by the fish of the Arges than be led into captivity by the Turks." Vlad could not have agreed more, but he was unprepared for what Miruna did next. Dashing across the room, she hoisted herself into the tower window and giving one last look at Vlad, threw herself into the river far below.

Vlad stood frozen in shock for valuable seconds before striding to the window. Miruna was already lost to the current. Vlad saw no sign of her nor of the deep crimson gown she had been wearing. His heart cried out in anguish as his mind insisted that he still had time to escape with his son.

His mind was right. He would mourn for Miruna later. Now, he had no time to waste. He called for Mihnea and his nanny as well as a couple of other servants and they were soon making their way toward the secret passage, carrying as much as their strength and time would allow.

Vlad led the way to Transylvania, seeking refuge with King Matthias Corvinus, where he would spend the next nine years in his custody while Radu occupied the throne of Wallachia.

Ginny

THE WATER IS HOT, and although it feels good massaging her body, it's making her drowsy. Ginny adjusts the temperature to luke-warm, then to cool and finally stands beneath a stream of cold water for a full minute before she turns it off.

"Brrr," she says, wrapping a dove grey towel around her shivering shoulders. "But at least I'm awake," she mutters, wiping the last of the steam from her bathroom mirror. The purplish smudges beneath her eyes make her look like one of Edward Gorey's Gashlycrumb Tinies. "C is for Clara who wasted away . . ." Which makes her think of another Clara. "Better stop there before I think unkind things," she turns toward her bedroom.

Really more than anything in the world right now, she would like to go to sleep. She gazes longingly at her bed. Her eyelids rub across her eyes like sandpaper each time she blinks.

I need those eye-openers like what's-his-name had in "Clockwork Orange," she thinks, then laughs at the image of someone following her around with eyedrops. So much for that idea.

She pulls on a red sweater dress and knee-length brown suede boots, grabs her purse and heads out the door while calling goodbye to her cats.

She backs her dark green Bug out of the driveway. The car is older than she is. The 1972 fully restored Volkswagen Beetle was a present from her folks when she was graduated from high school. With the help of a Chilton's guide that she'd found on eBay, she'd managed to keep it running for almost 10 years.

Ten years, she thinks, astounded, I'll have been graduated from high school for 10 years, next year. Jesus. Even under Ginny's loving care, the little car is on its last legs. She decides she sounds like a wedding when she drives. I sound like a bunch of tin cans rattling, she thinks, I ought to paint "just married" across the back of my car so I don't have to explain the noise.

Ginny sits down at her small desk hoping no one will see her. If I sit here quietly maybe Terry won't give me anything else to do.

But, of course, as soon as he realizes she is there, the editor bustles over with some last minute news releases.

Damn, she pouts, sometimes I hate being the fallback reporter. At first, the fact that they trusted her to cover any beat felt like a compliment. Now, she just feels used. There was always a skeleton crew on Monday because the reporters who worked the weekend, got the day off.

And then Abe walks in, his face exploding in a happy smile when he sees her, and Ginny's heart drops to her feet before resuming its place in her chest and pounding unnaturally. The last thing she wants is a run-in with Abe. She still hasn't had time to process the previous 24 hours.

Her chagrin at being handed several news releases turns to glee. She is glad she has something to do so she doesn't have to talk to him. She quickly picks up the phone to make her first phone call. When Abe passes by, she holds up her hand and indicates she is on the phone. He sits on the edge of her desk.

Shit, she thinks, angrily. She hates people sitting on the edge of her desk, despises people, especially Abe, listening while she is making a phone call. Caught between a rock and a hard place, she decides, now hoping no one will answer the phone. On the fifth ring, she hangs up.

"Not even an answering machine," she informs Abe.

"You look tired," he answers.

"Thank you," she says, sarcastically, "I didn't sleep well last night."

"I'm sorry," he says, assuming it's his fault, or actually his mother's. Ginny realizes this and doesn't correct him. God, how egocentric can you get, she thinks, amused. Why does he always think that if there is something wrong with me, it has to be because of him or his mother? He's either incredibly confident or paranoid.

"How much do you have to do this morning?"

"I just have a couple of things," she shows him the releases. "I was hoping I could take off early? Maybe if I go home and try to nap . . ?"

"Sure," he says, "on one condition."

"What's that?" she asks, cautiously, dread filling her veins with ice.

"Another date. Another chance. This time without my mother."

That's what she'd been afraid of. Damn. Son-of-a-bitch. She ought to refuse him, and take off early anyway.

"Not tonight," she says, instead, playing for time.

"How 'bout tomorrow?"

"You know, probably, but let me check," she smiles, but it is forced to her lips, does not reflect in her eyes. She scrambles through her purse for her iPhone. She sees it glinting at the bottom of her purse but pulls a disappointed face. "I must have left my phone in the car. Can you give me a call later? I'm sure if I nap, I'll be up by sundown."

Abe is clearly disappointed but has no choice but to agree, "Sure. I'll let you get back to work so you can get on home." He hopes that after a nap she'll seem much less grouchy. He hates seeing the lifelessness in her eyes.

By 10 a.m., she is finished with the releases, and decides to get the heck out of Dodge before Terry can find something else for her to do.

Before heading home, she decides to cruise through the tiny town because it always relaxes her. She loves driving through the residential areas looking at the older homes. Hansel and Gretel houses is how she thinks of them. Today Corazon resembles a scene in a country-English postcard, only the misty and heathered moors are missing. With its narrow streets and English-village architecture, Corazon has an air of not having quite awakened to the 21st century.

The sun sparkles on the leaded and whimsical windows. The sapphire-blue sky frames chimneys and gambreled roofs. Ginny admires the curious curve of a cornice, a capricious cupola while smiling at her talent for alliteration. Other than her mother and David, and occasionally Abe, she doesn't have any one she talks to on a regular basis, no boyfriend or girlfriends, for that matter. She has long since learned to amuse her self.

She passes into a neighborhood influenced by the Spanish style of architecture. Although she prefers the fairy tale houses, she also enjoys looking at the redwood and adobe homes.

She drives through the carefully executed oasis of the town on her way back to her beach-side cottage. Even in such a practical era, there are very few sidewalks, street lamps or street signs. They would have marred the effect of the tumbled gardens and rock-walled homes, anyway, she decides. She is glad that there are rules governing construction in this town. The gas stations with their wooden eaves might be hard for tourists to identify, but she knows where they are, appreciates their unobtrusiveness.

Ginny finds it amusing that a tree cannot even be cut down without the permission of the police. I'll bet that frustrates a lot of people, she thinks, pulling into a park on the outskirts of the town.

Walking across the already-fading grass of the park, Ginny settles herself on a swing. Next to riding Merlin on the beach and through her small strip of forest, swinging relaxes her the most. It is a beautiful fall day. The sky almost looks alive it is so blue. The sun splashes through the leaves, dappling her as her feet reach for the leaves.

Ginny loves swinging. When she is swinging she can promise herself anything. Her first promise is always that she will never care what people think about her again.

"Never," she laughs at the tree, "ever, never, ever again." The motion and the warm sun on her face make her sleepy. With the tension she had built up at work released, she forgets about Abe and his badgering her yet again for a date. But she cannot stop thinking of Wolf, even though she knows her fantasies will never come true. She can still feel his face buried in her hair, his strong hands around her as she and Merlin carried him home last night.

The arc, which originally carried her pointed toes closer to the tree, is narrowing. She is startled out of a doze when her feet scrape the dirt beneath the swing. She looks around, embarrassed, forgetting her promise not to be bothered by other's opinions. She is the only one in the park.

When she gets home, she walks down to the beach for a moment. The sun reflecting off the surf stings her eyes. She looks at the tree where the bat had perched. She can still see some of the footprints she and Wolf and Merlin had made walking to her house. Her heart thumps, painfully, and the footprints blur as her eyes swim with tears.

"You're hopeless," she tells herself. "It's hopeless. Everything is hopeless." A fly lands on her face, and she reacts violently, slapping herself hard in the process of shooing it from her face. Lack of sleep and this new sensation of hopelessness have left her feeling more than grouchy. A vampire for God's sake. She can't fall in love with a vampire. It's just too impossible.

She yells in frustration, then cries hysterically, finally laughing at her histrionics. But, most importantly, she feels much better, sane again.

"Time for bed," she tells herself, gently. She imagines Wolf asleep in his log cabin, wishes she were sleeping next to him.

She closes the curtains in her bedroom and dropping her clothes on the floor, slides naked between the warm flannel sheets. Within five minutes she is sound asleep.

Ginny & Wolf

THE HOUSE IS DARK WHEN WOLF ARRIVES. His heart fills with dread. Is something wrong, he wonders.

"No use panicking until you find out," he rebukes himself. He sees her car parked in the driveway, and he knocks on the back door. There is no answer, so he tries the knob. The door is unlocked and he steps inside.

"Ginny," he calls. Still no answer. His heart pounds, arduously. He walks down the hall toward her bedroom convinced that he has brought his bad luck down upon this woman. Her bedroom door is open and he peers inside. His legs go weak with relief when he sees her sleeping peacefully, and deeply.

Wolf enters the room and stares at Ginny for a while, trying to decide whether or not to wake her. He wants to talk to her too badly not to. He sits on the edge of the bed, gently touches her bare shoulder.

"Ginny," he says quietly into her ear. "The sun has set." She stirs and reaches for him. He lets himself be taken into her arms. She presses her body against his, and he wishes desperately that he could give himself to her.

"Wake up," he says, face once again buried in her hair. He kisses her ear, her cheek. Her mouth searches for his, finds it. He breaks away from her passionate kiss, heart slamming against his rib cage. He is growing weak from lack of blood and from the remembrance of desire.

"Am I awake?" she asks, voice muffled by his chest.

"Yes," he whispers.

"No wonder you stopped," she sighs. "In my dreams you don't." She sits up and asks Wolf to turn on the lights. He reluctantly lets go of her.

"My robe's on the back of the closet door," she says, pointing. He hands it to her hoping to catch a glimpse of her body as she pulls it on.

She knows he would like to see her, and lets him catch a brief glimpse. Might as well, she thinks, it's not like he's going to take advantage of me. Not that I would mind that at this point.

Her breasts are like Hannele's, he sees, firm and full with small nipples. Damn, damn, damn, he thinks, why me?

"I'm starving," she says, "I haven't eaten yet today."

She looks hard at Wolf. "And what about you? How long can you go without eating?"

"I'll have to go out tomorrow night," he tells her.

"Just as well," she replies, heading for the kitchen, "I guess that means I have a date with Abe tomorrow night, after all." She doesn't see him grimace behind her back.

"**W**ow, I just thought of something wild," she says, cracking an egg and letting it slide into a frying pan.

"What's that?" he says, watching as she concocts a fried egg sandwich. He's never before seen one made.

"You've never eaten at McDonald's," she laughs. "You've never had a Big Mac or fries or a Coke. That's pretty amazing considering they're in practically every country now."

She looks at him, still laughing. He looks bemused by her meal.

"All right," she confesses, "I'll admit that I don't make the standard egg sandwich, but it's not that uncommon. I happen to like pickles and cheddar cheese on my fried egg sandwiches. I know a lot of people who eat theirs with ketchup, and I happen to find that disgusting."

"I wouldn't know," he smiles, "I have never had a fried egg sandwich of any sort."

"Then you haven't lived, my friend," she teases, "you haven't lived."

She takes the thick sandwich and a tall glass of milk into the den.

"It's kind of chilly in here, isn't it?" she suggests, hopefully.

"A bit," Wolf agrees, sees the look in her eyes, and asks, "Would you like me to build a fire?" Ginny nods, happily and takes a huge bite out of her sandwich.

"Yummy, yum yum, in my old tum tum, as we used to say when we were kids." Wolf likes the way her eyes crinkle at the corners when she's happy, the dimples that appear beside her mouth.

"You really said that?" he asks, taking some kindling from the basket next to the stone fireplace.

"Believe it or not," she says, doing a poor imitation of Jack Palance. Munching on her sandwich, she watches as Wolf builds the fire. He is not wearing his gloves tonight and his hands move surely and quickly at their task. Strong hands, she thinks, hands that held her closely less than half an hour ago. And his mouth . . . Better not to think about that, she decides. She gulps down the last of her milk, wipes away the white mustache it leaves behind.

Wolf joins her on the couch and pulls her into his arms. She looks at him studying her.

"You're beautiful," he says, kissing her gently. She tries not to respond, but can't help it. It feels too good. He pulls away and she leans her head against his shoulder, sighing. She wants him too badly to discourage him. How frustrating.

He tightens his arms around her, and whispers into her ear, "Now tell me about your self."

"I don't know what to say, where to begin. I haven't led that exciting a life."

"Then begin at the beginning. Where were you born?"

"I was born in Brunswick, Georgia" she began. "We actually lived on Saint Simons, a small island off the coast of Georgia, but the hospital is in Brunswick. The island is mainly a resort, and my father ran a hotel there. The Shipwreck Villas and the Crow's Nest Pub. Pretty silly, huh? I grew up there, and actually I loved it. I love the ocean, Atlantic or Pacific. As long as I am near the ocean, or sea, I guess, I'm all right. The thought of living someplace like Kansas scares the hell out of me. I'm afraid I'd suffocate. I love the beach. It's another world, especially at dawn and dusk when it's empty. You can walk along, listen to the waves, watch the crabs scurrying across the sand, the sea birds diving into the waves and you're at peace. No one can get you. I don't know what I would have done if I hadn't come out here . . . Well, that's irrelevant. The main reason I came out here was because David had this house on the beach for me. Otherwise, well, 'what ifs' are useless."

"If wishes were horses, beggars would ride."

"Exactly," she replies, "and if "ifs" and "ands" were pots and pans..."

"There'd be no work for tinkers!"

She looks at Wolf. It is clear he is watching, listening, intently to her story. She smiles at him, and he smiles back. She settles more comfortably against him.

"So," she continues, "I grew up at the beach. I was born March 1, 1981."

"So, exactly eight months before me."

"Well, not exactly. I'm still a year younger than you; or rather, a year and four months because I turned 27 this year."

"You knew what I meant," he squeezes her.

"Yes," she admits, "just being difficult. Anyway, I'm the eldest. My brother, Jack, just passed the bar exam in Georgia and has been offered a job with a law firm in Atlanta. My sister, Carolina, the youngest, is still in college."

"Carolina? Is Ginny short for Virginia?"

"Yes, heaven help us. My father insisted; something to do with recognizing where we had come from. Though, if that were the case, shouldn't he have named me for some town in England?"

"Could have been worse."

"Don't I know it. I thank the Lord everyday that we didn't migrate southward from Pennsylvania or Delaware. So, my mother agreed, with the proviso that we get more normal middle names."

"So?"

"Virginia Marie."

"Well that makes sense. The Blessed Virgin Mary."

"My mother is too Catholic to pass that opportunity by."

"And what about you?"

"My faith is strong, but I prefer to keep it on the quiet side. What about you?"

"There was a time, but religion doesn't take too kindly to my kind. There's something about not being of this world nor of the next that leaves one stranded in the middle."

"Not unlike a living purgatory."

"Closer to hell than purgatory, but yes."

"I'm sorry," she holds him more tightly, head against his chest. There his heart continued to beat solidly just as it has done for more than 400 years.

"Back to the beach," he prompts.

"I have to admit my childhood was pretty much idyllic. We weren't rich but we had enough. Enough for me to keep a horse at the local stable and ride often. We didn't travel a lot but I didn't know to miss it. When I was fairly young, maybe about eight or nine, David Tucker, came to St. Simons. I don't remember why—a family reunion, maybe. Anyway, he was staying at our hotel and he and his wife and my father and mother hit it off pretty well. A couple of years later, we got the news that his wife, Susan, I think her name was, had died in childbirth. I remember because I was shocked that that could still happen.

"My father insisted that he come back and stay a month or so, and he did. Dad really helped him through his grief. He continued to visit us every other year or so for years, and then when Dad was diagnosed with pancreatic cancer," tears fill Ginny's eyes and she paused to take a deep breath. "David was there for us during those last painful months. And when he asked Mom to come out here with him, it seemed the best thing for her. We sold the hotel and pub, and as I was fresh out of grad school, I came out here too."

"Grad school? I know you studied German in Heidelberg. Is that what you studied here?" Wolf asks.

"Journalism and German," she answers. "An odd combo, I know, but I had to take a foreign language and German just came to me so easily. I really enjoyed it and that's why I took part in the study abroad program at the University of Heidelberg one summer. I just wanted to learn some more and really be able to speak it. At the time, I wasn't majoring in the language, but by the time I got back from Germany, I decided to go ahead and make it my second major."

"Did you stay in Heidelberg or did you get a chance to see some of Germany?"

"Unfortunately, we mostly stayed in Bavaria. And an end trip took us to Austria and Switzerland."

"Did you get over toward Nürnberg, Erlangen, Marloffstein?" Wolf names some of the larger towns. "That is not far from where I lived, and very close to where Uschi was from."

"Actually, Marloffstein sounds familiar. I think maybe that is where we tried Beerenwein one night."

"Did you like it?" Wolf makes a face. "It's too sweet for my taste."

Ginny cocks an eyebrow at him, "I thought so to," she says of the wine made of berries—strawberries, blackberries—there were several different kinds, "but I would imagine that by now even beerenwein would be a delightful change of pace. Speaking of which, I need to stand up for a minute," she says, sliding out of Wolf's arms. "I think I'll have a glass of wine." She picks up her milk glass and plate and walks in to the kitchen and places the dirty dishes in the sink.

When she re-enters the room, Wolf is standing by her bookshelf, surveying a shelf of books bearing such names as Stephen King, Peter Straub, Anne Rice, Charles Grant, H.P. Lovecraft and other authors of the same genre.

"Looks like you are as fascinated by horror as I am," he says over his shoulder. "At least I have an excuse."

"Can't help it," she says, trying to peer over his shoulder but he is too tall, "For some reason I have always loved those types of books. Next to books about travel and historic romance, I love horror and suspense."

"And mysteries."

"Well," she corrects him. "Some mysteries. I really like Sharan Newman's Catherine Le Vendeur series, but honestly, I usually tire of most series pretty quickly. The characters always seem to grow disproportionately superhuman if not caricatures of themselves. It's one of the reasons I don't really watch television. For example, my mother is really into that series, "24." She is always talking about it and all I can think is: how many intense 24 hours can Jack Bauer have?"

"I never watch TV anymore. I used to in the earlier days of television, but I've grown weary of it. And I don't think I've read any Sharan Newman, and I have read a lot. Sometimes, it's the only thing I have to do to wile away the long hours of the night."

"So, I've been keeping you from your reading?"

He smiles, "I'd never read again if it meant I could spend every night talking to you."

"Thank you."

"I mean it."

Ginny returns to the sofa, stretching out along its length.

"Does that mean I'm no longer welcome," Wolf asks.

"Of course not," Ginny laughs. "It just means you either have to support my head or my feet on your lap. Your choice."

"I'll start with your head in my lap," he smiles. She sits up so he can sit down, then lays back using his legs as a pillow, looking up into his face. Her neck curved back, begging for a kiss or, perhaps, a bite.

"You're definitely at the advantage," she says, pointing to her arched throat, "or can you still be hit where it hurts."

"Unfortunately, yes."

"I'll keep that in mind.

"Do you expect me to get out of hand?"

"Unfortunately, no," she grins. "I used to have a book like that when I was a kid."

"Like what?"

"I think it was called "Fortunately, Unfortunately," but I'm not positive. It was about a guy who fell out of an airplane or something, and his parachute wouldn't work and fortunately, he was going to land on a haystack, and unfortunately, there was a pitchfork in the haystack and so on."

"So continue. Tell me about college. Your friends, uh . . ."

"Lovers?" she finishes his question. Something flashes behind his eyes. He's already jealous, she realizes. That makes her illogically happy. "Friends," she says, slowly. "I didn't really have any friends in college, still don't. I had acquaintances, people I did things with, but no one I would have poured out my heart and soul to.

"You see, I had a best friend once. At least, I thought she was my best friend. But all the years we were friends, she was really just using me. I guess because she could talk me into doing anything—sneaking out, lying to my parents—that type of thing. Anyway, we went off to college together, and the using turned to pleas for money. We shared an apartment and eventually she stopped paying the bills. It really got messy and I haven't spoken to her since. Unfortunately," she can't help smiling, "I haven't really trusted another female since. And unfortunately, again, there really isn't a "fortunately" to go with that.

"You know that Bob Dylan song . . ."

"I Want You," he interrupts. She glares at him.

"Ha ha, as if that's a possibility. No, I'm talking about 'Positively 4th Street.' I was thinking of it because that's exactly how I feel about her. I still won't even say her name. She really hurt me deeply."

"I'm sorry."

"I'll probably get over it someday. The truth is, I have forgiven her. And, logically I understand it was her problem not mine, but I still haven't found or allowed myself to get close to anyone since then. Even when I lived with Ken, I just never let him get that close to me. I guess that's why when he graduated and moved away, we just drifted apart."

He was staring at her, "You lived with someone."

"Oh come on Wolf, it's a different world than the one you grew up in. Yes, I lived with Ken during my sophomore and junior years. He was an art major. I think I was more entranced by his weirdness than I was attracted to him. He was into sculpture, strange sculpture. He always had to tell me what his stuff represented. I still sometimes wonder how we managed to stay together two years. I guess maybe that was easier than breaking up. We got along. That's the easiest way of explaining it."

"Was he the first man you slept with?"

"Whoa, that's a personal question, and I'm not sure how it really matters," she says in amusement, but he appears to really want to know. "Yes, as a matter of fact, he was. It wasn't earth-shattering—the way I'd always dreamed it would be. But, I didn't really know what it was supposed to be like. I've dated off and on since then," she laughs. "but, I haven't been attracted to another man since then, and I wasn't even really attracted to Ken. I guess the type of guy I'm attracted to is never attracted to me. How fair is that? "

"You're not attracted to Abe?"

"Most definitely, certainly, not Abe," she shudders. He moves so he is lying down next to her. He uses a finger to follow the lines of her face, tracing her eyebrows, her nose, her lips. He stares at her, thoughtfully.

"I have a 'believe it or not,'" he says. She waits for him to tell her. "I am jealous of Ken, and I am jealous of Abe. I know I can never have you, but it kills me to think that someone else did, that someone else wants you and it can never be me."

"Says the guy who has had a wife *and* met the love of his life," she says, but not unkindly. She wonders, if perhaps, he is projecting his love of Hannele on her. At the moment, though, she can live with that. She wonders if it is possible to feel so strongly about someone so quickly. He pulls her on top of him, holding her tightly.

"Hold me," he says, squeezing her, "and don't ever let go." She clings to him, urgently, fervently wishing that there could be more than this thrusting of bodies together. Never in her life has she so wanted to make love to a man. And now that man, the one she has been waiting for, is a vampire, and can do nothing more than hold her. Again, she wants to cry, scream in frustration. But she also does not want to feel those arms loosen from around her, does not want to feel him draw away. She buries her face in his neck, gently kissing the vein that throbs there. She kisses the strong line of his jaw, his chin and finally, his lips.

A pounding on the front door causes them to jump apart like guilty-of-necking teenagers. The color burns high in Ginny's cheeks as she stares wildly at the front door. Who could it possibly be? Her mother or David would have called first before coming over from the Corazon Valley ranch. That left only one person. Abe.

"Shit," she says, tightening her robe around her. Wolf's hand had been seeking her breasts when the knocking began.

"Coming!" she yells, smirking at the double meaning there. It is too damn close to what she'd like to be the truth. "Shit," she curses again under her breath.

She looks back at Wolf, who is pointing toward her bedroom. She nods. How the hell could she explain spending an evening with the local vampire? She is smiling when she opens the front door.

"Well, hello, Abe," she says, as cool as a cucumber, she reflects, considering. "What brings you here, unannounced," she glances at the clock, which reads 9:40, and back at Abe, "at this time of night?"

"I wanted to check on you," he says, "because you didn't look so well when you left today." He isn't looking at her but rather around the room as if he expects someone else to be sitting there.

"I thought I heard you talking to someone when I came up," he says, bluntly.

Heard or saw, she thinks. At the time he would have been coming up the walk and extending his hand toward the door to knock, she and Wolf hadn't been talking. She glances at the window to the right of the front door. There's a good two-inch gap in the curtains. She is no longer smiling.

"Then you were mistaken," she says, coldly. It's none of his darn business if she has a male guest.

"I could have sworn," he says, still looking around. It's obvious he would like to search her house, although Wolf could very easily have escaped through the back door. His brow wrinkles in puzzlement, "I didn't know you had a dog."

"I," she follows his stare, there is a huge wolfish looking animal sitting in the hall which leads to her bathroom and bedroom. "Wolf," she blurts without thinking. She takes hold of herself, continuing slowly. "Yes, that's Wolf. I bought him today. For protection. I haven't been sleeping well because I've felt as if I've been being watched lately," she says, pointedly.

Abe does not even have the decency to blush. Evidently, he does not consider his eavesdropping unusual, she thinks. The little shit.

Wolf is sitting calmly in the hall, watching every move Abe makes. Ginny is not only pleased with his manifestation but also by the jealousy that has spurred it. Nice to finally have a guy she's interested in equally attracted to her.

"Does he bite?" Abe asks, looking warily at the beast.

"That's a good question," she laughs, "Why don't you try him out?"

"Ha ha, very funny," Abe says, "He looks ready to tear my head off."

Now that would solve all my problems, Ginny thinks, and then shudders. Wolf looks too ready to do just that. And despite the fact she is disinterested in Abe as a boyfriend, she really does like him as a person.

"Cold?" Abe asks, concerned, "Are you running a fever?" He places his hand on her forehead, and Wolf growls, quietly.

"Nothing like that," she assures Abe, and stretches out on the couch. "A rabbit ran over my grave, that's all."

"A rabbit? That's good. We always say . . ." Wolf trots into the room and joins Ginny on the couch, silencing Abe.

"Bad boy," she says, slapping him on the back. "Down. No dogs on the couch. Only cats."

Wolf gets down but looks at her reproachfully. It is all she can do to keep from laughing. The big dog settles himself at her feet and watches Abe.

"I don't think your dog likes me," he tells her.

"Isn't that amazing? I only bought him today and already he's very protective. I'm sure you'll grow on him. Would you like something to drink?" she asks, belatedly.

"Whatever you're having," he points to the solitary wine glass on the coffee table.

Of course you would, she thinks and intercepts a second reproving glance from the dog. But, she has asked, and at this point, it is necessary for things to seem as normal as possible. And Ginny is nothing if not a good hostess.

Abe follows her into the kitchen noting the dirty dishes in the sink. She's hardly the neatest of people, he thinks, his lip curling in disgust at the drying egg on the plate.

"You ought to wash that before it hardens," he cannot help but say, and immediately regrets it.

He doesn't miss the anger that briefly narrows her eyes, before she smiles sweetly, and says, "You're right. You pour the wine, I'll wash the plate and glass." But the line of her jaw is hard from where she is clenching her teeth.

God, why did I say that, he chastises himself. I need to learn to keep my mouth shut. He realizes he's already pushed Ginny too far with his possessiveness, particularly as they've only had two dates. I can't help it if I'm jealous, he rationalizes to himself, but his mother's behavior is going to take a lot to overcome.

Wolf is getting angry. Actually he is already angry and is pushing toward enraged. He is jealous of every moment spent with Ginny because he has so few. That bastard can see her during the day. The thought sends an arrow of pain through his heart, and the black lips curl back to reveal his gleaming white fangs.

Abe is stopped in midstride. "Is he going to attack me?"

Ginny looks at Wolf, and says, "I hope not." Wolf backs down, but still keeps an eye on Abe.

"So," says Abe, sitting down in the armchair occupied by Wolf the previous night, "you still haven't told me how you're feeling."

"I'm just tired, that's all," she explains, glancing over at Wolf. What she sees causes her hand to shake so hard that her wine spills. Wolf is sitting, cross-legged, at her feet. She looks up at Abe who looks worried for her. Not because of Wolf, whom he can't see, but because her hand is shaking.

Abe jumps up to take the wine glass from her hand and is met by the snarling beast, fangs bared once again.

"I think your dog is too damned protective," he tells Ginny.

"Damn, you can't even make any sudden moves around him."

"Perhaps, I'll have to get rid of him," she says. The dog whimpers and sits down again.

"Are you sure you're all right?" he asks her. "Your hand was shaking so hard I thought you were going to drop your glass."

"To tell you the truth," she lies, "I really don't feel that well."

"Why don't you take tomorrow off," he says, concern in his eyes, "and if you still don't feel well tomorrow night, then I'll take a raincheck on the date."

Why does he have to be so darn nice, she thinks. It would be much easier on her if he were always a jerk. But, she can see behind the concern, suspicion. Is he wondering if the reason she is so tired is because of the man he saw with her on the couch? Ginny is confident that when he leaves, he will return on foot just to check what he is sure he saw.

She drains her glass and suggests to Abe that she would really like to go on to bed now.

"I understand," he says, "and hopefully, I'll see you tomorrow evening."

"I'll let you know otherwise," she smiles. "Goodnight." She leads him to the door, and watches until his taillights have disappeared from view. She carefully locks the door and turns to Wolf.

"I don't like him," he informs her.

"Why is that?" she is finding it hard not to smile. She turns off all the lights in the room while she awaits his answer.

"I think he's sneaky," he says, simply.

"So do I. That's why I am turning off all the lights. I would not at all be surprised if he were on his way back to the house, now, on foot, to spy on me. Isn't that terrible? I hate to think that way about him, but there was something in his eyes. Not a good sign that we're not even a couple yet and he is already overly possessive."

"I saw it too," says Wolf. "So what are we going to do?"

"First, we're going to get away from that window," she finds his hand and leads him down the hall toward her bedroom. Her curtains are still closed from her nap, and she leaves them that way. "Now, we have two choices. We can sit here in the dark and talk or I can get dressed and we can go over to your house and talk. Which will it be?"

"I don't want to have to cower here in the dark," he decides. "Let's go to my place."

She pulls on jeans and a sweater, laces up her boots and is ready to leave within five minutes.

"Now," she says, "the only question is, is Abe still out there?"

"We'd better give him another 10," Wolf says, sitting down on her bed. Ginny sits beside him, reminding him to keep his voice low.

"In case Abe has his ear to a window," she says.

"So what are we supposed to do for the next 10 minutes? I feel like we're trapped here. And, I can't even talk to you. Damn, that guy is really making me angry."

"Shhh," she whispers, rubbing her smooth cheek against the coarse hair on his. "Do you have a beard because you can't see to shave?"

"I decided on the first evening I woke up as a vampire that it would be easier to let my beard grow out and just keep it trimmed," he murmurs in her ear. "We wore our hair longish but were clean shaven back then although men did still wear beards and mustaches. I have found throughout the centuries that there are always men who have facial hair so I never stood out that way. I did try cutting my hair once after World War II because I really stood out, but within hours it was back to its regular length."

"What did you do?" she whispers back.

"Wore a wig or a hat when I had to be out. And you're right, it would be very difficult to shave when you can't even see yourself in the mirror; possible but formidable? You know, I haven't seen myself in nearly four centuries. I don't even remember what I look like. But, obviously I can't be too bad if someone like you, well, you know."

"Perhaps it's just that vampire charisma," she teases, brushing her lips against his.

"Thanks."

"You're welcome," she says, nipping his chin with her teeth.

"Never tease a weasel," he murmurs, solemnly.

Ginny laughs, then claps her hand over her mouth as if to keep any more laughter from escaping, "I haven't thought about that book in years. How does it go? 'Never tease a weasel,'" she continues, remembering, and quoting from the book, "This is very good advice. A weasel will not like it and teasing isn't nice.' That was one of my favorite books when I was a kid. My dad had a friend who told me and my brother and sister that weasels eat potato chips and drink rootbeer."

"I thought we were supposed to be sitting here quietly?" Wolf prompts.

"It's impossible not to talk to you and besides, you shouldn't have brought up weasels, you weasel," Ginny laughs, but quietly. "We spent one entire summer bugging Mom for rootbeer and potato chips all the time. Why on earth would you have read a children's book?"

"I've kept up with children's books as well as others," he explains. "You have to admit they are fun to read."

"Yeah, especially the Dr. Seuss books."

"I do not like green eggs and ham. I do not like them Sam I Am."

"That's another one of my favorites."

"We have a lot in common."

"Hmmmm, perhaps."

"What do you mean?"

"Nothing. Surely, it's been at least ten minutes; Abe must be gone by now." She stands up and crosses to her bedroom window, pulling the curtain aside, carefully. She peers into the dark for a minute but sees no movement. "I think he's gone, that is if he ever came back. I'm taking it for granted he did. And if he is gone, we can stay here. We don't have to go all the way to your place."

"Actually, if you don't mind. I would prefer to go back to my house. It's a lot safer for me," he says, standing up and joining her at the window. "But, if you don't want to go there, I'll stay here with you."

"I'd love to see your home."

They slip through the darkened house to the back door, which is closer to the woods.

The evening is chilly and silent except for the sounds of night. The faint moonlight provides enough illumination to see the path. They walk hand in hand, listening to the night noises—the singing of the crickets, the rustle of small animals in the underbrush, the occasional flap of a wing and the hushed pounding of the Pacific on the shore.

"I love the night," Ginny breaks the silence, but her voice is hushed.

"It's all I know," Wolf drops her hand, and slides his arm around her waist. "If it weren't for movies, I wouldn't even remember what daylight is like."

"Do you miss the sun?"

"Sometimes. The problem is that I am so afraid of the sun that I hide myself way before dawn, just so I don't have to take any chances. The general myth is that a vampire will get burned alive by the sun. The truth is we can actually stand the sun but it makes us so weak that we are really vulnerable and the morning coma, as I like to call it, that we slip into is very difficult to fight as well. But honestly there are times when I want to see the sun so badly that I am almost willing to take the chance and put my so-called life at risk just to see it again. But I never do. Survival always wins out in the end."

They reach the point where the path veers off toward Wolf's home. It is starting to match the well-trodden appearance of the trail used by Ginny and Merlin.

Mephistopheles bounds up to Wolf, happily, then draws back, suspiciously, when he notices that Wolf has a guest. The man has never had a guest since Mephisto started taking care of him. It is the same woman who brought him home on the horse the day before. He does not know how to react.

"This is Ginny," Wolf says, looking into the dog's eyes, "she is my friend. Remember that."

"The dog stares at her for a moment, and she cautiously stretches her hand toward his nose. Mephisto smells her hand as if memorizing her scent, then licks it.

"You'll be safe with him from now on," Wolf says.

"He won't attack me?" she says, remembering the bared fangs of the previous day.

"He'd better not," he says, pointedly. Mephisto licks her again.

Ginny's breath catches in her throat, "Oh my God, they're beautiful."

Wolf follows her eyes to the abstract pattern of his stained glass windows.

"They remind me of sea glass."

"Sea glass?"

"You know, glass that's been buffed by sand and bathed by the sea. It washes up on shore. I used to collect sea glass when I was a kid because it looked like jewels to me."

"Let's go inside," he says, but he's imagining a young Ginny with a treasure chest full of sea glass.

When Wolf opens the door, Ginny's mouth drops open.

"Wow," she says in awe. There are thousands of books lining one wall of the big room that serves as his den. Half of another wall is taken up by a huge stone fireplace, but Ginny's eyes are on the books.

There must be more than 100 years worth, she thinks, and says, "I feel just like Belle in Beauty and the Beast."

He looks at her quizzically but explains, "When I built this place a little over 100 years ago, I started buying books to keep. Before that I was doing so much traveling, I couldn't keep them."

"I'll bet you have hundreds of first editions that are worth big bucks now," she says, perusing the titles on one of the lower shelves. "Oh my God, is this an original *Dracula?*" She picks up the tome next to it. "*Varney the Vampire?* You have a copy of *Varney the Vampire?*" She pulls a slim volume from the shelf and stacks it on top of Varney. "I can't believe it. *The Vampyre* by John Polidori. It's like the first vampire novel. Wow. I'm speechless."

"For obvious reasons, I have a lot of vampire literature," Wolf says, as he kneels down next to the magnificent stone mantle of the fireplace. "And twice as much vampire trash."

"Can I read it? Trash?"

"Hmmm?" He arranges the kindling, strikes a match on the stone and sets it to the paper.

"Can I read *The Vampyre* and *Varney the Vampire?*" she is already thumbing through the book. "And what do you mean by trash?" Ginny turns to see what he is doing and her jaw drops once again.

"You could roast an entire cow in that thing," she says, "it's bigger than the fireplace at the Boar's Head."

"When this place was built, it probably wasn't unusual to do just that. Though, actually, they probably roasted deer rather than cows. Except for the bedroom, which I altered myself, this place was built in the traditional architecture of the time. At least, standard for a ranch house. I've added to it since then. For example, when bathrooms were brought indoors, I couldn't very well say not to build me a kitchen or bathroom if you know what I mean. Besides, for a while, quite a while, my caretakers would stay here."

Ginny glances down at the books in her hand and holds them up so Wolf can see them. "Well, can I?"

"Of course you can. You can read anything you want."

"What did you mean by trash? I don't see any vampire trash here. Certainly you can't mean *Dracula?*" She sits down on the soft leather couch that faces the fireplace. On the other wall, a widescreen TV and a shelf containing dozens of DVDs offers another form of entertainment. The fire is blazing now, and Wolf joins her.

"You don't see any trash because I got rid of it all. And by trash I mean any books that over-glorify the vampire or its lifestyle."

"It?"

"We might as well be. Vampires are freaks, monsters, whatever you want to call us. We are neither living nor dead and to survive we have to prey on other humans. Unconscionable."

Ginny's eyes begin to prick with impending tears. It never occurred to her that a vampire might not actually want to be a vampire. Not that she has given it much thought as she has always assumed that vampires, like werewolves and Big Foot and Nessie, are just products of overactive imaginations used as a literary device. How does one redeem a reluctant vampire? The answer comes back to haunt her as it had done the previous night—by killing the vampire that had created it. But, she no longer wants to risk losing Wolf, at least, not yet.

"My turn to lie down," he says, laying his head in her lap. He props his feet on the armrest. "So where were you when we were so rudely interrupted?"

"No where near where we were supposed to be. If I recall correctly, we had been sidetracked."

"Oh, yes, you were talking about Abe."

"I wasn't talking about Abe. You're the one who brought him up. I was talking about Ken and the fact that I haven't been attracted to anyone since we drifted apart."

"No one?"

Ginny looks down into Wolf's eyes, "Except you, of course, and a lot of good that does me."

Wolf looks away, hurt. But of course it's true, he thinks. A lot of good it does her to be attracted to me when I can't do anything about it other than hold and kiss her. Damn.

Ginny rubs his forehead as if she can erase the deeply etched lines of pain there. She traces his eyebrows with her finger, then his nose and finally his lips.

"But don't worry about it," she smiles, "for now we'll just pretend this is the old days when you had to court someone forever before you got to the wedding bed."

Wolf grins back, and she tentatively touches the sharp teeth that change his handsome face to a horrid one when he smiles.

It's not like they're that sharp, she reflects, and they're not even that pointed, but just enough so you notice. And when he smiles, the dog-like canines become too prominent.

"Can I lie down with you," she asks. He nods and sits up so she can stretch out beside him, stuffing a throw pillow under his head. "Anyway, back to my history," she lays her head on his chest.

"Let's see . . . college, Germany, grad school, then Dad died and with Jack and Carolina in school and Mom having moved out here, I decided I needed a change of scenery as well. A year after Dad died, Mom married David. I think I can honestly say that there was no romantic interest between them while Mom and Dad were married. But, once Mom moved out here and began the year-long process, with the help of her priest, of grieving for my father . . . well, I'll just say that it didn't take long once Mom got out here for the interest to develop. They both seem truly happy now, and I really am glad that they both have found a second chance at love."

"I know I've had a couple of chances, but I would really like another," Wolf grouses. "But it's all so pointless."

"Why can't you find a nice female vampire to love?" she jokes. Wolf looks horrified.

"I don't even like being a vampire. Why would I want to develop a relationship with one?"

"Good point, but your future seems so bleak. Of course, I say that knowing you've already managed to exist for four centuries, so maybe it's not as bad as all that. I guess from a human perspective it seems bleak."

"So, you're saying you don't see me as human?"

"I didn't mean it that way, I just meant that our perspectives differ because not only will I age but I have a limited life expectancy whereas conceivably you could live forever at age 28. You have to admit that would make a relationship with a human impossible. It might be fine, assuming I decided I wanted to live without sex and children, for the next ten to twenty years, but I will start looking much older than you eventually. And I will die. I mean, I guess you could find another woman after me, and then another, and so on ad infinitum, but that seems a desolate existence in it own way."

"Thanks for cheering me up."

"I'm sorry, I'll change the subject. We'll return to my pathetic little life and I can be depressed instead," she teases. "Where were we? Oh yes, my decision to become a west coast rather than east coast person. It all worked out rather well because a job opened up here at the *Daily Sun* not long after I moved out here. I had already visited Mom out here a couple of times, and I liked it. I especially loved the cottage, which David offered me. David has also known Abe for quite awhile and spoke to him about me. And, Abe said I was welcome to come out here and give the position a try. So, here I am."

"I take it you're happy or at least, content?"

"Actually, no. As much as I love this town, I hate the job. I don't want to be a reporter for the rest of my life," Ginny says, vehemently.

Wolf laughs, "What do you want to do?"

"If I could do anything I wanted, I would travel. I would have my own home somewhere, probably here, and I would take off half the year, traveling. But, of course, that's unrealistic. I can't afford to do that. My plan is eventually to write travel stories for magazines, and if I'm lucky travel books. Maybe I can even try my hand at fiction. That way I can finance my travels. Unfortunately, I am going to need a break for that, but it may happen. Right now, I am saving up for a trip to Nepal. It's going to take about $5,000 to do it easy. If I save that much, I can stay there a couple of months and still have some money when I get back. I thought I would write some magazines before I go and ask them if they're interested in anything on Kathmandu. I can also take pictures."

"When are you going on this trip?" Wolf asks. He doesn't look very happy.

"Well, I'd been hoping for next spring but there's no way I can save another two-thousand by then. I guess it'll have to be the spring after this one . . ." her voice trails off as she notices the expression on Wolf's face. "What's wrong?" He suddenly seems so still. She pulls herself up to look into his face.

He looks at her, almost embarrassed. "I know this is presumptive of me but I had already begun to think of you in future terms. I know that's stupid, especially given your speech about the futility of a vampire/human relationship, but I just met you and I feel actually alive again for the first time in centuries. I know the trip is nearly a year and a half away, but it seems so soon. Damn, it's not fair."

She looks at him. It's no doubt true, she realizes, that in vampire time, a year or so might seem like a day. And as much as she enjoys talking to him, being with him, there is no way it can last forever and two years might even be pushing it. She does hear the clock ticking, and at 27 she is more than ready to find someone to settle down with before she misses her time. She doesn't want it to be Abe, but he does care for her, can offer her security. It's all so complicated, and as jealous as both Wolf and Abe are now, how could they all possibly remain friends through her marriage to another man, particularly if that other man turned out to be Abe?

As if reading her thoughts, he says, "And I can't stand to think of you with another man. No one would ever be good enough for you."

"And you are?" she teases, gently.

He looks at her, sees her smile, the warm look in her eyes. He cups her face in his hands, "I'd like to think I am." He pulls her face toward his, kisses her tenderly.

She snuggles her face between his neck and chin wondering why she is the object of such a cruel joke. *I've waited years to find someone who desires me as much as I do him, and along comes Wolf and he's* everything I've ever wanted in a man, she thinks. Except for one thing—one very important thing. And if I can live with the constant sexual frustration, would I be able to give up children, as well? I'm just not sure I can give up my entire life for a vampire.

Wolf is also thinking. Were he a normal human, he would be ecstatic at the turn of events. A beautiful woman is falling in love with him. And he knows that if he were not a vampire, he would be as in love with her as he once was with Hannele. Damn Vlad, he thinks.

"Why didn't I kill Vlad?" he says, aloud.

"Why don't you?" murmurs Ginny, who's frustrated by the fruitlessness, literally, of a long term relationship with Wolf. And since she mentioned it, he continues to bring it up. Either kill him or shut up about it, she thinks, peevishly.

Suddenly, it's all so clear to Wolf. Just because it has been 400 years doesn't mean he cannot still kill Vlad. So what if he dies, he can't have Ginny anyway. And if he kills Vlad, he'll be killing two birds, or bats rather, he manages to smile, perhaps more, with one stone.

"You're right," he tells Ginny. "I am going to kill Vlad."

"I wasn't serious," Ginny says, pulling herself up so she can look into his eyes. "I thought you were just complaining again. I don't want you to kill Vlad, you'll die."

"I know."

She stares at him in disbelief. He wants to kill himself, she realizes. Is it because he can't have her? "Why?"

"As much as I'd like to believe otherwise, I know that there is no way we will always be together. Even if I could handle your having a husband, a family, I still believe we'd drift apart. I'd have to be a secret. What man is going to understand your being friends with a vampire, even if he were convinced that I am. How would you explain me to your children? Not to mention the fact that you would probably move away from Corazon and definitely from your cottage."

"What if I say I'll give up that kind of life for you?"

"It wouldn't work and you know it."

She does know it. She wants a family too badly. Hell, for that matter, she doesn't exactly want to remain celibate for the rest of her life, either. She realizes that it wouldn't be long before she began to resent him, hate him, perhaps. No, she decides, she would rather remember the short time they spent together than grow to hate him.

"I don't ever want to hate you," she says, tears forming in her eyes. "But I don't want you to die."

"I've already made up my mind," he says, "and this is not even quite like suicide although I suppose it is murder. But at least I'll be killing something evil. Really, I'll be killing at least two evil creatures, if not more. I have no idea how many vampires Vlad's produced."

"You're not evil, Wolf," a tear slides down Ginny's cheek.

"I am a vampire, that makes me evil."

"But you said you never killed anyone."

"Taking their blood is bad enough."

She looks at him, sees that he is determined, that nothing she can say will change his mind. This must be how he looked the night he set out to kill Vlad the first time. How is it that I can already be so deeply in love, she wonders. "When?"

"There's no time like the present," he says, trying to smile.

"I'm going to help you," she decides. "That way we can spend as much time together as possible."

"Wrong. Absolutely not. I am not going to let happen to you what happened to Hannele. Vlad was a dangerous man then and is probably even more dangerous now. No, this is something I am doing on my own."

"Do you know . . . No, of course you don't know where Vlad is. You're not even really sure he is alive. We only assume that through what we know of vampire movies and legend. So, if you don't know where he is, much less if he's alive, then there is no way you can do this on your own."

"Why not?" It is the angriest she has seen him look so far. He looks almost ready to pout.

Ginny is unable to keep from laughing. "I'm sorry, but you look like a little boy about to throw a temper tantrum."

Wolf's frown deepens. Ginny laughs again and kisses him where his forehead is creased between the brows.

"You're not going to get rid of me that easily," she smiles, but her eyes reflect her stubbornness. Wolf tries to interrupt, but Ginny hushes him with a hand over his mouth.

"First of all," she explains, "if you couldn't gallivant all over Europe in the 17th century without a caretaker, how the hell do you think you're going to do it now?"

"I didn't gallivant, and I can get the Brauers to send me another caretaker."

"So, you're saying you want some strange man to take care of you instead of me?"

"I don't want to risk your being hurt, or worse, killed," he repeats, inflexibly.

"Fine then, fine," Ginny almost yells, "Have it your way. But I'll tell you right now that even if you do get the Brauers to send you a fucking caretaker, I'll follow you anyway. Do you understand?"

Wolf is taken aback by her anger.

"Don't you understand," she continues, her anger collapsing, "I've had so little time with you, and if you're going to have to die then I want to be with you until you do. Please. I'm begging you to let me help you, but I'll use my Nepal money if I have to, just to follow you. You've got me whether you want me or not."

"You'll have to quit your job," Wolf says as if that will change her mind. But even though he is aware of the dangers, he is more relieved that she wants to be with him.

"You know darn well I won't mind quitting my job," she says, beginning to smile.

"How will you explain it to Abe, your mother?"

"I don't have to explain a darn thing to Abe. And I'll just have to come up with some explanation for my mother."

"This is craziness you know. I'm not easy to take care of."

"I can imagine," she replies, tracing his lips with her finger, then his chin and throat. With the same finger she runs her finger down his chest to the waistband of his jeans.

"I guess here is where I stop," she says, eyes gleaming, mischievously.

Wolf smiles, "I'm afraid so."

She begins unbuttoning his shirt. "I want to see your chest," she explains. "Is that all right?" She stops, momentarily.

"Of course it's all right," Wolf says. It will be nice to feel a woman's hands caressing him again. Not since Hannele . . . No I don't want to think about that.

"Mmmm, nice." Ginny murmurs, and kisses the soft hair there just the way Hannele had 400 years earlier.

Wolf sits up and gathers Ginny in his arms, bride-over-the-threshold style. He carries her to his bedroom.

"Verdammt," he curses when he throws back the comforter.

"What the hell is that?" Ginny blurts. "It looks like . . ."

"Soil. Earth from Fürstensteinbrück. It seems silly but I have to sleep on the soil of my grave."

"But you were never buried."

"Had I been buried it would have been in the family cemetery in Fürstensteinbrück. I don't understand, I know only that the one time I didn't sleep on it, I did not recover my strength by sundown. And now it's nearly dawn and I want you to stay with me," Wolf confesses.

"You mean sleep here with you all day?"

"Yes. You don't have to sleep on the dirt. I'll put a sheet on your side. Besides, you have the day off, right? Or do you have something else you need to do?"

Ginny spends one guilty moment considering her cats, her horse. They'll make it until sundown, she decides. The desire to sleep and to spend that time sleeping next to Wolf is too great. Her time left with him is limited.

"Yes, I'll stay," she murmurs, pressing her soft, warm body against his.

"Thank you," he says, already resenting the time he must spend away from her that evening. Maybe he will not go quite as far so that he can be back in Corazon by dawn.

"I don't suppose I can leave this room until sundown?" she asks, worrying that she might need to use the bathroom.

"You know, I don't know. I guess it really doesn't matter as long as you shut the door if you must leave the room. A little bit of light coming in from outside for a brief period of time shouldn't affect me too much. I've never been brave enough to take the chance; just too distrustful. I always lock the door from the inside so that should something happen to Mephisto, at least I'll have advance warning that someone is trying to break in. If you leave the door will be unlocked . . ."

"Don't worry, if I leave, it will be only to use the restroom; it won't take long. Are you really worried about someone breaking in? What would you do if someone actually tried?"

Wolf pointed to the high ceiling, beamed with roughly hewn logs. "There's a trap door up there that opens onto a small room."

He thinks of everything, Ginny smiles, but the trap door is a good 10 feet or so above their heads.

"How the hell do you get up there," she asks, "especially when you're in a hurry."

"I can jump that far, but I could also climb."

Ginny looks around, sees nothing to climb on or with.

Wolf is grinning. "Vampires can scale walls. Didn't you read *Dracula?*"

Ginny remembers Jonathan Harker watching Dracula descend the stone walls of his castle, head down. She shivers. "God, that scene was so spooky to me. I can see him like some kind of slimy lizard or something oozing down the walls."

"Thanks."

"You'd be hard put to remind me of a lizard."

"What do I look like?"

"With that blond hair of yours, more like a big cat—a lion, perhaps."

"Really?"

"Well, you know, as much as a human can."

"I'm not human."

"You are to me. You're too damn hard on yourself. Why don't you give yourself some slack for a change. As a matter of fact, I don't want to hear even one more self-deprecating word come out of your mouth."

"Until when?"

"Until you die," she says, and sobs. He holds her, tightly, until the tears that fall from her face to his chest have stopped.

"I'm sorry," she sighs, "but I'll probably do this many more times until . . . I don't want to think about it. The sun's about to come up and it's time to go to sleep. Better show me where the bathroom is first? You still have one in working condition, I hope?"

He points to the room's far corner. The wavering light from the candles barely reaches the dark corners of the room but she can see the dim outline of a door there.

"You mean you had one in here the whole time? Then I guess I won't have to leave the room after all. Gee whillikers, or as Tom says in *Little Men*, 'Thunder Turtles!'"

Wolf laughs, "That's why I want to spend all my time with you. I never know what you're going to say next.

She is back within a minute, nestling against Wolf's body under the warm comforter. "You know, I should go ahead and call Terry and let him know that I won't be coming in today. We usually get in before Abe, and even though Abe knows, he probably won't think to tell Terry until he gets in and I don't want Terry to be calling my home and not getting an answer. He's bound to tell Abe, and that will worry him. If I go ahead and leave a message saying I'm turning my phones off so I can sleep, things might go better."

Once she has made the call, Ginny turns off her phone and snuggles into a comfortable position against Wolf.

Outside, the first orange rays of the sun gently touch the roof of the cabin. As if that is his cue, Wolf's eyes close, and head on Ginny's chest he is soon fast asleep. Ginny runs her fingers through his thick blond hair, wondering for a moment what she has gotten herself into. But Wolf's rhythmical breathing soon lulls her to sleep.

Abe

FOR THE FIRST TIME IN HIS LIFE, the oak-paneled walls depress him. Usually, when feeling low, his bedroom offers him the illusion of peace. It is his sanctum. It is where he goes to get away from his mother's ever-watchful eyes, ever-dominating tongue. When his father had died, he had spent two days in this room, lying on his bed and staring at the ceiling. He had cried off and on during those two days in the twelfth year of his life, the hot tears pooling in his ears. But mostly he had thought, staring at the ceiling as if it were a screen where all the memories of his father played for one last time. He had desperately tried to remember every word, every touch, every look.

Since that time, he has never cried, but his bedroom is still his refuge. Now, it is where he goes to think of Ginny.

But tonight, instead of providing comfort and sanctuary, the dark wood seems to enclose him like some small animal in a trap. His thoughts keep returning to a cottage, a beckoning window and a couple embracing on an overstuffed couch.

Abe is dumbfounded. He could have sworn he had seen Ginny lying on top of a man when he had peered through her front window. But when she had opened the door, there had been no one there. Only Ginny in a robe, a fire dancing merrily in the hearth and the dog.

"That huge whatever it was," Abe thinks, because it was no breed he could identify. Maybe a cross between a wolf or coyote and some other large breed. He was sitting, as he had done only a few days earlier, on his bed and staring into the mirror. His mother is out at the moment; some kind of women's meeting or charity event, he isn't sure.

Abe plays the scene over in his mind for the umpteenth time since he left Ginny's cottage. He had driven over to her house to check on her, that much had been true. He had been worried because she had seemed so tired at work, her eyes had had a bruised look about them. He knew he had promised to call but he was afraid of waking her. He thought, perhaps, if he drove by and her lights were on . . .

And, he had seen the light shining through her curtains, and had thought, good, she's awake.

Although he didn't make a practice of peeping through people's windows, he couldn't resist the two-inch gap in the curtains masking the living room window that looked out over Ginny's front porch.

Had he been asked why he succumbed to the urge of peeping Tomism, he would have probably said that he had just wanted to see Ginny being herself, see if she behaved at home the same way she interacted with him.

He had been shocked to find her in the arms of another man (he already thinks of Ginny as his) whose face he could not see because it was curtained by Ginny's long brown hair. But, when he had seen the man's hand pulling open Ginny's robe, a surge of anger swept through him and he had knocked on the door harder than he had meant to.

And when she had opened the door, she had seemed surprised and not a little disturbed at his sudden appearance. And there had been no one there, unless of course he had been hiding in Ginny's room or the bathroom.

Abe stands up to pace the expensive oriental carpet, which is spread over the hardwood floor of his bedroom. It is mostly rusty red, the color of dried blood, he thinks and is even more depressed.

He remembers the solitary wine glass and the single plate and glass in the kitchen sink, remembers with a grimace the egg drying on the plate. But that hardly proves anything. So the fellow didn't want anything to eat or drink.

He recalls how good she looked in her robe even if it was just an old and raggedy terry cloth; she had looked like an angel to Abe.

When he had driven away, he had parked his car where it could not be seen from her house. He had then quietly walked back to her cottage. All the lights were off and he had not been able to see through any of her windows. He had assumed she had gone to bed.

Still, the dog puzzles him. Abe knows Ginny well enough to realize that her two cats are nearly children to her and that things would have to be really dire for her to take on a dog. He would think she'd add locks to her door or purchase an alarm system first, if that is, she really is afraid of her house being broken into. And other than a few domestic disputes, there haven't even been any violent crimes in Corazon in the past few months.

Perhaps, he decides, it is another present from her stepfather, Yet for some reason he finds this hard to believe. Why would David buy her a vicious dog, especially when she already has two cats and a horse? Besides, the dog looked like he would eat cats for snacks. David would be more likely to buy her a gun, Abe thinks, standing up, hands freezing on his tie.

And anyway, she had said she had bought the dog just today so her stepfather could not have given it to her. Where in the hell did she find a dog like that in Corazon? It's not that big a town. Surely the Humane Society wouldn't adopt out a ferocious animal like that? It looks like the type of animal that would be turned in just because it is too temperamental. Those types of animals were usually put under soon after they arrived.

The dog had also been mature, at least three or four years old.

"This is too weird," Abe says, aloud. He wonders whether he should check on her in the morning, wonders whether she will break her date with him. He decides against checking on her. She had been angry enough when he had arrived unannounced earlier. And what if she were sleeping. That means I can't call her either. I'll just have to hope that she doesn't break the date.

Just after sundown, the phone at the Bar El house rings. It has an ominous tone to it, and Abe is afraid to pick it up lest it be Ginny calling to break the date. But he doesn't want his mother to answer it either.

It is Ginny, but she is just calling to make sure he still plans on taking her out. He still is and tells her they have reservations for eight o'clock at the French restaurant in town.

"I'll pick you up at quarter 'til," he says. His mother takes one look at his smiling face and grimaces, but says nothing. Her plans to pull them apart have pushed them closer together.

Hanging up the phone, Abe carefully avoids looking at his mother as he heads up the stairs to get ready. He is excited at the prospect of seeing Ginny. Also, someway or another, he is going to get some answers from her.

Vlad

My dearest Miruna,

Beloved, I know that you will never receive this letter, but I needed to put into words just how vast a hole you left in my life. I feel that there is now an empty space where my heart once resided. And while I understand completely why you felt death was a better option than risking capture by the Turks, I am devastated by the loss of the one person who seemed to understand me completely.

No longer do I have anyone with whom to share my hopes and dreams. No longer will I be able to look into your beautiful eyes and see the love shining there. I will miss you more than I ever dreamed possible.

Fortunately, despite the fact we are currently "imprisoned" in a tower room (Solomon's Tower, of all things!) in Visegrad Palace, Matthias is doing his best to make us feel welcome here. Mihnea and I made it across the Carpathians and into Transylvania without mishap and threw ourselves on the mercy of the king, who was vacationing at Brasov. Much to my surprise, he was more than happy to take us into his custody as his prisoners. And I had been planning to seek his alliance to help us fight the Turks. Ironic, isn't it, that once again it is a Hunyadi that will determine my future? Sometimes I feel that I have spent more of my life as a prisoner than as a free man. And trust me, I have learned from my past imprisonments that

I can in no way count on a quick return to freedom. It could be years before I see Tirgoviste again.

Unbearably, it is now that wretched sodomite Radu who sits on my throne. And yet again, the Turks have control over Wallachia and I can only imagine how long the Hungarian king will stand for it. Are the Turks really so much better than I?

Meanwhile, I must bide my time and pray that I can win the good graces of Matthias. I need to convince him that I am much better suited to the throne of Wallachia than Mehmet's "catamite" or any Danesti prince. I fear he doesn't understand the threat we, as a nation, are under. Everything I have done, I have done to protect my people from foreign invaders whether they be Turks or Germans or even rich and selfish merchants whose only goal is to oppress the common man for financial gain. And I would do it again.

Farewell, my beloved, and many thanks for allowing me to pour out my heart to you. I miss you, desperately. Mihnea, too, misses his mother. He is fine but a tower room is no place to raise a child. In some ways, I had more freedom in Adrianople.

It seems to me that your spirit is about me and that brings me a certain peace. And for now, I can continue to live in the hope that in due time I will once again occupy the throne of Wallachia.

Yours always,

Vlad

A startled gasp jolted Vlad from his intense concentration on his handiwork. He turned to find a wide-eyed Mihnea studying his current project, which covered about four-square feet of the chamber floor.

"Papa, what are you doing?"

"Practicing."

"Practicing what?" Small birds and mice, in various stages of impalement on miniature spears, were arranged in a pattern that to the six-year-old boy looked like a star within a circle.

"Someday I will be king again," Vlad explained, "and when I am, the Turks are going to pay for invading my country and killing my wife and your mother."

"How does killing birds and mice punish the Turks?"

Vlad laughed, but not unkindly. "I don't think Matthias would take it that well if I practiced on him or his family, do you?"

"You mean, you would do this to people?" Mihnea indicated the twitching animals.

"My son, I *have* done this to people. How do you think I managed to rule such a safe kingdom? Did you know Wallachia was so safe when I ruled it that I was able to keep a golden cup on display in the central square of Tirgoviste and no one ever touched it."

"Really?"

"Yes, really," Vlad ruffled his son's dark hair. "Now, you go on and play and let me get back to work. I heard there is a new litter of puppies. Why don't you go and play with them?"

"Yes, Papa," Mihnea replied, obediently. Vlad watched him leave before returning to his birds and mice. They had only been relegated to the tower for a few months and for more than a year now had free reign of the castle and its grounds making it much easier for Vlad to round up the creatures he required for his "experiments."

Taking a deep breath, Vlad once again centered himself as he surveyed his current project. The truth was that this particular pattern was being constructed for more than his amusement. He was concocting a plan, and if he had to use it, he wanted to be sure that he would not fail.

The pattern of his own life—from freeman to prisoner in a seemingly never ending circle—had made him realize that once he was free from Matthias, and once he had regained his throne; he was sure to have to fend off the Turks once again.

And one day, his luck was sure to run out. And when it did, he must be ready. Meanwhile, he continued to placate Matthias—rejecting his own Orthodox faith for Matthias' Roman Catholicism and even wooing the king's cousin, the Countess Ilona Szilagy, whom he would marry in a fortnight. Once they were married, he would be allowed to come and go as he pleased as well as attend banquets and other social functions at the castle. And while he was sure Matthias would eventually support his retaking the throne of Wallachia, there was still no sign as to when that might be.

"**I**t's finally going to happen," Vlad called out, triumphantly, as he entered his family's quarters in the small town of Badu, Transylvania. The silence echoed against his ears.

"Ilona? Vlad? Janos?" Only silence. Silence and stillness. Which was completely unnatural in a home that claimed two young boys among its residents. And, just as the fingers of fear began to worry the fringes of his heart, he heard Vlad's ringing laughter bouncing off the stone walls that marked the short carriageway to their home, and he stepped outside to survey their progress up the drive.

The statuesque Ilona towered above the boys and their tiny nanny, Crina. The women's arms were laden with packages and the boys were laughing excitedly over some new toy.

Ilona glanced up, and seeing her husband waiting at the top of the stairs that led to their doorway, murmured something to the boys, who, shouting excitedly, began racing toward their father. Vlad's first son, Mihnea, had recently come of age and was now serving in the court of King Stephen of Moldavia.

Once the children had regaled their father with the morning's shopping adventure, Crina squired them off to their rooms for some quiet time. Finally alone with his wife, and after having been served tea, Vlad began again, "It's going to happen."

"You're finally going to regain the throne?" Ilona asked.

"Yes, Matthias has officially granted me a pardon, and now Matthias, Stephen and I will be able to set our plans in motion and remove Radu from the throne."

"That's wonderful, my love," Ilona smiled. Vlad smiled back. He had been lucky to be allowed to wed Ilona. In some ways, she was everything that Miruna was not—tall, blond, steady, patient. And while he missed the passion and deep understanding Miruna had given him, he had actually needed the stability that Ilona had provided him during the past decade.

One of the major reasons he had not had the support to return to the throne of Wallachia since Radu had taken over had been the boyars, who still despised him for his reign of terror.

But Ilona had been a calming influence on him, allowing Vlad to remain on his best behavior. And in public, there had been no fits of anger or angst; and more importantly there had been no impalings.

At least none that they were aware of, Vlad smiled, inwardly. Humans were so easily deceived. Did they really think he was hunting only wild boar on his solitary trips into the Carpathians? For that matter, did they really think he could kill hundreds of thousands of people and suddenly be content with insects, birds and rodents? Even the pleasure he'd experienced when he'd managed to torture and kill a few cats and dogs paled in comparison to what he could do with humans. But, he'd been very careful and had disposed of the bodies completely before returning from his hunting trips.

Now the final preparations were being made to once again attack the Turks and re-take the throne, and then Vlad would make his own preparations. Because, following twelve years in exile from what should have been his throne, Vlad's daily scheming for his own version of "Lex Talionis" had become a constant in his life.

Ginny & Wolf

GINNY WAKES SHORTLY AFTER 2 P.M. Wolf sleeps soundly next to her. The sleep of the undead, she thinks, studying his nearly motionless form; only his chest rises and falls gently as he breathes. There is no way she can remain in bed for another four hours. Sliding as silently from bed as possible, Ginny pads toward the huge door and looks back at Wolf, guiltily, before unlocking it and retreating to the living area where she can make more noise.

Mephisto watches her, warily, but his tail thumps against the floor a couple of times and she scratches his ears. Wolf had said she could leave the bedroom, but she still feels bad about doing so. On the other hand, she is anxious to start doing some "research." She peruses his DVD collection before selecting "Noseferatu: A Symphony of Horror."

As it is a silent film, she can watch it while quickly reading Polidori's *The Vampyre*. Before settling in, she finds the bathroom and then heads for the kitchen. To her great disappointment, the room is empty. No refrigerator. No food in the cupboards. She finds an ancient coffee mug in one of the cabinets and realizes that until Wolf awakes, she will have to content herself with water.

"Oh joy," she informs Mephisto, sarcastically. "It looks as if water is to be my breakfast. Or is it lunch? Either way, that's going to have to change if he wants me to stay the night, or day rather, again."

After retrieving her books from the coffee table in front of the couch, she puzzles out the complexities of getting the DVD going before making herself comfortable in the armchair in front of the television.

"Nosferatu," she reads out loud to Mephisto when the movie starts, "Does not this word sound like the call of the death bird at midnight? Take care you never utter it, lest life's pictures fade into pale shadows, and ghostly dreams rise from your heart and feed on your blood."

Mephisto watches her, almost knowingly. "Yes, I know," she continues, "Kind of pointless to tell me not to utter the word once I've uttered it. Nosferatu," she croaks, then caws. "Or do you think it sounds more like the call of an owl? You know, as in *I Heard the Owl Call My Name?*" Mephisto just blinks at her. Sighing, she opens the book.

Following a long introduction to the introduction, in which she learns, interestingly enough, that this particular novella was just one of a number of works produced after an evening of ghost stories, the most famous work being *Frankenstein*, she finally begins the book, itself. But not before pondering what it must have been like to listen to ghost stories being told by Lord Byron, Percy Shelley and Mary Godwin, as well as Polidori and another unnamed woman. Whether it was or not, she pictures it being a stormy night in Geneva, the waves of the lake, lashing the shore, angrily, as the party, gathered about the fire in the sitting room, sipped their sherry or claret and tried to scare each other.

Less than two hours later, the movie has ended and she has finished the tale and she is wondering how she will fill the next hour or so. Perhaps, she should re-read *Dracula*. After all, it has always seemed like the most real of the vampire tales to her; wildly romantic, yes, but no more so than any of the books by Anne Rice. Her stomach complains, loudly, for food, but it is only another hour or so until sun set and she figures she can wait that long.

She is well into the book when the door to Wolf's bedroom swings open.

"Goot Even-ing," she greets him in her best Bela-Lugosi-Dracula voice.

"Very funny." He looks more pale than usual.

"Looks like you could you use a transfusion," she jokes. "Do you realize you have nothing to eat or drink here? Not even an extra bottle of Tru Blood in your lack of refrigerator."

"It has to be living blood."

"Geez, Wolf, did you even have a sense of humor *before* you were a vampire?"

"I don't remember."

"Great. Well, you certainly seem to have woken up on the wrong side of the coffin."

That actually brings a slight smile to his lips. "I'm sorry," he apologizes, "I guess I am feeling a little weak." He sits down on the couch, and Ginny wonders, briefly, whether she should join him. "How long have you been up?"

"Since 2 p.m. or so."

"Really? That long? What have you been doing?"

"Well, I decided there was no time like the present to start researching, so first I watched 'Nosferatu.' Damn. I uttered it again. Life's pictures will surely be fading into pale shadows now."

Wolf pulls her closer, chuckling. "Don't worry, I won't be the ghostly dream feeding on your heart," he assures her, breathing in the scent of her hair. "Did you learn anything?"

"The continuity kind of sucked. At one point it says they live in caves, tombs or coffins filled with earth from fields of the Black Death and at another point the movie states that vampires can only draw their strength from the cursed earth in which they are buried. Obviously, it's an adaptation of Dracula as well as a really early film, but the latter does seem to fit with what you were saying. And, unlike in the book, Count Orlock just disappears when struck by dawn's light. But, and this is silly, the most interesting thing about the movie to me was the fact Murnau used footage of a striped hyena to represent a werewolf. Of course there was no Discovery Channel or Animal Planet back then so people weren't as animal savvy."

"So, a waste of time?"

"No, I'm glad I saw it. I also read *The Vampyre* and I'm well into *Dracula*. I have read *Dracula* before, but now I'm really paying attention. When I get home, I'll do some research online."

"What exactly are you researching?"

"I don't know, exactly, I just want to be prepared before we begin this so-called adventure. And I've been meaning to ask you something. You said the name of the vampire that created you is Vlad Dracula. Is this the same Vlad Dracula as Vlad the Impaler?"

"You know, I'm not sure."

"But in the Dracula movie with Gary Oldman, they kind of imply that, don't they?"

"Yes, they do, and I'm not sure why I never checked on that."

"Do you have a computer here?"

"No, I left my MacBook in San Francisco."

Ginny bursts out laughing. "I'm sorry," she tries to explain, "it just sounds like a modern cover of the song . . ."

"I Left My Heart in San Francisco," Wolf sings.

"High on a hill it calls to me," Ginny continues. "Yeah, who sang that?"

"Who hasn't? Tony Bennett, maybe?"

"Or Frank Sinatra."

"Probably both. At any rate, I forgot to bring it with me."

"Well, perhaps you can pick it up tonight. Meanwhile, I'll google Vlad when I get home. I imagine you need to be on your way soon. And so do I. I have a date with Abe tonight, remember? And, we're both starving, in a manner of speaking."

"Do you have to go out with Abe?"

"Unfortunately, yes. I need to call him and let him know the date's still on. I'm turning in my notice tomorrow and I really need to let him know first. When will you be back?"

"As soon as possible. I'm not sure I'll go all the way to San Francisco. I just want to be with you," he pulls her more tightly to him.

She is reluctant to remind him of the fact that he might have to make arrangements to "close down" the apartment in the city, not to mention his property here. After all, what they're planning is a suicide mission.

Ginny & Abe

O N THE WALK BACK HOME, SHE CALLS ABE and tells him that she feels up to going out that night. He informs her that he has made reservations for 8 p.m. and will pick her up fifteen minutes prior to that.

After ending the call, she picks up her pace. She has about an hour to get ready and still has a good half-mile left to walk; in addition, it is rapidly getting darker and the last rays of a magnificent sunset do little to illuminate the woods.

She is glad when she reaches the comfort of her cabin, and for a change the complaining cats amuse more than irritate her. "Yes, I know," she informs them, "I feel like I've been gone a long time too." She feeds them quickly and before getting dressed, rushes out to the stable to check on Merlin.

When she returns to the house she is left with just enough time to change clothes for her date with Abe. She gazes longingly at the shower, before turning toward her closet.

While she searches her closet, she wonders where Wolf is. He had offered to drive her back to her cabin, but she didn't really want to call Abe while he was listening. He had kissed her lightly goodbye and when she glanced over her shoulder as the path entered the woods, he had still been watching her. She wonders when she'll see him again, whether or not he is driving the three hours to San Francisco or if he has gone somewhere closer.

Pulling her no-fail little black dress from a hanger and over her head, Ginny begins to worry about how she is going to tell Abe she is leaving. She and Wolf had failed to concoct a story and she is sure Abe will have questions.

She had very briefly considered calling Abe and canceling. But then she had decided she would be better off—well, better thought of—if she told him herself that she plans on quitting. She doesn't want to hurt him by having him hear it from Terry first.

She wonders if his face will betray anger or rejection or whether he'll hide his emotions.

She wonders if he'll mention Wolf.

Wolf. Wolf out there, somewhere, searching for blood at this very moment. She imagines his almost azure-blue eyes carefully scanning a crowd for a woman. A woman, her heart pangs, jealously. A woman who, before the night was through, would feel his soft lips on her throat. And who, unlike Ginny, would feel the softness replaced by enameled smoothness as lower and upper canines met to produce two miniature holes in the jugular vein.

Ginny shudders. I haven't thought of that before, she realizes. It would have been hard enough to handle aging while Wolf remained young, close to impossible to live a life without husband and children, but there would have been no way I could have controlled the jealousy that would surge through me like acid each time Wolf needed blood.

Between Wolf and Abe, she decides, she ought to be a nervous wreck.

"How am I going to handle this?" she asks Tigris, who's weaving around her ankles. "What have I gotten myself into?" She buckles a wide black belt around her waist, causing the dark wool to cling to her hips and buttocks. She gazes appreciatively into the full-length mirror and decides against a necklace.

Only two more weeks of work, she thinks, and then how long. How long will it take them to find Vlad? How long before Wolf is dead?

"I don't want to work these last two weeks," she tells Euphrates, bending over to stroke the soft, reddish brown fur. He meows in sympathy. "I want to spend every minute with Wolf." But at least by giving two weeks notice, she has that much more time with Wolf. And there is still a lot left for them to do; most importantly figuring out where Vlad might be and how to get there. That reminds her of looking up Vlad on the internet, but she still has to brush and put up her hair and pull on some hose . . .

She is half way to her desk when the doorbell interrupts her progress. "Just a minute," she calls while quickly scribbling on a sticky note to remind herself to google Vlad when she returns.

Sliding her black-stockinged feet into a pair of black flats, Ginny grabs the matching jacket and heads for the door.

The atmosphere is perfect and the food smells wonderful but Ginny just can't eat.

"What's wrong?" Abe asks. "You've hardly touched a thing."

"I'm just not very hungry," she says. "I don't know why." She had been so hungry when she left Wolf's; starving by the time she got home, but now her appetite has disappeared completely.

"What's going on?" Abe asks more harshly than he means to. He clears his throat and begins again, more reasonably, "You've been acting differently ever since our first date. If it's me or if there's someone else . . ."

Unwilling to meet his eyes, Ginny had been concentrating on stacking the asparagus on her dinner plate when Abe first spoke. Consequently, he had missed the flash of anger in her eyes.

So, he had been looking through the window.

"That's not it at all," Ginny says, frostily, "it's just that I am going to give Terry my two weeks notice tomorrow."

With some guilt and a good deal of enjoyment, she watches the shock spread across Abe's face as her news registers.

"You're quitting?"

"Two weeks from tomorrow."

"It's that man isn't it?"

"What man?" The frost has turned to ice.

"The man you were with the other night."

"As a matter of fact. So, you're admitting to looking through my window. Or perhaps you saw us elsewhere together?"

"Who is he?" Abe ignores her accusation.

"That's hardly any of your business."

"Are you getting married?"

Ginny laughs, "No, we're not getting married."

"Then why are you quitting?"

"We're going to travel," she falters. It is time for the cover story and she still hasn't come up with one.

"Where?"

"Well, um, we've talked about Germany." But she doesn't sound convincing as she says it, and quickly lifts her wine glass for a fortifying gulp.

Abe stares at her, not knowing what to think. Why won't she give him a straight answer to his questions? If she'll admit that there is another man, then why won't she tell him anything about him? She's still hiding something, he decides.

"So where did the dog come from?" Abe asks, hoping to throw her off guard.

"The dog is his," the lie rolls smoothly off her tongue.

"Then why on earth did he hide when you answered the door?"

"He has his reasons for not wanting to be seen," she says.

"Does he live around here?"

Ginny laughs again. "If I won't tell you who he is, why would I tell you where he lives? Besides," she decides it's wise to add, "He has already left the country." The last thing they need is Abe snooping around hoping to get a second look.

"He's left the country before you've even decided where you're going?"

"He's making arrangements. I'll meet him in a couple of weeks."

"So, how long will you be traveling? Will you ever return to Corazon?"

"I don't know how long I'll be gone," she replies, and Abe detects a hint of sadness in her eyes.

"But you will be back?"

"I suppose so. Maybe in a month, maybe two. Maybe a year. I just don't know."

"You mean until he gets tired of you." The son-of-a-bitch won't marry her, Abe thinks, and she's so in love with him that she's willing to be used by him until he either gets bored with her or finds someone new. Abe's heart aches for her. Maybe when she gets back, he hopes, she'll be ready for someone more stable like me.

"If you say so," Ginny replies, and Abe wonders what that is supposed to mean. What the hell is going on?

Ginny looks into his eyes, sees the hurt and puzzlement there.

"Please don't ask me anymore questions, Abe," she pleads. "When I get back," (if I get back) "I promise I'll tell you everything."

"Thank you," he says, reaching across the table to take her small and surprisingly cold hand in his.

"Cold?"

"Maybe some coffee?" she suggests.

Abe orders cafe au lait, before assuring Ginny that she doesn't need to quit. "Take a leave of absence," he says. "As long as you need. But, if you can still give me the two weeks, I'd appreciate it. I need to find someone to fill in for you."

"Thank you," she replies, glad for the distraction of the waiter bringing their coffee. She feels on the verge of tears.

Abe watches her in silence, but is thinking of the suitcase he must pack when he gets home. He has already decided he will follow Ginny—and her mysterious companion—wherever they might go. He has enough contacts to pretty easily discover which outbound flight she'll be on. The two weeks will give him enough time to make sure all his business is in order, as well.

He signals the waiter. "Can we have a box for that," he indicates Ginny's uneaten food, "and the check? Thank you."

Ginny & Wolf

IT IS PAST MIDNIGHT WHEN THERE IS A KNOCK on the back door. Ginny is not surprised, but neither is she thrilled to find Wolf at the door.

When Abe had dropped her off about 10 p.m., she had decided to take Merlin for a ride before turning in. As they rode along the moonlit beach, she had murmured to her horse all that had happened in the past couple of days and her anxiety had finally begun to melt away. She took time over his grooming and the repetitive motions helped soothe her even more. By the time she got herself ready for bed in flannel pajama pants and long-sleeved t-shirt, she was finally hungry again.

She placed the meal she hadn't eaten earlier in the microwave and while she was waiting, turned on her laptop computer. She had just gotten her Google page to come up and had typed "Vlad Dracula" into the search line when the microwave dinged.

She carried her laptop into the kitchen with her and decided to read the Wikipedia article on Vlad while eating her chicken cordon bleu and asparagus.

It was nearly midnight before she decided that she needed to at least attempt to fall asleep or else feel miserable the next day. She had just crawled into bed and was weighing the benefits of taking half an Ambien when the knocking on her door jolted her to her feet.

"Wolf," she says, opening the door, "I didn't expect you back so soon."

"How did the date with Abe go?" he asks without preamble.

"How did your date with someone's neck go?"

Wolf blinks a couple of times in confusion before his already ruddy face turns a shade redder. "I'm sorry. That was unfair."

"Well, what were you expecting? You come charging in here as if Abe might at this very moment be waiting for me to come back to bed. I really don't understand your jealousy. His, definitely, but yours, no."

"You're right, of course. You've given me absolutely no reason not to trust you. I guess more than anything I am jealous of any time he gets to spend with you because our time together is so limited."

"It really sucks, no pun intended, that you have to 'disappear' occasionally until you feed; nor does it help that I work during the day while you're sleeping. It really cuts down on the amount of time we can spend together. And I really really really have to sleep at night because most of my work has to be done during daylight hours. The next two weeks are going to be tough, but it won't help me if we set out on this quest with me suffering from exhaustion."

"I know, I know."

"I am willing to get by on a little less sleep, but we've got a lot to do during the next two weeks in order to get you out of the country."

"I've been thinking about it most of the night," Wolf sits down on the sofa, pulling Ginny onto his lap. "Even if we charter a plane, which I am sure we're going to have to do in order to avoid a host of problems, I still need a passport."

"We also need a cover story," she says, snuggling closer. "I had no idea what to tell Abe tonight when he asked me why I was quitting."

"What did you tell him?"

"Well, first of all, he did see you through the window so I couldn't deny your existence, but I refused to tell him anything about you. The only thing I told him is that we plan to travel, which sounded really lame."

"I'll have to think about that as well."

"He wouldn't let me quit. He told me I could take a leave of absence, as long as necessary."

"That's decent of him, considering," Wolf says, impressed. "He really does care for you."

"It *only* adds to my feelings of guilt," she yawns. "I did look up

Vlad, by the way. What a monster. He literally impaled hundreds of thousands of people. And do you know, they're not really sure how he died. There are several versions to the story. I don't know if it's the same guy, but I sure as heck wouldn't be surprised." Ginny suddenly slides out of Wolf's lap. "Come look," she says, excitedly, "I saved his picture to my computer. I want you to look at it and see if it's the same guy."

Ginny brings her computer out of sleep mode and suddenly Vlad's face fills the screen—the angular face with the jutting lower lip, accentuated by the man's underbite, the heavy mustache beneath the long, sharp nose, the large and hooded brown eyes and long and curly brown hair.

Wolf looks ill.

"I take it that's the same man?" Ginny slides her arm around Wolf's waist.

"A little younger," Wolf's voice is barely a whisper. "But, yes. That is the demon who killed Hannele and destroyed my life forever." They stare at his picture in silence for a while.

"I wonder what he's looking at," Ginny murmurs.

"Hmmm?"

"I don't know. It just looks as if he is doing more than posing for a portrait. It looks like he's thinking about something that makes him sad. He doesn't look particularly evil."

"No, he doesn't, does he? But, in person, believe me, he was quite different."

"Well, you're living proof of that. Where do you think he is now?"

"I don't know, but as I would like to go to Germany, first, perhaps we can begin our hunt in Berlin. There's sure to be a vampire or two there. Big cities are easier to hide in, and, of course, hunt in."

Ginny glances at the clock and yawns again. "I'm assuming you didn't make it all the way to San Francisco?"

"No, I was anxious to get back."

"In that case, you're welcome to stay here tonight and use my laptop if you need to. As you noted, you're going to need a passport. I'm not sure how we're going to pull that off in two weeks, but they all have that electronic device in them now, so it seems like a "fake" is out of the question. I know you can pay extra for rush service, but getting a birth certificate quickly is harder . . ."

Wolf watched her expectantly as she quickly typed "birth certificates California" into the search engine. More than two million results popped up.

"Two to three days," she mused. "So, the real trick is finding a child who was born and died between 25 and 35 years ago, and sending off for his birth certificate . . ."

"Oh, I see, and I can take over his identity."

"Exactly. Unless you can think of some other way? I really don't know much about this type of thing so I'll leave you to it. If I don't get some sleep, I'll be worthless tomorrow."

"I understand."

"I'm assuming you'll leave at some point?"

"I feel safer in my home right now."

"Because of Abe?"

"Yes."

"You're probably right although I told him you'd already left the country. Will you come tuck me in?"

"Gladly."

Ginny

THE SUNLIGHT FEELS GOOD ON HER FACE. She and her mother are sitting at an outside table at her mother's favorite café—Amber Waves. It's really more of a brew pub but their food is also good and their beer is excellent. Ginny is savoring a chocolatey stout as she waits for her burger to arrive.

This might be a good moment to bring up Wolf, she thinks, remembering his beer connection, but she chooses to wait. She can already see the waiter approaching with their food, and her mother will insist on saying a blessing. Fortunately, it is a hurried grace as the scent of the food has set both their mouths to watering.

"Bless this food to our bodies and our bodies to Your service, in Christ's name we pray. Amen."

"Amen," Ginny choruses, thankfully. She is suddenly ravenously hungry, and wonders, briefly, if this is what Wolf's hunger for blood feels like.

She and Wolf had waffled over how much she should tell her mother. He was getting a birth certificate and passport in the name of Matthew Nicholas, and while they would have to use that name exclusively once they started traveling, Ginny was sure that Abe would be contacting her mother to find out just what she knew. It was seemingly a catch-22. If she told her mother about Matthew Nicholas, they would be easily traceable, assuming Abe wanted to do that, once they got to Europe. But, if she told her about Wolfdietrich Fürstensteinbrück, Abe might track them to the town of the same name. She could always go with Wolf's "American" name—Nachttier—but she thought her mother would find it reassuring to know that Wolf has money, and making up a reason for him being wealthy seemed risky. So, the truth or not the truth?

Ginny opted for the truth because, in the long run, it would make them less "findable." So, now the only thing remaining was to actually inform her mother.

"So," her mother initiates the conversation, once they've finished their lunch, and ordered another beer. "what's going on?"

"What do you mean?" Ginny flushes, guiltily.

"Come on, honey. I know you. You've got something on your mind and it must be pretty important if you felt you had to invite me to lunch to tell me."

Ginny gazes into the depths of her lager for a moment before raising her eyes to meet her mother's. "I'm not really sure where to begin. I . . . well, let me ask you something. Remember when I asked you and David about the guy in the Prius?"

"Yes," Jessie said, light beginning to dawn in her eyes. "You met him?"

"He lives in the house on the beach about a mile south of my cabin."

"And you've fallen madly in love with him?"

"Well, I am questioning my sanity . . ."

"Why is that?"

"He's asked me to quit my job and travel with him."

"Good Lord, for how long?"

"We're not sure how long. I already spoke with Abe, and he told me rather than quit, I should take a leave of absence."

"Wise man. How long have you known this guy? It can't have been long. What's his name? What does he do?"

"I met him Sunday night."

"You haven't even known this man a week and you already want to quit your job and take off with him?"

"Mother, I'm not that foolish. There are extenuating circumstances."

Her mother just raises her eyebrows, questioningly, as if to say, "convince me."

"Wolf has . . ."

"Wolf?"

"Wolfdietrich. He's German. Anyway, Wolf has been estranged from his father for years, and he has just found out that his father's health is failing and he wants to return to Germany to make amends before his father dies."

"And he just wants you to tag along?"

"No, I guess I'll kind of be playing a part. Wolf's an only child and he thinks it will be reassuring to his father if he thinks his son has settled down; that he might produce an heir . . . you know."

"Producing an heir is that important?"

"In his family it is. His name is Wolfdietrich Fürsten-steinbrück." Ginny holds up her beer. "His family owns Furstenbrau."

This silences her mother for a moment.

"So," she finally manages to speak, "he is the heir. Strange that David has lived here all these years and didn't know he had the heir to a brewing fortune living next door."

"Actually, the cabin was Wolf's. He sold it to David."

"Good God, Ginny, how old is this guy? David bought the cabin more than twenty years ago."

"Well," Ginny faltered, "I guess I should have said that it belongs to the Fürstensteinbrück family. Wolf's only 28. I guess his parents were having marital problems and Wolf and his mother came to live here for awhile. It probably stayed empty for years, as well, when Wolf was sent off to boarding school and then university."

"Am I going to get to meet him?"

"When he gets back, maybe I can have you and David over for dinner."

"Gets back?"

"He's in San Francisco. On business."

"Furstenbrau?"

"Yes. The reason I was going to quit is because Wolf wants to re-main in Germany until his father dies, and we're not sure how long that will be. And then, as we'll already be in Europe, we can do a bit of traveling. Assuming, of course, that I still want to be with him. The truth is, I haven't known him that long. But, I do know that when I am with him, I'm the happiest I've ever been. That could change, I know, but I am willing to take that risk."

"And if you're not happy, you'll come back?"

"I'll be back either way," she lies, because it has occurred to her that this is a really dangerous man that they are wanting to kill, and her chances of dying are probably as likely as Wolf's. She'd like to think she is invincible, but if Vlad was able to overpower an enraged Wolf . . . well, she was going to have to start coming up with some contingency plans, in the eventuality that Vlad somehow gets to her, as well. "This is where I want to be. But, I was hoping you might be able to take care of my kitties for me."

"Do you want me to go by the cabin every couple of days?"

"I want you to do what's easiest for you. If you think it will be best for me to take them to y'all's house, I'll be glad to do that. Either way is fine with me. But there is one more thing."

"What's that?"

"Wolf has a dog. He could find another home for it, but I hate for him to have to do that."

"What kind of dog?"

"It's a Akita Inu. His name is Mephistopheles."

"I'll have to check with David. Is he well-behaved?"

"He is actually extremely well trained. I don't think he'd be a problem."

"I assume Wolf will be paying all the expenses for the dog as well as the trip?"

"I offered to use my Nepal money but he refused. I will make sure any bills I can't pay online are paid in advance, though."

"The wonders of modern technology, huh?"

"It is amazing. I could be sitting in an internet café in Amsterdam, and pay my power bill or balance my checkbook." Ginny's iPhone begins to chime.

"What's wrong?" her mother asks.

"Nothing wrong," she sighs, catching the waiter's eye, "It's just reminding me that I have an interview in 15 minutes."

"As I said, the wonders of modern technology. No wonder you don't have to wear a watch."

Once the bill is paid, Ginny hugs her mother and tells her she'll call. Normally, she'd be at home on Saturday to pick up Merlin, but tomorrow she has an Earthquakes game to shoot. She's ticked, but the previous Friday she was lamenting the fact that she didn't have a game because she didn't want to go out with Abe.

Life sure can be ironic, she shakes her head as she unlocks her Bug.

Vlad

T HE END WAS NEAR. He could feel it approaching more quickly than the advancing Turkish army. How quickly things had gone awry.

The three men—Stephen, Matthias and Vlad—had begun a massive campaign against the Turks the previous autumn. Vlad's first objective, dethroning Radu, was easily met. Radu had died as a result of syphilis, a rather fitting death as far as Vlad was concerned, and had been replaced by Basarab the Old.

So, with troops numbering 5,000, they rode southwards, stealthily cutting their way through small contingencies of Turks until they reached Sabac, which they destroyed; then Srebrenica, Kuslat and Zwornik. Along the way, he had impaled thousands of Turks with the claim the impalements were for the honor of freedom, and for the honor of God.

The victory was theirs—Mehmed II, still the sultan, had been weakened and Vlad and his compatriots returned to Romania in March of 1476. The fighting didn't end there, however. Before the summer ended, the trio's forces had cut a wide swath through their own homeland, routing the Turkish invaders from the Carpathians.

By that November, he was finally back on the throne at Tirgoviste. Unfortunately, the boyars weren't happy with his return and with the armies of of Matthias having returned to Hungary and those of Stephen to Moldavia, he found himself in an unsupportive kingdom. Stephen and Matthias left Vlad with a meager garrison—barely two thousand men comprised mostly of Moldavians—with which to defend Wallachia. The problem was that he needed many more able-bodied males to rouse to his call of arms when the Turks soon began to threaten once again. No one responded.

It had not taken long for Mehmed to recover from his defeats and revise his strategy. Despite all the territory lost, he still held onto Bucharest, a major city near the Danube, and from there was amassing what was left of his battalions—tens of thousands of men compared to Vlad's paltry 2,000.

Stefan Bathory, the recently appointed governor of Transylvania, was working with Hungary on an invasion of Bucharest and called on Vlad to prepare the way. His assignment was to skirmish the Turks in the area just north of Bucharest, an area of woodland and marsh, which, if it went according to plan, would cause confusion and help serve as a decoy to cover Bathory's approaching army.

Vlad found himself both undermanned and over-anticipated—a precarious situation. Marching out of the gates of Tirgoviste in early December, he had followed the Dimbovita River south to the monastery at Snagov, where he would finalize his battle plans, and if necessary carry out the preparations for his approaching "demise." It had been his hope that Bathory would assign reinforcements to meet him there and he would have a chance to return to Tirgoviste in triumph. But as he feared, no one came.

And now at last his end was near. It was on this cold morning not long before Christmas that Vlad and his vanguard encountered an overwhelming body of Turks in the Vlasia Forest, adjacent to the monastery. The fighting was fierce and Vlad had little time to put his final plan into action. The Romanians, though greatly outnumbered, fought like devils. And while they were occupied, Vlad just needed to find his way to the special circle he had prepared the previous evening.

Ginny & Abe

MORE THAN A WEEK HAD PASSED since Ginny had given Abe her notice, and he, with great restraint, he thought, had managed to keep his distance from her. But, each time he saw her, he had felt as if a long sharp blade had been sunk into his heart and twisted.

Yet, as her two weeks narrowed down to one week, he began feeling more and more desperate. Soon she would be gone. Perhaps for good. So, unable to take it any longer, he had begged her for one last "date" before her departure.

"I promised myself that I was going to leave you alone and let you do what you felt you needed to do," Abe confesses as he fills their glasses from a pitcher of draft.

"But?"

"But I just couldn't let you leave without spending some more time with you. I'm afraid I'll never see you again and I couldn't live with myself knowing that I just let you leave without telling you how I feel about you."

"Oh Abe," Ginny sighs. "Don't think I don't know how you feel. I do, and I'm flattered. It actually hurts me deeply that I can't share those feelings, but I just don't."

"What does this mystery man have that I don't?" he asks, jokingly, but his eyes tell a different story.

"It's not a competition, Abe. It's not about who has what—more money, greater intelligence, funnier, whatever. It's really all about the way I feel when I am with him. I can't help the way I feel. I like you and I think we could always be friends, but I feel differently about him."

"Does 'him' have a name?" Abe interrupts.

"Of course. I just haven't decided yet if it's wise to let you know."

"Wise? I don't understand why not."

Ginny takes a long, slow drink from her glass of ale while she considers how to respond. How does she explain to Abe that she just doesn't trust him; that she knows that as soon as she is out of his sight, he will be using his numerous contacts to find out more about Wolf. And that, of course, would be disastrous because he doesn't actually exist. What he would find is nothing and then he would be really worried.

She was able to tell her mother because she knew that she would be satisfied with the story, take it at face value. Abe, on the other hand, is already jealous and she has no doubt that the first thing he'll do is set out to prove why "Wolf" is not the right man for her.

"All I can say," Ginny finally manages to respond, "is that I promised him I wouldn't. Not yet, anyway. Maybe I can talk him into letting me tell you right before we leave."

"Humph," Abe grunts, unhappily, as the waiter places their sandwiches in front of them.

"I know it seems unfair," Ginny tries to placate him. "It's just that he's not around right now and I don't want to break a promise."

"So I take it I'm not going to get to meet him, either?"

"I . . . " Ginny trails off, reuben half-way to her mouth. "I can't make any promises. But, my mother wants to meet him, too. So, I'll ask him, ok? That's the best I can do."

Lord have mercy, she thinks, this is a lot harder than it has any right to be. If they knew the real stakes involved, she thinks while slowly chewing her sandwich. She swallows with difficulty. A lump has suddenly appeared in her throat. Yeah, if they knew the real stakes involved there'd be no way they would let her leave the country. A vision of Vlad's face flashes through her head. She tries imagining him with elongated canines and blazing eyes and shivers.

"You ok?"

"Yeah," she shivers again, "I guess I have a whole herd of rabbits racing over my grave." Shaking her head as if it will rid her mind of thoughts of the impending hunt, Ginny changes the subject. "You know, I've been wondering . . ."

"What's that?"

"Well, if you're interested, I would really like to do a photo essay before I leave."

"On anything in particular?"

She launches into her idea for a photo essay on local architecture.

Ginny

GINNY TAKES A DEEP BREATH and mentally fingers her rosary. "Hail Mary," she murmurs while consciously inhaling in an effort to still her thundering heart. "Full of grace," she exhales.

She glances again at the clock. Her mother, David and Abe will be here any minute now.

The fajita meat—chicken, beef and shrimp—is keeping warm in the oven while the sautéed onions and green peppers simmer on the stove. The tortillas are keeping warm in the oven and all the accoutrements for fajitas sit ready in the the fridge: the pico de gallo, guacamole, grated cheese, sour cream, cold Coronas and lime wedges. Chips and salsa await her guests in the living room. The only thing that isn't ready is Wolf.

They had worked out a complicated plan in which he would be "arriving in Corazon from San Francisco" despite the fact he is actually just a mile away. He is "due" at 7 p.m., but about that time Ginny will receive a phone call from Wolf making his apologies. "Business has left him in San Francisco until 6 p.m. and he is still two hours away from Corazon. Go ahead and start without me," he will say thus preventing his inability to eat from causing any unnecessary awkwardness or rousing undue suspicion.

He will show up about 9 p.m., instead, and Ginny prays that they've come up with stories to cover any possible question from "Why are you so pale?" to "So, tell me about your work . . ."

There is a loud knock on the door and Ginny jumps, heart slamming against her chest once again. Must be Abe, she thinks, heading toward the door. Her mother always gives a distinctive rap, for politeness' sake, before walking in, calling "hello."

She ushers him in just as the headlights of David's truck mark their entrance into her driveway. She gives a silent prayer of thanks. She won't have to spend much time alone with Abe, after all.

"Would you like a beer?" she asks over her shoulder as she heads back to the kitchen.

"Sure," Abe says, following her. "I'm assuming he isn't here yet?"

"No, he's coming from San Francisco, but I'm expecting him any minute," the lie rolls more smoothly off her tongue than she cares to admit.

"Hmpf," Abe grunts as Ginny opens the refrigerator and grabs a beer in one hand and the bowl of lime slices in another.

"Here you go," she hands him the Corona after she pops the cap and inserts the lime. "You want to come sit in the living room while we wait?"

As they pass the front door, Jessie and David arrive.

"I brought my famous sangria," her mother says, holding up a pitcher. "I'll put it in the fridge."

"There are also Coronas in there," Ginny adds, "if David prefers . . ."

"So," her mother asks as they join Ginny and Abe in the living room, "when does the guest of honor arrive?"

"I was just telling Abe that I expect him any minute." As if on cue, Ginny's cell phone rings. "Oh no," she says, shortly after the initial hello. "What time do you think you'll get here?" She can feel the weight of the trio listening to her every word. "Ok. Yes, I will. See you then."

"I take it that was Wolf," her mother says after Ginny slides the phone into a pocket in her jeans.

"He wasn't able to leave San Francisco until six."

"Which should put him here about nine," Abe interrupts.

"Yes, unfortunately. He said to go ahead and eat without him," Ginny does her best to try to look disappointed.

"I'm sorry honey," her mother says.

Abe looks skeptical, but asks, "But he is on his way, right?"

"Yes, definitely," Ginny replies. "He really thinks he can make it here by nine."

"Well, then," David chimes in, "how about another beer?"

"I'll join Mom in some Sangria."

"I'm fine," Abe says, holding up a mostly full bottle.

Shortly after nine, the sound of a car pulling up to the cabin alerts them to Wolf's arrival. Ginny and her mother are finishing up the dishes in the kitchen. Ginny feels her stomach lurch as her heart simultaneously leaps with the anticipation of seeing Wolf again. She shakily puts down the rag she is drying dishes with and heads to the front door.

This is the moment they've all been waiting for and the moment she has been dreading all night. She is surprised that Abe hasn't tried to beat her to the door.

She and Wolf share a grim look before she leads him into the living room and begins the introductions. As a concession to Ginny, Wolf shaved his palms and removed his gloves before driving over to her cabin. No need to raise eyebrows. As a further concession, his hair has been pulled back into a neat ponytail. His instincts tell him that Ginny's mother will be easier to win over than the jealous Abe, but he needs to make as good a first impression as possible.

Fortunately, in his exquisitely tailored suit and with his practiced but disarming smile and lightly accented English, he comes across as both the knowledgeable businessman he is supposed to be while still exuding an Old World charm. And with that natural vampire charisma, even Abe seems to fall under Wolf's spell, albeit grudgingly.

"Thank God," Ginny groans as she shuts the door on the retreating taillights. "I'm so glad that's over with. I was beginning to think I'd scream if I heard one more question."

"Why? You weren't the one being bombarded." Wolf pulls her into his arms.

"Maybe I felt your pain, so to speak."

"Hmmm," he sighs, burying his face in her hair and inhaling the lavender scent of her shampoo.

"So, do you think you assuaged Abe's suspicions?"

"Does it really matter if I did?"

"I guess not. I think the thing they were all most interested in was whether or not you're a real person."

"Well, that's debatable."

"Ha!" Ginny laughs, pressing her body more firmly against his. "You're real enough."

"Thanks for the vote of confidence. Is everything ready for tomorrow night?"

"Just about."

"One last walk on the beach together?"

The tightness in her throat almost prevents her from speaking. "I'd love to." Outside, the stars sparkle against the velvet black of the sky and the moonlight shimmers off the crest of each wave. Ginny breathes deeply, the salty air filling her lungs and wonders when, if ever, she'll see her beloved beach and cabin again.

Vlad

IT WAS LATER TO BE RECORDED by the monks who lived nearby that the body of Vlad Dracula was found mutilated in a nearby bog. The only way the priests could tell who he was came from the medallions and the princely vestments he wore. He was decapitated, seemingly in ritualistic style after death. His head was nowhere to be found.

What people would never know is that it was all part of Vlad's plan to not only disappear, but to live forever. Once he had removed the clothes from the body of the man he had killed the evening before, a man similar in size and build to himself, Vlad stripped and dressed the corpse in the distinctive clothes of his office, including his precious medals.

Then reciting an indecipherable prayer, Vlad raised his keenly sharpened sword and severed the corpse's head from its body. Pulling the body to the center of his pentagram, Vlad awaited dusk surrounded by the impaled bodies of Turks he has sacrificed to the demon Azazel.

It was his hope that once he performed the ancient rituals, Azazel would grant his special request.

Finally, the sun began its descent. Vlad could barely see the bodies he had sacrificed. In the gathering gloom, they bear as much kinship to men as to the beetles and rodents Vlad first tortured in his youth.

He feels magnificent, ready to take on the world.

And while Christianity had long since forced underground those ancient religions that called for blood, Vlad had done his research. As far as he was concerned, it was still an age when men spoke to gods and demons, alike, and their sacrifices guaranteed an answer.

Vlad prepared to call forth the demon that he believed was mostly likely to answer his request.

Sprinkling a mixture of herbs, roots and ashes around the huge pentagram, the king began to chant. The words were garbled as if he were speaking in tongues. To the best of his knowledge, Vlad had determined that his best chance was to recite the rituals of the ancient Dacian god, Zamolxis—backwards. Once he completed the ritual, Vlad knelt in the center of the pentagram, and waited.

Five minutes passed and nothing happened. For the first time, it occurred to Vlad that he might not get his wish.

"I didn't do all this work for nothing," he screamed at the impaled bodies, shaking his fist at the unanswering mound, and stamping his foot, childishly, in frustration and anger.

"So impatient," a baritone voice, rich and rolling, boomed from behind him.

The king's head whipped from side to side trying to locate the source of the voice.

Something moved at his feet, and Vlad squinted into the gloom, stepping backward, away from the center of the pentagram. Everything was still, there. He wondered if his eyes had deceived him. Perhaps, he had so wanted to see something that the shadows from the dancing light of the torch he had just ignited . . .

Again there was movement. It looked as if the body at his feet was sitting up.

Vlad experienced his first thrill of fear. The body of the man he had decapitated, the body he intented to use to replace his, was sitting up. It must be Azazel.

But the man was dead, the king took a step backwards. And, he can't possibly speak! He has no head.

"Neither do I have a heart," the voice sounded again like thunder during a summer storm. "Metaphorically speaking, of course."

Vlad watched in horror as the headless body of the man now wearing his clothes took a step toward him. The voice did not sound angry. It struck the king as amused, pleased even.

So, Azazel had chosen to manifest himself in Vlad's final sacrifice, his proxy, so to speak. Vlad smiled. It seemed his god had a sense of humor, as macabre as it might be.

"You called me up in such an interesting," the demon Azazel lingered over the word, as he extended his arm toward the impaled bodies, "manner, that I was just curious enough to answer your call.

"Although," the voice continued, "you never assumed I wouldn't come, did you?"

Vlad stared at Azazel, and a brief lightning stroke of anger flashed in his dark eyes.

"Why would I assume otherwise?"

Laughter resounded from the stiffening corpse. It rolled past the king like a tremendous wave.

Vlad felt as if every hair on the back of his neck stood on end, but it was important that the demon remain ignorant of his fear. On his face, the king maintained a look of almost patronizing amusement.

"You don't appear to have any good qualities at all," the voice chuckled. It was deep and rich like spoiling meat.

A dark and finely arched eyebrow was raised, "So?"

Laughter issued forth from the body's neck once again. "I like you," the voice spoke once the laughter abated. "Perhaps I will grant your wish. I assume you have something to ask for. Or is there another reason you summoned me?"

"I want everlasting life," the king demanded.

"You realize, of course, that I do not grant anything freely. I have my price. If I had wanted to do good, there would never have been a need to rebel in the first place."

"I'm willing to negotiate."

"There will be no negotiations," and the demon's voice was as cold and barren as the moon. "You will take what I give or nothing at all." And the god laughed, but this time it sounded like the fiery furnace of hell. "Take what I offer or leave it. Either way I win."

Vlad's debauchly-full lower lip went razor-thin with anger. He had no choice, and that infuriated him. He no longer had the upper hand. Actually, he did have a choice. He could regain his position by refusing the offer. But that would mean he would have to sacrifice eternal life. Some choice!

"What is your offer?"

"First of all," the headless voice explained, "I am afraid I cannot offer you eternal life without a few strings attached.

"You may live forever but it will be on your own recognizance. In other words, I will expect a new soul from you at least, and here I am being lenient because I like you, at least once a year.

"Now you may ask, how will I deliver these souls into your hands? Well, each year on the night of the winter solstice, I expect you to make a sacrifice—a human sacrifice.

"Also, you may not live forever as you are now. I am afraid that is impossible. Human bodies are not meant for immortality. The only way you can live forever is if you don't live. By that, I mean you must accept life as one of the undead."

"Undead," the king interrupted, "what do you mean by undead?"

"Had you given me time, I would have explained," the voice sounded irritated. "To survive as the undead, there are a number of things you must do. While you will give up a number of earthly pleasures, you will gain other powers." The voice stopped as if to observe Vlad's reaction to this news.

"Go on," the king snapped.

The silence was deafening, but Vlad stood his ground. "Don't expect me to be eternally grateful yet. So far, it appears as if you're the only one with anything to gain in this situation."

"You're the one who requested everlasting life. I'm only explaining the terms of the contract. You still have the option to refuse my demands."

"I may do that."

"To spite me? Yes, you just might."

It was nerve-wracking to hear this voice issue from the zombie-like body of a headless man. The very emotional voice did not match the motionless and mutilated body it came from.

"Anyway," the voice continued, "you must give up food, sexual intercourse and sunlight. On the other hand, you will become twenty times stronger, you will be able to see in the dark, you will be able to control some animals and even move like some of them—climb walls or sail through the air—and you will have the ability to present yourself as an animal."

"And I will never die," the king added.

"Well, let me amend that. You won't die but you can be killed. And, because sunlight will return your strength to that of any mortal man, if you are not protected during the day, a stake through the heart will end your life. So will decapitation. Otherwise, your wounds will heal and you will not be susceptible to any illness."

"Is that it?" the king asked, sarcastically.

The demon's adopted body began to shake with laughter. Deep red and clotted blood began to gush from the gaping wound where once a head had been attached. Bits of lung and egg-sized clots of blood spattered the ground, and even Vlad retreated backwards from the grisly display.

"Ah, yes, I've forgotten the most important part. You must feed," Azazel continued once his laughter had abated.

"You said I must give up food."

"You must give up what you consider food or shall I say, what most consider food. I happen to know you already have a passion for this kind of sustenance. You drink it every time you kill an animal and you glory in spilling your fellow man's."

"Blood! You mean I must live on blood. You're talking about making me a vampire."

"That's exactly what I am offering. I see you've heard of my creations."

"I've heard the stories, but I assumed they were only myths designed to scare bad children."

"Oh, they're very real."

"Then why all the restrictions?"

"Because why should I make it easy on those who wish for eternal life? You're lucky people, you must remember that."

"So, I must exist on blood."

"But, you can't drink the blood of the animals you track in the forests. If you drink their blood, it will be as if you have tasted poison. No, you must feast on the blood of your fellow man. And the human must be living when you do so; the blood needs to be pumped straight from a beating heart. Should you neglect to do so, you will die. I don't think you would find this form of nourishment unappealing. Am I correct?"

The king felt his excitement rising. The thought of subsisting on humans, on their blood, washed over him in a wave of lust. The throbbing of his erection was almost unbearable.

Azazel laughed. "I knew you would enjoy that. The release you will feel each time you feed will be very similar to an orgasm. I suspect that that alone will sway your decision my way."

"I need time to think about it," his voice was already hoarse with desire.

"You have one hour. If you choose to live forever, you must be away from here and in hiding before dawn."

But Vlad was already walking away. He must relieve the ache in his groin before he could think rationally.

Sitting, back against one of the tremendous oaks that grew at the edge of the bogland, the king imagined living forever, feasting on the blood of women and men. He could almost feel the pulsing jugular vein beneath his lips and taste the salty-coppery blood. His hand slowed as he came, but he continued to stroke himself. It might be the last time I use this organ, he thought, but the idea was not unappealing. How nice it would be to have the pleasure he often had to bring about manually, without the bother. As much as he enjoyed masturbation and the fantasies that brought about the always-gratifying release, he always felt as if he were somehow degrading himself.

But, if all it took was to feel the throbbing vein beneath his lips, the gushing blood in his throat . . .

Once again, he was reaching a climax. "Yes," he grunted as the hot semen geysered onto the cold earth and fallen leaves. "Yes."

"You've decided." Azazel's back was to him as he approached but the demon knew he was there, had probably been with him the entire time.

"Yes."

"Good. I'll arrange it so it is never known that you were here." Azazel, arm lifted stiffly, pointed toward the pentagram and its contents. I see you already arranged for the misidentification of your body."

Vlad surveyed the scene. He had to admit that he had not considered the evidence created by the pentagram and its grisly sacrifices. He had planned to leave the headless body in the swamp and to burn and bury the head.

"Outside," the demon ordered.

Vlad stepped away from the pentagram, standing side-by-side with the headless corpse. As soon as he did, the five stakes that marked the outer pentagram, and the five stakes that marked the inner pentagram burst into flame. Within seconds, the bodies impaled upon the stakes ignited as well. Finally, and quite eerily, the lonesome head in the center of the pentagram imploded in a tiny but brilliant ball of fire.

"They will find nothing," the voice said. The king felt no emotion as he watched his handiwork burn to ashes, only a mounting excitement. Now, he would live forever. He smiled, broadly, his face flushed with the heat of the fire. He could not see the sharp teeth that reflected the rosy light.

He listened with only half an ear as Azazel issued a few more rules of vampire life.

A dull but almost liquid thump alerted him to Azazel's departure. The body lay at his feet, deserted by the demon. Vlad pulled the corpse disguised in his clothing the hundred yards or so to the bog and left it there.

"Yes," he murmered. "Finally a life I deserve."

The demon neglected to inform him of his new appearance, and failed to mention that he would never again see his reflection. The hair on his palms would be discovered soon enough.

As Vlad left the woods in search of a decent hiding he place, he recalled the last of Azazel's directions:

"First of all, when you feed, should you gorge yourself on blood and the human dies, unless their neck is broken or unless they are buried with wild roses and garlic, staked through the heart, decapitated or cremated they will continue to live," he had said. "Unlike you, they will not be able to roam far from where they are killed or buried. They, too, will be undead and they will cause holy hell for you because they must subsist on the flesh of dead humans. Should a rash of this occur, you will be hunted. It would be easier for you to go ahead and put them out of their misery."

"I don't understand."

"If you kill someone with that foul mouth of yours, you bring a similar curse upon them. But you may also lift that curse by making sure they are actually dead or by not killing them in the first place."

"Which do you prefer?" Vlad had asked.

"I, of course, prefer that you kill them. Unless they are staked through the heart or buried with wild roses and garlic, they will become mine. If you break their necks, decapitate or burn them, they are more likely not to receive a proper burial."

Vlad had laughed. "I knew there had to be more in it for you than just one soul a year."

"But don't forget that soul. I will consider it a breach of contract if you do."

"How often must I feed?" Vlad had continued, ignoring the threat.

"That will depend on your needs, but I would suppose once every two to three nights. But your guess is as good as mine," and the voice had snickered, evilly, "I'm not going to tell you everything."

"What?"

Laughter had boomed then faded. "It will make life a little more interesting.

"People have always desired immortality, Azazel had then mused, "and there have been a few who were evil enough and desperate enough for me to grant their requests. And, there always will be those willing to make a deal with me. There may even come a day when millions are sacrificed in my name."

"Anything else," Vlad had yawned.

"You may make others of your kind. In that if you want companionship, you may allow a fellow human to drink your blood after you have fed briefly on them. They will immediately become very much like you."

But Vlad's attention had slipped by that point. In his mind, he was already walking away, trying to think of a place he could stay, safe from the light, until the next night's fall.

"And remember," the voice had whispered in his ear, "if you die, you're mine."

But the demon's last remark didn't sink in until dawn, as Vlad curled up in a small cave to sleep.

"Don't worry," he chuckled, as he whirled down into the sleep of the undead, "I'm never going to die."

Ginny & Wolf

THE LONG FLIGHTS FROM SAN FRANCISCO to New York and New York to Nürnberg are finally over. Ginny stands in line at the Europcar counter waiting to sign for the Peugeot 207 she has reserved via the internet.

Chartering a plane had been a stroke of genius, she muses, and says a quick prayer of thankfulness for Fürstenbräu and the small fortune it provides to Wolf. There had been ample time to sleep and the small crew had been both very accommodating and very discreet, taking care of as much of the legalities as possible. Ginny and Wolf had had to do little more than flash their passports.

Now things would get progressively more difficult. The plan is to first drive northeast to the small town of Fürstensteinbrück whose major industry is the Fürstenbräu brewery, the only remaining sign of Wolf's family.

A descendant of the Brauers still maintains ownership of the brewery in Fürstensteinbrück but the beer itself is now brewed in numerous locations throughout Germany, some of which are designated for the export beers.

But, Wolf not only wants to see the original brewery, but has business to discuss with Gunter Brauer.

"I thought you weren't really involved in the business," Ginny had said when Wolf made a trip to the brewery part of their plan.

"There are just some things I want to sort out," he had replied mysteriously and no amount of coaxing had forced him to reveal what he had in mind.

The day is brisk and the sky a deep blue as they begin the short drive with Ginny at the wheel. Not only is Wolf weak and exhausted and fighting off the need for sleep that sunlight brings, but Ginny has the feeling that Wolf may be overwhelmed by the changes that have occurred since his last visit.

"I'm assuming it's unrecognizable," she says after glimpsing the visible shock on Wolf's face.

"That would be an understatement."

Ginny shakes her head in sympathy. "I'm so sorry. Do you think you'll find anything that reminds you of the village you grew up in?"

"Perhaps the *frauenkirche*? I just don't know."

Ginny knew that the forest in which he had both consummated his love with Hannele and lost her to Count Dracula must be foremost in his mind. Did that part of it still exist? A bit of web research had turned up the fact that Fürstensteinbrück backed up onto the Naturpark Nördlichen Oberpfälzer Wald, not far from the Czechoslovakian border. It was possible, but she has to admit to herself, highly unlikely. And even if the actual spot were there surely it would now be unrecognizable. Trees would have died and fallen or, more likely, been harvested in the past 400 years.

Pulling up in front of an imposing and very modern looking brewery, Ginny's heart sinks. So much for the original, she sighs, inwardly. Wolf looks dejected as he walks toward the main lobby doors. But, as she pulls away from the main part of the building, she spots what appears to be an older, and much added onto remnant. Perhaps, she hopes, somewhere amidst the odd conglomeration is something Wolf can recognize.

Returning to the village, Ginny finds her way to the Schwarze Katze, the bed and breakfast at which she has reserved a room for the night. After checking in, she carries her small suitcase up to the room, eager for a shower. The trip may have been luxuriously easy compared to commercial flights, but she still feels like she reeks of air travel.

Both the hotel and the room are charming. The timber-framed building was once part of an 18th century Dominican cloister, and Ginny loves the contrast of the white stucco and black-painted timber. The windows in their room open to reveal a bird's eye view of a lovely garden, still abloom with fall flowers. Unfortunately, the chill breeze forces Ginny to close them sooner than she wishes.

"Shower," she reminds herself. She has another hour or so before she has to return to pick up Wolf from the brewery.

Before she makes the drive back to the brewery, Ginny pulls on her most comfortable pair of jeans and a thick cream-colored cable-knit sweater to ward off the autumn chill. After running a brush through her long hair, she quickly twists it into a bun and secures it with her hawthorn chopsticks.

Once she arrives at the brewery, Wolf instructs her to park the car, then leads her inside to meet Gunter Brauer. The middle-aged German has clear blue eyes and blond hair that is rapidly receding from his hairline. Serious, but with a dry sense of humor, he takes Ginny on a personal tour of the brewery, explaining everything about the brewing process from fermenting and conditioning to filtering and packaging.

In the tasting room, she samples the half dozen brews this particular establishment produces before proclaiming the hefewiezen her favorite.

"The yeast beer? Really?" Wolf asks.

"Yes. I don't know why but I've always liked that little swirl of yeast that gets poured out at the end. But don't give me rauch beer. It's just too smoky for me."

Gunter laughs in agreement.

"I'm pretty sure I never tasted it," Wolf says.

"**I** can't believe you're still awake," she tells Wolf when they finally get back in the car. They had arrived early in Nürnberg about the time Wolf would usually be crashing for the day. Instead, it is now well past noon, and her stomach is signaling its displeasure at its emptiness. She glances at Wolf. He looks paler than usual and she has no doubt he'll have to "hunt" that night. She still hasn't come to terms with what to call his need for blood, she feels like she's either always joking about it or euphemizing.

"I suppose, considering that it's getting closer to sundown than sunrise, I'll be up until dawn tomorrow."

"Can you make it?"

"Do I have a choice?"

"I just worry about your strength," Ginny says.

"I have no doubt I'll regain most of my strength when the sun sets," he assures her.

"Well, if you want to shower once we get back to the room, I'll go in search of some food. I'm starving and I don't think I can wait until sunset."

"I will take a shower if you don't mind, but I had Gunter's secretary call to have a picnic lunch prepared for you. It should be delivered shortly. Again, if you don't mind, I would like to drive over to the Naturpark." Ginny sends him a quick, sidelong glance. "No, I don't really believe I'll find anything there, but I would like to be in those woods once again."

"Ok, I can do that."

"Thank you."

A call to the room announces the arrival of the picnic basket. But, Wolf is already out of the shower and they decide to pick it up on the way to the car. Ginny's stomach grumbles loudly in protest.

"Oh don't be silly. You can wait another half hour or so," she answers it.

But, she is greatly relieved when Wolf pulls on his leather jacket. "Ready?" She jumps up from the bed in obvious anticipation.

"Yes," he smiles at Ginny's eagerness, but his eyes look tired. He doesn't remember what it feels like to feel human hunger pangs. When the blood lust strikes, but is denied, the effect is more like a mind-numbing exhaustion.

Wolf carries the basket to the car as Ginny grabs another chance to skim over the directions to the part of the park they wish to access before she begins driving there. Wolf can once again be her navigator, but she likes to have a general idea of where she is going.

It's a short drive as the park virtually surrounds the small towns and communities in the area. But Wolf knows exactly where he wants to go. Ginny pulls into a small parking area that offers access to a a couple of picnic tables and hiking trail.

The picnic tables are inviting, but Wolf asks if Ginny would mind a short hike down the trail.

"I am sure we can find a suitable area to picnic and I want to be assured of a little more privacy."

"Sure, if that's what you want." The late afternoon sun slants through the birch trees that are rapidly shedding their golden leaves. It's a beautiful afternoon, the path is easy if a little rocky and it isn't long, perhaps half a mile, before they find a sunny spot in a clearing about 10 yards off the trail.

Ginny spreads the tablecloth that was provided with the basket on the fallen leaves and grass. She looks around. "This isn't the spot?"

"No, no," Wolf quickly assures her. "The forest has changed, yes, but I am sure our rendezvous was further south. But, it is not unlike the glade in which we met."

The immensity of the moment fills her for a second and she feels the tears pricking at the back of her eyes. Four hundred years ago, Wolf had once made a vow of love to the woman he adored in a spot not unlike this and not very far away. And here he is again . . . she glances at him and realizes he is watching her, and the look in his eyes causes the tears to spill over her lids.

"I'm sorry," she says, brushing them away, "I'm just so so sorry."

"My love," he traces the line of her jaw with his index finger. "I cannot tell you how much it means to me to have found a woman that I can love as much as Hannele."

His image blurs through the tears. Damn, she thinks, damn it all. Why does he have to be a vampire? It's so unfair. She wants to sob. She wants to throw things. Instead, she blinks away her tears and lacking a tissue, wipes her nose with her hand.

"You know for a split second there," she says, her voice cracking, "I almost begged you to make me one of your kind."

"Never." Wolf states, harshly.

"No," she agrees, softly. "Never. So, what's in the picnic basket?" She quickly changes the subject, reaching her hand in and pulling out a bottle of a Riesling spätlese. "Mmm. Spätlese, and a good one. Hopefully there's a corkscrew." She rifles through the basket. "Yes!" she cries, triumphantly holding up the implement.

"Let me do the honors," Wolf smiles, almost sadly, as he gently removes the bottle from her hand while reaching for the corkscrew with the other.

"Thank you, kind sir," she says but there is a smile in her eyes as she peers into the basket.

"Thank you God," she breathes a prayer as she removes some cold baked chicken.

"I know you're not overly fond of processed . . ."

"Or fried."

"Meats."

"Vielen dank, mein Schatz."

"Nichts zu danken."

"Ach, und hirtenkäse auch!" Ginny laughs, pulling a block of cheese from the basket. "You know me so well already." She pulls some chicken from the bone and stuffs it into her mouth before looking for a knife to cut the earthy cheese.

"Is there a glass in there?" Wolf asks.

Ginny hands him a plastic mug. "Close enough." She pulls some crusty bread out of the basket and tears off a piece, adding some chicken and cheese to it. "Perfekt!" she claims after taking a bite. Wolf hands her a glass of the spätlese, and she takes a sip of the crisp, refreshing wine to wash it down.

"Thanks," she says again, with meaning. A few more bites of the cheese, chicken and bread tame the hunger and she is once again able to think more clearly. "You know this is really nice," she tells Wolf, looking around. The birds are still singing, the wind whispers in the remaining birch leaves and the late afternoon sun shines warmly on her head. The wine has relaxed her, the food has sated her hunger, and for just a moment she wishes to forget why they are here in Germany. She moves around so that she is leaning against Wolf, encased in his strong arms. Physical contact with him is both reassuring and almost painfully sensual.

"This is one of those times when you think nothing can or will ever change," she sighs, wishing that she, too, would have the chance to consummate their love. The frustration, at times, is nearly unbearable.

Wolf kisses the top of her head. "Oh how I wish it were true." And yet they both know: tomorrow Berlin and the beginning of the actual hunt.

"I have something for you," Wolf says, removing Hannele's ring from his pinky. Ginny sits up quickly, sloshing her wine.

"What?" She turns to face him, alarmed.

"No matter what happens to me I want you to have this," he slides the amethyst onto Ginny's index finger.

"Hannele's ring?"

"Yes. And when we find Vlad, I will give you my ring. The one I gave Hannele. And you will know that in my heart, you are the one. Forever."

Ginny contemplates the gem that sits heavily on her index finger. The clear purple stone glows warmly. Suddenly, her head is reeling as the full impact of what they are about to do hits her. There is no doubt now. Wolf is serious. Not only does he intend to search down Vlad and kill him. He knows that he will die in the process and is willing to sacrifice his life to redeem himself and to hopefully destroy any other vampires the Count has created.

Once back at the Schwarze Katze, Ginny prepares for bed. It may be only 4:30 p.m., but the sun is already setting. Wolf is preparing to return to the much larger town of Nürnberg to assuage his hunger.

Ginny really doesn't want to think about it too much and as soon as he's out the door, she swallows an Ambien to ensure that she sleeps away most of the time he is gone. The sun is scheduled to rise about

7:15 a.m. Before climbing into bed, she hangs the German equivalent of a "Do Not Disturb" sign—Bitte Nicht Stören—on the door.

She opens the book she is reading—*Twilight*—and settles down to read until the Ambien kicks in. She wonders if animal blood would be an option for Wolf. Somehow she doubts it. Surely he would have taken that route long ago had it been a possibility.

Not surprisingly, Ginny awakes, feeling well rested, shortly after 2 a.m. Wolf has still not returned. It's too late to take another Ambien. She has to drive into Nurnberg in the morning to do some shopping and she doesn't want to be groggy when she goes.

Fortunately, there is a small coffee maker in the room and she heats herself some water for tea, and makes herself a snack with some left-over bread and cheese. Settling back down with her book, she waits for Wolf's arrival.

A few hours later she has finished the book and the minutes seem to be passing very slowly. Wolf has still not returned and her anxiety is mounting. She decides she'll try to waste some time and take her mind off the waiting by showering and getting dressed for the day very slowly. The whole process—from hair washing to lotioning to blowdrying to make up and dressing—can take nearly an hour if she takes her time.

While she is luxuriating in the hot water streaming over her body, she feels a pair of arms encircle her waist. The touch of his cool skin and his telltale scent identify Wolf immediately. Ginny sighs and leans back into his embrace. His naked flesh is soft as silk but as solid as a column of marble and his lips are firm against her throat as he kisses his way down to her collarbone, and she turns to face him, moaning in pleasure. His mouth and his hands may be his only instruments for pleasuring her, but he is taking her places she has never been before.

"I have to say that that is the best shower I have ever taken," Ginny confesses as she pulls her black woolen dress over her head.

"I'm glad I could be of service," Wolf chuckles. He is checking the drapes over the windows, arranging them in such a manner that not even a single ray of sunlight can gain entrance to the room.

He removes a paper bag from the pocket of the leather jacket he tossed on the chair when he entered the room earlier. Before Ginny can ask what's in it, Wolf starts apologizing. "I'm sorry I have to do this," he says, walking over to the bed and pulling back the covers.

"But you were able to dig up some new dirt, right?" Ginny asks with dawning understanding.

"Yes, for the first time in more than a century. I had some earth shipped to me when I first moved to California, but I obviously haven't been here in a while."

Ginny watches in amusement as he scatters the fresh earth on a towel he had purchased just for the occasion. At least that was one thing they wouldn't have to explain away to the innkeeper.

The sky is just beginning to lighten as Ginny exits the room, leaving Wolf recumbent on the bed, still as a statue beneath the duvet as he sinks quickly into his peculiar brand of sleep.

Ginny considers *Twilight* again and the vampires that never sleep. It seems impossible that they can have such superhuman strengths and abilities and never a need to re-charge, so to speak. But, she has to admit there is something incredibly appealing about Edward.

She is able to find a parking space near the downtown pedestrian zone near Kaiserstrasse. Her first goal is to find an open restaurant. She can use a little breakfast (read coffee) before she begins her shopping.

She spies a small restaurant with an open door and welcoming lights squeezed between two shops and heads for it, stopping to pick up a copy of Spiegel from a newsstand in order to practice her German, on her way in. She is seated immediately and quickly orders coffee, rolls and cheese, preferring to keep her breakfast simple before shopping for clothes.

She takes her time, perusing the newspaper and enjoying two cups of coffee before finally paying the bill and heading out. She has brought very little in the way of clothes with her; she and Wolf had decided it would be better for her to purchase some new clothes once they had arrived to make sure she blends in better.

Wolf had handed her a credit card before she left that morning, "I want you to spend what you have to to look stunning. We'll be going to some nice clubs in Berlin and I want you to look like you spend money on your clothes."

So she wanders through the shopping district looking for high-end boutiques and designer stores feeling incredibly guilty. She usually spends next to nothing on her clothing and now she has a chance to buy the type of clothes she often drools over in magazines. She isn't sure if she can do it.

But after wandering around for more than a couple of hours and trying on more than one dress, Ginny happens upon a little shop that sells gently used designer clothing. Now that she can deal with, she thinks, happily, entering the store.

Once inside, she finds a Christian Dior dress that she feels will work no matter where she goes. The little black dress is not only the essense of sophistication, but the short-sleeved dress is cinched at the waist with a thin black belt, sports a Peter Pan collar and hidden buttons down the bodice. She finds a pair of Christian Louboutin shoes she thinks rounds out the outfit nicely—the black suede Mary Janes have a platform sole with a silver wedge.

She leaves the store feeling somewhat high. Not only has she not had to spend too much, but she has managed to buy two things from designers named "Christian." Surely that has to be a sign, she thinks, practically floating out of the store. All she needs is a purse to complete the outfit and maybe a bracelet and some earrings. And at least one more complete outfit, she reminds herself.

An accessory boutique provides her with a silver metallic clutch shimmering with rhinestones, some silver and rhinestone bangles, and chandelier earrings, also glittering with faux gems. She feels like she has taken a sophisticated yet modest outfit and glammed it up a bit. Hopefully, she'll look as good as all these purchases make her feel and not stand out too much as an American rube.

More wandering and more searching. Ginny decides that if she doesn't find something promising in the next ten minutes, she'll stop and search for lunch instead. Seven minutes later she happens upon a consignment shop. And it is there she find two dresses she can't decide between—an Emanuel Ungaro sand silk dress with a printed-organza neckline or a Nina Ricci salmon jacquard jacket and dress? The colors make her skin glow and bring out the flashes of copper in her hair.

Finally she decides, what the hell, she'll take them both. This opportunity may never happen again. As she leaves the stores, cheeks flushed with both pleasure and guilt, she decides to go ahead and rest awhile with a long lunch before beginning the search for shoes, accessories and a coat she can wear over all her purchases.

Despite the fact she's wearing flats or maybe because of it, her feet are beginning to ache. She is thankful to find a small and very German restaurant nearby. Mittagessen was once the main meal of the day, but like America and a lot of the rest of the world, industrialization has slowly changed that—midday meals were now a quick affair, leaving the big meal of the day to families at home. But, of course, even that was changing now. It seems like more and more people eat out rather than at home, Ginny muses as she waits for the waiter to bring her Radler, a mixture of lager and lemonade.

When he returns, she quickly orders a luncheon portion of schweinsbraten (pot-roasted pork) and pommes frites, the German version of French fries, served with mayonnaise.

As soon as he leaves, she takes a long thirst-quenching swallow of her Radler before sneaking another peak at her dresses. She is happy with her purchases and can't wait to get back to Fürstensteinbrück to try them on for Wolf. He being male, has carted along a couple of suits— the ubiquitous Armani and a recent purchase, a Tom Ford suit and shirt. Always nice to look cool, she sips her Radler, smiling inwardly. They'll make a smashing couple.

It isn't long before the food arrives and Ginny dawdles over her meal and a second Radler. As much as she wants to complete her shopping, she might as well waste as much time as possible. Wolf won't be waking up til nearly 4:30 p.m., anyway.

She finally drags herself away well after 1 p.m. and begins the hunt for another pair of shoes. She finds a number of pairs of strappy and very high-heeled sandals that would no doubt do just fine but she just can't bring herself to buy a pair. Her penchant for clumsiness (she's been known to trip and twist her ankle on more than one occasion) makes her worry. They're hunting vampires, for goodness' sake. She snickers out loud and quickly turns it into a cough. Well, they are hunting vampires for "goodness'" sake, bizarrely enough. Anyway, what if she gets chased? Suddenly she recalls the vampires of Twilight again.

"Faster than a speeding bullet," she murmurs quietly and hiccups another giggle, remembering their lightning speed. She ducks behind a rack of shoes and slaps herself. Pull yourself together, she demands. She can feel the hysteria bubbling just beneath the surface. She exits the store quickly before she makes a bigger fool of herself.

Passing another store selling more casual footwear, a sparkling pair of Chuck Taylor All Stars catches her eye. She enters the store entranced by the glittering champagne shoes. It would work perfectly, if not too funkily, with the dresses she just bought. She has to have them! She loves shoes but she has seldom lusted after a pair; these seem to be calling her name. Of course, she has always kidded herself that she is part raven because of the way sparkling and shining things have always appealed to her.

One more boutique yields a champagne gold raw silk bag decorated with creamy faux pearls and the rest of the jewelry she needs to complete her outfits. There is still a coat to buy but she can't stand the idea of another moment spent shopping. The black velvet opera coat that once belonged to her grandmother will have to suffice. Breathing a huge sigh of relief, she heads back to the Peugeot to dump the bags before calculating how much more time she has to waste before heading back to the Schwarze Katze.

She probably has just enough time to quickly visit the Albrecht Dürer-Haus. She's always loved his artwork, but she argues with herself, you're already exhausted and you still have to drive to Berlin. And, most importantly, there is not a doubt in her mind that Wolf will want to hit a couple of clubs, at least, tonight. Before they left, she came up with a list of possible clubs at which they might find leads to Vlad, himself, or the Berlin vampire culture. She sighs hugely and regretfully, the Albrecht Dürer-Haus will have to wait, possibly for another life-time.

They arrive at their lodgings, the Hotel Palace in the city center, about 9:30 p.m. and before 10 o'clock, they are comfortably ensconced in a park suite. The canopied four-postered bed beckons to Ginny; instead, she finds herself taking a quick shower to re-invigorate her tired body and soon she is dressing to go out in her new "Christians."

Wolf nods, approvingly, as Ginny twists her hair into a neat chignon, pinning it into place and sliding one moonstone-tipped chopstick through the bun for decoration.

"You look," he pauses, "breathtaking."

"Thank you," she says, stifling a yawn. She lifts the decanter, delivered by room service while she was in the shower, and pours herself a glass of wine. "To finding what we came for," she says lifting the glass in a toast before taking a fortifying sip.

"Amen," Wolf agrees. "Where do we go first?"

Ginny consults her list. "Keeping in mind that I'm already exhausted, I suggest that we don't try more than two or three places tonight. Is that all right with you?"

"I understand. And, of course, you can catch up on your sleep during the day tomorrow, nicht wahr?"

"Absolutely. Anyway, I'm thinking we might want to start with Bar am Luetzowplatz, which seems kind of trendy as does Watergate. SO 36 has quite a history, but is currently very alternative with both gay and straight clientele. That should give us a wide enough variety for our first night, don't you think?"

It is nearly 3:30 a.m. before Ginny lets herself back into the room. Wolf is out stalking—he has to keep up his strength—Ginny grimaces, remembering his last words before he took off at a steady pace toward Kurfürstendamm and its bars and clubs, still going strong at this time of night.

"Morning," Ginny corrects herself, grumpily. It's actually morning and as far as she is concerned, it has been a very long day. Hard to believe she had awakened in Fürstensteinbrück that morning, spent a day shopping in Nürnberg, had driven to Berlin and still managed to pack in several clubs. She had also managed to consume no more than one drink at each club, keeping her alcohol level as low as possible while still managing to stay fairly alert. Still, there had been nothing and no one to alert them and carefully worded questions had elicited no useful information. The only consolation, she thinks, slipping off her shoes, is that she won't wake up with a hangover. The problem is, unlike Wolf, she won't be able to sleep until the sun sets the next afternoon. Between her bladder and hunger, she will probably sleep no more than eight to nine hours.

Despite her exhaustion, she hangs up the Dior dress before slipping naked between the soft sheets of the queen-sized bed. She hopes she sleeps through Wolf's arrival. He should be back within a few hours. The sun rises late this time of year.

Sure enough, Ginny awakes shortly after noon. Wolf lies comatose next to her.

"At least I slept through his arrival," she thinks, sliding quietly off the bed, and then wonders if that is necessarily a good thing. During the remainder of this trip she might be better off to be a bit more aware. She has no idea what might come up. Just because they aren't aware of any vampires in Berlin doesn't mean that those vampires aren't aware of them.

"Just because you're paranoid doesn't mean that everyone isn't out to get you," she murmurs, closing the bathroom door. She wants to get dressed and hit the streets—first lunch and then she wants to check out some of the local occult stores.

Dressed comfortably once again in Levis and the wool fisherman's sweater, Ginny stops at an outdoor food stand and orders a Dürüm Döner, strips of lamb with the typical turkish toppings wrapped in a flat chewy homemade bread. She wishes she could enjoy a beer with it, but pulls the bottled water from her purse and hails a taxi. She has the addresses for several stores specializing in the occult and she wants to get to all of them before Wolf wakes around 4:30 p.m.

Unfortunately, the first store on her list is not only out-of-business, but looks as if it has been sitting empty for quite a while. She can barely read the letters that still remain in paint above the door—Baphomet.

The second store she visits, as well as the third, is more commercial than she is looking for. The sales people seem to consist mostly of Goth-dressing young adults and the stores apparently specialize in books and jewelry, oils and incense and other mostly-Wiccan items. Ginny has a feeling that she needs to find a store manned by someone genuinely interested in all aspects of the occult. A store that sells not only the typical candles and pendants, but actual herbs and maybe even silver bullets.

The taxi drops her off at the final store on her list—Mandragora. The archaic lettering on the sign, and the store's location in an older section of Berlin, raise her hopes by a fraction.

As she enters the small shop, a bell rings to announce her presence. Ginny inhales deeply the aroma of all the herbs and dried plants that fill a shelf lining one wall of the store. Incense and candles add to the headiness of the shop's perfume.

A door opens at the back of the shop, and a tall and not unattractive man strides down the aisle to where Ginny is admiring a blackstone scrying bowl. He appears to be Turkish, one of the Germany's many guest workers who have emigrated from that country.

"May I help you?" His German is perfect, which means he's either been here awhile or is the son of immigrants.

Suddenly, Ginny is unsure of how to begin. "Um, do you mind if I just browse around for a little while?"

"Certainly," he says, returning to the counter, which is made of solid oak, dark with age, and which boasts an ancient cash register. A small credit card machine next to the register gives evidence that despite its apperance, the store has joined the 21ˢᵗ century. "Let me know if you have any questions." He sits on the stool behind the counter and picks up the novel he is reading. No, not a novel, she notes as she begins to wander down the aisle. It was clearly something by Malcolm Gladwell—*Blink* or *Outliers*—she didn't catch the title but it looked like one word, and she is pleasantly surprised. People never cease to amaze her.

You just can't judge a book by its cover, she smiles to herself, as she studies the spines of the books that fill a shelf at the back of the shop. There is an entire section devoted to vampires and vampire lit, and isn't long before she is immersed in *The Vampire Book: The Complete Encyclopedia of the Undead* by J. Gordon Melton.

"Interested in vampires?" a voice asks quietly from behind her. Nevertheless, she is startled, and nearly drops the book.

Once again, she has only a split second to come up with a suitable lie. "Actually," she begins, and blushes, for once being thankful for its telltale hue. Perhaps the clerk will misread it. "I'm working on a novel about vampires and I've been trying to find out the different ways they can be killed."

"The different ways?"

This is harder to explain in German than she had realized. "Mein Deutsch ist nicht so gut," she apologizes.

"Amerikaner?"

"Ja," and Ginny laboriously tries to ask whether a stake through the heart is really worth the effort or if there is a better way . . ."

"Oh yes, a stake," he laughs, touching his heart. "And then you must cut off his head and burn him."

"That's a lot of work. You wouldn't happen to have any stakes here?"

"You want a stake?"

"I'd like to see one so I can describe it," she explains although she really wouldn't mind purchasing a few just in case.

"Nein," he laughs, "We don't stock any stakes. Vampires don't really exist."

"Of course not," she laughs, "and I guess you don't sell silver bullets, either."

"The only 'weapons' we sell are the athames, the daggers for witchcraft."

She smiles, hopefully charmingly, at him. "In that case I'll just get this book."

But as she leaves the store, she feels his eyes boring into her back. For a split second, after he'd claimed that vampires don't exist, his eyes had flicked toward the door to her right, and she knew he was lying.

Мeнmеt

Aᴦᴛᴇʀ Gɪɴɴʏ ʟᴇᴀᴠᴇs ᴛʜᴇ sᴛᴏʀᴇ, Mehmet stares after her for a long time. Despite the fact that her story had sounded genuine, there had been something about the beautiful young woman that sounded the warning bells in his head.

He has been Mustela's keeper for less than ten years and never in that time have his suspicions been raised in the slightest.

There had been that split second there, after he'd told her vampires weren't real; a look in her eyes that said, 'we both know that's not true.' But the look had been so brief and her story about stakes so charming . . . he suddenly wishes Herr Leipold were still around.

Mustela's former keeper had passed away several years ago, and Mehmet is now entirely on his own. He will have to wait until Mustela awakes. He picks up his book again, but he doesn't see the words. He is remembering that fateful day eight years ago when Herr Leipold had asked him whether or not he wished to take over Mandragora and become Mustela's personal assistant.

"So, what do I have to do?" Mehmet mumbled, avoiding Herr Leipold's sharp eyes.

"The shop, you know and understand, and we believe you are fully capable of running it. As for Mustela—and that is a name someone he loved gave him very long ago—he does not need much caring for," Herr Leipold said.

Why would you call someone you love a weasel, Mehmet wondered, but asked, "OK, but *how* do I take care of him?"

"First of all, you are welcome to live here, if you wish. But, if you don't, you must be here at the crack of dawn."

"I'll live here." He hated the apartment he shared with five other workmates. It was crowded and it stank.

"Wise choice. Also, once you awake each morning, you must not leave the shop until sunset."

Mehmet made some noise of objection.

"If you should do so without good reason, Mustela will be very angry. Especially, should someone enter the store in your absence and discover him."

Mehmet's brow was wrinkling in confusion. So what if someone saw him? He didn't understand. "But what if I have to go to the hospital or something like that? And what about vacations?"

"At night you are free," Herr Leipold continued, ignoring the youth's obvious puzzlement. "From sunset to sunrise, you may do as you please. Unless, of course, Mustela has something he wants you to do. As for vacations, you will only leave the shop and Berlin if Mustela is so inclined.

"Think about this. If you accept this position, you will be agreeing to serve Mustela, hand and foot, no matter what. You may say no now if you wish."

"Can I think about it? Don't I even get to meet this guy?"

"You have until sunset. If you do not say 'no' then, you will have the opportunity to meet with and talk to Mustela at that time. Then you may decide for sure. You must be willing, remember, even after you meet him, to give your life for this man."

"What about eternal life?" When Herr Leipold had asked to meet with him earlier, he had mentioned immortality.

"That will come in time."

"What if I meet him, and then decide I don't want to take this job?"

"We'll kill you. That is why it is so important for you to decide before sunset."

He left the youth sitting shocked and staring into space.

It finally dawned on him later that afternoon, and he began putting a number of things together.

Ever since he had started working at the shop, Herr Leipold had always been careful to have him out of there by sunset. The reason he hadn't thought of it before was because the sun set at different times throughout the year—early in winter, late in the summer. But he'd always been on his way home by sunset.

And, Mehmet remembered, Herr Leipold had once let slip the fact that he'd been with the owner since he was sixteen. He had to be well past 80 now, and the owner needed a new shopkeeper! Either the owner was incredibly ancient, Mehmet imagined the mummified mother of Norman Bates in *Psycho*, or, and this seemed hardly believable but more likely, the owner was immortal.

But Mehmet knew of only two things that were truly immortal—Allah, and he doubted very much that a god would reside in a dusty old occult shop. The thought of it made him laugh out loud then grimace as the noise echoed through the silent shop. And, of course, vampires. Although he guessed they couldn't be considered truly immortal because they could be destroyed. Nevertheless, vampires were capable of living forever.

And that made sense. That brought it all home. All those hours Herr Leipold had discussed vampires, and his extensive knowledge of the creatures! Why it all made sense!

He also knew enough of the creatures to know that vampires must avoid the sun—it made them weak, stripped them of their powers. From sunrise to sunset, he smiled. Only vampires would need someone around to keep the amateur Van Helsings from seeking them out in the daylight hours.

"And to keep them away from stakes!" he laughed, aloud. He began pacing the shop, happily. He could handle this. He understood now why they would kill him if he met the vampire and then refused the job.

"For everlasting life! Hell yeah, I'll guard a vampire!" he whispered, jubilantly.

He supposed Mustela was his testing ground. They wanted to make sure he could take care of a vampire before he became one. Mehmet wondered how long that would take. He wondered how long Mustela had been around.

He stopped in his tracks. But what about Herr Leipold? Why hadn't he been made a vampire? He would definitely ask him that question *before* he met Mustela. And, he wasn't about to let on that he had guessed their secret. He could lose his life!

A customer, one of the few who frequented the place, entered the store. It was Marlen Becker, a not unattractive woman whom Mehmet guessed to be around thirty. She fancied herself a witch, and was always buying the ingredients she needed for her love potions.

She had dyed-black hair with a white streak down the center like a skunk. He and Herr Leipold jokingly called her as much behind her back. They didn't laugh at her breasts, though. Mehmet tried hard not to stare at them each time she entered the shop. Her breasts were magnificent, and she knew it, and everything she wore was designed to draw men's eyes to her best asset.

Excited by the coming meeting with Mustela and by the tremendous, eggplant-sized breasts rising from Marlen's chest, Mehmet felt himself hardening, uncontrollably. He hoped he could hide himself behind the counter, but as per usual, Marlen wanted some mandrake. The devil's testicles, Mehmet thought, and his member throbbed in response.

The root was, of course, on the highest shelf, and even though he stood more than six feet tall, Mehmet was forced to use a stepladder. The shelf was then another couple of feet above his head, and he looked down to find that the quite obvious bulge in his pants was directly in line with Marlen's face.

Oh, great, he thought, flushing. She was staring at it.

When her hand caressed the swelling there, he almost fell off the stepladder. He looked down at her in surprise, but there was also more than a little hope in his eyes.

"I can take care of that," she told him, quite frankly.

His legs buckled and he sat down on the stepladder to find his face directly in front of her breasts. He moaned and buried his face in them.

Marlen laughed, and had he seen her face, the look of victory and power etched there would have sent a surge of coldness through him that would have left him limp and feeling as if he'd been raped.

But his face was nuzzling her ample breasts, and he felt as if he might explode. This is my lucky day, he thought, as she coaxed him up and into her arms. He took her mouth, eagerly, pressing his erection against her stomach. Slow down, he ordered himself, as he felt himself falling toward climax. He stepped back and let her unzip him.

When she took him in her hand, he had to bite his tongue to keep from coming. Frantically, Mehmet scrambled to pull her dress up, and discovered she was wearing only a garter belt and hose. Her hair down there was as blond as wheat, and he vowed to talk her into never dyeing her hair again. He touched it, slipped his hand further between her legs and was delighted to feel the wetness there.

She hadn't been counting on this. The movement of his fingers was bringing her quickly to the edge. Her feeling of victory was joined by surprise and delight as well. Mehmet lifted Marlen with ease, settling her on the heavy oak counter. She shuddered with pleasure as he brought her to a climax. Grunting something in Turkish, he picked her up and settled her upon him and before the contractions of her orgasm had faded, she felt herself rising toward another.

He was strong and so masculine. And, she thought, he seemed to be able to control himself better than any man she had yet had sex with. Her moans soon out-paced his, and they both cried out in pleasure as they came.

The look men got in their eyes when they wanted her was her greatest aphrodisiac. And, Mehmet's had been especially exciting. Behind the hard glaze of lust had been something else, something she couldn't fathom. And, she would definitely return. She wanted to find out just what that look had meant.

After Marlen had left, Mehmet had a hard time controlling his patience. For the final hour before the sun set, he paced again. He was ecstatic when Herr Leipold finally emerged from the back of the shop. There was a door back there that always remained locked, at least during the day. The old man had said it was a storeroom for some of the owner's private belongings. Now, Mehmet knew better.

"Now?" he asked, "Now?" He absolutely forgot his promise to ask the old man why he had never received eternal life.

Mehmet was adequately impressed by Mustela even though the man was obviously gay. The truth was he no longer cared. He wanted to live forever and Mustela was his ticket to everlasting life.

And now, nearly ten years later, he wonders when his day will come. Sure, he is only in his thirties and Mustela is about the same age. But, he would rather live forever at say, 32, than at 42. Still, knowing Mustela, he will probably have to wait another ten years. He curses, silently, as another thought jumps to the forefront: Just how long will the promise, alone, of eternal life keep him serving Mustela? Ten more years? Twenty? Why had he never asked Herr Leipold that suddenly all-important question?

And if that thought alone isn't enough to sink his spirits, what is he supposed to do about this woman interested in vampires? Damn, damn, damn!

The shop's bell sounds and Mehmet looks up to see Marlen, her hair now the color of corn, arriving to bring him a late lunch. She is still heavy-breasted and beautiful, and after eight years, they have still not lost their passion for one another. And, she still has not found the meaning of that mysterious look in his eyes.

As always, he feels himself rising to greet her. Because of Marlen's work schedule, their lunchtime rendezvous are rare. He'll worry about the other woman later. He has until sunset, after all.

Ginny & Wolf

WOLF IS CONCERNED about Ginny's little "shopping" trip but for another reason. "It appears as if a vampire may have found us first."

"What do you mean? That guy wasn't a vampire."

He just stares at her.

"Oh, you mean maybe he was a keeper?"

"It would make sense. If that's the case, you were incredibly lucky. Of course, I could be wrong, but I'll bet we'll find out tonight. If this Turk is a keeper, we'll be approached; actually followed and then approached.

"There are so few of us, that any newcomer is found almost immediately. We have a rather efficient network, actually. I knew we'd find someone quickly, but this is almost amazing consider the size of the city."

"I had no idea that I would find a vampire at an occult store. How obvious is that? I just wanted to see if I could find anything about vampires in general, and maybe see if there was a club where the local vampire culture liked to hang out. I thought maybe someone might know something without realizing they actually knew something."

"Not a bad idea, really, but damn, I don't like them having the advantage. We need to find Vlad but no one else is going to want us to find him, especially if they know I want to kill him."

Ginny's heart sinks. "I screwed up, didn't I?" she asks, mournfully.

"Well, maybe not. Let's be optimistic."

"That's easy for you to say."

Wolf takes her into his arms, kisses her. "I love you," he whispers into her ear.

She clings to him, tightly. It's all going too fast. Is it possible they will find Vlad himself, tonight?

Wolf has never been to Berlin, and Ginny had stayed here only briefly during her trip to Germany while in college. Slipping out the list she'd downloaded from the internet, Ginny scans the list of bars and dance clubs for that evening's choices. Pulling a flyer from the back pocket of her Levis, she hands it to Wolf.

"Transilvania?" he lifts an eyebrow. "Erotic vamp night?"

"At least it's a starting place," she says. "They claim to have 'vampires and victims, coffins, skulls and horror-drinks'."

"Horror drinks?"

"A Bloody Mary, no doubt."

"Very funny."

"Well, I'm sure it's not real blood," she pauses, "although I suppose they could serve animal blood." She shudders.

"Not your cup of tea?"

Ginny rolls her eyes, "But it does sound like a good place for a vampire to be incognito, so to speak. The club is in a dark cellar, and the review claims that the bar is 'reminiscent of an eerie ghost house'."

"What, may I ask, is a ghost house?"

Ginny giggles, "I think they probably mean 'haunted.' Poor translation would be my guess.

"Hmmm, and if Transilvania disappoints?"

"It's all beginning to seem so arbitrary. Maybe their following us is actually for the best. But, should they not show up at Transilvania, I also wrote down the Green Door, Eschloraque and I even picked out a few gay bars just in case—Schad und Rauch, Connection and Lenz."

"You're right, of course, I'm not sure that it really matters where we go," Wolf says. "I really do expect to be visited no matter where we go."

"Maybe we can hold them off a bit if we go to Transilvania first," Ginny mutters.

"What?"

"Nothing. I just meant that maybe they'll be too embarrassed to show up there." She looks at Wolf. Damn, he looks so good, she thinks. He looks like a model in his Tom Ford suit, very Duke-of-Windsorish despite the long hair and short beard. She loves the way his beard scratches her face when he kisses her. It feels so real, and these days she seems to need a lot of reminding that everything that is happening to her isn't a dream.

"How do I look?" she asks, unnecessarily, fidgeting with her hair.

"You look incredible," he says. He never gets tired of looking at her, and tonight she looks unbelievably sexy, almost as if she's stepped out of a previous era. In the salmon jaquard dress, she looks as if she should be going dancing on the Titanic, not heading out to a nightclub called Transilvania searching for vampires. "You look incredible," he repeats.

It is nearly midnight and Wolf is thinking that it is time for them to move on.

Wolf seems disgusted, Ginny, relieved. Perhaps they had been too embarrassed to show up at Transilvania.

They decide to try out a club recommended by the bartender at the club—Katacombe.

"What are we going to do now," Ginny asks, as they find a seat in a corner where they can keep watch on the door. The club is designed to look like the famous tombs of Rome, and Ginny shivers despite the fact the temperature is very comfortable. Wolf scowls. He had been so sure about the Turk.

Ginny hides a smile with a faked cough. Wolf so often reminds her of a little kid when he doesn't get his way. She supposes it has something to do with being the only son of a rich family. And, although it amuses her, she really likes the way his lower lip thrusts outward when things aren't going the way he wants them to.

He's really sexy when he pouts, she grins.

"What are you smiling about?"

"I was thinking that you look really sexy when you pout."

He appears nonplussed, as if he'd been unaware that he'd been visibly sulking.

"I wasn't pouting."

"Oh," she nods her head in agreement but the dimple that appears at the corner of her mouth betrays the smile she is trying to hide.

"I wasn't."

She smiles at him and he smiles back.

"Young love is so wonderful," a sarcastic voice comes between them.

They look up to find a stylishly-dressed man standing before them. Wolf squeezes Ginny's hand, painfully.

Damn, she thinks, he was right.

The man now blocking the view of the door they'd stopped watching is of medium height and very thin. He appears to be in his mid-30s and is wearing a well-tailored herringbone wool suit. His spiky mouse-brown hair would have looked more appropriate on a teenager but he seems to carry the style well enough. Cold grey eyes regard them out of a face as hard and pointed as a ferret's. His mouth is a thin, bloodless line.

Ginny suddenly realizes, instinctively, that were this man not a vampire, his preference would be for men. Actually, probably still is, she decides, recalling the Turk. The Turk seemed like a man's man, but she could see how one could appreciate him no matter their sexual preference.

"I am called Mustela," he says as he takes a seat.

Ginny feels the corners of her mouth lifting in a smile that she quickly tries to hide.

"I see you find that fitting," he says, speaking to Ginny.

She blushes. Never tease a weasel, never tease a weasel, repeats in her mind. This is definitely one occasion when she'll keep that advice close to her heart.

"I understand you wish to learn how to dispose of vampires," he says, ignoring Wolf.

Ginny blushes again. "Not really," she mumbles, "only in writing."

"Not really?" Mustela's left eyebrow raises in mock dismay.

It is as if a coating of ice freezes her face. "It was none of his damn business why I was interested in vampires," her voice is as wintry as her face.

"Perhaps," he smiles, acidly, "but I must admit, I felt some concern when I discovered someone had entered my shop trying to purchase stakes."

Ginny laughs, and Mustela seems taken aback. "Why on earth would I want to kill vampires?" she smiles, snuggling up to Wolf.

Wolf slides his arm around her shoulders, protectively.

"I happen to be in love with one," Ginny adds.

"It strikes me as a rather unsatisfying relationship," Mustela states, while shooing away the waitress.

"The heart has its reasons which reason knows nothing of," she quotes Blaise Pascal, but her tone is once again glacial.

Mustela's mouth slowly parts in a genuine smile. It greatly improves his appearance even though it exposes his long, sharp canines.

"Immortality, perhaps?" he smiles at her, but his eyes are cold.

Wolf's hand tightens on her shoulder.

"But it's really none of your business," Wolf speaks for the first time.

"So, what is the reason for your visit," Mustela continues as if Wolf had never spoken. "Is this your honeymoon?" The latter word drips with sarcasm.

Ginny can feel Wolf's anger rising. "Be calm, my love," she whispers into his ear. He takes a deep breath but his grip on her shoulder does not relax. Mustela opens his mouth to speak, but Wolf interrupts him.

"I didn't realize I needed a reason to travel," he says. "Is there some new 'law' that requires it?"

Mustela stares at them. Perhaps, Mehmet had been right. Perhaps, Wolf had sent the woman to see if she could scare out some of his kind. What was their relationship? They actually appeared to be in love, not that he believed in that emotion, personally. But, she is still human? Surely if they were 'in love,' they would want to be together eternally.

Human love is something a vampire could not possibly give her.

"Actually, I'm looking for a man I met nearly 400 years ago," Wolf goes straight to the point.

"A man?"

"Well, that's one way of putting it. Obviously he was no longer human at the time."

"Does this man have a name?" Mustela asks.

"Shit," Ginny moans, face paling.

"What is it, Ginny?" She looks as if she's seen a ghost.

"Wolf, oh God, I could have sworn I just saw Abe!"

"Abe Van Helsing?" Mustela laughs, referring to the famous vampire killer. "So, you are here to kill vampires."

Wolf and Ginny stare at him as if he has suddenly switched from German to Martian while speaking. He has the feeling he's struck closer to the truth than he's first realized.

"Are you sure it was Abe?" Wolf asks. A jealous ex-love is the last thing they need around right now.

"No, no, I can't be sure. I was watching you, and then I looked away and I could have sworn I saw him there, lurking just beyond Mustela's shoulder. But, you see, I was already turning back toward you when I saw him. When I looked back he was gone. What the hell is Abe doing here? If you think about it, it makes sense. Damn him!"

"It seems you have greater problems at hand," Mustela says, standing up. "Perhaps, we can meet again tomorrow evening, after you have worked things out?" He is almost desperate to discover Wolf's reason for being here, but he hopes that by the next evening he will have learned more about this strange couple. Like Wolf, he dislikes being at a disadvantage.

"No, don't leave," Wolf calls, but Mustela has already disappeared. "Scheisse."

"I'm sorry," Ginny apologizes, "but Wolf, I know that was Abe. He's followed us here." Of course, one phone call will confirm that, she realizes. "I'll phone Mom as soon as we return to the hotel. She was supposed to call Abe and tell him everything once we left. Everything but where we were going, that is. I have a sneaking suspicion she never had the chance."

"I hope you're wrong," Wolf tells her. "Because he could ruin every-thing."

Maybe that wouldn't be so bad, Ginny thinks. She's beginning to wonder whether she couldn't live with Wolf for the rest of her life—one way or another. Maybe someday she could even convince him to make her a vampire. Maybe . . . Her eyes begin to glow. Then I could spend all of eternity with him.

She looks at Wolf. His jaw is set and he is staring moodily into the crowd. No, she realizes, there is no way he'd even consider something like that. He might even hate her for suggesting it. The glow fades. No, Wolf will die. She can see it in every line on his face.

Wolf suddenly turns, stares madly into her face. "Don't ever forget me," he demands, and kisses her long and hard. The kiss is soon mixed with tears, but they are his, not hers.

Ginny & Abe

S HE DECIDES TO CALL HER MOTHER as it is still late afternoon in
California. Her mother agrees it has to be Abe that she saw at the
nightclub. He had left town on "vacation" the same day they had.

And, as he doesn't yet know that Ginny spotted him at Katakombe,
there is really little she can do at the moment.

Besides, it is time for bed. The sun is rising and she is exhausted.
She curls up next to Wolf and is asleep before the first ray of sun touches
the hotel's eastern face.

O nce again, she awakes just after noon. Sliding from the bed, she
grabs a bathrobe and enters the living area of the suite where she quickly
brews some coffee in the in-room coffeemaker. She finds herself pacing
the small area as she worries about Abe. She wonders if he is watching
the hotel now; if he even knows where they are staying. Surely, he must
sleep, too.

Her stomach growls, loudly, and she realizes she never got around
to eating last night, although Wolf had, naturally.

If you can call that eating, she thinks. He hadn't taken that long,
and as per usual, he hadn't wanted to talk about it. He is so repelled by
that part of his life that he refuses to admit to her that it exists in
anything but the most euphemistic of terms.

She pulls on her jeans, one of Wolf's white t-shirts and his black leather jacket. So what if they're his, wearing them makes her feel as if he's with her.

She scans both sides of the street for Abe when she leaves the hotel, but she does not see him. She turns left, and begins searching for a restaurant. She finds a German restaurant first, but passes it up because although she loves the language and one of its countrymen, she doesn't particularly care for the food. She finds a Turkish restaurant less than two blocks away from the hotel, and enters it. She knows that to find good Greek-style food in Germany, she must find a Turkish restaurant.

She hasn't had good dolmades since the summer she spent here in college, so she orders the stuffed grape leaves and a glass of retsina. But because she is alone, and in a city where people are now looking for her, she does not linger over her meal. She also has a nagging feeling that Wolf needs her.

That's just your vanity speaking, she rebukes herself. But, the meal has made her feel much better. She feels more awake, alive and in love despite the danger. And I'm not going to think about it too much, her lips curve upward slightly, or I'll get depressed.

She steps up her pace a bit because she remembers that there is a book she's been dying to read and hasn't had the chance. And it's not the vampire book she purchased yesterday. She had glanced through it while waiting for the sun to set the previous night. Unfortunately, it hadn't revealed to her anything she didn't already know. If she hurries, she may finish the latest Stephen King novel by the time Wolf wakes up. Things are starting to move quickly and she may not have another chance to read it.

Not only that, she grimaces, if I don't read it now, I may never be able to. There is no way I could later finish a book that I had brought to read on this trip, not if Wolf dies first. It would remind me of his death. Of course, that's probably being ridiculous, isn't it? She chides herself, for all you know, you may want to be reminded of Wolf in the future.

As she turns down the hallway to her room, something strikes her as amiss. Her mind flashes an image of a door clicking shut.

Was that my door I saw closing? It had been so slow and nearly silent she isn't sure.

"The Turk," she gasps, aloud. Wolf! She runs. She'll kill him, herself, if he's after Wolf. She'll kill anyone who attempts to hurt him.

The key card slips through her fingers as she tries to insert it in the lock, falling like a leaf toward the hallway carpet. She tries snatching it before it lands, but misses. Breathing heavily, panicky and trembling, she grabs it off the floor and tries again, begging the light to flash green instead of red. Success! She slams the door open, not sure what she is going to do but ready to do whatever is necessary.

When the door bangs against the hotel wall, Abe whirls around in surprise. It had taken him a lot longer to work the encoder than he thought it would. It hadn't been quite as hard to get the room number from the desk clerk, but he had finally been able to convince him he was indeed Ginny's boss, and that he was worried she was being held here against his will. The clerk had, of course, remembered Ginny. What man, straight or gay, wouldn't notice her beauty, her style? His knowedge of Ginny and a healthy tip had secured him the room number. But he still hadn't expected Ginny for at least another half hour.

He had watched her leave the hotel less than an hour ago; had followed her until she entered the restaurant. Once she was seated, he was satisfied she would not return immediately. He had then rushed back to the hotel and had spent almost half an hour working the encoder with the small machine he had purchased (illegal and *very* expensive). It always looked so easy on CSI, and he hadn't accounted for the occasional appearance of a hotel guest or maid.

He had known they were going to Fürstensteinbrück; Ginny's mother had mentioned it the night they had all finally met Wolf. Fortunately, the town was small enough that he had easily picked up their trail there. He limited his tailing them to when they were together and it appeared as if they were to remain in Wolf's hometown for a while. Jessie had said the visit was to help mend relations between Wolf and his father. He was quite surprised, therefore, when they loaded up the small car and headed north to Berlin.

Until yesterday, he had been trying to figure out their peculiar relationship. Why did they seem to travel mostly at night, and sleep during the day? Why was it he rarely saw them both together between dawn and sunset? Until yesterday, that is, when things started to become a lot clearer.

Last night, he had followed Wolf when he had left the hotel after dropping off Ginny at the lobby entrance. The taxi had gone on and Wolf had headed off on foot. It hadn't been easy to keep up with him, but, after a while, he had understood that this man was also following someone.

Why on earth would he be following some Goth girl, Abe had wondered. The girl's pale skin almost guided them like a flashlight. She had led them to a several-storied parking garage.

Maybe he's a rapist, Abe had hypothesized. Maybe he's paid her but for propriety's sake, he is keeping his distance.

Bewildered, he continued following the two until first one and then the other entered the mostly empty building.

He had decided to wait until Ginny's lover (he had scowled when he thought this) left the premises before he began following him again. But after a few minutes, Abe had been unable to withstand his curiosity or the silence any longer. Carefully, and quietly, he had entered the garage.

At first, he had thought they were necking, and an almost-insane anger rose in him. Poor Ginny, he had thought, his heart aching for her. But, then he'd realized that that was not what was going on. The girl had been hanging limp in Wolf's arms, unconscious.

Then, with almost eerie silence, Wolf had pulled away and let the girl slide to the ground. There had been blood around his mouth and on her throat. Dark and wet. Only his fear of being caught kept Abe from retching. He had watched as the man wiped the blood away from his mouth, a disgusted look on his face; had been mystified by the self-hate he had seen reflected there.

But, that had been enough for him. Before he could be seen, he had turned, and running as quietly as possible, threw himself behind a parked car just as that creature had emerged from the gaping door of the building. Then, Abe had waited until Ginny's friend, without even a final glance over his shoulder, returned the way he had come.

Rather than follow the monster, he had known where he was go-ing—back to poor, sweet Ginny—he had checked on the girl.

She had not been killed, he'd been surprised to find out, and she had started coming back around when he touched her. Abe had de-cided it would be wise, since the girl seemed all right, to be well out of her sight before she opened her eyes or he might be blamed for her condition.

He had returned to his post outside the hotel and fumed. How was it fair that such a freak, such an aberration, say it, Abe—a vampire—could have attracted someone as beautiful, intelligent and as good as Ginny? Perhaps, he has her under his spell, he had thought. Can't vam-pires do that? Hadn't Dracula done the same thing to Lucy and Mina? Poor Ginny, I'll save you, Abe had vowed.

An hour later, he was sure that Wolf had beaten him back to the hotel. He returned to his own lodgings in order to catch a few hours sleep. If things progressed as they normally did, Ginny wouldn't emerge until noonish.

Earlier that evening, or the previous evening, if you wanted to get technical about it, they had both appeared on the street shortly after 9 p.m. Abe's jaw had dropped when he had seen Ginny's outfit, and his jealousy had flared for the umpteenth time. It infuriated him in a way he could never explain to see her with Wolf. Abe had used his money to keep a driver waiting and followed them first to Transilvania, which he didn't dare enter; and later to Katakombe, which he found to be more crowded and where he stood out less.

Lurking in the darkness to the left of their table, Abe had been desperate to find out who the strange-looking man sitting with them was. He also was dying to know why Ginny had stopped at several occult shops earlier that day, including a lengthy visit to the latter shop.

There appeared to be some sort of confrontation between Wolf and the other man. He had been trying to read their lips when Ginny had suddenly looked up and over in his direction. He had turned and disappeared as quickly as possible.

Had she seen him? He had hoped not. It was doubtful that Ginny would be happy to see him here: as a matter of fact, she would probably be downright furious.

He had waited for them outside, and the rat-faced man had left first, joined by a tall, muscular man who acted like a bodyguard.

The two he had been waiting for left less than fifteen minutes later, arms wrapped around each other's waist. They had gone straight back to the hotel, and that's when he had followed Wolf.

And, here is Ginny now, staring at him not in surprise but in anger.

"What do you have in your hand?" She repeats.

He can't tell whether she is going to laugh or cry. He looks down, guiltily, at the object in his hand. It is a wooden stake.

"If you even so much as harm one hair on his head," she threatens him, "so help me God I'll kill you."

"Ginny, he's evil," Abe tries to explain. Suddenly, all his plans, his knight-in-shining-armor routine, seem to lie strewn around his feet like dead leaves. She seems so sane, so in control.

"I know what he is, Abe. I know better than anyone. And he is not evil."

"But I saw him drink someone's blood," Abe objects.

"Really?" she exclaims in surprise.

"Yes." He's puzzled.

"He didn't see you?"

"I guess not."

"Well, shame on him. He should be more careful." She hates to be so cold, but she has to make Abe understand that she has the situation well in hand. She is still terrified that he might make a wild dash toward the canopied bed and kill Wolf before she can stop him.

Abe stares at her in dismay. She's lost her mind.

"Perhaps I should tell you everything. Let's go get a beer. Wolf won't be up for a few more hours. Come on," she says, taking the stake from his hand.

He's too much under her spell not to follow her.

"I'll be damned," Abe breathes, "I'll be damned."

"So, will you leave us alone; let us do what we have to do?"

"No."

"No?"

"No."

"For God's sake, why not?"

"Because I love you."

Ginny regards him, sadly. "Oh, Abe," she sighs.

"I understand that you don't share my feelings."

"And I never will. Don't you understand, Abe? As much as I enjoy your company, your companionship, I will never be in love with you."

"I'll take that."

"But I won't," she cries, in exasperation. "I need love. I need everything that goes with it, including the sexual attraction. Abe, that's not something you can fake. I could love you as a friend for the rest of my life but I wouldn't be satisfied, I wouldn't be happy. Believe me, I know. It's terribly frustrating for Wolf and me, and we want each other. I can't imagine spending my life with a man that I didn't want. Does that make sense? Am I being selfish? I realize I can be too much of a romantic, but I'll never be pragmatic no matter how hard I try, and I do try, Abe. Please tell me you understand that. And, believe me; I'll understand if you can't just be friends."

"I'll take what I can get."

She lowers her eyes. He's a stubborn bastard, but the truth is a selfish part of her wants a friend nearby when Wolf dies; wants someone with whom she can share the agony of this adventure. "All right," she says, meeting his eyes again. "It's a deal. And, it's up to you. I think I can make Wolf agree to let you help us. But, you need to understand that we don't know how long it will take nor do we know how dangerous it will be. After all, a vampire who has lived as long as Vlad has will not give up easily. They're survivors. They're very strong and very tough."

"Says the petite woman sitting before me."

Ginny smiles, "I knew what your answer would be, I just had to let you know."

"So, what's next?"

"That's up to Wolf."

Vlad

MORE THAN HALF A MILLENNIUM, Vlad gazes contemplatively into the dancing flames, more than half a millennium spent, essentially, alone. He had not accounted for the extreme loneliness of being a vampire. Of course, he has to admit, that he chose that isolation. Most of the world's major cities, he knows, are host to a coven or two of vampires that gather together as much for support as for companionship. But he has always been a loner. A loner and a leader and it only took one attempt to lead a pack of vampires in Rome to dissuade him from undertaking another such venture.

Despite his reputation and the fact his reputation continued to grow throughout the centuries, he discovered that vampires tended to toady to the vampire who'd been around the longest—and there were plenty of vampires who pre-dated Vlad by centuries. And, after his one attempt at a coup failed (and failed miserably) he had spent the remaining years as a solitary. In eternal life just as in life, he could never quite be the king he wanted to be. Finally, he had decided it was much more fulfilling to be the ruler of his own kingdom even if he had no one to rule but himself. So he had chosen the solitary life.

Not that that is particularly unusual. There are vampires throughout the world who choose the solitary existence with and without keepers.

For centuries Vlad traveled to and spent time in some of the oldest cities in the world—from Jerusalem and Damascus to Athens and Alexandria, Delhi and Beijing, Istanbul, Rome, London, Paris. And as the centuries wore on the cities grew bigger and more numerous, and soon he found he was spending most of his time in Eastern Europe. Finally, his homeland had beckoned him to return and here he was, once again, hiding out in the Carpathian Mountains, glad to be alone with just the rats and wolves for company, depending entirely on his own wits for survival. With the occasional foray to big cities like Berlin, Vienna, Prague, Warsaw and Budapest, Vlad rarely has to resort to towns closer to home like Bucharest.

Of course, more than one thrill seeker searching for traces of the famous, Vlad, Count Dracula, has "mysteriously disappeared" when finding much more than bargained for.

Tonight, Vlad is trying to remember exactly how many vampires he, himself, has created over the years. Less than half a dozen, if he remembers correctly and most were early on—all but one were men. The female, who might have been his lover in a previous lifetime, was eventually hunted down and killed while they were living near Athens. The last vampire he had created was a mistake—something he had done in a fit of anger. To his great relief, he had never heard from or of that particular creature again. He had felt sure the way he had hunted him down while alive that he might do so again once he realized his new strengths. Nevertheless, Vlad had been careful never to return to that part of Germany.

But now it's time to prepare for his departure the next evening. He wants to make a quick trip down to Istanbul—a city he finds excellent for his purposes because it is teeming with people and he has never been able to exact revenge on the Turks to his satisfaction.

Ginny, Wolf & Abe

"**N**o."

"Wolf."

"I said, no." He is the angriest she has ever seen him but she enjoys it. Having known him so short a time, she wants to see every aspect of him before he dies, even if the anger is directed toward her. She only regrets that she'll never be able to see the way his face looks while making love to her. Right now, it is red with anger and his eyes are as gray and stormy as a roiling winter sea.

"Be reasonable," she tries to persuade him. "If we say no, he'll follow us anyway, he told me so. He could really mess things up."

"Then I'll kill him," he says, coldly.

It is her turn to be angry. "You would not. I know you couldn't do something like that. Say you wouldn't."

Wolf sits on the bed, head in hands. He doesn't want Abe along. He knows he doesn't have much longer to live; he wants to be selfish and spend as much of that time as possible alone with Ginny.

"He'll scare away Mustela," he says, but there is not much force to it.

"You know, I hadn't thought about that," Ginny agrees. "We'll just have to tell Abe to stay out of sight when we're meeting with him tonight." She sits on his lap, facing him, and pulls his head up until he is looking in her eyes. "I love you," she tells him. "Don't forget that."

He kisses her, tenderly. "Bring him in. I'm sure he has a lot of unanswered questions."

They are at Katakombe by midnight. Before five minutes have passed, Mehmet approaches them and asks Wolf and Ginny to follow him.

He takes them on the U-Bahn to a deserted building near the former Checkpoint Charlie. It is dark but Wolf is able to guide Ginny easily into the unlit building.

"I don't mean to be rude, folks," Ginny says as she feels her way into a seat, "but couldn't we have at least a little light. I can't see a thing."

Mustela obligingly lights a candle. As the wick ignites, his face is suddenly illuminated. For a moment, it looks as if he is being devoured by flames, and Ginny shudders.

"Is that better?" he asks.

"Yes, thank you," Ginny shivers again, and shoves her hands into the sleeves of her coat.

"Would you like my jacket, love?" Wolf asks, already pulling it off. And hanging it around her shoulders.

She smiles at him in gratitude.

"So," asks Mustela, "did you work out all your problems with Abe?"

Ginny glances up, alarmed. He had been paying attention the previous evening . . . "Yes," she sighs, finally, deciding it's better to impart as much "truth" as possible. "He's an ex-boyfriend of mine. When I told him I was leaving Corazon with another man, he wasn't very happy, but he seemed to take it all right. Actually, he was planning to follow me and win me back from Wolf or something like that. I caught him snooping outside my hotel this morning and had it out with him. He said he wouldn't bother us anymore."

"And you believe him?"

"After what I said to him, yes."

Mustela studies her for a moment, trying to decide whether or not she might be lying, but her eyes had been entirely guileless, had never swayed from his once. He wonders what her blood would taste like.

"So, how long have you been one of us?" Mustela asks Wolf.

"Nearly 400 years."

"Four hundred? You're a mere child. Why, I have been undead for the past thousand," he thinks for a moment, "and ninety-odd years."

He leans back, relaxing against the rickety chair and it squeals against his weight. But Mustela is not here but wherever he was more than a thousand years ago when he became a vampire.

"I was living in Rome at the time," he continues, "and was very happy with a young Venetian lad . . ." He stops, as he reminisces about the boy—his dark curls, his classic profile and skin white as marble. Mustela did not even remember the wife he had left in Germany. He had despised her horse-face and fat ankles. He had married her only because he wished to inherit his family money and her family money. When he was sure there was a son, he had left her for Rome and the education it would present him with, or at least that is what he had told his family.

He shakes his head, and goes on, "and then I met Phaon. I was 31 and he was only a few years younger, and although I was partial to young boys, I fell in love with him instantly.

"I saw him one night while I was stumbling through the streets, as drunk as a soldier, on my way back to the boy, Marco. I stopped to be sick in an alleyway. Unfortunately, the alley was already occupied, but I really couldn't wait. When I was finished, I looked up briefly to see if I had disturbed anyone, and that is when I saw him. I immediately flushed, embarrassed at my introduction to this amazing man. He was standing over the crumpled body of a young boy, who looked very dead. But I did not care; I could only stare into the eyes of that tall and imposing man. Those dark and piercing eyes. He had full black hair that fell in lush waves around his face. And full lips, I stared at them longingly. He looked like a Greek god. And then he was gone, like that. Just like that, not even a whisper of wind."

As Mustela describes Phaon, Wolf squeezes Ginny's hand, hard. She has been absorbed in Mustela's story, and looks at him sharply. It comes to her suddenly, that Phaon might be Vlad. Her eyebrows come together in a question. Wolf shakes his head. Disappointed, but still anxious for clues, she continues to listen to his tale.

"The next night I searched for him, and the next," Mustela continues, unaware of what has just passed between Wolf and Ginny. "Finally, on the third night, I saw him. He was striding down the street in front of me. I called to him, and he stopped. He seemed so superior, so alluring. He waited until I caught up.

"Are you feeling better tonight, he asked me. I flushed again. So in love was I already that I could not even speak. He seemed flattered, and putting his arm around my shoulder, he led me to a small but richly appointed villa.

"We talked for hours, and as the sun came up, he told me I must leave. I begged him to let me stay and he smiled at me. You can stay as long as you like, he told me, but you will never receive what you seek. I wondered what he meant, and he told me. I then begged him to let me be as he was. Come back tomorrow, he told me, and we will talk some more.

"I returned. We talked, earnestly all night long, and then he told me that he felt I was the type of man who could do what it takes to live an everlasting life."

Isn't that bizarre, Ginny thinks, the evil receive everlasting life on earth and the good in heaven. Is earth really hell? But Wolf isn't evil; she looks at him and the barely disguised disgust on his face. No, he's very good and this is definitely his hell, a hell he didn't deserve or ask for.

"I guess you know the rest," Mustela concludes.

"Have you lost track of him, Phaon?" Ginny asks, eyes shining.

"What a romantic little lady you have," Mustela comments to Wolf. But he is flattered. "Yes, I have kept track of him. He is living in Rome. He has his own villa just outside the city. Unfortunately, he does not want to leave his country and I rarely see him any more."

"But you do see him?" Ginny asks, smiling in wonder.

"Yes," he smiles at her, "I occasionally make my way to Rome."

"How romantic," she sighs.

Mustela's smile broadens. As much as he dislikes women, he has never been able to withstand adulation. "I still love him, dearly," Mustela continues. "Unfortunately, times are not easy and travel is difficult.

Ginny and Wolf heartily agree, remarking on how difficult their trip from California had been to arrange.

"And so, who is this particular someone for whom you seek?" Mustela asks, wondering if, once again, he has spoken out of hand.

"Actually, I would like to get back in touch with the man who created me," Wolf tries the truth. "Perhaps you've heard of him, his name is Vlad."

Mustela stares at him, obviously puzzled. "You don't mean 'Count Dracula? Vlad the Impaler?" He starts to chuckle. "That is just a legend. I won't deny that the man was evil incarnate but he died many years ago. What makes you so sure it is *the* Vlad? Did he claim to be?"

"Just once, and I'll admit I was in a state of shock, but he called himself Vlad Drakulya."

"What did he look like?"

"Exactly like the paintings I've seen of the actual count."

Mustela is scowling. Could the legend be true? Is there really a vampire out there who was formerly the Romanian king? "May I ask the reason you are looking for him? With a couple of humans in tow?"

"He owes me a debt and I intend for him to pay it."

Mustela's brow furrows but he only nods. Clearly this is a personal matter and it would be rude to push it; yet, still, something about all of this bothers him. Surely, he does not wish to kill Vlad, he thinks. That would be the death of him. He wants to know what is going on. He had been unable to find out anything prior to their meeting, tonight. Neither Rutger nor Armando, the only other vampires he knows in Berlin, have ever heard of Wolf.

"Are there any other vampires in Berlin that might know Vlad's whereabouts?" asks Wolf.

"One or two," Mustela answers, warily.

"Perhaps you know where I can find them?"

"That is something you will have to do on your own," he answers. "We have an agreement, you understand, not to endanger one another."

Wolf stands up, pulling Ginny with him. "Then maybe it is time for us to leave."

"Perhaps so," Mustela agrees.

The U-Bahn station is empty.

"Shall we head back to the hotel?" Wolf asks.

"Yes, let's go back," she assents, nestling closer to Wolf.

"We need to plan to get out of here as soon as possible. I don't think we're safe here anymore."

"So, do you think we ought to go to Rome and try to find Phaon?"

"That would probably be easier than finding any other vampires here. I have no doubt that Mustela will be sending them a warning. It was clear he didn't trust us."

A train pulls up, mostly empty, and they board. They do not see Mehmet and Mustela enter the car behind them.

"When they get off, kill them," Mustela orders Mehmet. But Mehmet and Mustela also are being followed, as well. Abe, who had agreed to stay away from their meeting with the vampire, had followed them, anyway. Just in case. And now, he doesn't like the fact that Wolf and Ginny are being followed by the big Turk and Rat-face.

When the train pulls in to Ku'damm Eck, Ginny and Wolf are the first to disembark. They walk, Ginny's arm around Wolf's waist, his around her shoulder, toward the exit. Wolf's head is pressed against Ginny's and they are so absorbed in each other that they do not notice that the station is empty, except for a crone-like cleaning woman bent over her mop.

Their footsteps echo emptily against the walls of the stairwell as they ascend the stairs. They are nearing the top when Ginny hears someone scream her name.

"Abe!" She turns and runs back down the stairs, her long velvet coat spread out behind her like a cape.

"Scheisse," Wolf curses under his breath and scowls. He knew he should have said no to Abe's involvement.

He begins slowly descending the stairs.

As Ginny breaks into the cavernous tunnel of the subway station, she sees Abe involved in a struggle with Mehmet. She does not see Mustela hiding in the shadows nor does she notice the cleaning woman cowering in a corner.

She skids to a stop several yards away from the scuffle, trying to figure out how she might help Abe. The men are fighting dangerously close to the edge of the platform.

The tunnel begins to vibrate slightly and she hears the crescendo of an approaching train. "No!" she screams when she realizes Mehmet is trying to push Abe in front of the on-coming vehicle. But her voice is lost in the roar of its appearance.

Hands imbedded deeply in Mehmet's thick throat, Abe hangs on. The train passes with a rush, and as it disappears into the far tunnel, Mehmet curses—a broad, rich and typically imaginative Turkish curse.

It is the chance Abe has been waiting for. He uses the lapse in Mehmet's concentration to his advantage. Releasing his grip on the Turk's neck, he simultaneously kicks and pushes Mehmet over the edge of the platform.

The Turk, arms spinning, topples onto the tracks of the subway, back landing squarely on the third rail. Ginny and Abe watch in horror as the life drains out of Mehmet's body, eyes wide and staring as his skin smokes and blackens.

And that's how death row victims are executed, she thinks, grimacing. How horrible.

A thud and an "oomph" recall her to the situation. She turns to see Abe sprawled against one of the columns supporting the tunnel. His eyes are rolled back so far she can only see the whites.

"Abe!" she yells, but her voice is cut off suddenly by a strong hand clamped over her mouth. She is turned, forcibly, to stare into the angry eyes of Mustela.

She does not even have time to struggle. As soon as her eyes meet his she is entranced by his piercing gaze. He lowers his head to her neck, and she finally knows how all the women Wolf has fed on have felt—the desire, the terror. The subway station begins to swim before her eyes, but Mustela has stopped.

Her heart freezes when she realizes what Mustela has in mind. He has ripped open his button-down shirt and using the long razor-sharp nail of his little finger, slices open his chest. And, while he seems to be hurrying, it's as if it is all happening in slow motion. He's going to make me drink his blood, she realizes. Wolf, she cries, silently.

Mustela is desperate. He has decided that the only way he can keep Wolf from killing him, which he would without a doubt do, is by making the woman he is so in love with a vampire. Surely, he thinks, he won't kill the woman he loves by killing him?

But, Wolf is already well on his way, running down the tunnel toward her. He had reached the bottom of the stairs just as Mustela had fastened his hand over Ginny's mouth. He had stopped in horror, all the strength draining from his legs, as he watched the weasel lower his filthy mouth to Ginny's neck, just as he had seen Vlad's mouth on Hannele's throat.

Furious and terrified, his strength had returned, sweeping through his body like a flash flood. He had grabbed the mop from the stunned cleaning woman, and as he ran, he broke it.

And, as Mustela pushes Ginny's head toward the blood oozing from his chest, much in the same way Vlad had to Wolf 400 years earlier, Wolf reaches them.

Pushing Ginny aside with his left arm, Wolf uses his right to plunge the improvised stake through Mustela's heart. Ginny crumples to the ground as her legs collapse beneath her.

Wolf pulls the trembling Ginny into his arms and the two watch as Mustela grasps the stake, trying unsuccessfully to pull it out. His hands flutter around the rod like dying butterflies. Deep red, almost black, blood wells out from around the wooden handle, which protrudes as much from Mustela's back as it does from his chest. Wolf's anger and fear had allowed him to easily thrust the broken mop handle through the rat's heart.

Mouth champing and foamy blood spraying from his lips, Mustela screams in pain, anger and defeat. His head whips from side to side, spattering Ginny, Wolf and the unconscious Abe with bloody spittle.

What they witness next is much worse in real life than in any horror movie they've ever watched. Before their eyes, Mustela begins to decay.

It is as if they are watching a speeded-up film of the decomposition process—skin pulling back from the hair and nails, the nauseating smell of gases, the putrefying and shrinking skin and the redolent odor of rotting meat. Then Mustela's hair and nails fall out, his body caves in, and degenerates, rotting away until only the bones remain, and even these slowly but quickly disintegrate until all that is left is a crumpled pile of clothing and dust.

Already pale from years spent living in darkness, Wolf turns a shade whiter still. Ginny, teeth clenched in a grimace of horror, is unable to turn her head from the dreadful scene. Only Abe misses the horror show, his body still and silent where it lies next to the column he was thrown against.

Staring at the remains of the vampire, and not even daring to glance at the burned body of Mehmet, Ginny clings tightly to Wolf. He is shaking as much as she is.

"I've never seen a vampire die before," he says, "except in movies, and that never seemed real."

"Wolf," Ginny can exhale no more than a whisper. "I think we'd better get out of here." She tugs at Wolf's arm, and he stares into her face, still dazed.

"I'm not sure I want to die like that, Gin." He looks scared and pitiful, and she longs to take him into her arms with his head cradled on her breasts, and comfort him. But, it will probably not be long before the police arrive, or the next train, for that matter. Ginny finally notes that the cleaning woman is no longer present; she doesn't doubt she's already looking for help.

"We'll worry about that later, my love," she pleads, "but right now, we'd better get out of here!"

Wolf shakes his head, and turns to leave.

"Abe," Ginny reminds him, pointing to where he lies next to the column. Wolf picks him up, fireman-style, and they begin to climb the steep steps to Ku'damm.

"Hey!" a weak voice says, "I can walk."

Wolf sets Abe down, and he stands, shakily, for a moment. Ginny and Wolf watch him, warily, wondering whether he is going to tumble backwards down the stairs.

Abe takes a step forward and leads the way, weaving but walking on his own. There is no way he is going to be carried like a baby by Wolf.

Rather than make the short hop to Rome by plane, Ginny convinces Wolf to allow them to make the 700-plus mile drive in a two- to three-day trip.

"I just think I need a couple of days to come to grips with what happened tonight," she explains once they are back in their suite.

"Well, I just wish that we'd been able to find out if Mustela had created any vampires," Abe complains. "For all we know there are vampires dropping like flies all over the world."

Wolf scowls. "I imagine Mustela never left Europe; he sounded like he always wanted to stay within traveling distance of Rome."

"Whatever," Abe sighs, removing the ice pack from his head, "we still aren't any wiser about what will happen to Wolf although I guess we do know how Vlad will die."

"Maybe," Ginny adds. "For all we know, how a vampire dies is dependent on how he is created."

"What do you mean?" Abe asks.

"Just that vampires surely didn't spring into existence like some god. The question is how were the original vampires created? I wasn't able to find anything really definitive."

"Perhaps Phaon knows," Wolf says. "We know he is an older vampire than Mustela, and he was around for more than a thousand years."

"He sure died more easily than I would expect a vampire that old to die," Ginny muses.

"I don't think our strength grows significantly the longer we are around. We might become more cautious, more adept at reading situations and people, but strength and speed are natural to vampirism."

"Well, he certainly wasn't being very cautious," Abe rubs his head.

"He obviously discounted you," Wolf muses. "They thought they had the element of surprise on us."

"They did. I had no idea we were being followed. Does that mean they would have followed us out of the subway tunnel? We were already heading up the stairs when I heard Abe yell."

"I don't know what his plan was but he was definitely following you when I stopped him."

"We need to be a lot more cautious. We can't risk that happening again before we find Vlad," Wolf says.

"We still have several hours before sunrise," Ginny stands. "I don't know about you guys, but I suggest we head south as soon as possible. We don't know if either Mehmet or Mustela contacted any other vampires before they," she pauses, hating to say it, "uh, died."

"Before we killed them you mean," Abe stands as well.

"In self-defense, but you're right. We killed them and we intend to kill Vlad and no matter our reasons, I guess that makes us murderers."

"Maybe it's better to think that way right now. All right, I'll head back to my hotel and pack," Abe says, heading toward the door.

"We'll pick you up in half an hour," Ginny adds.

They are able to make it as far south as Nürnberg before stopping for the night. They check into the Mövenpick Hotel at the Nürnberg Airport so that Ginny and Abe can turn in the car and rent a larger model when they wake up later that day.

Because it is Abe doing the negotiating, they trade up for a Mercedes and by 5 p.m. they are on the road again. A little over five hours later they check into the Grand Hotel in Trento, Italy. With more than six hours until sunrise, Wolf excuses himself, awkwardly.

"Why don't we see if we can find some place to get something to eat?" Ginny suggests after the door shuts behind Wolf.

"So we eat when he eats?" Abe says somewhat sarcastically.

"Very funny."

"I'm afraid that I'll never get used to his 'eating' habits."

"Well, if it's any consolation, he's not particularly happy about it either. Besides, if Wolf has anything to do with it, he won't be 'eating' for much longer."

"We'll see."

Leaving once again about 5 p.m. the following day, they are able to make it to Rome before midnight. After checking into Hotel St. George, Wolf suggests they get dressed and hit a couple of nightclubs.

Ginny groans, "Already? What is it about nightclubs, anyway?"

"I suspect it has something to do with 'easy-pickins'" Abe remarks, drily.

"That's one way of putting it," Wolf grimaces.

"Hand me the phone book," Ginny relents. "And I need a glass of wine."

"I'll call room service," Abe picks up the menu and turns to wine list. "Syrah okay with you?"

"Perfect."

Abe picks up the phone while Ginny persuses the club listings. "Hey guys!" She immediately has their attention. "This can't be a coincidence."

"What?" Abe and Wolf ask simultaneously.

"Another night club called Catacombe."

"You're right, that has to be more than a coincidence."

"Well, I guess we know where to start," Abe says.

An hour later, they hire a taxi to take them to Catacombe, as none of them know Rome well enough to brave the late-night traffic.

Unlike the club in Berlin, this Catacombe is brighter and airier and packed with 20-somethings dressed in designer clothes. Not a single Goth is in evidence.

"Strikes me as the very definition of 'the beautiful people,'" Ginny notes, glad that she purchased the Ungaro; she feels like she actually fits in here. Abe and Wolf, both born into money, blend in naturally.

A strikingly beautiful young man at the bar is staring at them, and if it weren't for the clothes, Ginny would swear that he'd just stepped out of a Caravaggio painting. He had that soft and pale look about him, the touseled chestnut curls and full lips.

Ginny nudges Wolf and whispers into his ear, "I may be wrong, but I'm willing to bet that guy is not quite human."

Wolf follows her gaze, and squeezing her hand, he stands and approaches the bar. Abe and Ginny watch as he introduces himself and it isn't long before the men move toward the exit and a more private place to talk.

"Well, I take it he was somewhat successful," Abe shouts over the pounding beat of the music.

Ginny raises her hand, fingers crossed, "Let's hope so," she mouths.

A few minutes later, Wolf re-enters the club and motions for them to join him. Once outside the club, he introduces them to the youth from the bar, "Ginny, Abe, this is Mario."

Mario nods, studying them.

It must be quite unusual, Ginny reflects, for a vampire to be accompanied by humans. First Mustela and now, Mario, seem perplexed by their presence.

"Mario has graciously invited us to a private party at the Catacombe San Callisto," Wolf informs them.

It occurs to Ginny that this probably isn't the first time humans have been invited to a private party hosted by vampires, but she says, "What is it about catacombs?"

"Humans tend to avoid them after dark," Mario explained in a strikingly melodic voice that causes Ginny to shiver in anticipation. Warning bells start to ring in her head and she is glad she has Wolf beside her. Mario is clearly a predator, and Ginny wonders if she and Abe should risk the trip to the party.

As if reading her mind, Mario assures her that because they are with Wolf, they will be safe at the party.

"Thank you," Ginny blushes. "We really would like to meet Phaon."

"And I have no doubt that he will be delighted to make your acquaintance as well. He has always had a soft spot for beautiful women."

Ginny blushes again and tries to look at her feet; she thinks she could drown in Mario's liquid eyes.

Wolf hails a taxi and suddenly Ginny finds herself in the middle of the backseat bookended by two vampires; just the touch of their thighs brushing against hers causes her to moan with pleasure. She'd forgotten that all vampires, not just Wolf, exude that sexual magnetism. Wolf places his hand on her leg as if claiming his territory; Mario smiles, and turns his head to look out the window. Abe seems oblivious to what's going on, but when he turns around to point out a landmark to Ginny, he is displeased to see Wolf's hand grasping her thigh. He scowls and turns back around, glowering at the passing scenery.

Phaon is exactly as Mustela described him—godlike and charismatic—no wonder he'd fallen so hard. She hopes Abe isn't careless enough to mention Mustela's demise. They have no way of knowing how Phaon will react, but she suspects he won't be happy about it.

"I understand you ran into Ratgar in Berlin?"

"Rat . . . oh, you mean Mustela," Ginny says.

"Mustela," Phaon smiles, wistfully. "He is using my nickname."

"He seems to be very romantic," Ginny is careful to use the present tense.

"Oh yes, I think it is what caught my notice despite the awkward circumstances of our first meeting."

"He claims you two still stay in touch."

"Yes, he visits me in Rome at least every year or two. But that's not why you are here."

"No," Wolf agrees, "I'm here because I am looking for Vlad."

"Vlad Vladiescu?"

"He created me."

"Indeed?"

"And you created Mustela?"

"I did."

"I know this might be a personal question," Ginny chimes in, "but I was wondering, yesterday, about original vampires. I'm not sure how they are created or how many "originals" there are. Mustela says you've been around a long time and I thought you might know."

"How many there are? No. How they were created? Not necessarily. I know how I was created, and Vlad, too, for that matter. I was created in the 2nd century B.C. by calling up the demon Azazel. He called up Azazel centuries later."

It takes every ounce of her self-control for Ginny not to cross herself. A demon. She'd never doubted they existed, but to willingly summon one? That is hard to imagine.

"You look shocked," Phaon murmurs, amused.

"I guess I always thought those that called up demons were evil themselves."

"I'm glad I don't strike you as wicked," Phaon continues, "but don't you find vampirism a particulary nasty species of evil?"

"Evil incarnate, perhaps?" Abe volunteers.

Ginny glances guiltily at Wolf, "I understand your point, but what if you become a vampire against your will?"

Phaon studies Wolf. "Vlad created you against your will?"

"I tried to destroy him after he killed my fiancée."

Phaon begins to laugh, "And he 'punished' you by making you one of our kind."

"You could say that."

Phaon continues to chuckle, "I am assuming you wish to find him to finally destroy him? Wolf neither acknowledges nor denies the statement. "Well, Vlad never played well with others, if you take my meaning. He left Rome a long time ago and I never saw him again."

"So you don't know where we can find him?" Ginny asks.

"I didn't say that."

"Or you have reasons for not wanting him destroyed?" Wolf adds.

"I didn't say that either. Destroying Vlad could punish you as much as him. And frankly, it's none of my business. No, I've only heard rumors."

"Rumors?" Abe prompts.

"Well, the vampire grapevine suggests that he has returned to his homeland."

"Count Dracula is living in Transylvania?" Ginny laughs out loud. "I'm sorry, but that seems too easy, not to mention too, too cliché."

"Yes," Phaon agrees, "but very like Vlad to return to the one place he ever had power."

Mario arrives with wine for Ginny and Abe, and Phaon says his goodbyes. "Stay as long as you like," he urges them. "I promise, you are off limits. You have my word."

But Ginny is beginning to feel claustrophic and takes her glass of wine and climbs out of the catacombs, glad to be back in the chilly but much fresher air. Abe follows her, leaving Wolf behind talking to a couple of vampires 'visiting' from Paris.

"Next stop Bucharest," Abe sighs, leaning against a tomb.

"This is all happening too quickly," Ginny chokes. "I'm not sure I want to go through with this."

"I'm sorry, Gin, I really am."

But she knows that this time tomorrow, they'll be in Romania if at all possible.

It actually takes them two days to get to Bucharest. Because of Wolf, it is necessary to charter yet another plane and arrangements for that have to be postponed until the following morning. So, while Wolf sleeps, Ginny and Abe make the necessary preparations.

Unfortunately, they inform Wolf when he wakes up later that afternoon, the soonest they were able to arrange a flight is the following day—but Wolf will be awake when the flight leaves at 9 p.m.

But, by the next night, they are standing in line at the car rental counter before 11 p.m. and picking up their Nissan X-Trail 4X4. They had decided they might have to do some driving over rough roads as Ginny's theory is that Vlad will have found a place to hide out as close as possible to the site of his former castle.

It is a quick drive to the Hotel Diplomat where they will stay until the sun sets the next evening before making the short trip to the town of Pitesti, which is the closest "big" town near the Arges River and not far from the ruins of Poenari, Vlad's fortress.

The next evening, they check into the Victoria Hotel and ask for recommendations for local pubs, where they hope to pick up some local legends about the infamous count. They end at Luceafarul, a bar recommended by the desk clerk.

The pub is dark and filled with men—hard and worn-looking men, although none of them can be much older than thirty, Ginny thinks as she surveys the bar, eyes adjusting to the gloom. When they had entered the bar, the talking had stopped and they had been stared at, warily.

"Touristin!" someone had laughed, in German, and the talking had accelerated and soon it was as if they had never interrupted.

Wolf orders them beer because he can speak a bit of Romanian, and they sit down at the last empty table.

"What are we going to do?" Ginny asks. "I mean do we just ask them out right if they've heard of Vlad or what?"

Wolf stares at the untouched beer sitting before him then at Ginny. "I guess I'm just going to have to ask," he says, standing up. Leaving his beer, he doesn't want to get trapped into toasting, he walks over to a table occupied by three big men—laborers by the look of them. Their work-dirtied hands encircle mugs of European-cold beer.

Their young-old faces peer up at him, curiously. It is not often that this bar sees tourists, especially people as well-dressed as these three. Usually, they get the jean-clad students with ungroomed hair. The ones that tried so hard to look European but were actually American. Or they got tourists of the same description but who really were European or Australian.

"We are looking for a man called Vlad Drakulya," Wolf states in Romanian, watching their faces carefully for reaction.

The men stare at him as if he's just announced that he is looking for Paul Bunyan and his blue ox, Babe.

"Vlad," one of them laughs, but his voice is shaky.

"Hey," another man bellows in Romanian, "this man is looking for Vlad Drakulya!"

The pub erupts in laughter, only the bartender pales, dropping a glass, unheard, in the commotion.

Wolf surveys the crowd in consternation. What had he said?

When the laughter dies down a bit, the third fellow at the table informs Wolf that Vlad is only a figment of their parents' imaginations.

"When we were young," he says, "our parents told us that if we were not good, then Vlad would take us away at night."

"They told us that he would open us up with his sharp teeth," another laughs, "and drink our blood like beer."

"Of course, it scared us when we were young," someone else says, "but by the time we were teen-agers, we realized it was just threats, that the man once known as Vlad Drakulya died a long time ago."

"There were always rumors, though," said the man with the shaky voice. "People disappearing elsewhere in Transylvania and particularly here in Pitesti. But they were only rumors," he says as if trying to convince himself of that.

Several of the men at his table jeer him and slap him on the back, and he quickly ducks his head and takes another larger swig of beer.

"Perhaps that is what I heard," Wolf responds, politely, and returns to his table.

"What was that all about?" Ginny asks. She and Abe had been astounded by the reaction to Wolf's statement.

"He is here."

Ginny looks around. "I hope you mean, here, as in this country, and not here—this bar."

Wolf smiles, "This country, but they do not believe in him." He tells them what had happened, what the men had said.

"I could use another beer," Abe says.

"Take mine. I can't drink it." Wolf pushes his beer across the rough wooden table toward Abe.

"No thanks," Abe refuses, standing up. "I think I can handle ordering a beer in Romanian."

Ginny is trying hard to hide her amusement. Wolf is angry. "Don't be mad," she squeezes his leg after Abe has removed himself to the bar.

"I should've said no," he takes Ginny's tiny hand in his, "but I just can't say no to you."

"That's because I love you," she explains.

"Is that why?"

"Yep."

"Now we have to find out where in Transylvania he is," Wolf changes the subject, much to Ginny's chagrin.

"I still think he's somewhere near Poenari. That was his fortress. It was where his first wife died. It just makes sense. Besides, you can't ask these guys again," Ginny says, looking again at the sad but patient faces trying hard to enjoy their lives. "They look as if they've said all on the subject they plan to."

She pulls Wolf's beer back across the table. "I'll drink this," she continues, raising the mug to her mouth.

"Don't get intoxicated," Wolf warns her.

She stares at him, coldly, frustrated by his seeming distance and the fact their time together is growing short. "It's only my second beer. Jeez, why would you say something like that? You can be a real asshole sometimes, you know?"

"What?"

She just shakes her head. She never bitches at him when he's out all night doing his particular form of drinking. Abe returns to the table, observing that Ginny seems to be agitated. Her face is set and her knuckles are white from clenching the mug too tightly.

If it's because of Wolf, I'm glad, he thinks, but says, "The bartender wants to speak to you, Wolf."

Both Wolf's and Ginny's heads turn simultaneously toward the bar. An older, heavy-set man is staring at them, almost fearfully, Ginny thinks.

"Come with me," Wolf says to Ginny as he stands up.

Her eyes ask him if he means it. He pulls her up and into his arms and kisses her, relishing the taste of beer on her lips. It's the closest he can get to enjoying the beverage.

"I love you," he reminds her, "and I don't want you to be mad at me.

She grins at him, helplessly, "Damn, I just can't stay mad at you."

"Sprechen Sie Deutsch?" Wolf asks the bartender.

"Ja," he assents.

"Dann, können wir auf Deutsch sprechen weil meine Frau kann kein rumänisch."

The bartender nods.

He had known as soon as they had entered the bar. The sight of the blond man had sent shivers running up his arms and legs until they reached his head, and the roots of his hair prickled, as if he had just jumped into a freezing shower following a steaming sauna. He could just tell—the pale face may have been the giveaway, or, perhaps, the way he had seemed to adjust to the light so quickly, leading his friends to a hard-to-see table in a smoke-filled corner.

But when he came to the bar to order beers, he knew for certain. The already rift-like lines that tracked from his nose to his mouth, deepened still more.

He couldn't miss the age-old wisdom in his eyes, the too-sharp teeth. He had waited on him, but he had avoided his eyes as much as possible. But there had been another look about this one—a look of determination, an appearance of goodness.

Goodness, how can that be? These creatures are always evil. And then he had said he was looking for Vlad. He had been so shaken, he had dropped the mug he had been drying. What on earth was he doing in this bar? So, he had asked to speak to him.

"**Y**ou're one of them," he states, boldly, although his hands clutch the countertop as if he would fall backwards if not for the support.

"What?" Wolf asks, startled. He knows what the bartender means.

"You are of the same kind as Vlad," but this time his voice is less than a whisper.

Ginny looks at Wolf, fear outlined on her beautiful face. What will he say? Will he tell the bartender?

"Yes," Wolf admits. The truth has worked so far. He wonders how the man knows. He can usually fool most people, but this man is apparently not most people. What is his interest? Does he know Vlad? And before the man can order him out of his bar—Wolf can see the hate in his eyes—he speaks again, "Yes," he repeats, "I've come here to kill Vlad."

Both Ginny and the bartender gasp, but for different reasons.

"But that will mean your death, too, that is if . . . "

"I know that," Wolf interrupts.

The bartender looks at him differently. Perhaps that goodness he had perceived had been real. Why else would a vampire want to kill his creator?

He studies the beautiful woman standing next to, almost on top of, the vampire. She is definitely human. Is it some perverted attraction? He would guess not. She has the look of naïveté, of seeing all the good in things—that American trustfulness—before it has been soiled by world-weariness. Only a good man, he decides, could win the love of this woman. And what of the man sitting moodily at the table?

"Who's your friend?" he nods toward the table.

"He's in love with me," Ginny informs him, following his eyes.

"And, what is he doing here?"

"He wanted to help us."

"You mean he hopes to win you once Vlad and ..."

"Wolf are dead," Ginny finishes the bartender's sentence. His insight is amazing. "To put it bluntly," she laughs.

"And why do you want to kill Vlad?" he asks Wolf.

"Do you know him?" Wolf counters.

"Perhaps," the bartender answers.

"I want to kill him because he is evil, because four hundred years ago he killed the woman I loved and because he ruined my life."

A shadow passes over Ginny's face and settles there.

"If it hadn't been for Ginny," Wolf pulls her even closer, "I would never have thought of killing Vlad. I only wish that I didn't have to die in the process. I loved Hannele but I love Ginny more than I ever thought it was possible to love someone."

"Really? Then why is she part of this?"

"It is only selfishness on my part that she is on this trek with me," he answers the bartender's question.

"It is not," Ginny nudges him. "I told him that if he didn't let me come, I would follow him, anyway," Ginny tells the bartender. "What is your name?" She adds as if it is a second thought. But she has been wondering for what reason does this man have so much interest in Wolf.

"Mihai Niculescu," he introduces himself.

They observe each other in friendly silence for a moment.

"Then I will tell you," Mihai breaks the silence.

Ginny and Wolf look at him, expectantly.

"Almost 40 years ago," he begins, but is interrupted by a request for beer. "Excuse me."

They wait, impatiently, as he waits on a number of customers, but the crowd in the bar is already beginning to thin.

"Forty years," Wolf reminds him when he returns.

"There had been rumors," he continues, almost as if he had never stopped, "that people were disappearing in the Transylvanian Alps near the upper reaches of the Arges River. There was a castle up there, a fortress, which was built centuries ago by Vlad the Impaler. Some said it was now inhabited by a recluse; others said it was Vlad the Impaler, himself, who was still lord there."

Vlad. The name struck terror in the hearts of wayward children. Even today, his heart would tighten when he heard the name. And when he had heard Nicolae shout that this man was looking for Vlad, he had broken into a fine sweat, and he had felt as if he had been plunged into the icy waters of the Black Sea.

"I was in the service and about twenty of us were sent to this fallen down castle to see if the rumors were true.

They arrived about midday. Mihai was not the only man among the twenty with sweating palms and fearfully pounding heart. Mihai knew it was because of Vlad. He had been terrified of the man since he was a child.

Others were complaining that the trek up the steep 1,480-step ascent to the crumbling castle was going to kill them. But Mihai knew that they were in excellent physical condition.

"No wonder the old hermit eats humans," someone laughed. "I wouldn't want to go down to town for groceries, either."

A turn in the path brought the castle into view for the first time. It seemed to glare down at them, forbiddingly. Mihai stopped. They were walking single-file up the relatively narrow path, and the man behind him bumped into him.

"Hey!" he complained, and then was silent. They were all staring at the castle.

"No wonder there are rumors," someone commented in an awed whisper.

Although marred by gaping holes, Mihai could see that it had once been a tremendous fortress. The sun disappeared behind a cloud, and the castle appeared to blink at them like some slowly-awakening beast. A chill settled over them, and the rest of the march was continued in silence.

Mihai was worried. If all the rumors about the castle were true, then what was to stop Vlad or, if it wasn't Vlad, this insane hermit from eating them as well? Had anyone in Bucharest thought of that before they had sent them up here on this crazy mission? No, of course not, he thought. This is just their way of appeasing all the people who had complained about the castle to the government. Their way of showing how much they 'cared' about the people.

"Why don't they just tear it down," he mumbled. But he knew why. Why spare such a great expense for nothing. If it were one day discovered that the land here was of value, maybe then they would do it. Mihai surveyed his surroundings, dourly. Unless gold or something of that nature were hidden in this rocky soil, then the castle would remain where it was until its bricks were dust.

And, if gold hadn't been discovered here yet, he doubted that it ever would be. Besides, he couldn't help but grin, Vlad would eat all the prospectors, anyway. It didn't occur to him that there would come a day when the ruins, themselves, would be a major tourist attraction.

They had almost reached the tremendous rocky outcropping that held the fortress, which had been built straight on the rocks atop the ruins of an earlier fortress.

It was a perfect defensive position for a castle, Mihai decided, but who the hell would want to defend this barren place? It most definitely was not built as a home; more likely just a hideout for the paranoid Vlad. Although Mihai had to concede with yet another grin, that just because Vlad had been paranoid, it hadn't meant that everyone wasn't out to get him. Mihai seriously doubted that other than the time arrows had arched from the castle into the valley below, killing the soldiers of his brother's invading army, the castle had ever been used as a defensive position. Who would want the place?

The rocky soil discouraged the growing of crops, and the slope was so rocky and steep that even livestock could not be grazed here. To Mihai, it looked as if whoever had built the place had been thinking of only one thing—isolation.

Despite the awe-inspiring view, Mihai thought he'd probably feel more at home in Antarctica.

As they approached the entrance, he noted that the great wooden door that once guarded entrance to the fortress, appeared to have been struck by lightning. It lay on the ground splintered, burned and rotting. Good target, he approved, too bad the blast didn't knock the whole damned castle down.

The men stopped before the arch that once held the tremendous door. It was more than twelve feet high and six feet wide. Fallen bricks and mortar lay scattered around what was left of the walls. The shingled roof had long since caved in and was a large part of the detritus that littered the floor.

Mihai shivered. The silence was even spookier than the castle. He had not heard a bird or insect since they had come in view of the castle. The shiver became a shudder. They were miles away from civilization. Should something happen . . .

A few feet away from the door, one of the many holes in the castle gave the men a glimpse of what lay inside.

Mihai could see what looked like brick floors through the dirt; the walls, too, were brick, stone and lots of mortar. And, except for crumbled and fallen bricks, shingles and lots of dust and dirt, the castle looked empty.

Someone half-heartedly tried the tapping on one of the stones that lined the arch, knocking as if someone might actually answer it. His knock was an almost silent tap, and a couple of other guys, laughing, pounded on the stone with their rifles, calling "anyone home!"

The stone shifted and made an odd, groaning noise, before, with a giant ripping sound, it fell away from the arch almost as if propelled.

Even though it was rolling away from them, the men scampered backwards in fear.

"Holy Mary, Mother of God," someone shouted, and crossed himself, as the carved stone continued to roll toward the cliff's edge, sending up a cloud of dust.

Mihai felt as if his hair were standing on end. Why are you so afraid of a rock, he berated himself, angrily. They were all acting like the little children they had once been, hiding beneath the covers, terrified that Vlad would come and whisk them away.

To where? Here? Had he known of this place as a child, Mihai would still be sleeping with the lights on.

Without speaking, they avoided the arch from which the stone had fallen, choosing to enter instead through the man-size hole a little more than a yard away.

Mihai had the creepy feeling that when he stepped on the floor, his foot would sink into the entranceway like quicksand until it had disappeared completely.

They entered the castle, feet crunching on the grit that covered the red-bricked floor. As soon as he was fully in the castle, Mihai felt as if a hand had tightened around him.

He came very close to turning back, then. He wanted to turn around, run back through the hole and away from the castle, as far away as he could get. And, he never wanted to look back. But, he didn't want to be thought of as a coward, so he gritted his teeth and moved further into the room.

The men stood, clustered in small groups, conversing in whispers among themselves. Something about the place discouraged loud voices.

Although, Mihai was tempted to shout just to make the bastard aware of their presence.

He was here. He could feel it. He knew that somewhere in this monstrosity the vampire was sleeping. But where? All was silence. He could see, now that he was inside, that none of the upper floors remained. And, the entire fortress room seemed open to the sky. Here, the high walls blocked the sun's rays. There were no windows. But the room was lightened by the great holes in the walls and the ceilingless rooms.

Obviously, most of the litter of fallen stones had been carried away long ago. Nothing had been done recently, though. Here and there tremendous pieces of brick and mortar lay where they had fallen from the great walls of the castle.

An especially big boulder lay against the remains of the room's furthest wall. Mihai wondered how it had ever been part of the wall. It was so big. Then he noticed something else, something very unusual for an abandoned home—not one sign of animals or insects.

There were no nests or cobwebs or excrement. Nothing to lead you to believe an animal had ever been in the place. That's odd, he thought, and mentioned it to a couple of men standing near him. His observance was whispered around the room. Soon all the men were standing together in a tight ball in the center of the room. Even the hairs on Mihai's hairy chest seemed to be rigid with fright. His testicles had long since retreated to the relative safety of his body.

And, suddenly, Mihai knew that they had overstayed their welcome. If we don't get out of here soon, he thought, they might never leave.

"It's quite obvious that no one is living here," he said, loudly, hoping that Vlad might hear and take heed.

A mumbled assent. They had been expecting glaring white skeletons and a raving madman with blood dripping from sharp teeth.

"I think we've seen enough to make a report," their commander agreed. The men filed out of the room, trying desperately to keep their feet from running.

It was easier to believe, once they began to descend, that the incline was speeding up their pace. Mihai did not feel safe again until he was out of the pass and on his way back to Bucharest.

"**W**e arrived there midday, and the castle was empty," he shakes violently and uncontrollably in remembrance. "As you can see it made quite an impression on me, and on many of the other men who made that trip. The castle was uninhabited or it appeared to be. But, I swear on my grave that there was something there, something so evil that it seeped into our bones and did not leave us until we were far away from that place. I cannot swear that Vlad was there. I did not see him. I saw nothing, not even a spider web. But I felt him. Or I felt *something* evil."

Ginny feels herself shaking in response to his story. I don't want to go up there, she thinks, I don't want Wolf to die in that awful place.

Wolf, on the other hand, seems to have grown stronger. He is close to his goal now. Soon it will all be over.

"How do we get there?" he asks.

"Things have changed a lot since I was last up there," Mihai explains. "The castle is now under reconstruction and it has become quite the tourist attraction. People come up from Bucharest or over from Sibiu all the time just to see the famous fortress of 'Count Dracula.' The truth is, he may or may not be there anymore. If he is, he is so well hidden that no one has reported feeling his presence while there; no workers have disappeared."

"What about sightseers?" Ginny asks.

"If they have, only their families, and perhaps the government, know they've gone missing; but no, nothing directly tied to the site."

"Sounds like he has become a lot more cautious," Wolf says. "But I have a gut feeling he is still around."

"Well, it's easy enough to get there," Mihai states. "Just take the DN 7c and follow the signs. There is a parking area not far from where the steps begin."

"We're staying at the Victoria," Ginny adds, "in case you remember anything else that might help us."

"I'll meet you back at the hotel," Wolf says, kissing Ginny. They are standing outside the bar. He won't answer the question in her eyes, and she knows he is going to feed.

This time, she feels no jealousy, only a vague pity for whoever his victim will be. She fingers the bruised mark on her throat. The two small holes have already scabbed over. She shudders in disgust. She had never considered the fact that she might be the vessel from which a vampire would drink. Although she should have, she realizes, after all the idea had been to find some. Why should they consider her sacred? Rather she should be amazed and thankful that Wolf has been able to maintain control over his blood lust while with her.

She looks up to see Wolf gazing at her with a pained expression marring his handsome face. He hasn't stopped apologizing for not returning with her to find out what was wrong with Abe.

He had let his jealousy rule instead of his wisdom, and it infuriated him that he had let Abe get to him. It was like saying to Ginny that he felt she would turn to Abe if the offer were good enough, and he knew that wasn't true.

She slides her arms around his waist, and hugs him, tightly. "I don't blame you," she tells him. "Besides, I'm fine. This will be gone in no time."

He touches the wound, "I'm so sorry."

"If you apologize one more time . . ."

"What?"

She looks at him blankly, "Hell, I don't know. I don't guess there's anything I can threaten you with."

"Sure there is," he presses his forehead against hers. "You can stop loving me."

"I would never do that. Not only would that be cruel, but it would be untrue. I'll never stop loving you, ever."

They kiss again, and it is only a "Good God" groaned from Abe that pulls them apart.

"Fuck you," Wolf says, before walking off, angrily.

Ginny is silent on the return walk to the hotel.

"I'm sorry."

"Good God, yourself, Abe!" Ginny finally explodes. "You knew full well what you were getting into before you came, and you and Wolf have been at each other's throats ever since." She pauses. "No pun intended. I wish to hell I'd told you to get the hell out of my life, now. I really do."

"I'm sorry," Abe apologizes again. "I just can't help it. You two are so happy together and, damn," he kicks a trashcan in anger, sending it clattering into the street, "I just can't stand it."

"Then leave damn it! Leave! Go back to your fucking newspaper! Just get the hell out of here!" she screams.

Abe stops and stares at her, aghast. He has never seen her this angry.

"You're the one who wanted to come along, remember?" she reminds him, her tone now subdued. "Please don't do this to us, Abe."

"Is that a 'you and me' 'us' or a 'you and Wolf' 'us'?"

She glares at him.

"That's what I thought."

"Abe," she sighs, on the verge of tears. "We know where Vlad is now. That means, at best, that I have a week left with Wolf. But, I know I'm not that lucky. Everything will be over in a few days." And the hollowness in her voice makes Abe want to take her into his arms and comfort her, but he knows she won't allow that.

"You're the one who said we could be 'just friends'," she continues, reproachfully.

Abe stands still, takes a deep breath and closes his eyes. He knows she is right. Damn, he knows it. And it's only a few more days. Maybe then he can make her change her mind. He could at least take solace in the fact that Wolf is impotent, so to speak. His breath comes out in a defeated rush.

"All right," he says, "just give me one more chance, that's all I'll ask for."

Ginny regards him, considering, "That is a chance to remain with me and Wolf without provoking him, isn't it? I've already told you that no matter what I'll never love you the way you want me to."

Abe nods.

"OK. I know this is stupid of me, but ok. I have this feeling I may need your support."

It is almost dawn before Wolf returns and Ginny is waiting, anxiously, sitting on the bed and facing the door.

"Jesus Christ," she stands up, "I didn't think you were going to make it back before dawn."

"I'm sorry, it just took longer than I thought it would."

"I had this terrible feeling that I was never going to see you again. I had even begun to think that you tried to make it to his castle before dawn."

"Don't worry so much," he ruffles her hair. "I am not going to die without saying goodbye to you, first."

If only she could slow things down.

"I assume that we will be heading up that way tonight?"

"Yes," he says, pulling the iron blue sweater Ginny had bought him over his head. "Do you want to take a shower with me?"

"With you?" she teases, and gently nips his chest. She could spend hours caressing and kissing it. She wishes she had the time to do so. She wants to memorize him, every hair on his body, every pore.

"Ow!" he looks down to see the impression her teeth have left. "Why'd you do that?"

She begins beating his chest with her fists, anguish and fear outlined in her face. "No," she moans, "no, no, no, no, no . . ." The tears splash from her eyes.

"Ginny," he grabs her tiny wrists. His thumbs overlap his fingers her wrists are so small. "Calm down, please." Her weight sags, and he picks her up, and lays her on the bed.

She stares at the ceiling, face red and puffy from crying, and the tears continue to leak from her eyes in miniature waves.

He lies down beside her, "I really don't know what to say to make you feel better about this."

"Nothing," she cries, bitterly, "you can't say anything. Oh, why did I ever let you into my house that night? I must have been out of my mind. Why couldn't you have . . . ah, shit, you don't kill, anyway." She sighs. "Hold me."

He takes her into his arms. Doesn't she know that this is as hard on him as it is on her? If he could live without ever having to drink blood again—even if it meant losing his strength or hiding in the dark for eternity or for the rest of a natural life—he'd do it. That's the only part of it he really can't stand. He even thinks he can get by without being able to make love to her (if I take a lot of cold showers, ha ha.), but not the blood. He despises that need in him. It makes the love he feels for Ginny dirty or evil, inhuman. It is too easy to confuse his lust for her with his lust for blood. And, he doesn't want her to be a part of his corruption.

"I'm sorry," she whispers into his ear. "I promised myself I wouldn't lose control again, that I wouldn't cry." She tells him about the fight with Abe as they finish undressing.

Damn, he has nice legs, she thinks, as he removes his pants—muscular thighs and calves and all that blond hair. Like his chest, his legs come close to driving her crazy with desire. And, his ass, she thinks, and his arms and his hands and his neck and his face and his hair. She could go on and on. And she wasn't forgetting that most important part of him that had been out of order, so to speak, for 400 years. She looks up at him. He is gazing down at her, glumly.

She smiles, brilliantly, and slides her hands up his stomach, over his chest and around his neck. She presses herself against him, "I love you."

He picks her up and once again lays her upon the bed, kissing her mouth, then chin and moving on down her throat. He lingers over her full, round breasts, taking each nipple in his mouth until they are taut and hard and she moans in response. His kisses continue down her belly and her skin quivers at the touch of his soft lips.

Picking her up, gently, he carries her to the shower.

Ginny & Abe

As soon as Wolf is soundly asleep, Ginny slips from he room and makes her way to Abe's door. She knocks lightly and when there is no response, pounds a little harder.

Abe opens the door, bleary-eyed with lack of sleep. "Ginny," he seems surprised, "the sun's coming up."

Ginny laughs, "We're not the vampires, Abe."

Abe grunts, "With the hours that we've been keeping, I've already begun to start craving blood."

"May I come in?"

"Sure, I guess."

Ginny giggles. Abe is dressed in a full set of flannel pajamas; when she had left Wolf's side, she had had to leave the cool and silky touch of his naked flesh against hers.

"All right, what's wrong? You're not the giggly type."

"Give me a break, Abe. I'm trying desperately to keep it together."

"So what gives?"

"I want to kill him, now."

"Who? Wolf?"

"Wake up, Abe," she says, sitting in one of the room's armchairs. "I mean Vlad. I think we should go and kill him now, while the sun is up."

"We?"

"I'll do it myself, if I have to. Oh, Abe, I just can't go there tonight with Wolf and see him die in the same horrible way that Mustela did. I don't think I can handle that. It would be so much easier on me, and I know I'm being selfish, if he were to die here while I am far away."

"What happens if he starts screaming in agony or something?"

"Abe," she protests, glaring at him.

"You said Mustela . . ."

"I know what I said. All right, say he does start screaming. So, the manager runs to our room and there's one of his guests, disappearing before his eyes. He'll probably call the police. So, we can take care of that. We'll just bring our stuff with us, and that way we don't have to come back."

"I suppose you want to leave now?" She is dressed in jeans, hiking boots she'd bought while in Rome, her fisherman's sweater and Wolf's leather jacket. Her long brown hair is pulled back in a bun, secured by her father's chopsticks, as she always considers them a good luck token.

She looks incredible, he thinks, she always looks so good.

"We have only until sunset."

"I'm going to have to take a shower to wake myself up," he warns her. "I didn't get much sleep last night."

"Quit complaining. I didn't sleep at all. But, I did take a shower, so I can at least do that for you. I'll meet you at the car in half an hour." She returns to her room to say her farewells to Wolf. It is something she has been dreading since he decided he must do this.

She stares at his sleeping form for a full minute. "Tomorrow would have been your birthday," her chin trembles. She takes a deep breath. She doesn't want to break down and cry. She'll have plenty of time for that later—on the drive back to Bucharest, on the flight back to America and the rest of my life, she thinks. Her heart feels as if it is trying to cave in on itself. She wishes she could tear it from her chest to stop, once and for all, the terrible aching there.

But there is one thing she has promised herself she will do before Wolf dies—give him last rites—because she believes that he deserves

God's forgiveness. She pulls a small bottle of holy oil from her pocket, oil she stole from the Catholic church in Corazon, she reminds herself, blushing. Hopefully, God will forgive her.

"Through this holy unction," she begins, anointing his forehead with the oil, "may the Lord pardon thee whatever sins or faults thou hast committed."

He continues his sleep uninterrupted and she leans over and gently kisses his lips. "Good bye Wolf. I love you."

She gathers all her things together and then wonders what to do with Wolf's luggage. Perhaps she should leave it here just in case they don't manage to kill Vlad by sundown? There is one thing she hates to leave behind, though. Wolf's family ring. It would be ashamed to leave the beautiful emerald behind, and along with Hannele's ring, she will treasure it forever; perhaps if she ever has a son . . . Well, she can't dwell on that. She slides it off his finger and stuffs it in her front pocket—another good luck charm.

Now, if she can just get out of the hotel as unobtrusively as possible; get out of the hotel without any questions from the desk clerk. She hangs the room's do not disturb sign—*nu deranjaþi*—on the door. The third language this week.

She glances both ways down the hallway. It is empty. "No problem," she says out loud. Her voice sounds strained and without hope. She drops her luggage outside the door, including a sword belonging to Mihai.

While waiting on Wolf the previous evening, Mihai had come to the hotel, and had offered her the sword to give to Wolf.

"It belonged to my great-great-grandfather," he had said. "It is a broad sword. And," he added, "I had it blessed and sprinkled with holy water. You may need it to remove his head."

"Remove his head?" Ginny had asked, accepting the sword with gratitude.

"One of the legends suggests that you must remove the head and stuff the mouth with garlic and roses."

Ginny had grimaced. That wasn't something she relished doing.

"Don't worry about returning it," he had said. "It may not be possible." And, he had walked away.

She returns to the bed and sits down beside Wolf. He is sleeping, soundly, as always. She wishes it didn't have to be this way, but admires Wolf's courage.

"Oh Wolf," she chokes, "I love you so much. Why did it have to be this way? Why couldn't you have been a normal human? Damn it, why did I have to fall in love with a vampire?"

Wolf moves, faintly, and she wonders if in his coma-like state, he has become aware of what is going on. Only vaguely aware, she hopes. She'd hate to think that he was trapped in sleep, waiting to die. She hates goodbyes, always has. She has always felt strained and awkward when saying farewells to friends and family.

With Ken, they had kind of just parted. But she loves Wolf as she has always hoped to love someone. And, now she must go and he must die.

"It's just not fair," she whispers. She kisses the roughness of his cheek and his motionless mouth. If it weren't for his softly rising chest, he could be dead already.

A sob escapes her lips, and she raises her hand to her mouth in surprise. She hadn't realized it was there, waiting to get out. She shouldn't have come back for a final farewell.

"I'd better leave, Wolf," she explains, "before I change my mind and before I break down. I love you. Oh darling, I hope you know just how much I love you."

The path is even steeper than she had imagined when Mihai had described it. And everytime they made a turn in the path, Ginny would hold her breath, expecting the fortress to come in to view.

When at last it does, she is still unprepared for what she sees. Mihai is right—a lot of work has been done on shoring up the ruins of the castle. It definitely looks more like a tourist attraction than Count Dracula's fortress.

"What's wrong? You look disappointed," Abe says, breathing heavily from the steep ascent.

"I guess I kind of hoped it would look creepier."

"Why on earth?"

"I don't know. I guess it would have put me in the proper mood." The early morning sun has given the stone and brick of the castle a soft and comforting glow.

"Well, maybe that will help," Abe says, pointing to a low-hanging rain cloud, which is quickly expanding across the sky. Ginny looks up in time to see the cloud move across the sun and completely block the warmth of its light. A few seconds later, the cloud hangs directly above the castle, casting a dreary shadow over the crumbling keep.

"Shit!" Ginny exclaims.

"What? You just said it was too nice a day."

"I left Mihai's sword in the Nissan."

Despite the fact that Abe almost hopes she wants to go back and give up until Wolf wakens, they're already here and he'd really like to get this over with. With the advent of the rain cloud, he is slowly being overwhelmed by the feeling of evil that now seems to seep from the castle.

"Ginny, we sure as hell don't have time to go back down and get it. Besides, I don't intend to make that climb again, only the descent."

"Then we'd better find a piece of wood to use as a stake," she says.

"I'm way ahead of you," Abe replies, sliding the day pack off his back. He opens it and pulls out half a dozen stakes. "And they're made of hawthorn, which is supposed to be especially potent."

"You're amazing," Ginny smiles at him. "But, I did remember both holy water and holy oil. And the garlic." She holds up her Nalgene bottle and a small vial filled with what looks like olive oil, which she's removed from her waist pack.

"Then I guess we're as ready as we'll ever be. We'd better hurry, the sun sets not long after 4 p.m., and if we fail, we need to be out of here well before Vlad wakes up."

It begins drizzling and Ginny prays that the weather will not get any worse. A fine mist has settled on her hair and her teeth begin to chatter. Abe studies her, even her lips are going blue with cold.

"Are you going to make it?" he asks.

"I'll be all right," she shivers. "Looking at that castle really gives me the creeps. Brrr."

"Better be careful what you ask for," Abe glances over his shoulder. It really does look like some beast waiting to pounce. His stomach growls. "We should have had something to eat, first," he complains. "My mother always warned me not to kill vampires on an empty stomach."

Ginny grins, "I was so desperate to get here, I didn't even think about it. Well, that certainly gives us a little incentive to hurry, doesn't it? The first one to kill Vlad gets a huge breakfast, that is, if we can find an American-style breakfast in this country."

"Come on," he commands, voice strong, "Let's get this over with."

Ginny, shaking her head and rolling her eyes, follows. One minute Abe seems to be a little boy, the next, the man in command.

There is now a cement walkway leading to the castle—walkways and stairs lead to its precarious perch atop the stony cliff. And rocky soil. She has never seen earth so full of rocks. The plant life has mostly died back for the winter; the trees are bare skeletons. She looks around, and her heart beats painfully against her ribs. If one looks closely enough there is an obvious circle around the castle, and in its circumference there is no plant life nor is there any animal life. Is it that the soil has been poisoned or is it just Vlad's evil?

"Kind of scary, isn't it?" Abe says, in an awed tone of voice.

Her teeth begin chattering again and she slaps her face, hard.

Abe is staring at her as if she is crazy; she's slapped herself so hard, she's left the bright red imprint of her hand upon her cheek. "Ginny?"

"I'm sorry, Abe," her voice is hard, determined. "I had to pull myself together. I just can't go in their shaking with fear. He'd like that. I know he would. He could win that way, and he can't win. I can't let Wolf down."

They have reached the entrance, and Ginny stares at the remains of the archway. Mihai had said something about not using the original entrance, but the wall has now been patched.

Ginny takes a deep breath and steps through the archway. The evil clamps its hand around Ginny as soon as both of her feet touch the brick floor. The strength of it almost suffocates her.

"He's here, Abe," her voice is strained as if she's speaking through a strangle-hold.

He feels it too, though not as strongly as Ginny. But he can't locate its source, it seems to hang in the air like the dust they've dislocated with their feet.

This clearly had never been a happy place, Ginny muses. No one has ever laughed here, she thinks, unless what small flame of happiness burned here was snuffed out by the death of Vlad's first wife. And then Vlad and his son had been chased from their hideout by Vlad's own brother. Years of exile had followed. No wonder he had become such a bitter man.

Where could he possibly be hiding, she wonders. Abe returns from the other rooms, and shrugs.

"The entire north wall has fallen, and there seems to be little left but ruins," he says. "Cleaned up, lots of reconstruction, but ruins nonetheless. And all of them are open to the sky."

"And to the sun."

Which at this moment is blocked by a monstrous cloud, Abe thinks, and shivers.

Ginny shivers, too, the dampness seems to be seeking the marrow of their bones. Where the hell is Vlad?

After another 45 minutes of searching, Ginny, exhausted and discouraged, rests against a huge boulder.

"He's here, Abe, I just know he is. I swear I can feel him," and she shivers as a finger of cold air caresses the hair at the nape of her neck. She hunches her shoulders against the chill. Abe joins her on the rock.

"What do we do?"

"I don't know," she trembles as she is kissed by another breath of frigid air, "but let's get away from this rock, there's a terrible draft here." She stands up and is stepping away before she freezes in midstride. "Abe," she looks around, and the expression on her face is hope mixed with fear.

"What's wrong," her expression scares him.

"Oh, Jesus, I could be wrong, but I think I've just found Vlad." The goosebumps on her arms have crawled into goosebumps and she is shaking so hard that Abe cannot determine which direction her hand is pointing.

He follows her behind the tremendous rock; there is a darker shadow there that looks like it could be the entrance to a tunnel. They look at each other, eyes widening, and back at the cleft formed by the rock and the remains of the wall.

"It's dark down there, Abe," Ginny whispers. She's not so sure she wants to complete this mission she's sent herself on. As a matter of fact, she's only a breath away from turning and running all the way back to Pitesti.

Abe pulls a couple of flashlights he's been carrying from the pocket of his daypack. Of course, he is prepared. Ginny is disappointed to see the electric torch. Now they must go on.

Abe flashes the light down the dark corridor; it does little to dispel the gloom. Rather than reflecting off the moist walls, the light seems to be sucked in by them.

"Look at this," he points the beam at a small gutter running alongside the corridor's wall.

They have walked only a few feet into the earth-made cleft, but the gutter is definitely the work of a man's hand. The water from the walls seeps into the gutters, there's one on each side, and flows in a slow-moving stream over brackish algae, downwards.

"I wonder where it ends up?" Abe asks. They walk on in silence, descending, slowly, another 20 feet.

"Listen!" Ginny hisses.

They stop and Abe feels like his ears are going to explode, he's listening so hard.

"Ginny," he bitches, she's so tightly wound, she's hearing things, he thinks, "all I can hear is the water dripping into the gutters." It sounds like some kid is plunking away at his toy piano, like the one Schroeder uses in *Peanuts*.

"No, listen, I hear something else." Just under the plinking noise of the dripping water she hears another sound. It sounds like someone is rubbing two pieces of silk together.

That's stupid, she thinks, unless two people wearing silk are danc-ing down there. She strains her ears. Yeah, that's exactly what it sounds like—silk being rubbed together—and, what's that? Interspersed with the rubbing noise are little clicks. It kind of sounds like someone's drumming their fingernails against a table or something.

"Abe," she begins, "I can't figure . . . Shit!" Her curse echoes off the walls.

"Shhhh," Abe glares at her, but she can't see him. "You're going to ruin any element of surprise we might have."

"Abe, I forgot my waist pack."

"What do you mean you forgot your pack? Why the hell did you take it off," he whispers, loudly.

Ginny cringes from the anger in his voice. "I set it down beside the rock," she says, meekly. "It was uncomfortable."

"First the sword and now the holy water and oil. You had better go back and get it," Abe says, slowly, trying to contain his anger. His tem-perature is rising from the pressure. He's scared too, and he just wants to get this all over with.

"But, Abe, it's dark back there."

"Jesus Christ, Ginny," he explodes. "You've got a flashlight. And at least we know what's back there. Just go and get it."

"Why don't you come with me?"

"Because I'm not the one who left the pack!" His whisper is as loud as a shout. "Not to mention the fact that I'm already exhausted and I still have to ram a stake through the son-of-a-bitch's heart. Don't worry, I won't move."

She heads up into the darkness, "Fuck you," she whispers, under her breath, but she is actually glad she has him here with her. She hears the rustling-clicking noise again as she ascends. She shakes her head in confusion, maybe it's all inside her mind but it seems to be growing louder.

She emerges into the grey-white light of the castle. And there's the pack, right where she left it. She shakes her head again, this time in amazement at her own forgetfulness. What had she been thinking? She really needs that sword. If Vlad doesn't die like Mustela, she may have to cut off his head.

Wait a minute, Abe thinks, pausing, I can hear it now, too. That rustling noise; it must be what Ginny heard. The sound is growing louder, and he can barely hear the musical water any more.

"Ouch!" Something nips at his ankle. He turns the beam of the flashlight toward the floor. His skin crawls in disgust. A huge, fat, sleek rat is staring up at him, its beady eyes black and bulging as if its ancestors have spent thousands of years in the dark. It looks as if it would like to eat him for lunch. Using the butt of the flashlight, Abe bashes the black-hearted little monster in the head. It lands in the gutter.

"Jesus," he whispers, stomach heaving in loathing. He pauses suddenly as something occurs to him, and his heart freezes in his chest. His light picks out the dead rat in the gutter. Surely not?

He shines his light down the tunnel. The floor appears to be moving. It looks as if a wave is rolling beneath the stone floor. Not beneath, Abe thinks, the adrenalin surging through his body like an electric shock, above the floor. He turns to run. But the rats are faster.

"Abe?" He hears Ginny's voice at the top of the tunnel.

"Ginny," he screams. "Run."

She takes a few steps into the stone corridor. "Abe, are you all right?"

The rustling sound is echoing off the walls, and besides the clitter, she can hear squeaking now.

Squeaking? She hears Abe grunting and mewling in fear.

"Ginny," he bellows, "Rats! Run!"

Rats? Oh, shit, rats! She finally identifies the noise. Oh, Jesus, Abe. He's being attacked by rats, she whimpers.

"Abe, I can't leave you!" she yells.

"Ginny," she can barely hear him; it sounds like he's yelling through a pillow. "Run! Before they . . ." His voice is silenced, and the horror of what's happening down there finally hits home.

She runs. All the way back to Bucharest, she thinks. She hears a strange sound, like a pig snuffling for truffles, and she turns around expecting to see a boar, like the one over the fireplace in Corazon, charging after her. There is nothing there, only the castle growing more distant with every step. But the noise is still there. She screams in terror, and then realizes that she is the one who has been making the sounds.

The tears stream from her eyes, blinding her. Oh what has she done? Why had she talked Abe into coming? She remembers now what Wolf had told her—about vampires being able to control certain animals. No wonder there are no remains to deal with, she thinks, tripping on the last step in the path and falling hard to her knees. The denim rips and the blood oozes from her opened knees, but she gets up and keeps running the last hundred yards to the parking area.

Oh, Abe, what are they doing to you? She worries. The thought of Abe being devoured by rats makes the bile rise in her throat.

But had she known what the rats were doing with Abe, she would rather he be devoured.

When the rat had inserted its head into his mouth, Abe could take it no longer. The feel of those sleek bodies with their rough and oddly reptilian tails scampering all over him, nipping him with their long, sharp teeth had been nearly impossible to bear. Yet he still forced himself to warn Ginny.

But then, a rat that had been clinging to his throat tried to silence him by pushing its oily little head into his mouth. He'd tried to pull it away, but rats were crawling all over his hands, as well. And then the little bastard that was trying to insert its head into his mouth had bitten him. The feel of its whiskers brushing his lips, the cold and wet nose against his tongue had been too much. Abe had bitten back. The rat screamed in pain, and Abe, mouth full of rat's blood and hair, had passed out.

The rats carried him back down the passage deep into the heart of the mountain. Abe was alive but unconscious. They had a present for their master. Their marble eyes glowed with anticipation. For, once Vlad had his fill, Abe would be theirs.

Ginny & Wolf

"**W**AKE UP," SHE MOANS, SHAKING WOLF. "Wake up."

His eyelids flutter in protest but he continues to sleep, deeply. It is at least another half hour until sunset.

Trembling and cold, Ginny strips off her clothes and tosses them on the bathroom floor. She returns to the bedroom and crawls into bed, cuddling up next to Wolf. But, as tired as she is, she can't sleep. She keeps hearing the rats, and her mind rebels at the thought of what they might have done to Abe.

"Go down sun," she begs, "please go down."

Finally, Ginny feels Wolf's arms tighten around her and the relief is so great, she sobs.

"What happened?" Wolf asks. He sounds angry, and she removes her head from where it is lodged at his neck to look into his eyes.

He is angry. Although he is not sure what has happened, he does know that something occurred during the day, something terrible. He had sensed Ginny's distress as he slept that morning, could feel her terror when she had tried to shake him awake, earlier.

"What happened?" He repeats, and then, knowledge as he fits the pieces together, "You tried to kill Vlad today, didn't you? Where's Abe?"

She flinches from the coldness in his voice, and she can't meet his eyes.

He forces her chin up, orders her to open her eyes.

"Wolf," it's more pleading than explanatory. His eyes appear nearly gray with anger. They stare into hers, unyielding, and the anger rushes through her, exiting through her mouth.

"To hell with you!" she yells, pulling away from him. "We went up there for you, damn it, and I don't have to apologize for it. You can pout as much as you want to, but we failed, all right! You'll still have your chance to kill that monster, you son-of-a-bitch!" And she bursts into tears.

Wolf pulls her into his arms, holds her as if he'll never let her go.

"I'm sorry," he whispers, "I was just scared. Damn it, Ginny, you could have died!" She feels his heart beating faster at the thought of her death.

"I just couldn't bear the thought of watching you die," she explains. "I thought it would be easier on all of us, if you died here, and Vlad died there. I didn't realize—the rats."

"The rats?"

"You know what you told me about being able to command animals?"

Wolf nods, remembering one of their many conversations.

She tells him everything, even about forgetting the sword and later, the pack which contained the holy water and oil along with the garlic.

"That forgetfulness probably saved your life," Wolf remarks, grimly.

"Oh God, Abe," Ginny begins to cry again. Never in a thousand years would she have wished this upon him.

"Mourn for him later," Wolf says, not unkindly. "Unfortunately, if we're going to finish this thing off tonight, then we'd better get moving."

Ginny regards him fearfully. Go back up there? Tonight? She's not sure she can do that.

"You can stay here," Wolf tells her.

"Don't tell me what to do," she snaps. "I'll go back up there if I damn well please, and you can't stop me."

"I . . ." he starts, then decides against it. The shock appears to have made her irrational.

"If that's what you want."

"Of course it's not what I want. But I don't really have any choice in this, do I? Never have, have I? Ever since you decided to do this . . ."

She stops in midsentence, remembering that the orginal idea was hers and hers alone. Closing her eyes and taking a deep breath, she continues. "I'm sorry, Wolf." The pain on his face is killing her. "I'm just so scared."

"I understand," he pushes her long strand of hair away from her face, kisses her. "We'd better get moving."

She looks at her clothes, scattered on the bathroom floor. Maybe she'd better put those back on rather than ruin another set. No telling what might happen this time.

She hands Wolf his leather jacket.

"You wear it," he says, he knows how much she likes it.

"How will you keep warm?"

He pulls on the sweater she gave him over a long john shirt. "I'll be warm enough in this, don't worry."

As his head emerges through the collar, he sees her winding her hair into a bun, and securing it with the chopsticks.

"Are you sure you want to risk losing your father's chopsticks?" he asks.

"They're a good luck charm for me, Wolf."

He considers her for a minute. "I imagine you're right. You are the one who made it back here alive."

"Wolf?" She sounds a little sheepish.

"Yes?" he is anxious to leave.

"You might want this back," she removes the ring from her pocket and hands it to him. He looks at her questioningly. "I thought, well, if we did manage to get Vlad, and you did die like Mustela . . ."

"I understand. Keep it."

"Wolf?"

"Yes?" He sounds very impatient now.

"I really need to have something to eat before we go or at least get something to take with me. I haven't eaten since last night."

"You can't wait?"

"Ha, ha, real funny. Just because you can go a couple of days without food, doesn't mean I can. And while Abe and I were running around preparing for tonight's battle, you were asleep. And, while I was climbing Mount Everest today, you were sleeping once again. No wonder you don't have to feed but a few times a week. But I, being the wimpy little human that I am, must eat for energy. Especially if you expect to climb back up to that castle. Believe me, it's one hell of a walk, and I'm already faint from hunger, and I haven't gotten any sleep in more than 24 hours."

"Are you finished?"

"Yes."

"You can pick up some food at the hotel's restaurant on the way out. Will that be all right with you?"

"Yes," she says, storming out ahead of him. Jesus, what am I doing, she thinks. Why am I bitching at him like this? He's about to die.

"I'm sorry," she says, sliding on to the driver's seat of the Nissan. She glances over her shoulder to make sure the sword is still in the back seat. She sees its leather-scabbarded bulk and sighs with relief.

"It's something I have to do, Ginny."

Her mouth is watering for the chunk of cheese she is holding in her hand, but she kisses Wolf's cheek and promises not to bitch at him again. "I love you, I really do," she says, "but I'm so afraid of losing you. And, I'm afraid of what Vlad might do. What if he sends out the rats again?"

"I don't think so."

"Why not?" she says around a mouthful of cheese.

"Because he's a cocky bastard. I'm sure that he is thoroughly convinced that he is invincible. He'll want to kill me himself."

"I hope you're right, I don't think I can handle those rats again after the way I heard Abe scream."

"I love you," he smiles at her, a genuine smile but his sharp teeth no longer bother her.

"Might as well," she smiles back at him.

He laughs.

Abe & Vlad

"WHAT DO WE HAVE HERE? Vlad strides from his upright bed to stand over the dazed Abe. Despite the pitch dark of the cavern, he knows instinctively when the sun has set. He created the bed centuries ago because he found it made for a less vulnerable position, and he despises being vulnerable. Vlad lights the oil lamp on the wall above his sofa, and adjusts the flame so that Abe can see into the far reaches of the cavern.

So this is Vlad, Abe regards him, silently. He looks just like the paintings Abe found while surfing the internet in Rome except his face looks crueler somehow.

"My friends here tell me you are not alone," Vlad lifts Abe, stares longingly into his eyes. He'll make a good meal. But not yet. First he wants some information.

Weak from the ordeal with the rats as well as hunger and the desire brought on by Vlad's proximity, Abe faints.

Vlad slaps him back to consciousness.

"Wake up," he says, nastily, "we have some business to attend to."

"Fuck you," Abe whispers. He must save his strength.

The anger that flashes in Vlad's eyes is terrifying and Abe bites his tongue, hard, until he tastes his blood. In the midst of the pain, Abe is able to tear his eyes away.

Vlad chuckles. This is a smart one. He throws him against the far wall, like a spoiled child with an unwanted toy.

Abe passes out again, and after making his way over to where Abe is sprawled on the rocky floor, Vlad kicks him back to consciousness.

"You'll tell me what I want to know," Vlad informs him.

"Over my dead body," Abe grunts, his head feels as if it's split in two. He feels it to make sure it is in one piece. It is, but if the anger that has frozen Vlad's face is any indication, it may not be for long.

Abe wishes he had one of those cyanide teeth—just a crunch and instant death. He has a feeling that if Vlad has his way, his death will be most unpleasant.

The rats are staring at him with what appears to be anticipation, and his skin crawls. They look almost too human, lined up at the far end of the room as if they are an audience watching a most interesting show. He is surprised they have not yet applauded. Unfortunately, he thinks, I seem to be the villain in this production.

Vlad kicks him, hard, in the crotch, and Abe curls up in pain. He will not speak. He doesn't care what Vlad does to him. He will not endanger Ginny's life; that is, assuming she got away. He can only pray that she turned and ran in time.

"Do I have to tell you what I will do to you to make you speak?" Vlad spits, his face is crimson with rage.

"Oh, I have a pretty good idea," Abe forces himself to smile through his pain and his still bleeding tongue. "You strike me as the nail-pulling type. Or, maybe, you'll cut off my genitals. I bet you'd like that, you faggot."

Vlad screams in frustration. He'd love to tear this man from limb to limb, but he needs his blood too badly. What if the other, the woman, shows up? What if she brings someone with her? He needs his strength.

He looks at his rats. Their beady, marble-sized eyes are moist with expectation. It has been quite a while since they have feasted on a human. Abe had killed two of the rats, Vlad had been informed, but if he drains Abe of enough blood, he won't be able to kill any more of his little friends.

Yet, he also does not want to kill him. He wants this man to suffer as much as possible for refusing to talk to him. He briefly longed for the old days when a sharpened stake, inserted in a most tender area might produce the desired results. Ironic, that he, too, must now beware of stakes.

"You're going to get off lucky," Vlad tells Abe. "I need your blood too much to waste it by spattering it all over this room, which is what I would like to do.

"I had a mistress, once," he digresses, remembering the way in which he had killed her for lying to him about being pregnant, "and there was so much blood . . ." He stares, longingly, at Abe's throat, he can almost see the blood coursing through the jugular vein.

Vlad pulls Abe into his arms, and Abe finally understands how Wolf had been unable to resist this man. His face burns in shame as he tries to will away the erection that is rising, immodestly, where it is pressed against Vlad. The disgust and loathing in Abe's face further excites the vampire. He always enjoys the desire he evokes, especially in heterosexual men. He fondles Abe's erection, and smiles wickedly. He now knows how to get his man.

He can stand pain a lot better than humiliation, I believe, Vlad thinks, licking his lips in anticipation. He caresses him again, and Abe groans in desire, but his face is the color of cottage cheese.

"No," Abe groans as Vlad unzips his pants. "No!"

"You'd like me to stop, wouldn't you?" Vlad says. "Well, there may just be a way out of this."

"Please, stop," Abe whispers.

"Who were you with today? And why did you come? Was it to kill me? My rat friends say it was."

"I can't tell you that." And to his great embarrassment Abe begins to cry. The tears leak from his eyes and he wants to wipe them away, deny that they are there, but Vlad is holding his wrists in a vise-like grip. His other hand is wrapped firmly around Abe's penis; and should Abe try something, he would lose it, Abe has no doubt of that. He can almost hear the rats snickering at his predicament.

"Shema Yisrael," he mumbles the Hebrew prayer, and Vlad laughs, squeezing Abe's erection until the pain is almost unbearable.

"Adonai Eloheinu, Adonai echad." Hear O Israel, the Lord our God, the Lord is One. Abe sobs, but he hasn't been to temple in years. Why hadn't he fought the rats off with the stakes? He could be holding one in his hand now, but he had allowed the backpack to be ripped from his back and now it lay useless on the other side of the cavern. "V'ahav'ta eit Adonai Elohekha," he can't hold on much longer, "b'khol l'vav'kha uvakhol nafsh'kha uvakhol m'odekha."

"And you shall love the Lord your God with all your heart and with all your soul and with all your might." Vlad snarls. "What is your God doing for you now?"

Abe screams as Vlad's teeth incise a small hole in his neck, and he collapses against Vlad, who is quickly draining the blood from his body.

Vlad wipes the blood from his mouth with the back of his hand, letting Abe slump to the floor.

"Here," he tells the rats. "He's all yours." Then he pauses, his hand in the air willing silence from the rats. "Wait, I believe we have visitors. Save him for later," he says, kicking Abe's unconscious form. "Come with me."

Ginny, Wolf & Vlad

N̲O̲ ̲W̲O̲N̲D̲E̲R̲ ̲G̲I̲N̲N̲Y̲ ̲H̲A̲D̲N̲'̲T̲ ̲W̲A̲N̲T̲E̲D̲ ̲T̲O̲ ̲C̲O̲M̲E̲ ̲B̲A̲C̲K̲ up here, Wolf thinks when the castle finally comes into view. The fortress looks even worse at night, dark and forbidding. He wonders if Vlad is waiting for them inside or if he will come out to greet them.

Ginny is puffing away behind him. Boy, it's been a long day, she thinks. It's still several hours till midnight, but except for the half hour before sunset, she has been constantly on the move. And, now, not only is it an effort to get up the mountain, but she often has to scurry to keep up with Wolf's strong pace. Even carrying the heavy sword in its old, cracked leather scabbard, Wolf seems to have no problem with the ascent.

He is excited. He is finally going to complete what he set forth to do 400 years earlier. And, as Vlad had earlier predicted of him, he doesn't mind dying in the process.

"I should have known," Vlad says. He appears just as they set foot inside the circle of death Ginny had noticed earlier.

"You won't get away from me this time," Wolf informs Vlad, who laughs, nastily.

Ginny shivers and cowers behind Wolf. She doesn't like the tone of Vlad's voice nor the look in his eyes.

"Don't look in his eyes," she whispers to herself. She hides her face in Wolf's back.

"Who is that sniveling behind you?" Vlad asks. "Perhaps it is the second of the two who invaded my palace earlier today while I slept?"

Wolf pulls Ginny out beside him, "Be strong," he encourages her. Ginny stares defiantly at Vlad, but she focuses her eyes on his forehead. She is afraid of what might happen if she catches his eyes. She doesn't want to end up like Hannele. Or Abe.

"I knew there had to be a third person," Vlad moves a step closer to the two. "But your friend would tell me nothing."

Ginny gasps in surprise. Abe! She had been sure the rats had killed him immediately. Is he still alive?

"No, he would tell me nothing, not even with proper incentive, so I was forced to dispose of him," he continues as if reading Ginny's thoughts. Vlad looks strong and powerful and his lips and cheeks are ruddy, a lot like Wolf's after he feeds.

Jesus, Ginny realizes, he fed on Abe. She wants to mourn for her lost friend, but she knows she must appear courageous, if only for Wolf's sake.

"I never did know your name," Vlad stares at Wolf. Except for the modern clothing, he has not changed a bit since that night in the Fürstensteinbrück keep. He takes another step closer. If I can get the woman, he thinks, it will be easy to take the vampire. Now that he is closer, the woman looks awfully familiar to him, too. His brow furrows in concentration. She looks a lot like the redhead, the one who the man had been avenging. But it can't be her. He had killed her almost immediately, hadn't he? Surely she wasn't a vampire, too? No, impossible, his god had said if he broke their necks . . . besides, she had been nosing around his fortress during the daylight.

Was it possible this fellow had found another woman who looked a lot like her? Vlad shudders, he feels as if he's stepped back in time. He was still edging closer. Another foot or two and he could grab the girl.

Wolf senses what Vlad is up to, motions Ginny behind him, and begins, in turn, to circle away from Vlad. He needs to be sure Ginny is safe, before he attacks the man.

I'm just going to have to rush them, Vlad decides, after they have completed a full circle, waiting, watching. Without a second thought he runs toward Wolf and Ginny. He has time because Wolf has not yet removed the sword from its sheath.

He easily knocks Wolf aside, and grabbing Ginny around the waist as if he plans to use her as a battering ram, Vlad runs toward the castle's entrance.

"Ginny," Wolf shouts, "remember what I told you."

Remember what he told me, Ginny is panicking, kicking her feet wildly. What the hell did he tell me? She pounds on Vlad's legs with her fist, but he just laughs. Then using all the force she can muster while swinging back and forth at his side, she kicks his knee, tripping him up. They fall to ground and Vlad drops her on her face, her lip bursting against a sharp rock, spouting blood onto the dry soil. It is soaked up, quickly.

She is trying to crawl back toward Wolf, who is running toward her, when Vlad picks her up, cradling in her arms. Looking over Vlad's shoulder to see if Wolf is any nearer, she sees him pointing to his head.

Why on earth is he pointing at his head? She can't think straight from all the bouncing and her lip is throbbing. And now she can no longer hit Vlad because her arms are behind her, wrists gripped painfully, by just one of his hands! His strenth is incredible. She begins to wriggle in his arms, and although the grip on her wrists tightens, she has wormed herself into a position she thinks she may be able to do some damage from. She lets her head sink on to her chest, then lets it fall back across Vlad's arm, the one that's supporting her shoulders.

It's going to take all her strength to sit up and slam her head into Vlad's left shoulder, but she hopes that it will cause him to drop her again. And this time, she needs to scramble toward Wolf.

One, two, three, she counts, silently. "Go!" She yells, startling Vlad. It works to her advantage and sitting up, she throws her head forward with all her might into his shoulder.

Vlad grunts in pain, but only grips her more tightly. In desperation, she sinks her teeth into this throat, ripping away some of the flesh there. This time, he drops her as his hand flies to his throat in shock, assessing the damage there. She lays stunned and aching on the ground, and a fresh gout of blood erupts from her bruised and swollen lip, but she quickly pulls herself together and begins crawling as quickly as possible toward Wolf.

"Wolf, the sword," she yells as she moves toward him. Vlad turns to face the man, face burning with hatred. He hadn't expected the girl to fight so hard, he should have broken her neck immediately, just as he had done to the other.

Wolf reaches to pull the sword from the scabbard, and Ginny screams, "No, Wolf, no! The sword has holy water on it!" What had she been thinking, what had Mihai been thinking? The sword had been blessed and sprinkled with holy water, it would burn Wolf's hand. Not only that, it formed the shape of a cross.

But, it is too late, Wolf is sliding the gleaming weapon from its sheath, and the metal burns with a blue fire, but he feels nothing. Has it really been blessed? He wonders.

Once he had tried to visit Franz at the cottage he had built for him, and couldn't get near it until all the crosses had been removed. When he had stepped into Franz' yard, he had started feeling ill, and the closer he got to his house, the sicker he became. He finally retreated, and yelled for Franz to come outside.

Franz, face pink with embarrassment, admitted that he had a number of crosses and crucifixes in his home. "I'm not afraid of you," he had been quick to say, "I'm just afraid."

Ginny is disappointed. She had thought that the holy water would work. She and Mihai had hoped they could burn Vlad with the blade.

Vlad begins to laugh, "I beat you at sword play before, what did she call you? Wolf."

"Perhaps so," Wolf's voice is as hard as the blade of the sword he is carrying, "but I am as strong as you now." Using both hands, Wolf swings the blade at Vlad's head, hoping to sever it from his body.

Using both hands, Vlad stops the blade in mid-swing. Within seconds he is screaming in agony. The blue light dancing on the blade begins to pop and sizzle as if an electric current is running between Wolf and Vlad. He can't let go, his hands seem glued to the blade, and they are blackening. A sick, sweet smell fills the air, the smell of burning flesh.

Ginny and Wolf look at each other in wonder. Why hadn't the blade burned his hands? Or perhaps, it was just the blade that was blessed, Ginny thinks. Maybe he can only hold the hilt.

Wolf is obviously thinking along the same lines for he loosens a hand and sets a questing finger lightly against the blade.

Nothing happens. That's weird, he thinks, and wraps his entire fist around the glowing metal. The heat is blistering with the fire that burns along it.

Still nothing. Wolf is mesmerized by this apparent paradox.

"Wolf, watch out," Ginny warns too late. Vlad, though his hands are misery—red and raw and weeping blood where they have not turned to charcoal—has taken advantage of Wolf's inattention.

Using the sword as his weapon, hands still affixed to the blade, he begins to swing Wolf in circles around him.

"Let go," Ginny screams, and Wolf obeys, but the centrifugal force sends him flying away from Vlad, and he lands, back-breakingly, against a large outcropping of rock.

Ginny runs to Wolf, praying that he is still conscious. She doesn't want to be left alone with Vlad.

As soon as he let go of the sword, the weapon had fallen from Vlad's hands, falling onto the dried grass where it began a small fire. Shrieking in pain and anger, Vlad turns toward Ginny. She is bent over Wolf, checking to see if he is still breathing. He is, but he is definitely unconscious. She doesn't know enough about vampires to know how long it takes them to heal from injury.

"There is no way to know how long he'll be out," Vlad says, advancing toward her. She doesn't want to risk Vlad advancing any closer toward Wolf, and quickly jumps up and begins running toward the vampire, throwing him off guard for a second. He expected her to run away from, not to, him.

A few yards before she reaches him, Ginny veers suddenly to the right.

"You can't escape me," Vlad tells her, slowly following her.

When she is at about ten yards away from him, Ginny stops and turns to face her opponent.

Vlad smiles, wickedly. He knew she would give in.

Ginny eyes him, warily, waiting for him to make his move. The sword lies a few yards away, with the fire burning a path away from it; but she knows she doesn't have the strength to use it. She has only one option she can think of, and she must make her move at the precise moment.

Vlad stops, confused. What is she doing? Has she given up? She is waiting for him, motionless, face pale in scant moonlight.

"Come any closer," she threatens, "and you're dead." She hopes she won't have to use her makeshift weapon. But, it is still hours until sunrise. Damn, why hadn't she met Wolf in the summer!

Vlad does not like to be threatened. "You don't understand," he says, taking a step closer, "I'm immortal. I can't die."

Another step.

She begins fidgeting with her hair. She is going to have to do this. Vlad is laughing. With her left hand, she pulls the Nalgene bottle from her waist pack.

"A drink before you die?" He chuckles. Another step. He is now within three yards of her.

She pretends to raise the bottle to her lips, before flinging the liquid toward Vlad. Most of the liquid patters harmlessly to the ground. What little falls on Vlad only makes him angrier. A whimper rises in her throat. Oh please, God, she prays, let this stupid little thing work.

Vlad takes another step toward her. He is now within an arm's reach. Both her arms begin to reach upward as if she is surrendering. With a final step, Vlad pulls her roughly to him. And, as he is encasing her in his arms, Ginny pulls her small hawthorn chopsticks from her hair and with as much strength as she can muster plunges them through Vlad's linen shirt and into his heart.

The shock of what she's done stops him cold. He stares down at the chopsticks, buried to their moonstones in his chest. He begins to run blindly for his castle. If he can make it inside, he can call on his rats. But he stumbles over rocks, and finally trips, falling to his knees.

Ginny runs after him, hefting the sword on her way. Despite the fact it has been in the midst of a fire, the hilt feels cool to her touch. He's not dying the way Mustela did. She is going to have to decapitate him, and she is not sure she has the strength to do it. He is still on his knees when she catches up with him. The miniature stakes seem to have weakened him considerably and thick, almost black blood oozes from around them. She raises the sword to strike the back of his neck, but just as it falls he lurches to his feet. His sense of direction seems to be lost as he wanders away from the castle, arms outstretched as if they are divining rods that will lead him to his lair.

Ginny stares after him in horror. She feels a warm breath on her neck, and turns, a scream rising in her throat.

It is only the wind. A light breeze touched by the warmth of the rapidly growing conflagration. The fire illuminates the scene—Wolf lying still next to the rock, Vlad wandering around, directionless.

She doesn't even want to think about Wolf. She doesn't have time to tend to him right now. Vlad is once again heading in the direction of the castle and she doesn't want to risk having to brave the rats, as well.

Vlad stumbles again, and Ginny realizes it's now or never. The chopsticks were enough to incapacitate but not kill him. The only thing she can do is chop his head off and make sure she rids the world of his body in the old way.

This time she can't miss. And as Vlad tries to regain his strength before standing again, she raises the sword above her head and brings it down slicing through his thick curls before the sword passes through his neck. She is surprised how easily it cuts through bone, muscle and tendon, and wonders if, indeed, the sword is more than blessed. Vlad's body slumps to the grounds as his head rolls away in the opposite direction.

Ginny watches his head with distaste. She knows that not only does she need to stuff his mouth with garlic (she forgot the roses), but she must bury it separately from the body.

The sound of hundreds, maybe thousands of rats, scrabbling over the rocky ground and emitting a high-pitched squeal causes her to drop the sword in shock. They are rushing to the edge of the rocky promontory and launching themselves into space, tumbling over the cliff like a dark waterfall.

As the last of the rats disappears over the edge, Ginny continues to stare after them. "Incredible," she finally breathes.

"It reminds me of lemmings," a voice replies. "Why do you suppose they did that?"

Ginny looks down at Vlad's severed head. It lies motionless, eyes blank and staring, at her feet. She turns around to see who spoke.

"Abe!" She throws herself into his arms, almost knocking him off balance. "Oh God, Abe! I felt sure you had been killed by the rats, but then Vlad mentioned you and then I thought he had killed you."

"Oh I think it was definitely his intention that the rats finish me off," he replies, fingering the wound on his neck. "But the timing of your arrival was impeccable."

"I'm so glad you're alive," she cries. "I was so worried. I don't think I would have ever forgiven myself if you had died. And I know your mother would have never forgiven me if I were responsible for your death."

"But you weren't responsible. It was my choice to come along with you on this suicide mission. Speaking of which, what happened to Wolf?"

"He's over there by that rock," Ginny points toward a darker black against the darkness. "Or at least he was the last time I looked. Now that Vlad is really dead . . . I'm not sure I can bring myself to look yet. Why don't we finish with Vlad first?"

"Finish with Vlad?"

"I need to stuff his mouth with garlic and bury his head."

"Oh boy. The vampire slayer's work is never done. What about his body?"

"I think we're supposed to burn it, but I'm not sure how to go about doing that."

"Can't we just toss him in that fire," Abe indicates the flames that are still moving away from the castle. Where did it come from anyway?"

"The sword started it."

"The sword?"

"Don't worry. I'll explain it all later. But you're right, we need to throw him into what's left of the flames first."

Ginny goes about the task of dealing with Vlad with intense focus, yet not so much because she wants to get the job done correctly, but because she doesn't want to think about Wolf. While she and Abe are finishing off Vlad, she makes a conscious effort not to keep her ears strained for what might be going on with Wolf. At one point she catches herself humming, inanely, "Three Blind Mice," as if to drown out any sound Wolf might be making.

Abe laughs and joins in, singing lustily, "Three blind mice, see how they run."

The soil is so rocky that it will be hard to bury his garlic-stuffed head. And, they don't have a shovel. She's going to have to use the sword; Abe pulls a now useless stake from the pack he retrieved on the way out of the cavern and begins hacking at the ground with it. The entire process takes them a couple of hours. As a kindness to Vlad, she buries his head as close to Poenari as possible. He may have been a monster, but at one point he had been human, and he had loved.

Later, trembling from exhaustion, they sink to the ground. Ginny silently gives thanks to God that Abe's life was spared and prays that she finds Wolf alive. She's still too terrified to go look at Wolf. But, if his ashes are there, she would like to bury them properly.

"You can't put off finding out forever," Abe says, his voice raw with exhaustion.

"I'll wait until the sun is up," she tells him. The fire has burned itself out and in the darkness that precedes dawn, she cannot even see if Wolf is lying there. "Yes," she closes her eyes, using any excuse to stall. "Let's wait until then. It'll give us time to rest and give me more time to prepare myself for the worst."

"If that's what you want."

"Abe, will you do me a favor?"

"Anything."

"Hold me."

She wakes with a start. She has dozed off. How long have I been asleep, she wonders, heart pounding.

It is a beautiful day and the sun is warm against her head. She is even beginning to sweat beneath the sweater and jacket. Abe is still asleep, now curled up on the ground like a little boy. She watches him with fondness. He might not like what she is thinking—that he has been like the protective big brother to her and she'll always love him for that—but he would be pleased by the look on her face.

She stands up, takes off the leather jacket and stretches. She turns to face the rock. Her heart is still pounding painfully. She doesn't want to look, but knows she must.

"You've got to," she says, aloud. She takes a deep breath, pressing her palm against her chest as if it might still the beating there.

Wolf is still lying where she left him. Is he dead? He certainly didn't disintegrate into ashes. Is he still a vampire? She walks slowly toward the boulder.

"Oh, the hell with this," she bitches, "just get it over with." And, with heart in throat and stomach at her feet, she kneels at Wolf's side.

He's still breathing. Her mouth opens in astonishment. But does this mean he's still a vampire? His face is already pink from the sun.

"I don't understand." She says, aloud, as if God will give her an explanation. They had all seemed so sure he would die once Vlad was killed. Tears are already filling her eyes. Is he still a vampire? What will that mean for them? She knows there is no way he'll make her a vampire. She also knows that it is impossible to watch herself grow old while he stays forever young; to give up the possibility of a family. Even if she did stay with him, they would have to be continually on the move. She'd have to say goodbye to her family.

"What are we going to do?" she cries, tears dropping onto his face.

"Is he still a vampire?" Abe asks from behind her.

"I don't know and I don't know what to do if he is."

"I still have some stakes."

"Very funny Abe."

Wolf moans.

Her heart begins to beat so fast it's slamming against her ribs.

"Wolf?"

He moans again, tries to open his eyes. But the sun is too bright. He squints, tears of pain leaking from the corners of his lids.

"Ginny?"

"Wolf, you didn't die."

"But?" He feels different. He doesn't feel that sense of exhaustion that usually greets a new day. He quickly runs his tongue over his teeth. The canines are only slightly pointed. He bares his teeth at Ginny.

She's taken aback at first, and then she sees the difference.

"Wolf," she says, pulling the gloves from his hands. His palms are hairless. "Wolf," she chokes, "you're human again."

He groans as he tries to sit up, clutching his head.

"Wow man, that's quite a knot you've got there," Abe states.

"Abe?"

"Here, try these," Abe pulls sunglasses from his pack and hands them to Wolf.

"Much better," Wolf says after putting them on. "I guess my eyes still aren't used to the light."

"True. You did wear sunglasses the whole time we were in Fürstensteinbrück," Ginny reminds him. "Do you think you can stand up?"

Ginny and Abe help him to his feet, and keep him steady until the dizziness passes.

"Think you can make it back to the car?" Ginny asks.

"I think so."

Ginny hefts the sword.

"You want me to carry that?" Abe asks.

"No. I've got a special relationship with it now. Do you think Mihai will let me keep it?" she asks.

"Well, you did say he didn't expect its return," Wolf reminds her.

"I think it has special powers," she admits. "Not only did it help me kill Vlad and sever his head, but it didn't hurt you, Wolf."

"That's true," Wolf says. "The sword felt cool to my touch despite the heat."

"It does seem like a miracle that you are alive and human again," Ginny says, taking his hand.

"Hey, if that sword does have special powers, maybe we shouldn't stop with Mustela and Vlad," Abe laughs.

"What do you mean?" Ginny asks.

"I'm feeling a bit like Jack Crow," Abe says, referring to the lead vampire slayer in John Carpenter's "Vampires".

"He's Catholic," Ginny jokes. "Maybe you should be Van Helsing."

"True," Wolf agrees. "And you're already an Abraham."

"As long as it's the Hugh Jackman 'Van Helsing'."

"Oh definitely," Ginny laughs, "You're much closer to Hugh Jackman than Anthony Hopkins."

"Thank you, Ginny, I appreciate that. And I guess that would make Wolf, 'Blade'." He says of the comic book-turned-movie-hero.

"Blade?" Wolf asks. "I don't look like Wesley Snipes."

"No," Ginny says, "but you are closer to being half vampire than we are."

"All right, but if I'm Blade, you're Buffy."

"Well, I am the 'chosen one'," Ginny giggles, giddy from exhaustion and stress.

"What do you mean?" Abe asks. "Chosen one?"

"Well, supposedly Buffy is the one chosen to kill vampires, and if Wolf hadn't chosen me, so to speak, there is no way we would be here in Romania right now; much less walking away after having killed two vampires."

"Three, if you count Wolf," Abe corrects. "After all, there are now three less vampires in the world. So, Wolf," Abe punches him lightly on the shoulder, "You've just won the vampire lottery, what's the first thing you want to do now that you're human again?"

"That's a dangerous question, Van Helsing," Wolf jokes. "Obviously the first thing I want to do is out of the question," he winks at Ginny. "So, my second choice, hmmmm." He thinks for a moment. "You're going to think I'm insane, but I'd really like to try a Big Mac, fries and a Coca Cola."

"How very American of you," Ginny laughs, "And I have absolutely no doubt that we'll be able to find a McDonald's even in Bucharest. I don't think there is a big city in the world without one."

"McDonald's it is then," Abe agrees. "Then on to the airport? I've got some phone calls to make."

"Sure, but if we have a choice, I prefer to fly back tomorrow," Wolf states. "We can stay at the Diplomat again. We're all wounded as well as exhausted, and it would be wise to get some sleep before we return."

Abe groans. "Why do I get the feeling I'll be spending a lot of time alone in the coming weeks?"

Wolf whispers something in Ginny's ear and she blushes.

Vlad III (1431-1476)

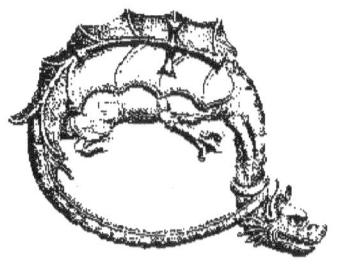

Afterword

WHILE THE NOVEL *REDEMPTION* is a work of fiction, the history of Vlad the Impaler in this book stays close to the known history of Vlad III (1431-1476). The fiction finds its starting place in many well-documented events in his life. Remembered for his passionate resistance against the Ottoman Empire and his signature form of retribution in impaling his enemies, Vlad was three times the prince of Wallachia. He and his brother Radu were indeed sent as hostages to the Ottomans at an early age. While no one knows what happened in that time to turn the young Vlad so violently against his captors, this book finds its beginnings there as Vlad began his path toward cruelty by using first insects and then animals before progressing to humans.

Vlad III's Romanian surname was Drakulya, which comes from his father, Vlad Dracul, a member of the chivalric order *Societas Draconistrarum* (Order of the Dragon). A member of this order would be referred to as "Dracul", a noun of the Latin word Draco, meaning "dragon." A son of Dracul was referred to as a "Dracula".

For its symbol, the order used a dragon wrapped in a circle with its tale wrapped around its neck (shown above). While the Latin word Dracul means dragon, in Romanian Dracul means devil.

Following his defeat, Vlad's headless body was buried at Snagov Monastery. His head was believed to be taken back to Istanbul. But how he died and whether the body found was his, remained disrupted. Vlad III inspired Bram Stoker's *Dracula*, who did not rely on much more than the name and his lust for blood.

I wanted to remain true to Vlad III, while speculating as to what might have gone on inside him. His downward spiral is played out against the story of Wolfdietrich von Fürstensteinbrück rediscovering his lost humanity through his encounters with Ginny Hunter. While Vlad descends into cruelty and madness, Wolf learns to love anew. It was the opposition in those stories which interested me in discovering the characters through writing this novel. I hope you have enjoyed taking the journey with me.

About the Author

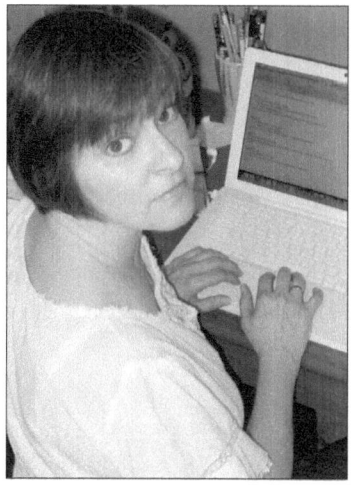

VICTORIA STEELE LOGUE is an award-winning newspaper reporter and editor. She is the author of a ten books on hiking and the outdoors as well as two driving guides. *Redemption* is her first novel.

Victoria and her husband Frank hiked the 2,130-mile Appalachian Trail from Georgia to Maine in 1988. They have traveled widely together with their daughter, Griffin. The Logues live in Savannah, Georgia.

www.ingramcontent.com/pod-product-compliance
Lightning Source LLC
Chambersburg PA
CBHW050601260626

47157CB00002B/654